# More or Less
# Crazy

~ ~ ~

*The Smokejumpers*

~ ~ ~

A Novel
by Murry A. Taylor

Proudly Published in the USA by
Books to Believe In
17011 Lincoln Ave. #408
Parker, CO 80134

Phone: (303)-794-8888

Find us on Facebook at
www.facebook.com/Books2BelieveIn

Follow us on Twitter at
@books2believein
#BooksToBelieveIn

Follow our blog at
bookstobelievein.wordpress.com
BooksToBelieveIn.com

#SmokeJumpers


Cover Design by
Mike McMillan
spotfireimages.com



ISBN: 1518644767

For the Smokejumpers

Evan Kelly stormed about his office on that hot July day in 1935.

As a staunch follower of the traditional ways of the U.S. Forest Service, the tough old fire officer had not risen to the position of Regional Forester in Missoula, Montana, by indulging in foolishness or tolerating it in others. But foolishness had reared its ugly head on his own home turf, among his own ranks. Such a cockamamie idea had no place on his watch. And he would put an end to it. Never mind that his superiors in Washington, D.C. seemed intrigued by this hair-brained scheme that had wafted out of the pipe dreams of a group of his young fire managers in the Northern Rockies. Given their apparent disregard for human life, rather than abide such nonsense, he was more inclined to recommend them for psychiatric evaluation. Kelly fired off a stiff letter to Forest Service Headquarters.

"I will remind you that you wrote some time ago about J. B. Bruce's scheme of dropping men from airplanes for firefighting. Pearson of Region Four was party to the scheme. I am willing to take a chance on almost any kind of proposition that promises better action on fires, but I hesitate very much to go into the kind of thing Bruce proposes. In the first place, the best information I can get from experienced fliers is that *all parachute jumpers are more or less crazy.*"

"I was transported to a wide plain, under a great dome of open sky, or to a forest dense, beneath a canopy of trees, and I began to understand how the voices of God spoke from the wind and the thunder."

Joseph Campbell
*The Power of Myth*

# Prologue

July 1973
Fort Greeley, Alaska

Two DC-3s circled ten acres of fire spreading in thick black spruce, eating its way south toward the Alaska Range. Both loads had rolled from Fairbanks. Jarvis Creek ran parallel to the left flank about 300 yards east. A dirt road bordered the north boundary of the fire near the tail. Back about a hundred yards was a clearing half the size of a football field. That would be our jump spot**.

"Fort Greeley," Johnny B. shouted, pointing out the window. Six miles north we could see several long runways, giant hangars and dozens of support buildings. Halfway between the base and the fire a fuel-break stretched east to west from Jarvis Creek to the Richardson Highway. Built by the Army to protect the fort from fire, it was four miles long and looked to be pretty wide. Ten miles beyond the fort I could see the little town of Delta.

The wind was calm and the jump went smoothly, with all the cargo and jumpers landing in the clearing. Shortly after the jump, a BLM pickup came from Delta with extra pumps and hose. The driver told Quinlan the fire had been initial-attacked the day before by a six-man helitac crew from Tanacross. They'd spent the day and had failed to do much more than secure the tail. I didn't get all of it, but part of the problem was not enough people. At ten the night before they had radioed for backup. Another six helitac were sent from Fairbanks. Both crews worked the fire during the night and had returned to Delta for rest only a few minutes before we showed up. He went on to say that smokejumpers had been requested the first day but Fairbanks dispatch had turned him down and sent helitac instead.

**Jump spot - One of many fire-fighting terms defined in a glossary on page 362.

By noon the fire was forty acres. A D-7 Caterpillar bulldozer arrived on a low-bed and began building fireline up the right flank on the west side. Matt Kelly and the second load of jumpers set up a Mark III pump in a small pond and followed the dozer line in with a hoselay. Quinlan and the first load, the one I was with, had run our own hoselay a similar distance up the left flank. Both crews talked about the winds that sometimes blew out of Isabelle Pass, fifty miles south. During its first twenty- four hours the fire had burned steadily south with typical pulses of active crown fire followed by periods of calmer fire on the ground. Since our jump the pulses had gotten stronger, each time gaining enough heat to make for a more continuously active head. Still, both flanks were holding. By 5:00 that afternoon, even with the progress we had made, the fire had grown to 70 acres. Just when both crews felt we had a chance to cut off the head, pinching it in from both sides, two things happened. Flames flared in the biggest pulse yet and put up a smoke column that blotted out the sun. It was one of those times when wildland firefighters stop what they're doing, look around, smell the air, listen to the fire, note the movement of smoke, look at the sky, and sense that they'd better watch out. It's not an easy thing to explain. It comes from experience and you either have it or you don't. Five minutes later the wind hit.

"Okay let's move," Quinlan shouted down the line. In no time, Kelly was on the radio telling his men to move back down the right flank, as well. I looked back during our retreat and saw a wall of 60 foot flames a quarter-mile wide spreading across the end of our hoselay. At the dirt road we held up, drank from canteens, and watched.

"Quinlan," I said, "there must be something we can do."

"Okay, we've got a few minutes. Let's pull this hose closest to the road into the jump spot. At least save that."

We started back in along the hoselay, spreading out and unscrewing hose couplings and gated Ys. I dropped off first and disconnected the 100-foot section closest to the road. No sooner had I got the hoses apart when there was yelling up the line. Along our flank a storm of flames whipped side to side, heading our way, a roar swelling in the dark sky. The wind suddenly doubled. Instantly the fire erupted from a fire that was getting away and going big into one was going big and threatening to burn us to death. Directly in front of the advancing flames, I saw Quinlan, Rake and several others abandon the hose lay and run in the direction of Jarvis Creek. I dropped the hose and started jogging back to the dirt road. The roar got real loud. Then, closer and louder, like a jet engine inside the burn somewhere. The air commenced to tremble. Dust and ash blew one way and the other, then started rotating in a wide circle. Then I saw it. Swaying side to side where it touched the ground, a pinkish-orange blur appearing then disappearing in a whirling fury, only to reappear again, each time closer, its black body swaying like a giant snake. Having grown up in Texas, I knew a tornado when I saw one. Out of the burn it came, leaving behind a storm of brown and gray ash to emerge on unburned tundra as a bright twelve-foot wide cylinder of fire, its outer edges a streaking blur of pink and orange fire that looked solid as a wall. I ran looking for a sump hole, a damp depression, anything wet enough to dive in. A blast of wind knocked me down. Fighting to get up, the wind rolled me in the tundra. Holding on to fistfuls of grass, I tried keeping low. I had seen fire devils before, some small, a few big enough to pick up small logs, but this thing that was coming, I'd never seen or even thought possible.

One thing was clear, I had to move. Staying as low as I could, I tried pulling myself away, all the time grabbing handfuls of tundra to keep from flying off. No matter where I went the fire tornado seemed to track my every move. Suddenly a storm of sparks flew all around me, and the tundra came alive with running ground fire. I was trapped. The vortex was forty feet away now. If I moved I'd be pulled off the ground. If I stayed put, I'd burn to death.

"Oh shit," I heard myself say. Having studied the stories of people trapped in fire, I had tried to imagine what it would be like. The fire is on you. Your body is burning. The pain. I knew enough not to breathe. Super hot air sears the lungs and then you die. That's what I was thinking when something strange happened. Motion began to slow down, the roar got quieter. All around me was chaos. Trees whipped back and forth as if trying to tear themselves free from the earth. Some part of my mind recognized that, in fact, my worst fear was to be my final reality. I was going to burn to death in a forest fire.

# 1

May, 1973
Bonanza Creek

We were out in a big yellow meadow looking up at a jumpship on final. Some lay back in the grass watching, others stood. All shaded their eyes. As the dark silhouettes left the door of Jumper 54, bodies fell away under the tail, deployment bags whipped up then back in toward the fuselage, suspension lines trailed out, and parachutes opened in a perfect blue sky. Like great jellyfish they floated and pulsed, turning one way, then the other. Way up high a jumper would yell something and his jump partner would yell back. Now and again a canopy would drift in direct line with the sun creating flashes of silvery white and International Orange that rotated through the T-10's radial seams and turned the already beautiful canopies into objects of momentary wonder. Jumpers landed in the meadow, rolled in the grass, got to their feet, pulled off their helmets and laughed as they began taking off their jump suits. In the last stick one jumper drifted a ways off to the east, then south like he was testing some new theory of windage or didn't much care where he went.

"He must be knocked out," John Rakowski said.

"He's not knocked out," squad leader Bob Quinlan, groaned. "He steered away from the spot the minute he opened."

"Well, he's not steering now," Rakowski said. "I think he's unconscious."

"Unconscious I can believe," Quinlan said. "Half the time it's hard to tell with you McGrath guys."

At about five-hundred feet I guess he decided to take things seriously because that was when he went after his steering toggles. That was also about the time the wind picked up. What he lacked in steering up to that point he seemed to be trying to make up for by jerking one toggle then the other and kicking his legs. None of it helped. With the forward part of his canopy caved in, the wind still pushed him backwards. At two-hundred feet he let out a big squall.

"He's over the pond," Quinlan shouted. "Get over there. I'll get a let-down rope."

Off we tore through a thicket of black spruce. Since I was closest to the pond to start with, I got there first. And sure enough, there he was, fifty feet offshore, floating in an ice hole, his canopy behind him on the ice, still inflated. The only thing I could see in the hole was his helmet, the top of his reserve parachute, and the toes of his boots. Serious trouble.

Quinlan ran up with a let-down rope. While he tied a stick to one end, I pulled off my shirt and t-shirt. Bob handed me the stick and some rope and I waded in, feeling my way through a unseen tangled of slimy objects, barely able to breathe. It was common knowledge that the coldness of Alaska water took only fifteen minutes to stop a human heart. The shore lead was ten feet wide, and by the time I got to the ice I was in above my waist and already gasping for air and finding it hard to go on. I broke off chunks with the stick, pitched them aside and moved on out, whooping and hollering at the cold. When the ice got too think to break, I stopped, coiled the let-down rope in one hand and swung the stick in the other like I was fixin' to rope a calve. Away went the stick, the coil flying behind. It missed the ice hole, six feet to the left.

"It's been five minutes," Quinlan yelled, his voice urgent.

I jerked the rope back, coiling it as best I could to keep it from twisting. The ice was three inches thick at the edge. I tried jumping up on it but it immediately broke off, and I fell back into the water with the rope tangled around my neck. The second throw landed past the ice hole to the right.

"Okay, that's enough practice," Quinlan said. "Now split the difference. Think of him as one of those Texas cows you used to rope."

"Cows got more sense than to get themselves into a mess like this," I yelled. "Besides, my fingers aren't movin' too well."

"Hurry up," Quinlan barked. "Time's running out."

I took a deep breath, whirled the stick over my head, then released it in a right-handed arc that landed five feet beyond the ice hole man.

"Get it to him." Quinlan was yelling louder now. First at me, then the ice hole man. "Tie it to the top of your harness. Pop your capewells. Leave the chute."

By the time I had struggled back to shore, those on the bank had commenced pulling. The body moved a little at first, then caught the edge of the ice. Ice-hole man broke off small chunks but he was too weak and slipped back into the hole.

"Turn around and backstroke up onto the ice," Quinlan roared.

Working his elbows behind him and with the jumpers all pulling, Ice-hole man tried again, then hung up the same and fell back just like before.

"Take off your pack tray," Quinlan said. "Your pack tray's catching on the ice."

Ice-hole man did not respond except for his hands waving around his head in a fashion no one could figure out. I don't know what possessed me then, but I lit into the water again, swam to the edge of the ice, took a deep breath, sunk beneath it, and started swimming for all I was worth. I kept my eyes closed for a while and just headed in what I figured was the right direction. When I opened them what I saw was right intimidating. There were three layers to it; the blue ice ceiling above, the terrible blackness of the lake bottom below, and me thrashing along in the clear space in between. The water was so cold my head felt like it was in a vice. I'd swam some in the cattle tanks on the ranch, but I never felt the panic of water like I did then. All I could hear was my heart racing faster and faster, pounding in my ears. I couldn't believe it. I'd come to Alaska to fight fire and now I was going to drown in a frozen lake. A shaft of light streamed down around the jumper then faded down into the black. As I got near the hole the jumper's left arm fell off his chest into the water, rotated slightly like he knew I was coming and was reaching for me. I grabbed his hand to pull myself up. Instead of me coming up I pulled him down. Once we got back to the surface, and after a quick gasp for air and some coughing, I thought I better introduce myself.

"Howdy partner, my name's Len."

"Duke," the gray face behind the mask stuttered, its eyes staring at nothing.

"Hold on, Duke," I said. "You've got to get yourself organized." I unsnapped the two capewell fittings that held the chute to the harness, then unsnapped the reserve and unbuckled the pack tray I put them both up on the ice.

"Y'all count to four then pull," I yelled to shore.

On four I kicked my legs, pried myself against the ice, and shoved him up as hard as I could. The body lifted some each time they pulled. Then, it came nearly out, slid back, then left the water and was moving away from me, dragging the reserve and pack tray with it. I dove under the ice and began frog kicking back the way I'd come. I got to shore right after he did. One group grabbed him. Another grabbed me. After I was dragged out of the water, I crawled over to a sunny spot and lay there shaking and shivering and trying to keep my teeth from rattling. My head ached with a sharp pain above my eyes and my hands felt like they were on fire. The ones that pulled me out went over to help Duke and left me to thaw out on my own.

Ice-hole man's jumpsuit, harness and various leg pocket items were waterlogged so he was too heavy to lift. Quinlan began unsnapping the harness, unzipping his jump jacket and pants, leaving only his Levis and long-sleeved plaid shirt. Once freed from his gear, Don Bell and Melvin Sheenjek pulled his corpselike body onto shore. The jumpers had gathered firewood, retrieved a can of saw gas and started a warming fire. Quinlan rolled him over on his back.

"Aackk," he said. "Johnny Bowen, another McGrath All-Star. I should have known."

Bowen's eyes were still staring at nothing. His lips looked like two dead earthworms. Then his jaw begun jumping up and down which made the worms look like they weren't dead but glad to be alive. Bell and Sheejek dragged him to the fire and held him up full-length to the heat. Bell unbuttoned Bowen's shirt and pulled it off. A jumper ran up with two sleeping bags. Rakowski grabbed them, saying to Bell, "Get his pants off."

"Oh no," Bell said. "I don't mind helping, but I'm not taking off a man's pants."

"You take women's off, don't you?" Rakowski said.

"It's not the same, Rake, and you know it. And I'm not doing it, either."

"Okay then, get out of the way."

I found out later that Rakowski was Rake, and that Rake was short for The Legendary Fucking Rake, a nickname he was right proud of. Rake undid the McGrath All-Star's belt, unbuttoned his fly and began slipping his pants down.

"See here," Rake said to Bell, "Johnny B.'s pants come off just like yours."

"Maybe they do," Bell said. "But I'm still not gonna help, and I'm not watching, either."

As Rake worked the pants down off the blue-gray legs, the All-Star groaned, tried to say something but gave up when his teeth went to chattering.

Quinlan wrapped a sleeping bag around him, then said, "Bowen! Keep your mouth shut. You're in bad enough shape already without biting your tongue off."

I crawled over to the fire and took off my boots and socks, everything down to my Levis. After a while Quinlan came over.

"That was good, you going in like that. How do you feel?"

"I'm fine, I reckon. Just a little tired is all."

"I want you to stay here at the fire. Keep an eye on Bowen. The McGrath guys call him Johnny B. He's a bit different. Dry out his gear. When he comes around he'll be embarrassed. Make sure he drinks some water. Tell him a jump story or something to cheer him up."

The crew went back to the meadow and their training, setting up pumps and hose lays, while the McGrath All-Star and I stayed at the fire. As time passed I began to feel guilty that I wasn't doing any work, just sitting there drying out my boots and enjoying the afternoon and still getting paid and all. When a man's getting paid it's only right for him to be doing at least some little thing. The All-Star was propped up asleep against a small spruce. After a while his eyes opened, but he just sat there with part of the sleeping bag over his head, staring at the fire, looking like an Indian with no friends. Five minutes later he uttered something that I didn't understand, then rolled over onto his side and went to sleep again. Finally warmed up, I got to my feet, washed the mud and slime from both me and the All-Star's clothes as best I could, then strung a line of F'er Cord near the fire and hung everything up using clothes pins I'd carved from willow sticks. Then I made a tripod of spruce poles and arranged his jump pants, jump jacket and helmet on it. In the right pocket of his jump pants I found his let-down rope, took it out, uncoiled it, then strung it in the trees. In the left pocket there was a soggy book, *Black Like Me* written by man named John Howard Griffin. According to the writing on the back he was a white man who smeared dye on himself and pretended to be a black man so he could find out what that was like. Of all the things in this world to do, to my way of thinking, that was about the craziest. In the same pocket I found a stuffed monkey with yellow buttons eyes and a small book of poetry entitled *The Way Home*. To my surprise the All-Star was the author. That was none of my business, of course, but I was curious, and didn't figure he'd wake up before I was finished. Even if he did he'd be too wore out to do much about it. So I read the first one:

## Times and Places

As a species projected forward by the thrust of an ancient past
the very forces that move us ahead sometimes seem to call us back.
Back to those times and places that formed and sustained us
back to where we can feel the flow of fate like that of a river
Forever flowing to the sea, forever returning to the sky,
to become rain, and then to fall once again into the headwaters of eternity

Well, I thought, the McGrath All-Star sounds like a drifter. From what he'd written I couldn't tell whether he was talking about good times and places or bad. Whatever it was, it was none of my business, so I flipped through the soggy pages, then set it in the sun next to the monkey with the button eyes. I left his PG bag alone. All jumpers were issued PG bags, and they carried their personal gear in them; things like dry socks, an extra t-shirt, a sweat shirt, rain gear, fish hooks and line, toothpaste, stuff like that.

The All-Star kept right on sleeping, and if it wasn't for a grunt now and then you'd have thought he was dead. That left me with not much to do, so I went to camp and sacked up some C-rations, two root beer sodas, a five-gallon cubitainer of water and a cargo chute. It was only my second day as an Alaska smokejumper and I couldn't believe how good I felt. The day before, half the crew and I hiked six miles down a ridge from the Parks Highway into Bonanza Creek where the BLM was holding its annual spring training exercise. Most all the crew had finished refresher training and all their practice jumps. Two Doug loads jumped that afternoon, then the one today with the All-Star on it. I already knew a few on the Alaska crew from my six seasons as a Region Five smokejumper out of Redding, California. Still, I didn't know them well enough to believe all the rumors I'd heard. In the Lower 48 the Alaskans had the reputation of being a heck of a lot of fun, pure and simple overtime hogs and, at times, a bit dangerous. Actually I didn't care much. It just felt good to be back out in the woods, camping with smokejumpers, hearing jump stories, and hearing them laugh. I hadn't realized how much I'd missed it.

Back at the pond I hung the cargo chute in a tree to provide the All-Star some shade. I opened a box of C-rats, and after a can of peaches and a few John Wayne crackers smeared with peanut butter, I lay back myself and was soon asleep. While sleeping I dreamed a dream I've had many times. I'm on the first load, standing by at a jump base I don't recognize. It's always the same, the siren goes off, I run to suit-up. Others are suiting up, too. But, because I can't find some part of my jump gear, the next thing I know the first load is on the plane with the engines running, ready to go. In a panic I ask some jumpers playing cards if they've seen my helmet, my harness or whatever. They look disgusted, laugh at me, then return to their game. Everything I'm supposed to be, I'm not. I have failed at the most basic smokejumper responsibility; I've lost an important part of my gear and I'm not fire ready.

I woke up feeling miserable and lay there a moment watching the sunlight flash and splinter through the seams of the cargo chute and thinking about the dream and how many times I'd had it. After a while I sat up, looked over at the All-Star, then grabbed a piece of firewood and put it in the fire. That's when I saw him, through the smoke, looking at me.

"How y'all feeling?" I asked.

The face in the sleeping bag said, "Do I know you?"

"I reckon you don't. Yesterday was my first day. Name's Len, Len Swanson."

The All-Star pushed back his sleeping bag, got to his feet, grabbed his boxer shorts, and pulled them on. He legs were white and gray with red splotches here and there, probably from the ice landing. His hair was blond, completely straight, and looked like it was cut with a bowl on his head. I figured him to be in his mid-twenties. Once he had his shorts on he looked into the distance, and commenced to holding his arms out like one of those swamp birds I'd once seen in Florida, all the time looking at the sky. After a time he lowered his arms, bowed his head, then looked up to the sky again. I began to wonder if something wasn't right with him. Quinlan had said he was different, and I sure didn't expect any medals but he acted like I wasn't even there. After he hobbled barefoot over to the clothes line he came back to the fire and looked at me like he was seeing me for the first time.

"My name's John," he said, reaching over to shake hands. "The guys call me Johnny B. You mind telling me how I got here, stuffed in a sleeping bag... naked?"

"Y'all had a wreck, don't you know that?"

"What kind a wreck?"

"On the ice, you broke a hole in it and we had to pull you out."

Johnny B. rubbed the back of his neck then looked out on the pond and saw his parachute.

"Where're my pants?"

"Right over there," I said, pointing. "Rake took them off so we could..."

"Rake took my pants off?" he croaked. "Well now. That's a scary thought, wouldn't you say?"

"I don't reckon I have an opinion on it, really. All I know is that you landed on the pond and caused a big ruckus."

Johnny B. stood a moment looking, then said, "Oh yeah... I guess I did."

"I swam out under the ice and shoved you up so the rest could pull you in."

At that he went over, picked up his monkey, rubbed its fur smooth, and of all things, commenced talking to it.

"Duke, just look at yourself. You're a fucking mess."

Johnny B. sat Duke on a clump of tundra next to the fire, making sure he was positioned just right. Next he did something I wasn't at all prepared for. Out of the top pocket on his PG bag he pulled a plastic bag and took out a small brass pipe and lit it and sucked in real strong, then held his breath for a time.

"Want a hit?" he wheezed, poking the pipe at me, still holding his breath.

"Oh, no. I don't reckon I do."

"Huh-huh, heeyuu," he said, letting his air out, all the time smiling.

"Hey man, this is not just regular weed. This is Matanuska Thunderfuck."

"It might well be, but I won't be having any. Hell, no wonder you missed the spot."

"Uh-huh, I see. Your first day was yesterday, right?"

"That's right. This is my second day."

"And you've never smoked dope or been stoned, right?"

"That's right. I been around it some, but I just don't care for it myself."

"How can you know you don't like something if you've never tried it?"

"I just don't, that's all. Besides, we're on duty. We're supposed to be working."

"Working?" Johnny B. said. "Is that what you call what you're doing sitting here? Is this you're idea of work?"

"I was told to stay here and look after you, and I didn't take it to mean smoke pot, either."

"Well, it'd be just as easy to watch stoned as any other way, don't you think?"

"No, I don't think that. You're strange enough to watch normal."

"So you're dead against it?"

"I reckon I don't need to escape reality."

"Reality sucks," the All-star said, taking another big puff.

"You might think that... I don't!"

"Besides," Johnny B. said shaking his head and grinning, "I don't smoke it to escape reality, I smoke it to escape madness."

I couldn't believe that, and after some thought on it, said, "Madness, hell. I'd be mad too if I'd fiddled around and landed in a ice pond and nearly drowned myself."

"Duke," Johnny B. said, looking at his monkey. "This is Len. He rescued us from the pond, so now he thinks he's a hero."

"I don't think any such thing. Where'd you get a crazy notion like that?"

The next thing I knew Johnny B. had lifted the monkey towards me, and was moving its arm from behind.

"Here, Len Swanson. Duke wants to shake hands with the man who rescued us."

"Look," I said, trying to settled him down. "I came up here to parachute to fires and to be a good smokejumper and enjoy the country, not to smoke dope and shake hands with stuffed monkeys."

But my words didn't faze Johnny B. one bit. He just smiled and kept moving the monkey's arm, its little hand going up and down. Hell, I didn't know what to do but I didn't see any profit in being contrary, so I took his paw between my thumb and forefinger and shook it with tiny little shakes.

"Good to meet you, Duke," I said quickly, hoping no one would come along and see it.

"Last thing I remember, " Johnny B. said, squinting up at the sky, "I was in the door looking down at the jump spot."

"Is that a fact?" I said. "Truth told, that was about the closest you ever got to it. Looked to me like you didn't care much where you landed."

"Hey, I missed the spot. Everybody misses the spot now and then."

"I know that. But you didn't just miss the spot, you missed the land."

"I must have hit my head or something when I went out the door, because I can't remember checking my canopy. There's a blank spot between leaving the plane and when I looked up and saw Denali. It was right there, you know. So far away, yet so big, so beautiful. I couldn't take my eyes off it. I guess I looked a little too long. When I finally got around to finding the spot, the wind came up."

I thought to myself that there was likely more to it than wind. I'd heard a few jumpers, mostly overhead types, tell about marijuana flashbacks, saying if you had one you might not be able to think straight.

"Well then, you deserved to go in the pond," I said. "On a jump you're supposed to be paying attention, not skylarkin' around."

"Well, I'll be damned, Duke," Johnny B. said, lifting an eyebrow to his button-eyed friend. "It's the sheriff of smokejumping."

I held up on that, and took a minute to remember the deep water of the pond, the painful cold, and how my body had begun to seize up under the ice.

"I'm no sheriff of smokejumping or anything else. But facts are facts, and if you'd been any further out who knows what would have happened."

"Hey, don't get me wrong. You rescued us and we're thankful. Right, Duke?"

Far as I could tell Duke didn't have an opinion one way or the other, so we just sat there and kept quiet until I decided to change the subject.

"They said you jumped out of McGrath."

"I did. But not last year. I took a year off and did some traveling."

"Oh yeah? Where'd you go?"

"Lots of places."

Johnny B. grinned at Duke. I don't know if it was the pot or just realizing he was still alive, but you could tell he was feeling better.

"Around the world. I flew to Japan from Anchorage. Stayed a month. Visited the island of Hokkaido. From there I went to Russia and took the Siberian Railway across Mongolia, around Lake Biakal and on to Moscow, then Turkey and Israel."

"Well, now. People talk about things like that but you actually went and *did it*."

"I did. Hell of a deal."

"That's a real adventure if you ask me."

"Yeah, all kinds of shit happened. In Israel I worked on a kibbutz. One day I was out in a field driving tractor and the field started exploding. I looked up and there were two jets dropping bombs."

"Bombing a man's field?" I said, disgusted. "That's downright uncalled for."

Johnny B. got quiet after that and just stared into the campfire. I was thinking about not asking him any more questions but he went on anyway.

"The explosions came across the field with the dirt flying up and passed me in a line. Then there was the boy and his bicycle on the road.

He saw them and started peddling as fast as he could. In my mind I said, no way. Then a bomb hit... right where he was."

Johnny B. glanced over at Duke, then at me. I didn't know what to say, so I just sat there feeling bad for bringing up the subject.

"If he hadn't pedaled so fast, the bomb would have missed him."

"I'm sorry," I said. "I imagine that's not an easy thing to forget."

Johnny B. rubbed the back of his neck, shook his head, "I was the first one there."

After he said that he didn't look at me or Duke or the pond or nothing, just at the fire.

"He died while I was trying to hold his head straight and stop the bleeding in his neck."

Caught off guard, I had no idea what to say. I figured he needed to tell someone about it, but I didn't know for sure, so I just kept still.

"That's what I mean when I say madness," he said after a time. "And what about you? You talk funny, like maybe English is your second language. You wouldn't be one of those lost hillbillies from Texas, would you?"

"Look who's calling people lost," I said, still feeling bad about his story. "But, yes. I am from Texas. And proud of it. Central Texas, north of Abilene a hundred miles. I grew up on a ranch. Cattle and hay mostly. That and horses. We train and sell most of the horses. My family's still there. And, I tell you what, man, if I were you I'd try not to take up the habit of running down Texas."

"You look part Indian?"

"Yes, and I'm proud of that, too. My grandmother was full Choctaw, from over in Louisiana."

"It's the cheek bones," Johnny B. said. "How'd you end up in Alaska?"

"I didn't *end up* here, I came on purpose."

"And what purpose was that?"

"Well, in a fashion, I reckon it was to figure my life out. I was getting confused down there with my so-called career and all."

"Confused?" Johnny B. asked, his interest now keen. "You do seem pretty confused."

"It was like this," I said, shaking my head, tired of his smart aleck wise cracks. "While I went to forestry college I jumped out of Redding in summers. That's how I got into smokejumping. When I got out of college I went to work on the San Bernardino National Forest as the Recreations and Lands Officer on the San Jacinto

District. I was responsible for eight campgrounds and the San Jacinto Wilderness. All that was fine at first, but then I had to deal with motorcycle gangs, late at night, go into their camps and talk with the head honchos when they were drunk and on drugs. They thought I was a cop and acted mean and called me a tree pig."

Johnny B. loved that and let out a big hoot and nearly fell over.

"*A tree pig,*" he cried. "I knew it, Duke. The sheriff of smokejumping was a *Tree Pig.* This is beautiful, man, I mean really beautiful."

He was so stoned he didn't understand I was telling a serious story.

"Tree pig or not," I said, "it was plain crazy. So I took a transfer to the Klamath National Forest marking timber and preparing logging sales. Things went all right for awhile there too, but then Nixon got involved and, without talking with anyone who knew the least thing about it, he raised the annual allowable cut, which is to say the *required* cut. A third. At the same time he only raised the budget to do the work three percent, said it was a matter of national security, that we needed to settle a trade deficit with Japan. That's when my real troubles began.

"Well, Duke," Johnny B. said. "It's plain to see that our friend here's had a tormented past."

"You're stoned," I said. "Now do you want to hear the rest of this or not?"

"Of course we do," Johnny B. said. "What are you waiting for?"

"I'm waiting for you to shut up, that's what. Now keep still and listen a minute and you might learn a thing or two."

Johnny B. got big-eyed when he heard that. He put his finger up to his lips signaling for Duke to keep quiet, which was strange since Duke never said jackshit anyway.

"So you see," I went on, "the only way to increase the cut by a third on three percent more money was to start clear cutting. I told them it was wrong, and they knew it, but went along with it anyway. All except me. We'd already spent a couple years complaining we didn't have enough help to check all our wet meadows and stream crossings as it was, and now we were expected to go off whole-hog and cut a bunch more. I told my District Ranger to tell Washington that we weren't gonna do it, that if they wanted that much cut then give us the money to do it the way it should be done."

While I was telling my story, Johnny B. opened a can of baked beans and was eating them with some John Wayne crackers.

"It wasn't long after that that the Forest Supervisor came out and took me for a ride up to Big Rock. We parked where we could see most all of the Mill Creek area where we were supposed to do the clear cuts. He put it plain and simple. It was my job to mark the sales, and if I wouldn't do it they'd get someone who would. Well now, as a young forester, that put me in a bind. I was still on probation so I told him I'd think about it. I did and I decided I better do like they said. But it wasn't a month later that I decided to take two years leave, come back to jumping, and see how things worked out."

Johnny B. spooned the last beans out, chewed for while, then said, "Let me get this straight. Tree pig goes rogue, gets in a hassle with Tricky Dick, draws attention of high-up boss, is threatened to have hams canned, feet pickled, and head turned into cheese. Is that what you're saying?"

I laughed about that. The McGrath All-Star laughed, too.

"I reckon that's it. And I'm also saying you're stoned. Right now you haven't got any more sense than that monkey there. What I'm trying to tell you is that when I left they weren't all that happy about it, and I have no idea what it'll be like when I go back. But now's no time to fuss about the past. I came up here to get back into jumping and enjoy life without having to deal with spineless bureaucrats."

Johnny B. looked over at his monkey and said, "Let's face it, Duke. Our friend, Len here, he's nothing but a damned trouble maker."

"Some's just hardheaded, too," I said. "Listen here. I don't want to talk about it anymore. That thunder business of yours has made you goofy as a shit house rat. And now here you are dreaming up stories and talking to a stuffed monkey. And to top it off, it's all on government time."

Johnny B. chuckled to himself, then unzipped a pocket on the top of his PG bag and pulled out a harmonica.

"No matter how tough life gets you can always make it better with a good mouth harp," he said. "This little tune's one of Duke's favorites."

Johnny B. blew through it several times to get the water out. Then, after a blues lead-in, he began tapping his foot and singing:

"There's a great big mystery...
and it sure is a worryin' me
This diddy wa diddy. . .
This diddy wa diddy
Won't someone tell me what
the diddy wa diddy means.
"Went to a church,
put my hat on the seat
Lady sit down and say,
'Daddy you sure is sweet'
Mister diddy wa diddy...
Mister diddy wa diddy
Won't someone tell what
the diddy wa diddy means.

Eyes shut tight, he kept on tapping his foot then lifted the harp and blew on it, making it squeal and moan and make animal noises. I couldn't help but smile and tap my own foot. With the harp still in his hand he rested it on his knee and — with considerable carrying on — sang a verse of his own.

"Well I turned to the left,
I turned to the right,
Landed on the ice and
went clear out of sight
Some diddy wa diddy,
that good wa diddy
Sure would like some sweet
wa diddy tonight."

About quitting time a wind came up and blew Johnny B.'s parachute to a place on shore where we could get it. Once we had everything packed up and our campfire put out we went to jumper camp for dinner. Sunlight burned bright in the orange and white panels of the two cargo chutes that covered camp. The apex of each chute was tied to a long spruce pole that stood at its center. With its shroud lines tied off to surrounding trees and brush, each canopy created an umbrella-like covering and provided some protection from the sun and rain. A large stack of firewood sat just inside the drip line of one. A chainsaw, saw chaps, and a Pulaski sat beside it. Two cooking fires were going. One-gallon goodie cans filled with water hung by wire bales over tripods made of spruce poles. Army issue P-38 can openers were hard at work opening C-ration cans whose labels offered things like "Beef Chunks, Cooked, Water Added," or "Chicken, Cooked and Formed," or "Eggs and Ham, Water Added." The stuff listed on the top of the cans sounded more like a formula for rocket fuel than food. Things like ferrous sulfate, thiamin mono nitrate, autolyzed yeast, acidity regulators, tripotassium citrate, tocopherols, monosodium glutamate, soy protein insolate, chicken powder, citric acid, and paprika flavorings. Although considered just another hazard of the job, most jumpers loved them. They tasted good, packed a lot of energy, and had four free cigarettes in each carton. We called them rats, short for C-rats.

Jim Kasson sat on a case of rats at the edge of camp, pulling feathers from two spruce hens he  shot sometime during pump and hose training. Spruce hens are a kind of grouse that live in the north country white spruce and paper birch woods. The jumpers called them fool hens since they're so easy to sneak up on and kill. I reckon Kasson was tired of eating rats in the war. He grew up in North Dakota, a little old place named Lisbon. As a kid he trapped and hunted. In a leg pocket of his jump pants he carried a sawed-off Winchester Model 12 pump-action shotgun that broke down into two parts. Lean and stringy, he had sand colored hair and kept to himself. I could tell right off he had a strong dislike for rules and the people who made them. After his rookie year in Missoula he went off to Vietnam. Fresh back, rumor was that he'd been in the mountains with a group of fighters and had worked secretly with what he simply called the agency. My first night in the barracks I overheard a  couple of the Vets talking. In Vietnam he was known as Killer Kasson.

Sitting there listening and watching, I thought back to the first time I saw Alaska smokejumpers. It was Missoula, Montana, August of 1967, during one of the busiest jump seasons in history. While Bobbie Gentry spent her summer singing how Billy Joe McCallister had jumped off the Tallahatchie Bridge, 425 jumpers spent theirs making a record 7,358 jumps to fires in the West. At one point all but fifty were jumping out of Missoula. The sky was filled with smoke from the Sundance, Trapper Peak, and Cotter Bar fires. A half million acres had burned. A hundred fires were out of control. Our twenty-man booster crew from Redding landed at five in the morning. Region 1 dispatch had 75 fire requests from Idaho's Nez Perce National Forest alone. Missoula was jumped out. After breakfast we were told to get some sleep. We went down in the cool basement where it was quiet. By noon dispatch had made up their minds and set priorities. That afternoon four of us jumped a fire in the River of No Return Wilderness in Central Idaho. The rest were spread here and there, mostly joining other jumpers working fires they couldn't catch. For a month we jumped fire after fire with no breaks. Pat Shearer, a Missoula rookie, made a record twenty-five fire jumps.

It was in the Missoula Ready Room that I first saw the Alaskans. I was checking my gear when a bunch came through the big bay doors silhouetted against the bright midday sun. After dropping their gear bags off their shoulders they stood talking casually, laughing and shaking hands with other jumpers. Although the Alaskans looked as fit and rugged as any, their dress and behavior were clearly different. Besides Levis and plaid shirts, one named Lance wore a pair of striped railroad overalls and a mashed-up baby-blue cowboy hat. His long black hair streamed nearly to his waist. Another wore dirty white Levis and—if you can believe it—a yellow cashmere sweater. Besides their flair for fashion, the Alaskans had a spirit wilder than most. They talked loud, held firm opinions and expressed them often, to anyone and everyone. But mostly, what set them apart was how much they laughed. They laughed at everything, including the Missoula squad leaders and their rules. In the eyes of a good many, the Alaskans were considered inferior when it came to basic smokejumper skills. Some of the base managers saw them as poorly trained parachutists, marginal firefighters, and flat-out oat hogs. "Oats" came from "OTs", which was what Alaska jumpers called Over Time. The Alaskans, I was warned, were a collection of rejects from the other jump bases, and best avoided.

Before fixing dinner at Bonanza Creek I decided I better go to my hootch and make a few improvements. My first night had not gone well. Somehow I had made a mess of my first hootch- building attempt in the bush. I held up on a little rise where I could look down on camp and out to the west. Camp smoke drifted in a blue haze across the yellow meadow as the crews settled in for the evening. Beyond the meadow was a band of red-bottomed clouds and a big frozen lake with pockets of open water. The red of the clouds had turned the ice a pinkish-gray. Beyond that was the interior of Central Alaska, eight-hundred miles stretching all the way to Nome.

My hootch looked more like a giant, black praying mantis than some sort of shelter. I stepped back to give it a good look over and figure out where to begin. I'd started with a ridge pole tied into the notch of two X-shaped end poles. That was a mistake since they both could move. So I threw the end poles away and tied the ridge pole to two trees. Thank goodness I was far enough from camp that no one would likely see what I was doing. Most times I did all right in the woods, at least in the Lower 48. But the Alaska interior, with its lumpy tundra, wet bog holes, and wobbly small trees was uncooperative, if not outright hostile to the entire notion of camping in comfort. How in the world could a man get the sides of a flimsy mosquito net stretched out tight and firmly sealed to the ground when there wasn't any ground to start with, just bushes, brush, jabbing sticks and clumps of cottongrass? Worse than that, how could anyone make a ground cloth and a rain fly from a 12 foot square of thin visqueen? Desperate, I cut some black spruce boughs with my Woodsman's Pal and arranged them under the mosquito net, hoping to smooth out the tundra. The bugs aren't bad yet, Bob Quinlan had told me earlier that day. Only the big, slow, dumb ones are out now, he said. The real mosquitoes report for duty in two weeks, once the nights get warmer.

I tore up some moss and spread it on top of the boughs for padding. By then the whole mess looked more like an area bears had dug up than a place you'd want to put a sleeping bag. That was another thing. The chicken bags—that's what the jumpers called them—were Army surplus mummies filled with chicken feathers. When you opened one up and held it up to the sun it let so much light through it looked like a cloudy day. Once the mosquitoes—even the dumb, slow ones—got under the net it wouldn't take them long to figure out how to drill through a chicken bag.

Anyway, I put the bag under the net, and then shook out the visqueen and threw it over the whole thing. With the corners tied down and the ridge pole ends sticking out, my praying mantis became a giant black beetle, a good deal like the one in the movie I'd seen as a kid, tearing around the streets of New York making a nuisance of himself. As much as I hated to admit it, I had a shitty hootch. Even with the changes it was little more a tangled mess of visqueen, EFF cord and mosquito netting. Before leaving I decided to clean up the area, the cut-off ends of F'er cord, the twisted and ruined scraps of fiberglass tape, some candy bar wrappers and other stuff that had fallen out of my shirt pockets. I took off then to join the others, glad to be leaving what felt like my first genuine, on-the-job screw-up as an Alaska smokejumper.

On the small rise I stopped again and looked down into the valley of Bonanza Creek, then beyond to the west. This is the interior of Alaska. Wilderness. Not like any in the Lower 48, with their boundaries and signs and campsites and trails. No sir! This was the real thing. It was big and it was empty and it was beautiful, but there was something terrible in it, too. Something that mocked man and the presence of man and efforts of man. Mean and savage-hearted, this place didn't give a damn whether you came or went, camped in comfort, lived or died.

While pulling a ball cap from my PG bag, out came a piece of paper, part of a form I'd signed when Al Mattlon hired me. I decided I'd better read it again.

### Smokejumper Job Description:

*Work Environment: The majority of work is performed in remote areas or in an aircraft flying at low level. While on fire duty (2-21 days per assignment) Alaska smokejumpers are subject to extreme fire behavior, use of hand tools and chain saws, black and grizzly bears, and low-level flights in helicopters from unimproved helispots. Living/working conditions involve rain and hailstorms with temperatures ranging from 30 to 100 degrees. Food is C-ration meals. Shower and latrine facilities are nonexistent. Sleeping facilities consist of a sleeping bag, a 12-foot square of visqueen, and mosquitoes are so numerous and miserable that they cannot be described on paper.*

*Smokejumpers risk serious injury or death while parachuting from aircraft. During flight duties, makes flights up to 5 hours over unplanned routes, across wilderness terrain, through frequent thunderstorms and turbulent air with sudden altitude changes in unpressurized aircraft and noise levels at maximum OSHA standards. While over a fire, must often work at open door, risk midair collisions, fly through smoke, and drop cargo from 150 feet above the ground risking a crash due to pilot error, sudden power loss or cargo snagging on tail.*

At camp I sat down on a five gallon cubitainer of water, a ways back from the rest, and took a minute to think about how great it was to be a smokejumper again. It had been three years since I'd last sat in a jumper camp. Smokejumpers were different, the Alaskans even more so. All are fit and rugged but the Alaska bunch didn't hold to a dress code like some did down south. It was the '70s and I believe it was the hippies that had inspired them. Levis and long-sleeve plaid shirts were common. Some wore canvas or leather vests. A few wore floppy crusher hats of various colors. Most wore baseball caps. All but a few had Buck folding knifes strapped to thick leather belts. Among jumpers, what the White boot was to boots, the five-inch Buck folding knife was to knives. With its sweeping rosewood handle capped at both ends by brass blocks, the Buck had an eye catching blade that curved to a fine point, the sum of which, when held in the hand, met the need for both function and art in a working tool. Alaska jumpers carried one thing others did not—a Woodsman's Pal. They called them Woody Pals, and used them to cut brush and spruce boughs. The Alaska version was a 16-inch steel machete with its tip cut blunt. It hung in a canvas holster from the hip.

The smell of fresh coffee was a perfect addition to a perfect moment, so I took my Army canteen cup out of my PG bag, knocked the dust out of it, and poured a cup. Squad leader Bob Quinlan sat off to the side reading a thick, dog-eared paperback named *War and Peace*. After a while he put it down and, looking across the campfire at the McGrath All-Star, filled his pipe with tobacco. Although small by smokejumper standards, Quinlan was strong and athletic, with a reputation of being fair-minded and tough. I could tell he was proud to be a jumper, and that he took anything to do with it seriously. He liked to get after people. I'd seen him light into them before. He usually did it by starting out with his trademark "Aackk". I reckon it was meant to bring extra attention to the subject, but mostly it just sounded like a worn-out duck call.

"Aackk, Johnny B.," Quinlan said. "You feeling okay?"

Johnny B. sat off a ways reading his book about the white man that wanted to be black. Duke sat on top of Johnny B.'s PG bag, staring at the campfire.

"Oh, I'm fine. Thanks for getting me out of the pond by the way. I got a little carried away looking at Denali. It's been awhile since I've seen Alaska like that. It was a bonehead move. But other than the fact that I screwed up, could have died, and now have to deal with the thought of Rake taking my pants off, I feel fine."

"Johnny B." Rake grinned. "How's it feel to have your nuts soaked in ice water for ten minutes?"

Johnny B. hesitated, then said, "Once they thaw out I'll give you a full report, Rake. Until then, just think of them as two frozen blue raisins."

"Maybe you can get your Johnson hot-wired when you get back to Fairbanks," Rake said.

Quinlan was taking it all in, sipping his coffee and puffing on his pipe. "Aackk" he suddenly said, "lucky we got you out when we did. A little longer and your heart would have needed hot-wired, too."

"I steered as close to shore as I could."

"Close is fine if you're playing horseshoes," Quinlan kept on. "But this is exactly the kind of thing this new District Manager's hoping for — that we'll hang ourselves with our own rope."

"Meechameandu," Melvin Sheenjek said. A Meechameandu, I learned later, was some kind of Indian devil Melvin's people believed in.

"Aackk," Quinlan said. "Then, we have Bell and Rakowski. The two that finished off the McGrath base."

John Rakowski and Don Bell, who were sitting side by side on a stack of C-rats, turned in unison towards Quinlan.

"Yes! I'm talking to you two. You're lucky they didn't fire the whole bunch."

Of those in camp that evening, besides Johnny B., it was Rake, a.k.a. the Legendary Fucking Rake, that made me the most curious. Rake had served a year with the U.S. Marines in Vietnam. Of average height, he was stocky, thick in the middle, and wore a Marine field jacket with the name tag torn half off. His brown hair was mostly wild, just like his mustache, eyebrows and sideburns.

"Bob Quinlan," Rakowski said. "Fairbanks squad leader and faithful devotee of the terminally mind-fucked overhead. Must you..."

"Meechameandu," Melvin Sheejek, said to Bob. "You look like a devil. You have the eyes of a devil." After pausing a bit, Melvin squinted mean-like, and said, *"You are the devil."*

"Aackk," Quinlan said again, this time worked up. "Don't go lumping me in with a bunch of overhead or any devils, either. I'm just saying, you went too far when you stole that plane."

"We didn't steal it," Bell growled, "we borrowed it. And I'm tired of hearing people whine about it, too."

"Meechameandu," Melvin said again.

"They needed some excitement," Bell added. "They needed some fun instead of all the time ruining ours, running around bitching about this and that, taking their pitiful little management jobs seriously. The mental stimulation did them good."

"Oh, no doubt," Quinlan said. "While they were away at a meeting in Anchorage, you talked the pilots into flying you guys on an 1800 mile, government sponsored beer bust across Western Alaska. I'm sure they got a big charge out of that."

"Meechameandu." Melvin insisted.

"Melvin," Bell snapped. "Stop it. So he's a Meechameandu. I don't really give a shit."

"Meechameandu," Melvin said with less heat.

As Bell told the story I learned how the McGrath overhead had finally had it with the crew of 1972. In a way it was a surprise, even though, during the three years I was gone from jumping, I did hear rumors that McGrath had become the wildest smokejumper crew in history. I never believed it, though. Stories always get exaggerated. But that night in camp, it was clear they had done some exceptional things all right. They had a few Vietnam veterans like Rake, just home from the war, a handful of ex-Air America bad boys, and a bunch of black sheep from the down-south bases. The more Bell talked the more excited he got. He told how they tangled with gold miners, bush pilots, local tough guys, and even employees of other government agencies like the US Fish and Wildlife Service, the National Park Service, and the Federal Aviation Administration. Not to discriminate, they had also thrown the National Weather Service weatherman in the Kuswowim River for his poor performance forecasting lightning storms.

Finally the McGrath overhead were called to Anchorage to explain things. Before they left they held a meeting in the cookhouse. They made it clear that they would be gone for two days, that they had had it, and that if there was one more minor infraction heads would roll. But only minutes after their plane took off, Rakowski went to the pilots of McGrath's DC-3 and said that, since the season was nearly over, the crew wanted to do something special to celebrate.

"The next morning," Bell said, "Rake and I wrote a supply order for 32 cases of premix fuel, then flew to Anchorage and got 32 cases of beer. Ha, ha. *Thirty-two* cases. Back in McGrath we loaded up the whole crew and flew to Unalakleet and landed at the airport along the beach. When the overhead called McGrath to see how things were going the cook told them they were going just fine, but that someone had left a note that we'd taken the plane and gone off to visit a village called Lickmanutsak. Ha, ha. Boy were they pissed."

The whole crew laughed.

"At least," Rake chuckled, "we hadn't gone to Kissmatoolchuk."

Again the crew went wild. All but Quinlan, who snarled and puffed out clouds of smoke from his pipe.

"We built this big driftwood fire and stayed up all night," Rakowski said. "A bunch of villagers turned out and got shit-faced right along with us. That was the best public relations BLM got with the natives all summer."

"Shit-faced!" Quinlan huffed. "Such a poetic swan song to the demise of a once great jump base."

"See it anyway you want, but it was fun, and I'm glad we did it, Rake said. "What were they gonna do anyway, send me back to Vietnam?"

"Hey? Anybody want some beaver?" asked another ex-McGrath jumper. "This is what mountain men used to eat."

He'd been sitting by the fire stirring a bucket of what looked like ink ever since I'd returned from fixing my hootch. Mountain Man—as he wanted to be called—was wearing some kind of cheap pirate hat with an eagle feather stuck in the side. On his belt was a long knife with leather fringe on the scabbard.

"Hey Mountain Guy," Rakowski said. "How about bagging the mountain man bullshit, okay? Do yourself a favor and have some Beanie Weenies like the rest of us."

Ignoring Rake's jab at his nickname, Mountain Man went back to stirring his beaver. Among smokejumpers, two basic rules apply when it comes to nicknames. First, never give yourself one. And second, if someone gives you one you don't like, don't let on about it. Even after obeying the rules, a fair number of jumpers wound up called things like The Fat Indian, Weird Bill, Chicken Legs, Airhead, Hairface, Stupid Man, Master Bates, and Old Leathersack.

The subject of Gloria Steinem and the feminist movement came up and Mountain Man was labeled a sexist pig who, by rights, should be called Mountain Person. Mountain Man flew into a rage, cussing and condemning all movements, modern or otherwise. Seeing his chance, Rakowski ran with it, and in no time Mountain Man went from Mountain Man to Mountain Person, which quickly went to Mountain Pussun, and then finally settled on the vastly more modern Mountain Puss.

"Hey Rake," Mountain Puss said, giving Rake the finger, "Beanie Weenie this." Rake just laughed. I thought it reckless of Mountain Man to get into it with Rake. It was clear that with one more change he'd simply end up being called Puss—not exactly an easy thing to explain to other mountain men.

Rakowski, on the other hand, loved being called Rake, the Legend or The Legendary Fucking Rake. Defying the rules, the odds, and thirty-two years of smokejumper history, he had given them all to himself. His favorite was The Legendary Fucking Rake. Other times he'd say, "Just call me The Legend."

"I know what your problem is," Rake chuckled, still digging at Mountain Puss. "You were one of those goosey Woodchuck kids that ran around in fake moccasins and dime store coon skin hats, right?"

Still ignoring Rake, Mountain Puss poked his knife into the black liquid and brought up a piece of something that looked like the sludge that collected around oil derricks where I grew up in Texas. He had killed the beaver with his .357 Magnum shortly after the All-Star went in the pond, skinned it, and commenced to brag on his getting some camp meat. His idea of cooking a beaver amounted to putting it in a bucket of water and boiling it for three hours, including the tail, which he claimed was a favorite of Louis and Clark. Mountain Puss held out a piece of the steaming black object, offering it to whoever might take it. Weird Bill pulled it off the knife, looked at it briefly, then said, "You missed some hair."

A few more decided to try Mountain Puss' beaver. Right off, Melvin spit it out.

"That beaver's ruined," Melvin said. "It was a good, fat beaver and you ruined it. Did you thank the animal's spirit? Hell no. You just shot it and started boiling."

"I didn't know they had one," Mountain Puss said. "I thought they were just hairy dumb shits with flat tails and buck teeth."

Melvin Sheejek leaned back and rolled his broad shoulders.

"Flat tails and buck teeth?" he said, trying not to laugh. "Sounds like some of those women you bring to the barracks."

Melvin was Neets'aii Gwich'in, and his people had lived in northeastern Alaska for over 6,000 years. Alatnuk, with its 150 residents, was just south of the Arctic National Wildlife Range. It was where he was born and had lived until becoming a smokejumper in 1970. Of Mongolian hunter descent, Melvin had high cheek bones, wide Asian eyes, a broad nose and a mouth that turned down at the corners like his stringy mustache.

"Crap," Bell said. "What'd you do, boil this in chainsaw oil?"

"Spirit or not, beaver's good for you," Mountain Puss said. "Lots of fat to keep you warm in winter."

"Well, this one tastes like shit," Bell said, throwing his piece into the campfire. "And it ain't winter, either."

"You ruined a good beaver," Melvin said to Mountain Puss. "You need to be Indian to know how to cook beaver. You're too white."

"Next time try taking the hair off," Rake said.

"Yeah, right!" Mountain Puss said. "Then you could glue it on your face and fill out those Elvis Presley sideburns.

"You're too white!" Melvin said, this time louder. "You don't know nothing."

For a moment no one said anything, then Mountain Man asked.

"Melvin? Is it too late? I mean, can we still do the spirit thing?"

Melvin shook his head. "I've never heard of it after cooking. Spirit had to leave on its own."

"Come on Melvin," Mountain Puss said. "I'd like to see how you do it."

Melvin and Mountain Puss got up and left camp. A few others got to their feet, grabbed their PG bags and said goodnight. On the way to my hootch, I stopped again on the little rise. The smoke above the meadow created the impression of an Indian camp. A few of the larger hootches were communal with lodge poles crisscrossed at different angles. Visqueen had been pulled tight across them, then tied off to the ground in various triangles that made the scene beautiful and complete. People sat in front of some and talked. Over 100 people were there from every branch of the BLM's Alaska wildland fire organization. Nearest the lake were the helitac hootches. For the coming season, they would crew the helicopters. Next to them was the camp of the roadside group. They would crew the engines stationed in Fairbanks, Tok, and Delta Junction. At the upper end of the meadow, across from the jumper camp, were the hootches of the office and clerical staff, timekeepers and administrative people—mostly women. The first afternoon they and the helitac people and a few roadside overhead had flown in directly from Fairbanks in a new blue and white Bell 205 helicopter. The jumpers had either jumped in or hiked in from the Parks Highway.

As for the upper-level fire staff, there wasn't a one there. The purpose of the campout was to review firefighting skills and equipment use, but more important, it was a good way to get to know the people you would be working with outside your group. Now and then I could hear laughter from the various camps. In the distance the Alaska Range stood a hundred miles to the south, a wall of jagged peaks bathed in alpenglow. Besides the late-evening activities in camp, the only other sound was the far off wing beat of the Nighthawk, diving for insects, making its fast wup, up, up, up, up sound in the cool evening air. Down at the edge of the lake Mountain Puss and Melvin stood side by side holding a bucket up to the sky.

# *2*

The next day at Bonanza Creek was clear and passed pleasantly with a session of map reading, area measurement, and compass work. All in all the Alaska smokejumper crew was about sixty men, thirty from Fairbanks, twenty-five from McGrath, and five or so transfers like me from different Lower 48 bases. After the talk the night before I could see there were some sour feelings between the Fairbanks crew and the fellas thrown out of McGrath. At one point a Fairbanks jumper said that McGrath was like the Keystone Cops of smokejumping. Mostly, though, it was just making fun. Jumpers always fussed with each other. I figured once fire season got going things would smooth out. But wouldn't you know, that night in camp they got into it again. I guess Quinlan felt he had to bring up the subject of the All-Star landing in the pond again, and how Mountain Puss had almost poisoned the crew with a boiled beaver.

"Bedeviled Bob," Rake said shaking his head. "Why make a mountain out of a mow hill? He missed the spot. We had a wind shift and some bad cooking. Hell man, that's as old as smokejumping itself."

"It's *mole* hill," Quinlan said. "A mountain out of a *mole* hill!"

"You better listen, Rake," Mountain Puss said. "Bob's right. We can't afford the bad press. They're talking about changing initial attack up here. Some loser from California's the new District Manager and he wants to use helicopters more. They're suppose to get all the close-in fires and we'll only get what's left."

Moans of skepticism came from around the campfire.

"Mattlon was talking about it just before we left," Kasson said. "There's eight new Bell 205s parked on the river right now, down where the tent frames used to be. Civilian models of the Hueys we had in Nam."

"Sheep have exhibited better critical thinking skills," Rake said. "These managers have been talking about replacing jumpers with helicopters for years. They like to hold our ass to the fire, then watch us shiver like dogs shitting peach seeds."

"Aackk, it's peach *pits!*" Quinlan said. "And, don't be so sure. I was here all winter. After Gary died, rumors started about downsizing the jumpers. The Anchorage Office was already eager to can McGrath, and Fairbanks was left without a foreman to stick up for us. This Mort guy, the new DM, he's all for it.

I sipped my coffee and pondered this news. The previous winter, Gary, the base foreman had come home late one night, put a pan of soup on the stove, then fell asleep on the sofa. His trailer house burned to the ground and he died in the fire. Al Mattlon, a squad leader with some experience on the operations desk, stepped in and took charge. Everyone assumed it would only be until they found Gary's official replacement. But, the first week in May, word came from the District Office that Al Mattlon was to be the new base foreman.

Right after I got to Alaska I visited Mattlon's office at 3.5 Mile, Airport Road. Al was tall and lanky with thin brown hair and a big Adam's apple. Unlike most smokejumpers, he moved slowly, like maybe he needed a new transmission, like the one he had was stuck in low gear or something. When he spoke he thought about it longer than most people. He would stop and hold up right in the middle of sentences and wait before starting again. Among the crew he was more widely known for his mastery of the barstool and jukebox than the basic skills of smokejumping. One time he and Johnny B. jumped a fire east of Nenana. They went to work right off. An hour or so after they had it contained, Johnny B. went looking for Mattlon. He went around the fire and back to the jump spot. Mattlon wasn't either place. After he got the fire safe enough to leave, he hiked a quarter mile out to the Parks Highway, then hitchhiked into Nenana. And there was Al sitting on a barstool in Moocher's Bar, smoking a cigarette and listening to hillbilly music.

In his office at 3.5 mile, though, he was impressed that I'd driven all the way to Alaska on the hope I could get on with the crew. He leaned back in his swivel chair, spent some time thinking, then explained that he wanted to hire me, but it depended on whether or not a couple guys came back. One had phoned from Guatemala. He was deciding whether to come back jumping or get on a sailboat with a friend and a couple German girls and sail to Tahiti. The other was in Khe San looking for a buddy who was MIA. Al Mattlon promised he would give me an answer by week's end. I had a feeling that he was a man of his word. Both guys called and said they would not be back.

"Ahh, well, ah, looks like you're in," he said as he hung up the phone, then turned to a blackboard behind his desk and wrote my name at the bottom of the '73 crew list.

"Anyone who drives all the way to Alaska for a chance to jump here... can't be all bad. Rumor is that you were a pain in the ass to the Forest Service... so you'll probably fit in here fine." At that he leaned across his desk, shook my hand, and said, "Welcome to the Alaska smokejumpers."

That was last Friday, and now just six days later there was this helicopter trouble. It wasn't at all what I wanted to hear my first week on the job.

"Well," Don Bell said after taking in the comments about the new District Manager, "he can run his mouth about helicopters all he wants. But he doesn't know shit about this country, how big it is, or how it burns."

A weak cheer went up around the campfire, but Bell wasn't done yet. "Puffy-fingered, potbellied, walrus-faced nerd. Wandering around his carpeted office in dress shoes, pretending he knows what's going on. Well, he doesn't. And he won't because he doesn't know that this country is a lot bigger than what he's seein' on his pitiful little maps with his pitiful little pins stuck in them."

More cheers, various Ah-uhhs and male madness. Bell was on a roll.

"Alaska's smokejumper country, always has been, always will be. And, I don't need to hear any more about it either."

Hearing that, the crew broke into a fit of arguing, and amid the ruckus didn't hear the Bell 205 helicopter that was, at that very moment, closing in on camp. By the time we did it was too late. On a low final, it came over the ridge right in line with our camp. Bell grabbed his Woodsman's Pal and ran out stabbing it in the air. The helicopter kept on coming. Camp smoke began to swirl. A rush of downdraft knocked Bell backwards off his feet. Instantly the cargo chutes over our camp began tearing at their ropes, pots and pans went this way and that, sparks flew. Hootches momentarily hopped up and down, then came apart as sleeping bags, mosquito nets, shirts, socks, and all kinds of stuff blew off in the brush.

The helicopter passed over, flew on a hundred yards, flared, then sat down in the meadow. Our crew was quick to offer a good amount of comments regarding the pilot's state of mind. Quinlan grabbed a burlap bag and lined-out a squad to fight the little fires that had started from flying sparks. Just like that our camp had gone from organized to looking like a bomb had gone off. Rake and Bell ran to the helicopter, shook their fingers, and pointed in the direction of our camp. A thin, young man carrying a black briefcase climbed out eager to shake hands with his enthusiastic new co-workers. I don't reckon much was communicated, though.

Five minutes later Rake and Bell were back in camp, growling around and cussing at the mess.

"Stupid nerds," Bell said. "Flying some district office jerkoff out here. Too bad they didn't burn up the whole camp."

I went to my hootch and saw that it had taken a direct hit. The visqueen tarp had been torn, and there were holes in the bug net. After a halfhearted attempt at repairs, I retied what was left and crawled into bed. I lay a moment thinking. All in all it had been a good few days in the bush, getting to know some of the guys and all. A pair of loons cried far out on the lake. Nighthawks dipped about in the cool evening air, the wup, up, up, up of their wings a pleasant reminder that all was well in the great scheme of things. In no time I was sound asleep.

The rain woke me at three. Just a sprinkle at first, then a steady tapping on my torn rain fly. A gust of wind pulled a knot loose from one corner, and I had to crawl out into the rain and fiddle with it. Back inside, the wind gusted, the rain fly flapped, pockets of rain water blew in the air then back on my head. Drips got to be steady streams. Desperate, I reached out from under the edge of the bug net and tried to do something about the dripping. I was messing with that when another wind gust tore the rain fly loose and set it to blowing in the wind. Rain streamed in. By the time I got out and got it corralled and back in again everything was as wet and dirty as if you'd stomped it in a puddle. Then, as suddenly as it had started, the rain quit. The woods got quiet again, except for this strange humming. Mosquitoes, I suppose cheered up by the rain, came tearing up out of the tundra in swarms, and easily gained entrance through the holes in my bug net. I tried poking the edges under the sleeping bag but that didn't work worth a damn. I'd doze off, only to wake up and see my arms covered with bloated, bloodsucking mosquitoes, the slow, dumb ones at that. In all my life I had never seen the likes of that many mosquitoes. Besides my arms, my forehead was lumpy and itchy too. I dug out my Army bug dope and squirted a palm full and then smeared it on my arms and forehead. I spilled some on the mosquito net and was downright discouraged to see it melt more holes. Shitfire! Having run out of plans that worked, I gave up and wiggled down into my soggy chicken bag and pulled my hard hat down low to keep the pesky bastards off my head. When I woke up a couple hours later my arms itched bad, but worse, the area across my forehead was nothing but raw skin. That was from a reaction between too much bug dope and the sweaty headband on my hardhat. Miserable as a lost calf in a dust storm, I crawled out, splashed on more bug dope, then crammed the remains of my hootch into a burlap bag and headed for camp where I built a fire, then sat in the smoke where at least I had a chance to fight them off.

An hour later the sun cleared the horizon. Lavender clouds sailed like tall ships against a pale green dawn. Suspended in the brush and trees, raindrops became pin points of rainbow light. A few jumpers got up, Quinlan, Johnny B., and Bell. Then, slowly, the rest came in. All but Quinlan were cranky. But, thanks to a balmy breeze and the glory of morning sunshine, it didn't take long until everyone was laughing and carrying on about our wet night. Some said it was Big Ernie, the smoke-jumper God, eager to test the new crew. The storm, they claimed, was his first dirty trick of the year. Big Ernie was known for behaving downright nasty at times, bringing on severe weather, broken helicopters, burned-over camps, slow seasons and even periods of low overtime. According to him, jumpers had to value hard work, drive on, and never give up. When things went bad, Big Ernie was often the one that got blamed. Melvin Sheejek, however, put the blame for both the rain and wrecked hootches — not on Big Ernie — but on Mountain Puss for turning a beaver into a pot of tar, and Quinlan for being a Meechameandu.

By midday the sky was full of undulating waves, sculpted curls and lacey strands of high vapor that caught the sunlight just right and created what, in Texas, are known as sun dogs. Large flights of geese and ducks and swans moved across the sky towards the northwest out into Minto Flats. Shortly after lunch we began breaking camp. I had to admit, except for a few minor troubles and one wet night, the week had gone well. Just before shouldering our packout bags, I took a long look at my first jumper camp in the Alaska bush. Then I turned away, grabbed up my pack, and fell in with the crew for our six-mile hike out to the Parks Highway.

We sat on the floor in two rows, one along each side of the fuselage, facing the tail. The DC-3's engines roared to pre-flight rpm checks. The Pratt & Whitney 1650s sent vibrations through the plane and my body and, for some reason, reminded me of a poster I saw while jumping out of Redmond, Oregon. Made by one of their jumpers, it was posted right next to the jump list. In its center was a photograph of a jumpship parked on the aircraft ramp at night. A lightning strike hammered down across the runway. All was black and dark and without form except for the jump-ship, the lightning and a bit of the sky. Beneath the photo, in stylish print, were these words from the German poet Goethe:  In Boldness there is Genius and Magic.

Following the run-ups the Doug sat idling, rocking gently side to side. I peered out at the flashing propeller blades. In the pit of my stomach I felt the strange uneasiness I get before a jump. Everything plays into it. Waiting for the announcement to suit-up, suiting up, checking gear, loading into the plane, the sound of great power and the smell of exhaust. With it comes the idea that, although slim, there's a chance that you could be living the last minutes of your life. Jumpers don't talk about it but it's there. Deep in your gut. Every time.

The brakes released and the big plane eased out onto the runway. Several jumpers raised their fists or gave a thumbs up. Pat Shearer, Johnny B. and Gene Bartell sat across from me. Hairface, Jim Cleermont, Charlie Wilbur, and Weird Bill Harlo were sitting behind them. Don Bell was right in front of me and would be my jump partner. Wearing Wellington boots, Levis, a plaid cowboy shirt, and an emergency parachute, Al Mattlon stood at the back of the plane by the open door holding onto the vertical cable and staring blankly at the ground. He would spot the load.

Out in the center of the runway the Doug stopped, held a few seconds, then released its brakes. The engines roared and off we went. I was looking through the blur of the propeller at the airfield when the tail lifted. Mattlon stood by the door with the wind blowing his hair. At 110 knots the Doug rotated and the land fell away, ten feet, fifty feet, a hundred. I heard the big wheels clunk up into the wheel wells. At 1,500 feet the engines cut back to cruising speed and settled into a steady drone.

That was my first time to see Fairbanks from the air. The Chena River ran in big loops through downtown, around buildings, under bridges, its amber-colored meltwater bordered by the town or mixed stands of spruce, aspen, and whitebark birch. We flew west, banking over the hills north of the University of Alaska. Mattlon had his headset on. From behind the wing there appeared a golf course, then some farms and an open field with a large log building. A snapping sound came from the door as Mattlon threw the first set of drift streamers. The Doug came around so that we could see them, ten-foot strands of red, blue, and yellow crepe paper sailing along in the great space between them and the ground. On our feet and crowding the windows, Bell turned to me.

"See those woods down there? he shouted, pointing to a patch of spruce near the University. "That's where we used to jump. But after Arden was killed we stopped."

I wasn't sure which woods he meant but hearing his words I put it together. During the let-down portion of refresher training, Arden Davis' death had been covered. Arden had missed the spot and landed in a black spruce that left him hanging only three feet off the ground. Following procedure, his jump partner yelled, Are you okay, and Arden had answered, Yes, I'm okay. Since a hung-up canopy is often caught so that some lines stretch tight and others to hang loose, shroud lines sometimes curl down around a jumper's shoulders. Figuring not to go through the whole letdown procedure for just three feet, Arden popped both fittings that attached his harness to his risers. Problem was, he did it without first checking for lines around his neck. As the group gathered up after collecting their gear someone noticed that Arden was missing. They found him hanged and dead, his feet barely a foot off the ground. From then on, the procedure was that a jumper would not respond with the words I'm okay until he was on the ground and completely clear of his gear.

"Arden was a good fella," Bell said. "He was a lot of fun. You would have liked him."

Mattlon tossed out the second set of streamers, glanced at his watch, then got down on the floor and lay on his stomach. That's the way spotters spot out of a Doug. With their heads near the floor, they can see farther forward under the plane for a good line-up. Timing the streamers helps determine the jump altitude, generally from 1200 to 1500 feet AGL - above ground level.

"Hey Bell, Duke wants to shake hands," Johnny B. said. I looked around and there was Johnny B. and his buddy with the button eyes.

"He what?"

"He wants to shake hands. This is his second jump," Johnny B. said, manipulating Duke's arm, up and down and extending it to Bell. "He wants to shake on it."

"Are you nuts?" Don howled. "I've got better things to do than shake hands with a monkey—especially a stuffed one. Throw that piece of shit out the door."

"Come on man, you're hurting Duke's feelings."

"I don't care if I am, I'm still not shaking hands with him."

The rest of the jumpers began shouting, "Come on Bell, Don't be a weaktit. Duke's a Bro."

Bell's hands flew around in front of him like he wanted something to choke not shake hands with. But the jumpers kept it up so that finally he reached out, took Duke's paw and shook it with little handshakes.

"Shit," Bell growled. "A damned monkey."

Mattlon looked up, said something into his handheld microphone, then held up two fingers signaling for the first two jumpers to come to the door. Johnny B. shoved Duke into his leg pocket so only his head poked out, then tied the cinch strings around his neck.

The first two jumpers went out. We were jumping in two-man sticks. That way each man is put out close enough that he has a chance to get into small spots in big timber. I was second man, fourth stick, and would jump behind Bell. As the first stick worked the wind the rest of us watched. Two sticks later, Bell and I stood waiting as Mattlon pulled the deployment bags into the plane, removed their static line clips from the vertical cable, then tossed them into the hellhole of the tail.

Mattlon yelled, "Next two."

Bell stepped into the door with me right behind.

"You see the streamers?" We both nodded. "You see the jump spot? "We nodded again.

"Okay, you got a little wind down low out of the southeast. Stay south of the road. I'll carry you long, you'll have plenty of room. There's a power line along the road, do you see it?"

We did. Al's transmission wasn't in low gear now, it was more like overdrive.

"Stay south of the road and you'll be fine. Bell, I'll put you in the door when we turn final. Go ahead and hook up."

Bell snapped his static line clip onto the vertical cable, inserted the safety wire and bent it so it couldn't come out. I did the same. As we turned final a sudden thankfulness came over me. Strange and unexpected circumstances had brought me back to smokejumping. I had given up all hope that I'd ever stand in the door of a jumpship again, and yet, there I was, looking out over Alaska, doing that very thing.

Mattlon stuck his head out into the slipstream and looked forward under the belly of Jumper 54 checking the line up. Pulling in, he said, "Right," and the plane yawed right.

Looking up at Bell he patted the threshold of the door with the palm of his hand.

"Get in the door," he shouted.

Bell stepped forward, grabbed the sides of the door and stood knees bent and straight-backed with the toe of his left boot a few inches beyond the threshold, out in the one-hundred mile per hour slipstream. Right off there was this sound like playing cards flapping against bicycle spokes. Bell jerked his foot back like he'd been snake bit. "Ha, ha. Did you hear that?" he said.

"What was it," Mattlon yelled. Don held up his boot. The stitching in the front had come loose, leaving four inches of the sole to flap in the wind. During the flapping, two or three inches of sock had been sucked out. The jumpers had a fit and commenced laughing and hollering at Bell. While the plane circled around, Mattlon grabbed a roll of hundred-mile-an-hour tape out of the spotter's kit, stuffed the sock back in, then taped the boot toe, making several wraps around it.

"Thanks Al," he said. "I appreciate it."

Mattlon yelled back. "You need new boots."

"I know it. And I intend to buy some. As soon as I get my first pay-check."

"If you can go out bar hopping every night, seems like you could afford a pair of boots."

"Bar hopping? Sounds like something a damned frog would do."

"I see you in bars all the time."

"I know, I've seen you, too. But it's not like I go there on purpose."

"Borrow some money, buy new boots."

"I better not, I owe too much already."

"Well you can't jump in those."

"I don't see why not. They're all right now."

"Here's the deal. Hop on down to Rocket Surplus on South Cushman, get yourself a good pair of boots. Put them on my account. Pay me when your first check comes... before you pay the rest. Okay?"

Bell looked puzzled a moment, then yelled, "That's mighty nice of you, Al, I sure will, you bet, but you don't have to do it if you don't want to."

"Maybe not, but it beats having socks blow in my face."

The Doug continued on around the jump pattern while Bell tested his boot in the slipstream. I couldn't believe it. There I was, fired-up to jump out of an airplane, and the next thing I know I'm listening to a conversation about frogs hopping about in bars and buying boots in a place that sells used rockets.

The Doug turned final. Mattlon spoke to his microphone. The plane yawed left. Mattlon's head was out, then back in.

"Get ready."

Bell braced himself in the door. I grabbed both sides of his main parachute for balance.

Mattlon looked up at Don, smiled, then slapped him on the back of his left calf, sending him out into a rush of noise and wind, leaving behind a door through which there was nothing but air for 1500 feet. Thrusting forward I cleared the door and felt the slipstream blow me sideways back along the fuselage, falling away in an accelerated downward arc. One one-thousand I counted. In a blur I saw my feet fly higher than my head and the big, broad tail of Jumper 54 pass above. Two one-thousand. I looked back at the plane and saw Mattlon's head out watching us. I felt like I was in slow motion. Three one-thousand. The plane was gone. Sure as hell, I'd gone and made a bad exit, not leaning far enough forward and letting my feet getting out from under me. Four one-thousand. The earth, the sky, then the earth again, then the force of the opening shock, and me jerked straight by the pull of the canopy. Just like that the roar was gone, and in its place came a startling silence. Looking around I saw Bell sail by. After checking my chute, I reached up and took the steering toggles from their elastic keepers on the risers. Facing the jump spot I saw jumpers on the ground gathering gear. A few vehicles were parked near the Musher's Field Lodge. Bell yelled something and I yelled, Okay, I see you. I looked again at my canopy. The thirty-two foot T-10 flashed International Orange and silvery white in the bright morning sun, rotating one way then the other, breathing in and out, catching and spilling air. I held upwind south of the road, just like Mattlon had told us. At three-hundred feet, running with the wind past the spot, I pulled my left toggle down as far as my arm would reach and came around facing into it. Bell landed forty feet wide of the big yellow X that marked the center of the spot. I held steady, making slight corrections that kept me aimed, more or less, at the X. The shadow of my canopy raced in a line across the ground, closing in on itself. A little gust of wind pushed me left, then right. In the next instant, there it was, high-speed dirt, rushing up. Just before impact I clicked my heals, pressed them firmly together, pointed my toes down, hit, rolled right onto my butt, my back, over my left shoulder, then flopped onto my side and stopped. With the canopy settling down beside me, I pulled off my helmet and began laughing, celebrating my good luck at completing a back flip on exit and still hitting the spot.

I turned off Airport Way onto Peger Road, and started looking for the District Office. Someone had left a message at the jumpshack that I had more hiring papers to sign. I felt on top of the world. That morning my refresher group had completed its first two practice jumps at Musher's Field. Smiling at myself in the pickup's rearview mirror, I recalled how good it felt to be standing in the door of a jumpship again, looking down at the world, feeling right with it all. I had the radio turned up and was tapping my fingers on the steering wheel, singing along with The Eagles, *Take it easy, take it easy. Don't let the sound of your own wheels drive you crazy.* It was Friday, a clear Alaska spring day and my second week on the job was nearly over. That afternoon I was to be put on the jump list.

It wasn't just the feeling of working in the company of capable, confident men, nor the notion that I could earn a lot of money. If I had learned anything during my years as a smokejumper, it was that the coming summer would involve people, places, and experiences beyond what a person might normally imagine. A summer parachuting to fires can't be scheduled. Rodeo people or sports professionals are special — any fool can see that — but they know something that smokejumpers don't. They know they will be in Dallas one day, in New York or San Antonio the next. As thrilling and satisfying as their lives may be, they are still tied to schedules, and to specific opponents at known places. Smokejumping is different. Jumpers have to live day to day, not knowing what will come next, what kind of fire they will jump, where it will be, or how they will deal with it. At the start of each season the savvy smokejumper accepts the fact that, for the next four to five months, the story of their lives will be written by the lightning storms that track Alaska and the mountains of the Northwest. No part of it can be foretold.

At the District Office I asked the receptionist about my hiring papers. She smiled, picked up the phone, said a few things, then hung up.

"Up the stairs. Second door on the right. The District Manager's expecting you."

"The District Manager? Oh, no Ma'am, there must be some mistake. I came to sign hiring papers, that's all."

"Uh, uh," she said, shaking her head. "No, you're the one he wants to see. I don't know about the papers but you can ask him."

That struck me as strange. Why in the world would I need to see the District Manager just to sign hiring papers? I went up the stairs like I was told and knocked on the door with the brass plaque that said, "Morton Twixtenblout, Fairbanks Area District Manager."

"Come in, come in," a voice blurted out. I stepped inside.

"Well now," the District Manager said, standing to shake my hand. "Sit down, please. You'll have to excuse me for... " He held up a while and looked a might confused. I was sure it was all a big mistake and was fixin' to leave when he finally said, "Oh yeah, here they... no."

Mr. Twixtenblout hesitated, squinted a moment, "Len? It's Len, right?"

"Yes, sir. Len Swanson."

"Mort Twixtenblout," he said, shaking hands again. "But just call me Mort."

"Yes sir. They said you had some hiring papers for me to sign."

"Papers? Oh, yes. They're right here, right here somewhere."

After a round of fake paper shuffling, Mort leaned back in his chair and smiled.

"You're probably wondering why I asked you here."

"Well no, not really. I was told it was to sign hiring papers."

"Ha, ha," he chuckled, glancing down at his fat hands folded on his desk. I don't often give much credit to people's looks — except in the case of real pretty women — but there was no way not to notice that Mort was a strange looking man. He got me to thinking of an article I read once in National Geographic about some fossil foot prints some ancient amphibian had made crawling up out of the sea. An artist had drawn it light brown with bowed-legs, a fat, football-shaped head with black marble eyes set close together, and a big, wide mouth with lips that looked like they were made from red garden hose.

"Let's get to the point," Mort said. "I'm new here and I need a little help. Help understanding some things about the smokejumpers. And who better knows the value of having a smooth running smokejumper crew better than a smokejumper himself? People here are proud of your crew and its work in the past. But, as you also know, nothing stands still. Things must move forward or they grow stale. Am I right?"

I shuffled around in my chair a little, not knowing what was going on.

"Well," I finally said after clearing my throat, "I reckon forward is a good as direction as any. Depends on the wind and the jump spot, of course." I instantly felt some regret for what might be taken as an insolent remark.

For a time Mort just sat there staring blankly at me. Then he blinked his eyes, gave a snort and went on.

"I checked your personnel folder. I know about your management background. That's why you're here, Len. It's about management. Management is the key to any organization's success. You see, I don't get out in the field as much as I'd like to, and it would be a big help if someone could keep me informed of things. First hand, you know. From a manager's perspective. Areas where I might be able to help with say... morale, efficiency, safety, things like that. With the new foreman and the McGrath men, I expect there'll be a few bumpy spots. Don't you agree?"

I didn't know what to say to that. He sat looking at me, and I just sat there looking at him. After a time his eyes rolled up in his head making it clear he thought he was dealing with a dimwit.

"I'm not like you think," I said. "I hardly know anything about the people here, and I don't know a thing at all about fighting fire in Alaska.

I appreciate the offer, though, but you'd best hunt up someone more constructed to your purpose."

"No, no. That's exactly the point. Experience is not what I'm looking for. All I need is objective reporting. You know smokejumping, I know management. Your file says you were a GS-9, so you must have written reports. This won't involve a lot of work. Just a weekly report. What went right, what went wrong, that sort of thing. I'll take it from there."

Here we go again, I thought. Another bureaucrat who can't tell the difference between a good bunch of smokejumpers and a bucket of horse piss.

"Like I was saying, you need someone local. Thanks for the offer, I do appreciate it."

Mort chuckled to himself. "Son," he said, leaning across his desk toward me. "I read your file. I see you had some problems in your previous position as a forester. Problems cooperating. Problems working as a team member to achieve agency goals."

The room got quiet. I commenced to get mad. I knew I better speak up before it got worse.

"I disagreed with their ideas on logging, that's all. In a couple years I'll have this jumping out of my system. Then I plan to go back. I left with good ratings."

"I saw that," Mort said. "But there's a future up here for a young man with the right attitude, if you know what I mean. Lots of new challenges with this oil pipeline and the road to Prudhoe Bay. Ratings are important here, too, don't you see?"

I didn't reply. Not because I hadn't heard, but because there was a photo on Mort's desk of a redhead that was so fine I couldn't look at her and think at the same time. The photo had writing on it. To Daddy Mo, it said. In the lower right corner it was signed, Love, Betsy.

Mort reached over, took the photo and turned it face down on his desk.

"Look, try it a couple weeks. If you don't like it, fine, we'll try something else."

Judging from Daddy Mo's persistence, I thought a straight-out refusal unwise.

"All right," I said. "I reckon it could help some. But I can't promise I'll be in touch every week. We're out sometimes longer than that, either on fires or at outstations standing by."

"Great! You can mail them in." Mort scribbled the address on a notepad, tore it off and handed it to me. "You'll be my eyes and ears in the field."

"I'll see what I can do."

I stood to leave. We shook hands.

"I believe you have some papers for me to sign."

"Papers? Oh no, there must have been a mistake. The only signatures needed to complete your hiring process are mine."

I waited, expecting him to sign the papers. Instead, he just smiled and put them in his desk.

That brought on a vicious feeling in me. One thing I can't abide is a liar.

"Well," I said, trying to control myself, if that's all then, I guess I'll be..."

Right then this roar came from outside. Mort jumped up and rushed to the window and I followed after him. Apparently driven by a maniac, a red carryall was barreling around the parking lot between rows of cars, splashing mud, sliding one way then the other.

"Ahhhh," Mort yelled, running to the door and out into the hall. "Call the State Troopers."

Roaring through puddle after puddle, the madman spun donuts and didos and splashed mud onto cars. I squinted at the muddy license plate, but couldn't make out a number. Mort came sashaying back to the window, his body twisting back and forth. We both saw it at the same time — on the passenger door — the not-too-mud-splashed inverted green triangle of the Bureau of Land Management.

"It's a government rig," Mort squalled. "One of *my* government rigs."

He took back for the door and into the hall again. "Don't call the State Troopers," he shouted.

After twisting back and forth a couple of times, he rushed back to the window again. He got there just in time to see the carryall roar through a big puddle and send a load of mud at another car.

"What the hell?," he said in a squealy voice. "That's my car."

The carryall disappeared around the north end of the building and tore off down Peger Road with its horn honking. Mort squealed again, did a few twists, then turned from the window and ran out into the hall and was gone. After a while I heard some yelling down stairs.

I reached over and picked up Betsy's photo, looked at it, then put it back face down. Mort's desk had all kinds of paperwork stacked on one end, including several letters carrying the logo of the Alnoka Pipeline Company, the umbrella organization coordinating the work of Standard Oil, Atlantic Richfield, Texaco and the various construction outfits building the eight-hundred and eighty-mile pipeline across Alaska from

Valdez to Prudhoe Bay. I'd been reading the papers and, from what I could tell, with the Alaska Native Claims Settlement Act nearly passed, Alaska's Indians and Eskimos had, at last, started to calm down. The largest construction project in the history of the world would soon be in high gear. And, from the looks of the letters, Mort's office was smack dab in the middle of it.

I was about to sneak another look at Betsy when Mort came in, huffing and puffing and twisting around excited-like. Flopped down in his chair, he sat a moment staring at the window.

"Some imbecile has stolen a government rig."

"Must not be too smart," I said, "or he wouldn't come back here and show it off driving around where y'all could see him."

Mort thought on that a second, then said, "It's hard to say, this place is different. Do you suppose it could have been a BLM employee?"

"I told you, I don't know a thing about this place. I just came here to smokejump. Enjoy the country. Do a good job."

"You do that," Mort scowled. "And while you're at it, keep an eye out for that red carryall. The driver and I need to have a little talk."

When I opened the door to leave, a man with a thin face and a black briefcase pushed by me and shut the door without saying Hello, Goodbye or Go to hell. Next thing I knew I was standing out in the hall alone, trying to figure out where it was I had seen him before.

An hour later I was back at Fort Wainwright, standing around with a group of jumpers, listening to them bellyache about electric wiring, running water and toilets, all of which they pointed out, did not exist in this great hulk of a building they called the T-Hangar. Al Mattlon had sent them out to inspect the place, saying that it might become our new jump shack. Hostile toward both the building and their role as inspectors, some had taken to sunbathing. The T-Hangar was this massive flat-roofed, box-shaped structure with peeling paint and big double doors that screeched along on rusted rollers and rails. Built during WW II to house airplanes ferried to Russia as part of the lend-lease program, it was later abandoned and used by the Army for storing aircraft parts and who knew what all. On the south end, nearest the runway, four old, weather-beaten windows held cheerless rectangles of opaque glass, some of which were cracked.

"Pigs wouldn't move in here," the McGrath All-Star said, loud enough for everyone to hear, especially Clark Mitchell, the squad leader in charge.

"Huh," Mitchell grunted, shaking his head. "It's not that bad."

"Not that bad?" Johnny B. said. "Then what's that yellow pool over there in the corner? It's dried sulfur or some other toxic shit the Army's hiding."

"Well," Mitchell said, "Al told us to check it out. The new District Manager is considering making it our new base of operations."

"What does he think we are, lab rats? Look at it, man. It's a hazardous chemical dump."

"Just the same, if management wants it, that's the way it'll . . . "

I immediately recognized the roar. From between two gray metal buildings a red, mud-splattered carryall threw itself into a skid and headed straight at us. Horn blaring, the carryall began spinning donuts in the gravel parking lot right in front of the T-Hangar.

"Hey," Johnny B. yelled. "It's Bell and the Red Lizard."

The jumpers began clapping, slapping knees and cheering. After seeing what I had at the District Office, I wasn't nearly as happy to find out who the driver was. Mitchell put his hand on his forehead like a visor, looked down and shook his head.

The carryall raced around in a cloud of dust; heads popped up in the back. The rig roared around a couple times, then slowed as the cargo door on the passenger side slid open. A man wearing goggles lay on his stomach on the floor holding a set of drift streamers.

"Hey, it's a jumper run," Johnny B. laughed. "A four-manner."

Passing by, the spotter of the Red Lizard load slammed the half-furled streamers into the dirt, then turned and watched them disappear under the rear wheel. Around again they went, turning final as the spotter looked forward to where the streamers had landed. A jumper crouched with his right hand gripping the aft side of the door, his left forearm over his reserve, and one foot out on the running board. At the streamers, the spotter slapped the jumper on the shoulder and he jumped out, feet together and wound up in some flip and skid thing that didn't look nothing like a roll.

"Jumper Away," shouted the spotter as the Red Lizard launched into another turn. In three more passes the spotter put out three more jumpers, with the inspection group cheering and raising cane each time. With all four jumpers safely on the ground, the Red Lizard made two cargo runs, each pass kicking out a used firepack. Held together by a single cargo strap, both immediately tore apart and sent shovels, first aid kits, C-rat garbage, files, and chicken bags flying. On the last pass the Red Lizard ran over a shovel and busted the handle.

Mission completed, the Red Lizard roared off, leaving behind four men who looked like they were modeling space suits in a garbage dump.

As the dust cleared and the laughing subsided, something caught my eye on the north side of the building. Peeking around the corner was Al Mattlon, with a cigarette dangling from the corner of his mouth.

# 3

An hour before quitting time the crew gathered in the Ready Room at our regular headquarters for a meeting. Mattlon was still in his office. A few guys were greasing boots, some were sharpening knives. Three women were busy in the loft checking and packing parachutes. Alaska jumpers, to my surprise and, truth be told, disappointment, didn't pack their own chutes or firepacks. All the jumpers did was train, fight fire or stand by. Everything else, including paracargo, was handled by non-jumpers under contract. At 5:15 Mattlon came in carrying a clipboard and a cup of coffee. Ambling to the front of the room, he pulled up a chair and sat down. The crew quieted.

"Ahh, well, I've got a few things to cover before some of you get away for the weekend. First, I'd like to hold a crew meeting every Friday about this time. I don't know how you feel about it, but it seems to me that... every crew needs a time to sit down and talk...  so feel free to speak up."

Mattlon took a sip of coffee, then looked at his clipboard. Ten seconds passed, fifteen.

"Organizations tend to evolve to where they become managed too much from the top down. I don't want that to happen here. It's already happened at a few other bases. So far we've done our job without it. But things are changing. To continue enjoying this job like we have in the past... we have to prove we can function on our own. And that takes people willing to... accept responsibility and manage themselves so that others don't have to. That doesn't mean we can't have fun, it just means we have to be careful. What's said here needs to go no further than the crew. So, like I said ... feel free to speak up."

Mattlon took another sip of coffee.

"Welcome to our new people. Also, thanks to all you guys who helped with refresher training. Other than a near drowning and a couple monkeys, one with button eyes, and the other with bad boots, things went pretty well."

"Don't go throwing Duke in with Bell," Johnny B. said. "Duke didn't have bad boots. Duke was ready."

The crew laughed. Bell squirmed.

"He better be ready," Bell said. "And he better watch out, monkeys can have accidents."

"Are you going to spank the monkey?" Pat Shearer asked, looking at Bell and slapping his crotch. "Bad monkey, bad monkey. Ayeeee, ayeeee."

After the laughter subsided, Al glanced at his notes again.

"I still have a few things here... so don't anyone run off at 6:00. I just got off the phone with Anchorage. It's dry on the Kenai, so they want two loads to stand by down there this weekend... one at Palmer, one at Soldotna. Mitchell's going through the list now. If you've already made plans for the weekend, check with him."

The news of weekend overtime caused a round of happy grunts and smiles, then Al went on.

"Mouse called from some place in Vietnam I've never heard of... and can't pronounce. You can get the details from Rake. He won't make it this season. A Marine buddy from his platoon is MIA and Mouse's looking for him. Jenson's not coming either. He left Panama two days ago with a guy and two German girls on a boat sailing to the Marquesas Islands. Who knows when we'll see him again. Other than Gene Hobbs, everyone is here and trained. Gene starts in two weeks, right after he finishes teaching high school."

"As some of you've heard... things may be changing up here. We've got a new DM, Morton Twixenblout, I think that's how you say it."

"Twist and Shout," Rake said. "That's what he does when he gets excited."

A chuckle rippled through the room.

"He has his own ideas about our work. According to him there's more to the job than jumping out of airplanes and putting out fires. Last week he called and asked to see copies of our jumpship contracts. Now he wants to be involved in who we select. He also knows that at times jumpers have... caused a few problems.

"Those helicopters parked by the river have been contracted to take some of our fires. At first just the close-in ones. But the state's bigger than he thinks. Keeping them fueled will be a problem. Still, that kind of attitude means we all have to do a better job. And... this is important. It means we have to keep our noses clean."

Al took out a cigarette, lit it, and after a long pull, said, "For you McGrath guys, the way I see it... that's history. Just the same, you're here now and we're under the gun. The new DM is going to be coming around, checking efficiency he says. We'll have to work with him. Your job is to keep putting out fires, like always. I'll take care of the rest."

"What's this talk about moving to Fort Wainwright?" Quinlan asked.

"Ahhh, well, ah... right now it's just talk. They need a place to house the new helicopter people, and since the copters will be based here, they're thinking of... taking this place."

"What?" Rake said. "Take it from us and give it to a bunch of rotor-heads?"

"Like I said, so far it's just talk. They've asked the Army about letting us use one of their barracks for housing and the old hangar for operations. The runway is a big plus, a mile and half long, and not busy and congested like International."

"Great," Rake scowled. "So we'll be stuck on a fucking Army post? Shit, I'm trying to forget the military, not move in with them."

"Let's wait and see. There's a lot to making a move like that. Let me deal with it."

I may not have known much about Alaska and the new crew, but I knew Fort Wainwright was an ugly mess of concrete towers, chainlink fences, and weeds compared to the green birch woods by the river and the old BLM buildings that we now occupied. Besides that, among smoke-jumpers there's an abiding distrust of any authority outside their own ranks. It's always been that way. If some rule or policy doesn't make sense they will, sure enough, raise hell about it.

"Anybody got anything else?"

The room stayed quiet, and I sat there impressed by a boss who spoke straight. Al Mattlon seemed to be a man who understood the value of including rather than excluding.

As the meeting broke up Clark Mitchell came out of Mattlon's office and went to the jump list. You could tell Mitchell considered himself a great judge of what it took to make a good smokejumper. As a rising star, he enjoyed it too. Five minutes after meeting a jumper for the first time, although some said it was more like five seconds, he was suspected of placing them into one of three categories; the physically strong and fully capable, like him; the physically satisfactory, but too smart for his own good, like Johnny B.; and last, someone he wished had washed out in rookie training. Mitchell was broad shouldered and handsome. Aside from his tendency towards instant size-ups, he was goodhearted, hard working and likable.

"Let's set these two loads," Mitchell said. They want you down there first thing in the morning, so you'll leave tonight. Be here ready to go at 7:30."

As the loads were set cheers flew up as individual names were called. After all the excitement of the week, it was a letdown to be left out while half the crew was on its way to the first good deal of the year.

Outside, I took a seat on a low rock wall to think about how I could spend a weekend off. Bell came out and, seeing me, sat down and said, "Don't worry about it. There's enough fire up here for everyone. Enjoy your time off. It won't be long until you'll be wishing you had more."

Mattlon hadn't said a thing about the Red Lizard and I was glad, even if it did put me in a bind with my reporting duties to Mort. The way Bell came and sat down and talked reminded me of an afternoon at Bonanza Creek. While the others cooked, I walked down to the lake, circled to the right and came upon Bell sitting on a high cutbank above a gravel beach.

"How you doing?" he had said, maybe a little bothered at having his solitude disturbed. When I started to leave he called out, "That's all right. Come on over and sit down if you want."

We sat at the opposite ends of a spruce log a while and took in the sky and its reflection on the lake. Bands of clouds had turned pink and orange between great expanses of light blue and green open sky. Canada geese circled, landed in a large pocket of open water, honked a little, then settled down. From the far end of the lake came the cry of a loon.

"They always amaze me," Bell said, his voice unexpectedly calm. "The way they live. The way they come back every year. They're the animal totem of the jumpers up here, you know. But they don't go around with a bunch of junk like we do. No hootches, no PG bags, rain gear, tarps, none of that crap. They got their own goose down and their own wings."

Some waterfowl squabble flared up near the other end of the lake, and the geese took off, rising together, cackling and honking and carrying on like they do. After circling a couple times they set their wings and glided back in, their feet reaching beneath them just before they splashed down, folded their wings and looked around.

"They're perfect in a way," Bell went on. "They live in harmony with the cycles and seasons of a whole continent, following the sun, going their own way, minding their own business. They don't worry about shit like we do."

Of the stories I'd heard about the Alaska jumpers, Don Bell stories were the most entertaining. Raised in a Quaker family in Virginia, from the time he was a boy he played and explored at the edge of the places where he lived. Even now, I'd seen him just stand and look into the distance at nothing but the country. But he had another side, too, edgy and volatile. He was likely to go off at the least little thing. As a teenager he marched with his family in parades, some supporting the Civil Rights Movement, others protesting the Vietnam War. One time a heckler spit on his father and called him a Communist. Don clobbered him with a peace sign, which caused a big ruckus. As a young man, he read books like *The Mad Trapper from Rat River, Ice Palace,* and *Jack London's Call of the Wild.* The year he applied to smokejumping, the Idaho City base foreman wrote him back saying that due to a tight budget he couldn't hire him. Don wrote back saying that he knew what it was like to have money troubles, but that ever since he was a kid he'd dreamed of coming west and becoming a smokejumper, and therefore he'd work the whole season for free. Upon receiving Don's letter, the foreman phoned him and offered him a position at full pay.

That evening Johnny B. came to my room upstairs in the jumpshack and said we had a fire call to Nenana. With the two loads gone to Kenai, and the rest of the crew on a tour of the downtown bars, we made the load. After picking up our gear, Johnny B. and I, two other jumpers, Mattlon and a pilot named Pickering drove to International Airport. While suiting up under the wing of Jumper 46, a red and yellow Grumman Goose, a call came on Mattlon's radio—Cancel and return to base. Dispatch said the fire had been contained by locals. Mattlon raised the radio to his mouth, then hesitated.

"Hey, hey you guys. Listen up. Start making airplane noises," he said, moving a hand in circles. "Like this, aauunn, aauunn, aauunn, come on. Make it sound like we're already flying."

"Aauunn, aauunn, aauunn," we commenced to yowl. "Aauunn, aau-unn."

"Ah... Fairbanks dispatch," Mattlon said, "this is Jumper 46. We're off the ground at this time, departing International enroute Nenana. What was your message?" Mattlon's hand was still waving as we were full-on aauuning and pretending we were airplanes.

"Ah Jumper 46... Roger that. Since you're already en route you may as well check it out."

Mattlon rode right-seat in the cockpit beside Pickering. He looked back and yelled. "Hey, good job on the airplane noises." All four of us gave him the thumbs up. At Nenana, Pickering made a low pass over an area of faint blue smoke on a dark ridge just west of town. A dozen people were up there digging in the dirt.

After seeing that the fire was in good hands, we flew the fifty miles from Nenana back to Fairbanks barely a hundred feet above the Tanana, a river filled with streaks of blues and pinks and yellows from a near midnight sunset. Sitting next to the open door I watched as the river bank slipped by with its dark woods, deep shadows, and sun flashing golden through the trees. Here and there I saw fish camps and remote cabins. The air was cool and sweet with the scent of cottonwood and willow. There we were, flying along in a magical space between the sky and its reflection in a river, the power of the engines roaring, the rush of the air beneath our wings, and I thought to myself, this is a moment too beautiful to be real, shared with people too good to be true, in a job too grand not to love. I looked away from the other jumpers to hide the fact that my eyes were filling with tears. No doubt about it, I was right where I belonged.

Back at the Standby Shack, Al wrote a charge number for the fire on the chalk board and put down Hazard Pay — Low pass over Fire # 3051. That meant an extra 25% tacked onto our wages for both the day we took off, and the one in which we were going off duty at 1:00 in the morning. A beautiful flight and extra pay, too. All for just making a few airplane sounds.

I took a shower and crawled into to bed, but couldn't go to sleep, so naturally I began thinking about things. I thought about Texas, and about how Texas was not just a state, but more like a state of mind. My family had been in Texas for a hundred and forty years, back to when it was the Republic of Texas. That made me a Son of Texas, a direct male descendant of the pioneers who settled the Republic prior to February 19, 1846, when it became the 28th state. In a way that troubled me some. I was one of those sons who had run off as soon as I got old enough to leave. Most people grow up happy where they are, living among familiar surroundings, family and friends. Content with their lives, they settle into them, probably thinking little about other places or ways. But I grew up different. From the time I found out I could think for myself, the world into which I was born became only a starting point. Raised on a cattle ranch in the big, flat country west of Novice, Texas, even as a boy, even though I'd only seen them in pictures, I dreamed about mountains with high green meadows and trees. Working cows, riding horses, and doing ranch work held its own rewards. But it wasn't enough to hold me. Shortly after my eighteenth birthday, I took a summer job on the Sierra National Forest in California, left the ranch and headed west.

It was a ragtag bunch of once-dreamy-eyed children that somehow wound up that afternoon in May of 1973, walking up Gordie Hensen's driveway into what would one day be remembered as the First Annual Alaska Smokejumper Pig Party. Jim Kasson had come via Vietnam where he had trained secret forces under the direction of the CIA. Rake had returned from that same country with half of his platoon dead. Johnny B.

had come by way of the Trans-Siberian Railway, Israel, Egypt, North Africa and Spain. Bob Betts had spent his winter digging for Mayan ruins on the Yucatan Peninsula.

Don Bell, on the other hand, had come in the Red Lizard after making stops at Goldstream Discount Liquors, Ed's Cut Rate Guns and Ammo, and Gorilla Fireworks. Still covered with mud, the Red Lizard sat parked near the start of the Henson's driveway with its nose rammed into a clump of diamond willow.

But that day, regardless of our varied pasts, we'd all came from Fort Wainwright where we'd spent the day moving smokejumper operations into the old T-Hangar. Having had little say in the matter, we had arrived at Henson's in a ornery and ready-to-party mood. Low-angled light filtered through the tops of birch and aspen as the crew gathered in the yard. Campfire smoke drifted in the trees where the light turned it various shades of blue. Surrounding Henson's cabin was a collection of oil drums, abandoned cars, wrecked snow machines, scrap metal, rolls of wire and stacks of firewood and lumber in varying states of decay. The party, it had been decided, would be called the Pig Party since a pig had been killed and was to be roasted over an open fire. Some thought that such a name might have a manly sort of appeal to the more hot-blooded women around Fairbanks. Clark Mitchell, the party chairman, had convinced Mattlon that a party, similar to one he'd seen in a Viking movie starring Kirk Douglas and Tony Curtis, would be the perfect way to show the McGrath jumpers that the Fairbanks crew was just as wild as they were. To keep drinking and driving to a minimum, Quinlan had volunteered to stay sober and drive a BLM school bus back to the barracks.

Bell, Rake, and Mountain Puss were standing around the cooking fire pissed-off about how the crew had been kicked out of the old base and banished to the fort. The rumor that the new DM was pushing for helicopters to be used on close-in fires was now a fact. A joint was passed around. Johnny B. walked over and pulled out a fifth of Crown Royal, took a big swig, then handed it to me.

"I better be careful with this," I said, taking a small pull. "I'm not much good at it."

"Don't worry, it's a self-instructing process," he said, taking another rip, then smacking his lips. "The more you do it, the better you get at it. See that geeky looking guy over there?"

I looked over and saw him, a puny looking fella wearing thick glasses and an Elmer Fudd hat.

"He was on the helicopter at Bonanza Creek when it blew our camp down."

I remembered, then. He was also the one who pushed by me that day as I left Mort's office.

Miles Morgan—we found out his name later—was looking around the yard like he was wanting someone to talk to. I had to wonder, what in creation would cause him to come to a jumper party? The Red Lizard was down the road run in the brush. If that weren't enough, several jumpers were smoking pot right in front of everyone, even the boss.

"This can't be good," Johnny B. said.

"I reckon not," I said. "Maybe we ought to run him off."

"Let's just watch a while," Johnny B. said, taking another swig of Crown.

At a food table, Miles helped himself to a plate of cheese, salami, raw carrots, smoked salmon, and potato chips. We moved closer to keep an eye on him.

"Excuse me, don't you work at the district office?" we heard a woman across the table say.

Miles didn't answer right off, but then said, "Yes, do you work there, too?"

"Oh no, but it's nice to meet you anyway. My name's Betsy."

Good lord, I thought. That's her, the redheaded Betsy in the photo on Mort's desk.

Charmed to be speaking with such a beauty, Miles stepped around the end of the table where they met and got into a long handshake. I figured her to be in her early twenties. She was a beauty, all right, with red, waist-length hair, fair skin and big brown eyes. With her ruffled white blouse, a beige suede jacket and faded Levis, she stood nearly six feet tall. Thin waisted. A right handsome woman, no question.

She held out a plate of sugar cookies.

"Here, try one of these," Betsy said to Miles. "I made them myself."

Miles took two, then stood munching his cookies, looking at Betsy like a cobra does a man playing a flute.

"Have a good one," Betsy said to Miles as she turned and walked away.

A call came on a BLM radio. "Pig Party, this is the standby shack."

Al Mattlon reached in his jacket. "Ahh, well. Go ahead standby shack."

"We're just getting off duty here and were wondering if there'd be a problem bringing the first load out to jump the party?"

Mattlon lowered the radio, looked up at the sky, ran his fingers through his hair, chuckled to himself, then asked, "You want to jump the pig party?"

"Affirmative!"

After some delay. "Ahh, well, ah... sure, why not? Use the big meadow, south of the cabin."

A half hour later we were in the meadow watching Jumper 54 circle overhead. Out came the streamers. Johnny B. and I stood watching, and looking out over the Tanana Valley to the Alaska Range. I couldn't believe what was happening. They were going to jump the Pig Party. That kind of thing just didn't happen at other bases, not unless it was Cave Junction where Mick and Dee run the Siskiyou base.

In no time the sky over the Henson homestead began to fill with parachutes drifting on a light breeze. Dogs barked and ran around raising hell. When the jumpers were safely on the ground, we handed them beers and helped gather up parachutes and jump gear.

Back in the yard, Gordie Henson and a couple other jumpers were busy taking the pig off the spit. It was charred black and its ears nearly burned off. The lips were mostly gone too, leaving its teeth to look fierce and warlike. Its eyes had turned white as marbles. The last thing I'd seen cooked that bad was Mountain Puss' beaver. Next thing I knew I was devouring chucks of savory barbecued pork, tossed salad, baked beans, and garlic bread.

By ten o'clock the first official Pig Party was going full-bore. An eight-track player sat on Henson's porch blaring Emerson, Lake and Palmer as they sang *Ooohhh, What a lucky man... he was.* People stood in groups around campfires talking and laughing and stomping around until most of the yard was nothing but mud holes. Things were moving fast now, powered by the voodoo of alcohol, weed, and a general Who-gives-a-Rats feeling. The exact time when a party gains the status of a complete blast, a total hoot, or a wild-assed mess, is rarely clear. But it was in one of those mud holes that I saw the very thing that qualified it for any one, if not all three categories. Of course, I was drunk by then, too. So, when I heard this ruckus behind me, I turned and was, right off, faced with two confusing emotions. First there was the pleasure of seeing two smokejumpers rolling in the mud, but then I saw that the one on the bottom, the one with his head down in a mud puddle, was Al Mattlon, our boss. Mattlon clawed pathetically at Don Tienhaara, while Teeny sat on top of him and cussed him.

"Join the Marines," Teeny growled. "Three years. See the world. It'll be fun... *fucker!*"

As much as the crew appreciated Mitchell's Viking party concept, they looked on their boss getting Teeny's mud treatment with some conflict. No one wanted to be seen as brown-nosing the overhead—even if he was a good boss—and, after all, the party was not on government time, and the puddle wasn't deep enough for Teeny to drown him in, and besides, neither one was doing the other much damage anyway, so we just kept out of it.

Evidently Teeny and Al had grown up together in the farm country south of Portland, Oregon. Ten years before, right after high school, Al had talked Teeny into the idea of joining the US Marines. After two months Al had been booted out while Teeny was left to serve out his four years, including one in Vietnam. Al's idea of seeing the world had turned out nearly getting Teeny killed.

"Bullshit!" Teeny said. "Four years. While I was getting my ass shot off, you were riding around in your new pickup, chasing women and snow skiing."

That called for another dunk in the puddle. One which left Mattlon gasping and the crew ready to save him. Then, Teeny stood up.

"There," he gasped. "I've been needing to do that for a long time."

He reached down and offered his hand to Al. Al took it, but instead of shaking it, he pulled Teeny down on top of him and they went to rolling in the mud some more. Minutes later the two stood at a campfire shirtless, Al staring into the flames and puffing on a Marlboro, while Teeny went on about how good he was feeling.

The first keg of beer was gone. A line formed at the second. The pig lay on a wooden table, a pile of bones and skin, its head cut off and turned up to the sky, its white eyes specked with ash. It was about this time that Miles Morgan began to act peculiar. Standing by himself on the porch he was smiling at everything, especially Betsy. Suddenly, for no reason he laughed real loud. Then, he lay down on the porch and stared at the sky, and laughed some more. The Moody Blues sang *Knights in white Satin, never reaching the end, letters I've written, never meaning to send. And I love you... oh how I love you."*

"I love you," Miles shouted, not quite in time with the tune. Next, he jumped up and pranced over to the food table, took up a bottle of tequila, took a big swig, grabbed a cold beer, then headed over to where Betsy, Don Bell, and Clark Mitchell were talking.

I reckon it was Mitchell's seeing Al and Teeny bare-chested, or maybe it was imagining a bare-chested Betsy, who at that moment was moving through the crowd and tossing her hair. More likely it was an alcohol blood level high enough to make it unsafe to drive anything but a Sherman tank, but whatever it was, it was strong, for at that point Al Mattlon's right-hand man peeled off all his clothes, including his cowboy boots, and stood in the mud, drinking beer and smoking a joint, all the time going on and on about how the cool night air had shrunk the very part he was trying to show off.

Betsy Twixtenblout ran to her car to fetch her glasses. Miles got his notebook out of his jacket pocket and dropped it in the mud.

"Curses!" The Legendary Fucking Rake said. "You've got the dreaded shrinking schlong disease. You better hope it doesn't settle into your legs or your knuckles will drag the ground."

Mitchell stood tall, unshaken by hecklers. Head high, his blue eyes cast occasional glances down on himself, not the temperature-altered part, but his chest and shoulders. Inhaling deeply, he occasionally exhaled short bursts of admiration that sounded like, cha, cha, cha. Rod Dow, fascinated by such goings on, stepped up and began asking questions.

"Is this," Rod began, "I mean, is it *normal* for you to do something like this?"

"I don't know, this is the first time, cha, cha, cha," Mitchell said.

"This is your *first time*?"

"Yes! My first time. I feel happy, maybe happier than I've ever been. Happy with myself. Happy to be in Alaska. Happy to be part of this crew."

"Right on," Mountain Puss said. "I dig it, too." At that Mountain Puss peeled off his shirt, then his shoes, pants, and skivvies, so that he, too, stood before the fire buck naked, except for the pirate hat with the eagle feather.

"Whoa there," Rake laughed, "What the hell is that, an albino mouse?"

"Grrrr," growled Mountain Puss as he leaped over the two-foot flames of the campfire. In a low crouch he stalked around, hands on his knees, repeating between different growls, "I ain't ashamed, and I ain't proud. Grrrr, I'm just me."

Bell ran to the Red Lizard and dug out a case of bottle rockets and Roman candles. Within minutes the party had become a war zone. Red, blue, and yellow flares sailed across the yard, hit the cabin, and soared out into the woods. Clark Mitchell remained unaffected by the barrage. One rocket did a big loop and flew back into the box that it came in. First there was a flash, then a blow torch noise, then clouds of pinkish-white smoke. Bell stood back as different colored explosions set the box to bouncing around the yard, sending rockets in all directions. While Bell stood there transfixed, I noticed that Betsy Twixenblout was looking at him with the same kind of fondness with which he was admiring the explosions.

"Spotfires," Quinlan yelled, as he ran off into the woods. Johnny B. and I took out after him, found some little fires and put them out, all the time having to listen to him rant about government liability, insurance claims, and private property rights.

Once the fires were out and the smoke cleared the party took on a more regular tone. Bell calmed down. Between Teeny and Al's wrestling, Mitchell's and Puss' disrobing, the rockets red glare and bombs bursting in air, I had doubts that by morning the Henson's homestead would still be there. But, as Bell saw it, he was still there, and so was another thing — a woman. A woman that had cornered him between the woodshed and the table that held the pig with the white eyes.

"Are you a rocket man?" Betsy asked.

"I like fire," Bell said, eyes wide with excitement. "Other things, too, not just fire."

"What about me?" Betsy said.

Quinlan started the bus and announced that it would be leaving for the barracks in five minutes. While Quinlan went into the cabin to round up jumpers, Bell took the burned pig's head and wired it onto the grill of the bus. With the pig's head in place, Dow declared a crisp, "All aboard!" leaped into the driver's seat, then roared off down the driveway with a load of drunk smokejumpers, honking the horn as Quinlan ran after it, yelling and waving his arms.

We had to work the next day. Somehow I had sense enough to put my alarm clock across the room so I'd have to get up to shut it off. Once on my feet, I figured I'd stay upright. I went down and woke up Johnny B., then took a quick shower. On our way to the T-Hangar, we saw the bus parked in the barracks parking lot, and decided we better check to see if anyone was still in it.

What we saw was a mess of empty beer cans, fast food wrappers and a human body. Miles Morgan lay unconsciousness in the rear seat and looked like he'd been in a fight with a wildcat.

"Get up from there," I said, poking him in the ribs.

"Ohh, that woman," he moaned. "Cookies. Oh... water..."

"He ate some of Betsy's pot cookies," Johnny B. said. "Wonder how many?"

"Parking lot... smoke... barracks."

"That's right," I said. "And from the looks of you, you're lucky you're not dead."

"Dead," he said, sitting up. "And sick, too."

He got to his feet and made for the emergency exit and opened it. The alarm went off. He scrambled down the rear bumper, fell to the ground and puked a couple times. Johnny B. shut the alarm off at the front of the bus. Rounding a front fender, Miles ran straight into the pig's head with the white eyes and scary teeth. He bawled like a sick calf, nearly fell again, then staggered off. We headed for the T-Hangar, hoping not to be late.

"He's a frigging spy," Johnny B. said. "Sure as hell he'll rat us out for the party."

God, I thought, what have I done? I'm supposed to be writing reports to the District Manager, and now I'm going to end up the subject of one. Ever since I agreed to that deal I hadn't seen anything to write about except things that would get us all fired. Last time we saw Miles he was down by Murphy Hall in a phone booth digging in his pockets for change.

"Look there," I said to Johnny B. Down a side street a Military Police car had started its engine and was rolling slowly in his direction.

At the T-Hangar we gathered up in what was to be our new Ready Room. It was still pretty rough. Keep A Goin' Construction, a group of would-be carpenters headed up by Mountain Puss, had hammered plywood onto pine studs and walled off one corner to make what looked more like a fairgrounds hot dog stand than a smokejumper operations office.

Quinlan called roll and set the first two loads. Some folks were missing. Probably in jail. Right after that everyone grabbed an Army chicken bag and threw it down somewhere to sleep. I tried to, but couldn't, so I lay there staring up into the high reaches of the T-Hangar, listening to the wind. The ceiling was 45 feet high and created a dim world of massive beams and cross-timbers held together by large iron brackets and great, long bolts. A wooden stairway ran up the east wall to various landings and walkways. The walls in the corner that became our new Ready Room had, sometime in the distant past, been painted a sorry pale green. Cabinets, fire extinguishers, and other wall fixtures had long since been ripped down, leaving ugly blank spots of splintered wood and tar paper. Wind rattled the windows. It commenced to rain.

"It's a big state," Johnny B. said, trying to bring some cheer to a bleak day.

"Aackk, sinners must pay," Bob Quinlan said. Bob had drummed up a poker game with Cleermont, a.k.a. The Fat Indian, and Mountain Puss.

"I hope we get a Yukon Flats gobbler today. It'd serve you right. Steal my bus and run around downtown with a pig's head wired on the grill. Obstreperous pups, yelling and drinking and picking up... I came here to work with... "

"I didn't see your name written on it," Rake said.

"Well, you would have if you'd looked in the transportation logbook."

"It's at the barracks. Turn it in tomorrow and clear your good name."

"Aackk," Quinlan said again. "With blood on the grill and pig fat in the radiator? I need a cup of coffee."

Rake shrugged his shoulders, "How about a hot steaming cup of shut-the-fuck-up?"

"It *is* a big state," Johnny B. said again, this time softer. "There's bound to be a fire out there somewhere."

I lay there thinking. Somehow I'd wound up on the bus, drunk with all the rest. My pickup was still out at Henson's—at least I hoped it was. The moaning of the wind and the tapping of the rain on the windows left me feeling sad, and I began to think about the great untruthfulness most people live with. I should have never agreed to make the reports. The only way I could make any kind of report, at all, was to tell a bunch of lies. And now there was this Miles guy from the District Office, and it was clear he was going to make some of his own. I had screwed myself good, and here we were, stuck on a damned Army post in an abandoned building nobody liked with no fires, all hung over and feeling like shit.

But that's wasn't all. There was the war in Southeast Asia, and the pain of those just home from it. You could see it plainly in some of the guys. Too much killing, too much lying, too many bad dreams. Most of it was denied or made into a story each one was trying to live with. For men like Rake and Kasson, and Doc Houston and Teeny, and the other Vets, the truth had been left behind in the jungles of Vietnam. Maybe it had to be that way to give them a chance to reclaim a sense of their own simple goodness. Rake, for example. He was often laughing and grinning and teasing people. My first day I saw him greet one of the other newcomers in our old Ready Room at 3.5 mile. He walked right up to the guy, leaned close to his face and said pretty loud, "Hi, I'm John Rakowski, an unregistered sex offender. I was just wondering if you had a girlfriend, a boyfriend, or any kinds of friends?" The guy stared at Rake, not sure what he was looking at. "I got two girlfriends," he finally said.

"Good, I'll take the ugly one," Rake said, stepping close so that the guy had to back up. "Does she have any big features that you'd like to tell me about?"

All the while Rake was talking he was doing these slow pelvic thrusts. The newcomer tried backing away until he was trapped against a wall. Rake moved to within inches of his face. The new guy wiggled from the wall and headed for the hallway. Rake yelled after him, "In my next life I want to come back as a size 40 bra."

But there was more to Rake. That same day, just before quitting time, the guy at the Operations desk sent me to Rake's room with a note. Before we moved to Fort Wainwright the barracks was on the second floor of the same building as the Ready Room and Operations.

I knocked and, when he asked me to come in, I opened the door and, right off, heard splashing in the bathtub.

"I'm in here, don't be bashful."

After him talking about sex offending and all, I wasn't sure I wanted to go in, but I had a note and when I told him about it, he asked me to read it. I went to the doorway and was surprised at what I saw. There he was, sitting in a tub of pinkish water, steam coming up all around him, a pair of tweezers in one hand and a pocket knife in the other.

"Something the matter?" he asked.

The message was from his sister, Lori. She wanted him to call the number on the note. Pinned to the wall next to the door was a photo of a group of about a dozen Marines, the front row kneeling, the others standing. In the back row he and another man stood side by side in full combat gear, their arms over each others shoulders, their rifle butts held against their hips, the barrels pointed in the air. In a corner of the photo was written, Goofy and me, Danang, May, 1972.

"Three hours later all those guys were dead," Rake said. "Except for me and a guy named Powell."

Rake asked me to call Lori and tell her he'd call at 8:00 that night, her time. He picked a piece of something out of his leg while he was talking.

"It's just metal," he said. "No medals but lots of metal. The Marine Corps said I could keep it. My blood. My metal. Hell of a deal."

Rake winced, then forced a smile. "Two weeks before timing out, I got hit by a mortar round. Probably saved my life since it got me sent home. Hot water opens the pores. The metal works its way near the surface where I can dig it out. The doc tells me I'll feel like a new man in a couple hundred years."

Lying there in the T-Hangar that morning, listening to the wind and rain, I was feeling hungover and thinking about things like that, how the world was beautiful and ugly, both.

"Hey Rocket Man," Quinlan said, tugging at Don Bell's sleeping bag. "What'd you do with the Red Lizard?"

Bell had a chicken bag down on top of a couple other chicken bags on top of a couple wood pallets. He'd been tossing and turning and mumbling a good deal.

"Get away from me," Bell said, jabbing a fist out at Quinlan. Rolling over, he jerked the sleeping bag further over his head. All at once he rolled over and started talking.

"There must be something wrong with me. I just had a bad dream. There was this charred pig with white eyes, and it was standing on its hind legs talking to a woman with red hair and big tits. It had on a trench coat and a stovepipe hat, and was pointing at the Red Lizard parked in front of Skinny Dick's Halfway Inn."

"Aackk," Quinlan said. "I could carve a better man out of a banana."

Just then the phone rang, and Quinlan went into the Operations office. "Alaska smokejumpers."

After a bit, Quinlan said, "Who wants to know?"

Quinlan put his hand over the receiver. "Hey Mitchell, wake up. It's the MPs. They want to know if we know anyone named Miles Morgan.

Mitchell was passed out in a swivel chair behind the Ops desk. He got up slowly and stepped to the phone, weaving back and forth, his hair in all directions.

"Hello."

I couldn't hear what was said on the other end, but I figured that the MPs we saw must have picked up Miles Morgan.

"Okay good," Mitchell croaked. "No, never heard of him."

Another moment passed.

"I don't care what he said, he's not with the jumpers. What'd he do, anyway?

Another pause.

"Drunk and disorderly. On the base? Oh, that's disgusting. Glad you got him."

Another pause, then, "Okay, great. That's right, never heard of the guy."

In one motion Mitchell chucked down the phone and wheeled back for his chair.

The afternoon passed much like the morning, except for the poker game that, at times, got too loud. I slept poorly, waking off and on, feeling sick for myself and the way I'd done at the Pig Party. Now that we'd turned our back on Miles, he sure enough would rat on us. I supposed a few would get fired. Johnny B. had taken up a spot at the Ready Room's main table and sat writing what looked to be a long letter. After he finished, he took out his guitar and played *He Was A Friend of Mine*, adding delicate guitar runs between the verses.

Bell emerged from his sleeping bag and spent the rest of the afternoon pacing back and forth in front of the windows that faced east toward a little trailer house that had been converted into a pilot's lounge. Beyond it there was just metal Army buildings and chainlink fences. By four o'clock only Quinlan and Mountain Puss remained at the poker table. After losing a big hand, Mountain Puss got after Bob.

"Dammit, you're cheating again," Mountain Puss declared.

Quinlan just grinned.

"Aackk, I don't have to cheat to beat a simpleton. Face it. You're just shitty player. It's your eyes. Your pupils turn into slits just like a snake when you've got anything worth holding, and they get big and round when you don't. When one man accuses another of cheating, it's a good sign he's a cheater himself, always pretending to be on the up and up, when deep down he's as depraved as a feral dog, constantly knocking over garbage cans, looking for a cat to eat or another dog with whom to copulate."

"This place is a looney bin," Mountain Puss said. "And Quinlan, you're the Bull Goose Looney. We've got to do something. It's like a morgue in here, dark and cold, bodies lying around. If we keep on like this, I'm gonna lose my fucking mind."

"A fucking mind is a terrible thing to lose," Rake said. "Just look at Bell."

Quinlan smirked and lit his pipe. "Aackk, human beings, the butt of mother nature's joke."

"This place is what's a joke," Mountain Puss said. "No electricity, no running water, no heat."

"My God, how the mighty have fallen, "Quinlan said. "We already have C-rats, free sleeping bags, and a phone. Next thing you'll want is blow dryers for your hair."

Mountain Puss shook his head, disgusted. "We need suit-up racks. Maybe hang up a cargo chute or two, get a pop machine and some lights."

Fists clenched, Quinlan began pounding the table.

"This is a standby shack for smokejumpers, not a country club. I came here to work with men, not... "

"Hey Bob, give it a break, will you?" someone said from inside a chicken bag. "All that grown men and work shit gets old."

"A pop machine," Rake said, clapping his hands. "That's the only smart thing anybody's said all day. We'll get a pop machine and then put beer in it."

# 4

hree days after the Pig Party Mattlon came to the T-Hangar,
went straight into Operations and had a meeting with Clark
Mitchell, Quinlan and the other squad leaders. Five minutes
later he came out and posted a memo on the bulletin board next to the Ops
window.

Fairbanks, Alaska<br>
May 29, 1973

To: Alan Mattlon, Base Manager, Alaska Smokejumpers
From: Morton Twixenblout, Fairbanks District Manager
Subject: Conduct

Congratulations on the completion of Spring training. I'm sure the responsibility of your new position must weigh heavily upon you at times. Despite the obvious successes, however, it has come to my attention that there have been a few problems. Be assured I will look into them further, but until I make my final decision, I want you to implement the following immediately:

1.  A two week suspension from smokejumping for John Bowen for unsafe parachuting at the Bonanza Creek Exercise.

2.  A one week suspension for Don Bell and John Rakowski for unprofessional conduct dealing with a representative from the District Office. Also Bonanza Creek.

As I've mentioned before, I feel the smokejumper program needs to be scrutinized more closely by my fire staff, especially in the area of personal conduct. The problems involve drinking, gambling, womanizing, and a general disrespect shown for the official decorum of the agency.

Also, there are some operational changes of which you'll need to be aware. Fairbanks District has ten Model 205 Bell helicopters on contract this season. Starting next week all initial attack fires within a 75 mile radius of Fairbanks and our regular outstations will be accomplished by helitac specialists.

My staff will be working with you to see that revised goals are identified and met. The key word here is performance. I'll be out one of these days to meet the crew and speak to them personally. Until then, feel free to call or drop by my office anytime.

~ Mort Twixenblout

Mattlon called for a meeting in the Ready Room.

"Ahhh, well, ah," he began, closing his eyes and pinching a point between them, just above his nose. "Looks like the DM has got some new ideas."

"Sanctimonious warthog," Bell said. "*I'll be out one of these days...* Jumpers have put out fires up here since 1959, slogging through miles and miles of muskeg, working their asses off, going without food, getting lost, chased by bears, doing things that fat-ass can't even imagine. Now he thinks he can walk in here and tell us about *performance*."

"We can't win against a guy like this," The Fat Indian said. "He may have some new ideas but he doesn't have any facts. He's already made up his mind."

"Mind," Bell said. "He doesn't have a mind. He better keep to his pathetic, fat-headed, office-loving ways and leave us alone."

"Helicopters will have trouble replacing jumpers up here," Quinlan said. "In initial attack anyway. The country's too big, and they don't have the fuel range."

"You're probably right," Mattlon said, still pinching the area between his eyes again. "But, he's the boss... and he's got ten helicopters. Apparently they're going to get first shot at the close-in fires. He claims they can get there quicker."

"Let them try," Bell said. "When the busts come we'll see who gets to what."

"In the meantime," Mattlon went on, " I want everybody to take this conduct thing seriously. The DM sees our crew as a problem that he needs to solve."

"Fuck it," Rake said, "I say we frag him."

"It's bad to be seen as a problem," Mattlon said, ignoring Rake.

"These managers have always seen us as a *problem*," Bell said, gaining heat with each word. "We just happen to be the *problem* that does all the work."

"That may be, but there's something we have to understand. It's no longer just a matter of good fire fighting. We've got to watch our backs. He's already overruled one of my choices of aircraft contracts. His new low bidder is out of Texas. They've been hauling turkeys from Texas to some factory in Louisiana. Two planes. They'll be here next week."

"*Turkeys?*" the McGrath All-Star said. "You mean *real* turkeys?"

"Yes," Mattlon said. "I mean real turk—"

"No fucking doubt," Rake interrupted. "Real turkeys and real turkey shit, too. We had a turkey Doug in Missoula in '67. The floor tracks were packed so full of turkey shit, the first time they opened the door in flight, turkey shit flew all over the place."

"It's that district jerk that came to the party," Johnny B. said.

"Bell," Quinlan said, "ask your girlfriend if she knows his name."

"She's not my girlfriend," Bell said, coldly. "And I'm not asking her anything."

"His name's Morgan," Johnny B. said. "He's the one that called here the morning after the party and talked to Mitchell."

"Morgan," Rake grinned, "as in Big M—little organ?"

The crew laughed.

"Miles Morgan," Mitchell said. "That's the guy. Claimed he was a jumper."

"Okay, that's enough for now," Mattlon said. "For the time being keep your noses clean... both at out stations and here in town. Be careful what you say to non-jumpers. I'll meet with the spotters tomorrow. We need to take a good look at our getaway times."

Mattlon halted, looked at his watch, stood up, then went to the bulletin board and pulled down the memo, wadded it up and dropped it in a trash can.

"And, as far as people pulled off the jump list goes," he said, "that'll be my call. Until you hear different, the list stays the same."

Mattlon was on his way out when he stopped in the doorway to the Ready Room, then turned back. "Ahh, well, just one more thing. Do you suppose that the next time we have a party, you could refrain from taking the BLM bus downtown and driving around picking up hippies and prostitutes, with a burnt pig's head wired on the front?"

The first time I saw McGrath it was raining. As we circled I could see the town set in a great U-shaped bend of a big muddy river. Across the middle of the U the runway ran bank to bank, north to south. Bell pointed to an opening in a thicket of Aspen, across the river from the south end where a DC-3 like the one we were in had crashed just three years before. Parts were scattered for a hundred yards. The twenty-man Stebbins EFF crew was on board. EFF is short for emergency fire fighter. Six were killed outright. The rest were seriously injured. The Doug's right landing gear had collapsed just as it lifted off. The pilot managed to keep his plane off the runway and get it across the river, but on the far bank the trees were too tall to clear and too thick to plow through, so the ship faltered, rolled forward on its nose and went in. It was a miracle it didn't burn.

"You're gonna love McGrath," Bell said, as we looked out the windows. "Look, there's Joe's."

We checked in with dispatch, then moved into two of the eight tent frames they had in the back. The McGrath Station was nice with its old log cookhouse, log sauna, woodshed, and shower room set in a stand of whitebark birch. Wooden walkways went in all directions across big areas of lawn. We settled in, which didn't amount to more than a trip to the warehouse for sleeping bags, pillows and bedding.

Two hours later we hit the trail through the woods to Joe's Roadhouse. For such a fancy name, Joe's Roadhouse wasn't much to look at, squeezed in like it was, on a bank above the Kuskokwim River with a dirt road running within four feet of the front door. Part log, part scrap lumber, wood poles and mud, it was the only bar in McGrath other than McGuirers. After thirty years of frost heaving, Joe's Roadhouse sat off kilter, its floors tilting this way and that, surrounded by dismantled snowmobiles, dead tractors, wrecked airplanes and discarded 55-gallon drums. Across the road a black bear hung upside down in a tree, completely skinned, even its head.

"Hey Joe," Bell called to the man behind the bar as we walked in. "It looks like those guys shot one of your relatives."

"Well, I'll be damned," Joe grinned, reaching for Bell's hand, "are you still alive?"

"Alive enough to wrestle your ass. I need something to drink."

"Price of booze just doubled," Joe said, still squeezing Bell's hand.

"Already?" Bell protested. "You usually get us half drunk before you do that."

Joe and Bell had finished shaking hands, but held on, squeezing hard.

"How much money did you get out of the gold mine?" Bell asked, the muscles tightening in his neck.

"More than you'll ever have," Joe answered, veins bulging on his forehead.

"Hell, you've got enough gold to buy the whole town now, but all you do is hide it." Bell face was red, and the hand which grasped Joe's trembled with the force of their grips.

"How the weather been?" Bell asked.

"The same as always," Joe answered, "shitty."

Bell looked over at me, lips pursed, trying to smile. "Some old sons-of-bitches think they're tough."

The two lowered their elbows to the bar where they switched to arm wrestling.

"Then, there's these young smart asses," Joe said, "who, just because they can jump out of a perfectly good airplane, think they're hot shit."

"There's no such thing as a perfectly good airplane," Bell groaned, the knot of fists trembling between them. "Start when ever you're ready."

"Anytime now," Joe grunted, the vessels in his forearms looking like big earthworms.

"Speaking of asses" Bell gasped, "I've got a question for you. What stretches the farthest, rubber or human skin?"

"How the hell would I know," Joe blurted. "Depends on the rubber, I guess."

"Human skin," Bell said, trying not to laugh. "It says in the Bible that Moses tied his ass to a tree and then walked forty miles into the desert."

Joe roared a great laugh as his fist slammed backwards onto the bar. Everyone laughed and yelled.

"Forty miles of ass," Joe howled. "You tricked me. You knew I was winning and you cheated."

"No, no. I was just waiting for you to start."

Joe set up drinks, glasses clinked and elbows bent.

"First round's on me," Joe said. "It's good to see smokejumpers back in town."

For the next four days, every one gray and rainy, the load on Jumper 56 was held on stand by in McGrath for reasons no one could figure. No one but Quinlan. For him it was clear. He claimed the move had Al's name all over it. Statewide things were extra slow for the first week in June, and the crew was getting cranky stuck in the old hangar.

"Aackk," Quinlan said, "out of sight, out of mind. You whine about the rain there and you whine about it here. This way he doesn't have to listen to it."

Also, Rake, Bell, and Johnny B. were on the McGrath load. This made Quinlan high-strung, but he had that figured out, too. Mattlon, he said, had friends in dispatch, and could move loads wherever he liked. If Mort got wind that Al had not pulled his three bad boys from the jump list, Al could calmly insist that they got away before he read the memo. Quinlan further speculated that in two weeks fire season would be in full swing, and Al's little problem would disappear on its own.

The days passed slowly with nothing to do but hang out in the tent frames behind the main station, sit around the woodstove reading, play poker or spades or crazy eights, read, sleep, then read some more. Someone had written over our door, Welcome to the McGrath Sleeping/Reading Institute. Since it was raining, dispatch said we could stay in the tent frames instead of down by the plane in our standby shack where there was no stove. An Eskimo woman was McGrath's head cook. Her six-year old son, Danny, hung out with us every day. One afternoon Rake went to the jumpship, got his gear and suited Danny up, helmet and all, and then Johnny B. took pictures and promised to mail them back to him. Besides entertaining Danny during the day and getting drunk at Joe's every night, the only other source of entertainment, besides eating, was playing fetch with a short-legged, black Scotty-looking stray that hung around the station. People said he belonged to someone in town. No one knew the dog's name so we called him Ripcord.

The reason there was no cussing during these long, boring days was the boy. From breakfast until quitting time he hung out in the tent frames, played Old Maid with Johnny B., practiced tying knots with Kasson, and listened to who knows how many jump stories. Except for when we went to Joe's he was always with us, even taking his meals at the smokejumper table. Truth told, Danny and the dog were about the only normal thing in our lives.

What it came down to was a struggle for mental health. Each morning we'd go through the same routine, rising for breakfast, then traipsing down to the standby shack, checking the plane, our gear, then traipsing back to the tent frames to read, play cards, listen to the rain, and wait out the day. Word finally came from Fairbanks. They were getting fires. The base had been jumped out for two days, and Al wanted us back. McGrath refused to let us go. Hairface, our spotter and jumper in charge, couldn't get a straight answer from the McGrath overhead as to why. Tension began to build. Over the phone Mattlon told him that both helicopters that were supposed to be sent to McGrath were in Fort Yukon working fires and that he suspected our load was being held to cover for them. When

Hairface related this to the crew, our self-imposed ban on cussing around the boy was tested to the limit. From that moment on, the crew became uncooperative at best and outwardly hostile at worst. That night at Joe's, Kasson walked right up to the Station Foreman and called him a worthless, brown-nosing kiss-ass.

The next day after breakfast McGrath dispatch told Hairface that we could no longer stand by in the tent frames but would have to stay at the standby shack. The reason, they claimed, was so we could make a quicker getaway. Everybody got pissed-off except Hairface and Quinlan.

The McGrath standby shack was a tent frame, too, but only half the size and no woodstove. Of the other two buildings, one was a small wood-framed shed that held firepacks, cargo chutes, and other jumper supplies; the other was a chicken coop looking thing where fuel cans, chain saws and pump kits were stored. It was sided and roofed with flattened five gallon fuel cans. With only four cots in the stand by tent frame and no room in the other two buildings, the only thing to do was hunker down in a cold room or a cold airplane.

"Were getting boned," Rake said. "I say we go back to the tent frames and tell them to fuck off."

"Al wants us to get along down here," Hairface said. "A bad report would fit right into the DM's plan. Al says to sit tight and let him handle things."

Initially Al's words calmed the crew some. If Al wanted us to sit tight, so be it. But then, at quitting time we were put off again at six, the fifth day straight without stand by overtime. As we walked to the main station a detection aircraft took off to look for fires. The question loomed big. If they were looking for fires, they must have expected to find some. And if they did, then why weren't we held on stand by like in the past?

"We're fucking hostages," Kasson grumbled. "They know we can't leave, so when they find a fire, they'll just round us up. In the meantime they don't have to pay stand by."

That night the rains came harder than ever, the kind Texans call a toad choker, and it was so depressing we even gave up on Joe's. The next morning, after checking his gear, Kasson was walking from the standby shack back to the cookhouse for breakfast when the Station Foreman drove passed in his pickup, hit a mud puddle and splashed Kasson good. Most of the crew was already eating when the door flew open and Kasson stormed in, stalked over to the table where the foreman was sitting, and without even saying hello, grabbed him by the scruff of the neck, lifted him off his chair, pulled the foreman's face to within inches of his own, and said, "You worthless pissant. If you ever do that again, I'll squeeze your head until it pops like a pimple. You got that?" Then he shoved the man back down in his chair and disappeared out the side door, leaving the cookhouse quiet as a church.

"Suit-up you brush apes," Hairface shouted from the cockpit. "We're fifteen out."

I woke from the deep sleep I get sometimes when flying, to the harsh reality of a spotter demanding that you wake up and get ready to jump out of an airplane. Alaska jumpers flew with chicken bags on every DC-3, each man had one, they stayed in the plane, and helped combat the long, and sometimes cold, flights. I pulled mine off and stuffed it in a burlap bag, then sat up and looked around.

Hairface made his way back through the jumpers towards the door. Other heads poked out from under chicken bags. Bell sat scratching his head. Quinlan was already suited-up. Melvin Sheejek lay at Bell's feet, passed out.

Because it was usually such a long way to fires in Alaska, jumpers didn't fly suited-up like they did in the Lower 48. Instead, we kept our jump gear in our gear bags and flew wearing regular clothes and the jump harness. Each man had his reserve and helmet close by in case we had to make an emergency exit.

Ten minutes later I was sitting by a window in my jump gear, looking down at miles of open sea. Forty miles behind us the coastline of the Katmai National Park ran south in a dark line toward the Pacific Ocean. Up ahead was Kodiak Island.

"The horrible one lives out here," Bell said, his voice reverent and his eyes flashing. "Biggest bear in the world. Kodiaks weigh up to 1500 pounds and stand ten feet tall."

The horrible one. That's what Alaska jumpers called grizzlies, after its scientific name, Ursus arctos horribilis. Kodiaks are a subspecies of the grizzly bear, bigger than its mainland cousin and isolated from other bears for over 12,000 years. Horrible or not, I was glad to get out of McGrath even if they were tall as redwoods.

The Doug throttled back and began descending. Johnny B. finished putting on his reserve, and then stuffed Duke in his left leg pocket. Duke looked a might scared. Since when did smokejumpers fly over an ocean to get to a fire?

"Coming up, left side," Hairface yelled over the engines. "Terror Bay, the Terror River, and the Terror River Ranch. Welcome to the Kodiak National Wildlife Preserve."

The Doug dropped its left wing and everyone moved to that side to see. Everyone except Bell, who was busy suiting up Melvin while Melvin was busy trying to maintain consciousness.

"Is he all right?" Hairface asked.

"He's fine," Bell said. "He's just a little too relaxed."

"Meechameandu," Melvin mumbled at Hairface.

Between Kodiak Island and the mainland the deep blue Shelikof Strait stretched to the southern horizon. Both North and South of the ranch a series of spur ridges separated several green and beige valleys that ran down from snow covered mountains to fan out into long, sweeping gray beaches. Terror Bay, an arm of water two miles wide and ten miles long, knifed deep into the central mountains. The Terror River emptied into the bay after its fifteen mile run from Terror Lake. A mile from the bay, on the south bank of the river, sat two log barns, a log corral with a few horses in it, a dirt airstrip, an airplane hangar, and a two-story building roofed and sheeted with plywood.

The head and both flanks of the fire were burning in thick forest and open grassland, moving away from the buildings up into a canyon. The tail was backing into the wind, moving steadily towards the ranch. Over the entire scene, a 6000-foot smoke column cast an ominous, dark shadow.

"Looks like about forty acres," Hairface yelled to Rake.

As first man on the list, Rake was fire boss, even though he wasn't supposed to be on it at all.

"See the people on the airstrip?" Hairface said, pointing. "Deal with them first. Let's hope you don't get a wind switch."

The first set of streamers drifted as expected then, just before they landed, blew in towards the fire. The next set did the same. Still, it was a big open field with a quarter mile between the fire and the barns.

"First three jumpers," Hairface yelled. Rakowski, Quinlan, and Mountain Puss moved to the door.

"Okay you guys. Hook up."

Coming around on final, the Doug cut through the edge of the smoke causing it to pitch up on a wing, right itself, then slam down hard. Rake's knees buckled some and he almost went down. The rest of us stayed seated on the cargo.

"Get ready."

With a slap to the back of Rake's left calf, the first stick took to the skies over Terror Bay. I pressed against the window to watch. Dow, Shearer, and Mellin were in the second stick. Then, it was Bell, Sheenjek, and me. Bell helped a seriously hung over Melvin to his feet and then to the door.

"What'd you say was wrong with him?" Hairface shouted.

"He's just a little hung over is all. This will sober him up."

"Hook it up," Melvin said.

"Yes, dammit, hook up," Bell said. "And get your helmet on. We're turning final."

Bell hooked up then checked to make sure Melvin was ready.

"Keep him between us," Bell said to me. "If he won't jump, push him out."

Hairface pulled his head in out of the slipstream.

"Two-hundred yards of drift, most of it high. Down low, it's in towards the fire, but I'm carrying you plenty long... you'll have lots of room. Any questions?"

We had none. Hairface thrust his head out and looked forward under the plane, then pulled it in, held the microphone to his mouth, started to say something to the pilots, then hesitated, and looked out again.

Bell turned to Melvin and yelled, "Melvin, listen. Just follow me. Hang on to my main. When I go out, you go out, too. Okay?"

Melvin's head bobbed up and down, but I wasn't sure if it was because he'd heard or because of the bouncing of the plane. Anyway, I grabbed Melvin's main and held him steady.

"Get ready."

The instant Bell got the slap he reached back with his right hand and grabbed the sleeve of Melvin's jump jacket then jumped, pulling Melvin with him. As I cleared the door I saw Melvin rotating sideways, then facing backwards, his arms wind-milling. It looked like someone had thrown a cat out of an airplane. Don's chute opened, then Melvin's, then mine.

Immediately after checking my chute, I looked over at Melvin. He was flying off with his arms dangling down, his head slumped forward. Either he was taking a real close look at the spot, dead, or just passed out again.

"Melvin," Bell yelled. "Pay attention. Grab your lines. Start steering." No response. I yelled, too. Nothing. Both Bell and I maneuvered our chutes closer to Melvin. He wasn't steering, just drifting along with his head down.

Bell turned right, then left, then right again, cussing and yelling at Melvin. I tried keep Melvin between us but it was hard, so I just decided to follow him. Suddenly he reached up with his right hand, pulled his right toggle all the way down and entered into a spiraling right turn. Around and around he went. Surprisingly, he was doing as well in the pattern as we were. That is, until the landing. He had enough sense not to spiral all the way into the ground — which was good — but not enough to avoid landing running with the wind—which was bad. It doesn't take a lot of skill to do a good roll when you land doing fifteen miles an hour, so it was no surprise that Melvin's was exceptional. So much so that he did two, maybe three, it was hard to tell.

On the ground, Bell and I quickly unsuited and ran over. Mountain Puss was already there.

"Man, that landing was scary," Mountain Puss said. "It's a wonder he's not dead."

"Well, he's not," Bell said. "Melvin's too tough for that."

Rake came over, knelt down and flipped up the mask on Melvin's helmet. Turning his face to the sun he lifted one eyelid. The large black pupil quickly shrank to a small dot.

"He's all right, Rake said. "I saw enough dead people in Vietnam to know when I see one. Hell, if he'd been sober, a landing like that would have killed him."

"Let him be," Bell said, pulling off Melvin's helmet. "I'll check on him later."

Bell took a canteen out of Melvin's PG bag, put it near his head, then pulled his parachute over him to keep off the mosquitoes.

Once all the cargo was on the ground, Rake radioed Hairface to go to the BLM station in Soldotna and load up two pump kits, three-thousand feet of hose and thirty gallons of premix. About the time Rake finished his order two men rode up, one on a fat, jug-headed horse, the other on a spotted looking thing that I figured was part donkey. Both wore cowboy hats and bounced rough in the saddle.

"Howdy," the first man said, reaching down to shake Rake's hand. "Name's Dave Sly, but you can just call me Dave. This here's Mat Leeder."

"Hi, I'm Rake," Rake said, shaking hands. "Of the legendary type. Nice to meet you."

"We didn't mean to cause y'all no trouble," Dave said. "We was supposed to catch some cows and brand them. But they's too wild. Then, the wind come up and our brandin' fire took off. I thought Mat here was tendin' it, and he thought I was. Oooeee, the boss ain't gonna like this one bit. His wife done radio-phoned Anchorage and told him. Ha, ha."

Dave and Mat chuckled briefly at the prospect of their boss' return, then turned solemn. Dave's horse was throwing its head a lot and turning in circles and farting, so that it was impossible for him to complete a sentence without having to pause between rotations. Mat's donkey stood with its head turned sideways. I figured it was blind in one eye. They looked like men that someone had dressed in kid's cowboy outfits. Dave was lanky and wore thick glasses and a black hat pulled down low over his forehead. Mat sported a gray Hoot Gibson with a stovepipe crown. He was swarthy and short, and had the peculiar habit of grinning vacantly at the ground.

"Plumb got away," Dave said, as his horse completed another revolution.

"Sure enough," Mat noted. "Took right off. . . ever which way. We was able to keep it from a comin' towards the barns for a while. Now they's no tellin'."

"Wife and baby's over in the cabin," Dave said, as his farty horse went around again. "That there's gonna be the new house." He was pointing at the plywood-framed two-story.

Lifting his eyes from the ground, Mat nodded in the direction of the smoke column. "Cows is getting' chased by fire now I reckon. We're hopin' they can find theirselves a snow patch."

"Let us know if we can help," Dave Sly said to Rake, his horse starting to crow hop backwards.

Then, grinning back at the ground again, Mat added," Cause if 'n they don't... well then."

Rake gave them a short list of chores, starting with letting the horses out of the corral, plus any other stock in the barns, then moving the jeep, the tractor and other equipment onto the airstrip. Next, he divided the crew into two groups. The first, led by Bell, would gather jump gear and cargo and pack it to the river. The second, led by Quinlan, would work with Dave and Mat to figure out the ranch's water system, and collect all the barrels, buckets and hoses, and get ready for a burnout in case the fire made a run at the buildings.

At that point the fire was moving away to the northeast into a canyon of white spruce. The area between the ranch and the fire's close edge was a forty-acre short-grass piece of ground which would provide us some time as long as the wind stayed in our favor. Not in our favor was the fact that the grass grew right up to most of the buildings.

A lot of people think wildland fire fighters, and especially smoke-jumpers are more or less crazy. Most see fire and the only thing they can think of is to get away from it. But wildfire is like anything else. It has a nature, a particular behavior. It's something you can observe and, over time, become familiar with. By the time a person applies to smokejumping, most have had several years of experience already. Each fire is different, though. Each burns according to a specific set of factors, like weather, time of day, the fuels it's burning in, the topography. Obviously, things happen that are beyond the range of usual prediction. Good firefighting requires, not that you fear it, but that you respect it. Wildfires sometimes have monstrous potential. The more refined the critical observation skills of the firefighter, the better the chance he will make sound decisions and catch it. To do it consistently, under so many different conditions, is what makes the work so satisfying.

I helped Bell, Johnny B., Mitchell, Dow, Scott Bates and Mountain Puss gather cargo. Right off, Johnny B. started in.

"Hey Len?" Johnny B. said. "Are you sure you're not related to these boys? They talk just like you do."

"Hell no, I'm not related to them. Why, I don't even know 'em."

"I'll bet you do. I hear everybody in Texas is related."

"This might come as a shock to a man who thinks he's an expert on just about everything, but if there's one thing you don't know shit about, Johnny B., it's Texas."

"That short one kind of looks like you, too."

He thought he was getting the best of me, but I just ignored him and went on gathering cargo. Quinlan, Bartell, The Fat Indian, Pat Shearer, Mellin and Kasson prepared for the fire fight by putting burlap bags, water buckets and barrels in several locations. Quinlan went to the closest part of the fire to see how easily it beat out with a wet burlap bag. The only spruce boughs were up in the hills, so that was going to put a strain on our burlap bag supply.

Bell sacked up Melvin's gear and carried it to the gear pile by the river. Then he helped him over to it, and after forcing him to drink half a canteen of water, left him with instructions that if the fire made a run at our gear, it was his job to protect it. Rake went to the cabin to speak with the woman. Moments later they appeared on the porch, her holding a baby wrapped in blankets, and Rake waving for me to come.

"Len," Rake said, "this is Jennifer. She wants to stay here for now. If the fire makes a run this way, you're to make sure she and the baby get to the river. It'll be your decision. You know what I mean?"

I said I did, although it was disappointing since it meant I would miss out on most of the fire fighting. Quinlan radioed Rake. The tail of the fire was too dry to beat out and was backing steady. Rake left to rejoin the crew.

"Ma'am?" I said to Jennifer. "Don't you worry about your cows. We had range fires where I grew up in Texas, and cows are smarter than you think when it comes to fire.

"Oh," the woman said, all the time watching the fire, not seeming to hear.

After a moment she turned and forced a smile, "Would you like some hot tea?"

"Maybe later. But for now... " I hesitated, wondering how to say it. "I don't want to frighten you, Ma'am, but it might be good to pack up some of your valuables. That way I can take them to the river. If the wind turns there's a chance we won't be able to save this place."

Inside the cabin Jennifer began collecting things: a file of letters and papers, a box of photos, some child's clothing, and a cardboard box of blankets.

"When the time comes, I'll put the cat in there," she said, pointing at another box. "This was the summer we hoped to finish the house."

While Jennifer set water on to boil, I sat on the porch and watched as the head of the fire crowned in the woods at the base of the mountain. Acres of orange and yellow flames roared above the white spruce, leaving hundreds of individual trees burned black, their branches waving like ghosts dancing under a great gray smoke column. Burning bark, spruce cones and branches flew into the air, then fell in showers. Like a thing alive, the fire raged and hissed and popped, an angry roar gaining strength. A half-hour later the column began to lean back over the meadow toward us. Embers trailing smoke began to fall. Spotfires took hold at the edge of the forty-acre flat.

Right then a bunch of things happened all at once. First, the smoke column collapsed and sent a violent wind down into the center of the burning woods. Next it flushed out onto the flat and sent a wall of running ground fire directly at us. Beyond the barns I could hear the jumpers yelling as they ran splashing buckets of water onto the dry grass, forming a circle of defense. Once it was wet enough, they would fire-out, waiting for the right moment to take advantage of the draft.

"Okay," I said to Jennifer. "No time for tea."

Off to the river we went, Jennifer carrying her baby while I followed behind balancing three boxes, one with a cat in it. At the river Melvin was moving gear bags onto a sandbar.

"Melvin," I said. "This here's Jennifer and Laura. You look after them. Jennifer, if you want to get a few more things from the cabin, do it now. But when Melvin says no more, you have to stop. Is that clear? Fire can move a lot faster than you can run."

"Yes, thank you. I understand. Are we going to lose everything?"

"Not if we can help it, Ma'am."

By the time I got to the barns the crew had started the burnout, lighting the edge of the wet area, then beating the flames out with burlap bags. Having tied into the river upstream from the farthest out barn, Quinlan's group was bringing the burnout line in a curve to a point where it would intersect a swampy area near the end of the airstrip. With the ground wind still blowing toward the advancing front, the burnout was in our favor. The wind calmed. Ten minutes later it picked up, reversed direction, and came straight at us. In no time the air was full of hot smoke. We couldn't see more than fifty feet.

Right then Jumper 56 roared over and dropped its first bundle of pumps and hose. Two chutes fluttered open, drifted a bit, then landed on the airstrip.

"Group one," Rake shouted. "Come with me. The rest, keep burning out toward Quinlan."

Rake, Bell and I tore into the first bundle, a Mark III pump kit and 800 feet of hose. The rest tore open the second and took off for Quinlan's group. The Doug circled out over the bay, then lined up on final and came roaring through the smoke with its navigation lights flashing green and white. Out came thirty gallons of premix. Within minutes we were on a gravel bank at the river with the pump, a Jerry can, five gallons of premix, a suction hose and strainer. We hooked up the fuel line between the Jerry can and the pump. Bell commenced to yanking like a crazy man on the starter rope, rrrrr, rrrrr, rrrrr. Bates put the fuel can on top of a pack box to hurry the fuel. Mitchell adjusted the choke. Bell cussed. I grabbed a handful of fusees and got ready to light them.

Next thing I knew Melvin was there, barging between everyone. Whipping out his knife, he cut a small yellow plastic band hidden behind the ignition switch, then said, "Anchorage District, safety shit. It's on all their pumps."

Three pulls later the pump sputtered, then roared to life. Melvin set the choke and ran up the throttle, then smiled big and yelled, "Now, back to baby sitting."

Johnny B. led the way on the nozzle, sweeping it back and forth as he went, while Bates and I lit the dry edge just inside the wet line. The rest beat out the perimeter behind us. With two hundred yards between us and Quinlan's bunch, we could only hope that his section was holding. Rake, in the meantime, moved back and forth in the smoke, talking to the plane on the radio, trying to reach Quinlan, helping where he could, moving up hose or beating out spotfires. Overhead the Doug roared past dropping the last of the hose. Rake got back on the radio.

"It's going to be close," Hairface said. "You've got about two-hundred yards between you and the other guys and the fire will get there about the same time you meet up. It's bumped the airstrip on the south side and appears to be holding, so no worries there."

The plane circled and the conversation ended with, "We'll keep an eye on things for a while here but we're getting pretty low on fuel."

At the front of the hoselay, Johnny B. crouched down out of the worst smoke. At times visibility was only a few feet. It hurt to breathe and, the red glow of the fire was getting brighter and hotter. I heard a funny noise, turned around, and there was Quinlan.

"Aackk," he said. "It's less than a hundred yards to the end of our line. The grass is shorter between us. We're holding what we've got. Don't let up. If it gets too rough, we've got the river."

Bob began pulling hose with Johnny B. Rake showed up with four more 100-foot sections, dropped two, handed the others to Quinlan, and said, "Take these to your side. Maybe it'll be enough."

My lungs were fighting for air, my eyes burned and my face was pouring sweat. The next section of hose was added as Johnny B. and the rest pushed ahead, keeping low, wretching and coughing, blindly beating on the fire, slowly moving up. About the time I didn't think I could take it anymore, I looked around and saw gray silhouettes moving against a orangish-pink background, burlap bags arcing through the air, slamming the ground, sparks flying.

Up ahead someone yelled. The last section of hose was put on. Two minutes later the two sprays overlapped. Johnny B. and Mitchell met, got down on their knees, and shoulder to shoulder leveled their nozzles across the grass. The flame front was 20 to 30 feet deep at that point and hot as hell. The boys with the burlap bags kept beating, the hoses kept spraying, and suddenly the gap closed and the flames were gone.

A great cheer flew up. Even though we could barely breathe, we started jumping at each other like a bunch of pups, high-fiving, whooping and howling and throwing burlap bags in the air.

"Quick," Rake yelled, "spread back down the line. Watch for spots."

Several were found and knocked down. Out in the burn, areas cooled into expansive sweeps of small flames, shimmering sparks and glowing embers. I told Rake I wanted to check on the woman. At the river Jennifer and her baby were huddled behind a wall of firepacks Melvin had built. Melvin stood facing the fire, his eyes shining.

"That was a good fight," he said. "Did you win it?"

"Maybe. It's too soon to say for sure. How's Jennifer and Laura?"

Jennifer pulled the baby away from her breast where it was nursing, then got to her feet. "We're fine. Melvin's taking good care of us."

I looked at Jennifer. She was the picture of loveliness, vulnerability and courage, standing there in that strange, unholy light, seeing her life surrounded by fire.

"Do you ever cry, Jennifer?" I asked suddenly, without even knowing I was going to.

She tugged her baby closer, looked me in the eye, and calmly said, "Yes, I do... but only about the important things."

Four hours later I carried my gear bag from the river to the main barn where Jennifer said we could sleep. It was 3:00 A.M. At that time of year, at that latitude, there was enough light in the northern sky to see without a headlamp. I looked at the buildings through a haze of blue smoke. Except for the roar up-canyon, a strange calm lay over the place. At the barn the crew sat around two campfires cooking and talking. They were too tired to make much noise, so they talked softly and only laughed a little now and then. I dropped my gear bag. Hungry and exhausted, I couldn't decide whether to eat or just sleep. Which ever I chose, I planned to enjoy it. A man can most times eat and he can just about always sleep, but not often with the satisfaction I felt there, in that moment, in that place, in the company of a handful of good men and a woman sleeping peacefully with her baby.

At one of the campfires, I dug into my PG bag for my coffee cup.

"We'll rack-out until six," Rake said. "Quinlan and Dow are going to stay up and patrol."

I decided to eat but didn't take long, just a can of baked beans, some John Wayne crackers, and then off to sleep in the barn on a pile of loose grass hay. Three hours later, I woke stiff and sore, my throat raw. Soft laughter came from outside. A few others were still sleeping. I had slept in my pants and t-shirt, so they were dry. But my fire shirt was still wet, just like my boots and socks. I took a pair of dry socks out of my PG bag and put them on. Then came the cold, stiff boots. Once up and on the move, I knew that both the boots and my body would loosen up. I knew it because I had done it many times.

"Top of the morning," the McGrath All-Star said from his sleeping bag.

"Well now, if you aren't a sight. Last time I saw you peeking out of a sleeping bag, you'd done steered yourself into an ice hole and almost died."

"I wish you'd forget that. Seems like every time I turn around you have to bring it up."

"Well then, I reckon I owe you an apology. It's just the most impressive thing I've ever seen you do, floating out there all alone, staring at the sky, blue-lipped and all."

Johnny B. reached over and set Duke upright on his PG bag.

"I'm glad I've got Duke. Duke's always cheerful and kind, not like some people."

"I can see why you are. You do all the talking and he does all the listening."

At the campfire I took a seat on a cubitainer of water. A thick smoke lay over the whole area, most of it up-canyon. Visibility was about 200 yards and the sun was no more than a dull, orange ball in a gray haze. The fire in the grassy flat next to the ranch buildings was all but out except a for few smoldering places along the river. Somehow the area looked smaller than when it was filled with fire just a few hours before.

Dave and Mat, came with a platter piled high with bacon and three loaves of fresh-baked bread. The cows had escaped, they said, and were grouped up in a wet meadow south of the airstrip.

"Lady of the house says her and the baby's doin' fine, and thanks to y'all," Dave Sly said. "She'd like to do more for ye. Claims she's never seen such a good bunch."

After breakfast, Rake split us into two groups again. All except Quinlan and Dow who had patrolled all night and were told to get some sleep. The first group was to check the fire area closest to the ranch, the second to work the perimeter up the north flank. That was my group. I took a chainsaw and began falling snags. Johnny B. was my swamper. Scott "Master" Bates and Mountain Puss moved one of the pumps up and got a pump and hose show going behind us. Bell took off to recon the south flank and the head so we could get an idea of how much total work we had. An hour later he was back. Near the head the fire had jumped the river, but he couldn't find a way across. He wanted to work that first, so we packed everything up, including the pump and hose plus enough fuel and rats for the day, then hiked up following Bell. I felled a white spruce across a twenty-foot section of waterfalls, then stepped carefully across, cutting the limbs off so the rest could follow.

The slopover was about half an acre. Mountain Puss and Master Bates set up the pump again and knocked down the hottest flames while I cut a line on the fire's edge right behind them, sawing through downed logs, cutting out small trees, limbing up the bigger ones. Bell scouted for more spotfires, then went back across the river to find Rake. He returned with a new plan. Everyone would stay on the slopover side of the fire, except for Johnny B. and me. After finishing the saw work, we were to go back and help Rake's bunch extend a hoselay up the south flank.

After five hours of pumping and sawing we tied into a snow field near the head, and Rake called for both crews to gather back down at a rock outcropping near where the steep ground gave way to the flat. He ruled the fire good enough, and told us an EFF crew from Kodiak was to be helicoptered in that afternoon to finish mopping up. It was time to eat and rest. Gritty and tired, we gathered up our tools and filed down off the mountain as happy as rats in a corn crib.

After eating, most of the crew sprawled out in the grass next to the rock outcropping to nap and enjoy the sun. Johnny B. wanted to hike up an open ridge a ways, so we did. It took us the better part of an hour to get up there, but the view was worth it. The smoke of the morning was gone, pushed higher into the mountains by a breeze off the sea. A hundred miles across Shelikof Strait we could see the mainland of Alaska. We were sitting there, taking it all in, when Johnny B. broke the silence with a poem.

"Ode to the Tumbleweed," he began, staring out to sea.

They bloom in a ways that few men see,

grow green and thorny, and die

In places where life is brittle and thin,

they tremble, break free and blow with the wind


And so it has been with much of my life

the good roads and bad, the trouble and strife

There are times on the road when I think I might stay

But I always move on, be that as it may


You never knew when Johnny B. would come out with something like that. And when he did, he never looked at you, just far off somewhere.

"I like your poems," I said.

"Oh, they're not poems, they're just words I hear in my head."

"I like them anyway, whatever they are."

"Good," Johnny B. said, still looking to sea. "Do you believe in moving on?"

"I damn sure did when we left McGrath. Hell, we do it all the time. I don't spend much time thinking on it, really. Do you?"

"I do when I'm doing it. And that was the case when I wrote that."

"What road was it?"

"Tibet. Didn't I tell you I went around the world?"

"A little, that day while you were thawing out by the pond."

"It took a year. I left right after the season of '71, caught a flight to Japan from Anchorage. From Japan I went across the Soviet Union on the Trans-Siberian railroad. From Moscow I went to Turkey, then Israel where I worked on a Kibbutz, then to Egypt, Libya, across North Africa to Spain, and then home."

"Did Duke go along with you?"

"Not until Israel. That's where Duke and I joined up, on the kibbutz."

"Duke's from Israel?"

"Yeah. Duke's a Jew. Didn't I tell you?"

"No, I don't believe so. That's not the kind of thing I'd forget."

"Remember when I told you about the boy on the bike and the bomb?"

"Of course I do. But I don't recall you mentioning Duke."

"Duke belonged to the boy. He was riding in a wire basket on the front of the bicycle. After the  ambulance took the boy away, I sat down near where he died, you know, maybe to say a prayer or recite a poem... something. Once I finished that, all of a sudden there was Duke, in the bicycle basket, covered with dirt. The boy had made a little safety belt out of two rubber bands and part of a wooden match, and had Duke strapped in. The boy wanted Duke to be safe. I got him loose, brushed him off, and introduced myself. We've been friends ever since."

I didn't know what to say. Johnny B. was still looking out to sea. After a time he went on.

"In the Soviet Union, at night on the train, I'd sit at a window and watch as it passed through cities, some with as many as 150,000 people, all barely lit by kerosene lamps and candles. In a small village in Turkey I met an English couple and spent a week sleeping on their balcony. The last morning I woke at dawn to a pink sky, the morning star, and the gray silhouette of a mosque. In the distance a woman began wailing. Her voice rose and fell and then rose again, on and on. It sounded like an agony so great it had taken over her entire being. Something had destroyed a part of that woman she knew she could never get back, Len."

I reached over and took hold of Johnny B.'s. forearm and held on.

"You need to write more, Johnny B.," I said. "That was good what you just told me."

While we were on the ridge, Bell went to the ranch, got a bag of something, then started back up, passing the crew at the outcropping, heading towards us. Melvin joined him. Together they made their way up a steep part of the ridge a hundred yards past where we were to a small cliff. I figured they were just out for a hike.

I took off my shirt and lay back, feeling the sun and thinking how lucky I was to be back jumping. Johnny B. pulled Duke out of his PG bag, brushed him off and said, "Dammit, Duke, just look at yourself. I know this firefighting is fun, but that's no excuse to go around dirty like our worthless friend, Len." After setting Duke in the grass, Johnny B. took out his harmonica and began playing Red River Valley. I think he played it because he knew I had some sad feelings about his story. Before Johnny B. finished his tune someone at the rock outcropping commenced yelling.

"Aackk," Quinlan called up the hill. "Don't you do that!"

I turned to look. There was Bell and Melvin at the edge of the cliff. Bell had his harness on and was facing into the wide open spaces. Behind him Melvin was shaking open a main parachute.

"Stop! Stop!" Quinlan wailed. "We don't have a trauma kit."

The canopy popped open in an upslope gust, rolled to the left, then right, then flew up and started forward toward the cliff with Bell running after it. I reckon that was his plan, but by then he had no choice. He could run off the cliff after it or be pulled off. Either way, for better or worse, through sickness and health, or until death do us part, Bell was airborne. At first the canopy rocked side to side, then forward and back. To everyone watching it was a plain fact; we were fixin' to witness the end of Don Bell.

The jumpers scrambled to their feet and began whooping and hollering. Down the steepest part of the ridge Bell flew with the shadow of his parachute racing right below him. All of a sudden an updraft took him up and out, then up some more until there he was floating alone high over the Terror River Ranch. For several minutes he steered back and forth, soaring like a bird while we looked on amazed. When he finally came down, it was near the barns. Getting to his feet, he waved to the rock outcropping where the jumpers had gone plumb wild.

"This crew's something else," I said to Johnny B., thinking that the same spirit that made them special would likely be their downfall.

"What do you think's going to happen with this new DM?" I asked.

"Who knows? He's just another one of these manager's who thinks he needs to boss around smokejumpers. It happens all the time with certain groups. Navy Generals screw with the Seals, Army brass screw with the

Green Berets. It's like if you can't be one, at least you can fuck with them. I think it's envy."

"You better hope he don't find out about you and Rake and Bell jumping this fire instead of being on suspension like in the memo."

"He probably won't. He's too removed from it. Once fire season gets rolling, those kind of things get lost in the shuffle." Johnny B. pulled a stem of grass and started chewing on it. "Why? Are you worried about it?"

I sat up straight, pulled a grass stem of my own, and thought a minute.

"Hell," I finally said. "I may as well tell you. The DM called me to his office the afternoon of our first practice jumps. He said I had more hiring papers to sign. Claimed he's right proud of the crew and that he's looking for ways to help us do a better job. Said he needed someone in the field to report on crew morale and efficiency, things like..."

"You're shitting me," Johnny B. said. "He wants you report on the crew?"

"I didn't want any part of it, but he had my personnel folder right there in his hand, and he shook it at me and said I was his man because I knew what it was like to be a manager from my time with the Forest Service. Hell, I felt like a cow that had just figured out the slaughterhouse concept."

"You should've told him to shove it."

"I wish I had. That low-down bastard pretended I had papers to sign. That was a trick to get me over there. Now I've got to finagle a way out of it. Or start lying. And as you might imagine, I'm not worth a shit at that."

"Was your meeting before the pig party or after?"

"Before! And I know what you're thinking. Listen, I haven't seen hide nor hair of him since."

"It's that district nerd, then," Johnny B. said. "He was at the party, and at Bonanza Creek. Bell and Rake got in his face about the helicopter blowing our camp down. Remember?"

I shook my head. "Good Lord, when I think of all of the stuff this crew's done, if I was to report half of it we'd all get fired."

"Well," Johnny B. said, scratching his head, "you can't say much about the Pig Party, that's for sure."

"That coyote-assed Miles will have something to say, though. You can bet on that."

Johnny B. turned to Duke, and said, "I've been wondering what was bothering the sheriff here, Duke. Turns out, he's a double agent."

"Why, I'm no such thing. And I don't reckon you intend to help much, either."

"Well," Johnny B. said, "you'll worry about it no matter what. But if I were in your shoes, I'd just relax and have a little faith. We may not see Fairbanks for a month. And when we do, tell him what a great crew we are. Tell him what a great boss Mattlon is. How would he know, anyway? Hang in with him. Spying works both ways. You ever think of that?"

"No, and I don't want to. I came here to enjoy smokejumping and that's all."

"Well, your ass is in a sling now. The least you can do is enjoy it."

"What if Mattlon finds out?"

"Maybe you should tell him."

"Johnny B., you're not suggesting I tell our boss that his boss wants me to spy on him and the crew, are you? Once that got out, no matter what, I'd be the one blamed. You just can't go and put your boots in the oven, Johnny B., cook them awhile and call them biscuits."

"Well, I guess you're stuck then. You're too hardheaded to take advice. It's important to fight the good fight, though. Just do that and, odds are, the rest will take care of itself."

"Aw hell, I reckon you're right," I said after a time. "Thanks for listening anyway. In the meantime, don't let on about this to anyone, on the crew or otherwise."

At eight that evening, while the crew was at the barn making dinner, a recon plane from Soldotna flew over and told Rake that, due to delays, we would be demobed at noon the next day.

A Coast Guard helicopter from Kodiak would fly in a crew and take us back. We would fly to Anchorage by commercial airline.

An hour later the rancher arrived in his Super Cub. Earl Deering was tall and lanky, wore Levis and a canvas jacket, and carried himself in a way you see in men who are comfortable with who they are. He shook hands with Rake, then with the whole crew. That night around the campfire, he visited with us and swapped stories. Mr. Deering had been ranching there for six years as part of a BLM project to see if beef cattle could be raised profitably on islands like Kodiak. Each year his herd got bigger and wilder. Newborn calves had run free and never been branded. Desperate, he had hired Dave and Mat off the street in Anchorage. They had come from Oklahoma to find work on the oil pipeline. Instead of catching calves—like they claimed they could—they had nearly burned up the place. If we hadn't saved his buildings, he said, he would have been forced to abandon the whole idea.

"This fall will tell the tale," Mr. Deering told us. "By the time you round them up and drive 'em to these holding corrals, then load them in the landing craft that hauls them to the cattle freighter, and then pay for it all, it's difficult to make any headway. We're getting better at it, but it's damn tough with the winters and the bears."

"Bears," Bell hissed.

"Most years they kill half the calves, sometimes more."

"That's just like them," Bell said, "running around killing and eating and shitting everywhere."

"One got my Romanollo bull last year. Brought him all the way from Italy. They're good for size and quality lean beef. He wasn't here a month when one day, while sitting on the porch, I heard him bellow. He was up by the edge of the woods with his head down, walking steadily towards something. I stepped out into the yard and, by God, here was this big Brownie. Damnedest thing. When they got to within about 20 feet of each other the bull put his head down and charged. Just before he got to the bear it raised up on its hind legs and the bull plowed into him and shoved him backwards a ways. Then the bear reached down over the back of the bull with his forelegs, grabbed it under the belly, and lifted the bull's back end off the ground. They danced back and forth like that with the bull doing a handstand with its ass in the air, and the bear on its hind legs, holding on. Then, just like he had done it a thousand times, the bear dug its claws in and ripped open the bull's belly and jerked him side to side until his guts fell out.

"I shot the sonofabitch from right in front of the cabin. Killed him with one shot. But it was too late. Apparently growing up in Italy didn't prepare my bull for fighting Kodiaks."

A pearl blue sky brightened above the mountains of Terror Bay as the sun broke through the clouds on the second morning of our fire. The snow-covered peaks stood creamy pink and white in the early morning stillness. Most of the jumpers were up and already gathered around campfires when the scent of fresh brewed coffee woke me. Shortly, I was up and feeling alive and full of energy.

"What a deal," Mountain Puss said. "A fire on Kodiak. Big Ernie's shining his light on us boys."

"Well, he better not turn it too bright on you," Rake chuckled. "You need to wash your face. Right now you could tattoo it on your ass and back into a lion's den."

The crew enjoyed a good laugh.

"Look who's talking," Mountain Puss said. "Those Elvis Presley sideburns of yours look like they were trimmed with a blow torch."

The crew laughed again.

"And the cowboys," Melvin said, when the laughing died down. "You know, you see cowboys chasing Indians in movies and on TV. But that's Hollywood. Here I get to see real cowboys in person, real cowboys in action." Melvin laughed his silent laugh, his eyes narrow slits. "They can't catch cows, they can't ride horses, so you know damn well they couldn't catch an Indian. They don't even... "

Bleep... bleep... bleep, bleep, bleep.

"Lookout," Mountain Puss yelled.

Sprawling backwards in a shower of sparks, jumpers tumbled away from the fire, cussing a storm. A smoking can with its sides ripped open fell to the ground not far from Duke, who lay face up covered with spaghetti.

"You almost killed Duke," squalled Johnny B. "Look, he's got spaghetti hair. Everything you do with food ends up a mess."

"No shit," Rake said, "I thought we'd been hit by a grenade."

A bleeped can had exploded. When jumpers cook a quick meal, sometimes they heat unopened cans by setting them in the coals. It's called bleeping, and comes from the bleep, bleep, bleep the cans make ten or so seconds before they explode. It's a quick and efficient way to cook, but of course, like with anything good, it involves some risk. A responsible bleeper must pay attention, listen for the first bleep, flip his can out of the fire with a stick, grab it with a gloved hand and shake it. If he doesn't, things end up like they did for Duke.

Mountain Puss apologized. Johnny B. reached over, grabbed Duke, started wiping him off, and said, "This has been a bad deal for Duke. First we got upside down coming out of the plane, then the wind dragged us through some cow shit when we landed. Now a damned spaghetti explosion."

"Duke's sure enough an action kind of fella," I said. "Look there, he's got some holes burned in his head, too."

Quinlan chimed in, "He's the star in the first spaghetti western ever set in Alaska."

We ate, drank coffee and packed up our gear. It was a fine morning. I went to a stack of cubitaineers to refill my canteens. I sat down on one and took a moment to look back through the camp smoke at the blue silhouettes of a band of men gathered around campfires. I saw something moving there among them, something greater than the sum of its individual parts. Something too old to name, too shadowy for language, yet something we all understood in our own way. It moved silently in the smoke, ancient and old, animated by laughter, calmed by solemnity. Something from the past. Something great, like the snowy mountains and the sky.

# 5

As soon as we landed in Anchorage we were met by a reporter from the Anchorage Daily News. With him was the Editor-in-Chief, who also turned out to be Jennifer's uncle. They were there to do a story on the Heroes of Kodiak, how the fire jumpers had saved a homestead, a women and child, and a family's dream. They took photos and names. Quinlan called Mattlon and warned him about it. To us it was a big fuss over nothing, but the story made the front page of not only the Anchorage Daily News but the Fairbanks News Miner as well. As soon as Mattlon saw it he phoned Campbell Field where we were standing by and made Quinlan the Chief of Party — the COP. As long as we were in Anchorage and close to sources of disaster, as Mattlon had put it, it was critical that Bob keep us in line.

Our school bus pulled into the parking lot of the Mush Inn, and we off-loaded gear while Quinlan went into the office to check us in. The Mush Inn wasn't anything fancy, but it was clean and not far from the bars on Second Street.

"Aackk," Quinlan said. "Motels, restaurants, the press. What's next? Sleeping bags and cots on the lawn were good enough in the old days and saved the taxpayers a lot of money. Next thing you know we'll be wearing Bermuda shorts and shirts from Hawaii."

"You in Bermuda shorts?" Rake beamed. "I can see it now. The guys would say, Hey Bob, are those your legs or are you riding a chicken?"

"Aackk, you girls know the deal. Mattlon wants us to mind our manners down here, not spend all night traipsing around town. Keep your gear bags in your rooms. Breakfast at Peggy's. Be in the bus ready to go at 7:30."

After getting settled, which included a run to the corner liquor store, Johnny B. and I clomped up the stairs of the Mush Inn to Matt Kelly's room. At the door we were met by a tall man wearing dark sunglasses and talking softly into the end of an empty beer bottle like he was covering a golf tournament.

"Ladies and gentlemen," Kelly said, "the tension here in room 221 continues to build as yet more guests arrive for tonight's event. This is Len Swanson, self-deluded Forest Service reject and his monkey-loving friend, Johnny B."

"Hey man, a cordless microphone," Johnny B. said, "I didn't know they'd invented those yet."

After a quick look outside, Kelly quickly closed the door behind us. Inside, two groups were gathered around two double beds. At the end of one was a table with two empty white plates. Charlie Wilbur emerged from the kitchenette carrying a bowl of white eggs. Before smokejumping, Charlie had studied cooking at the Brooks Culinary Institute in Seattle, and was best qualified to make sure the eggs were all alike. On the way to the Mush Inn, we had stopped at a store where Charlie handpicked two dozen of the Grade A Ranch variety.

"Here they are," Charlie announced. "The most perfect set of gems to ever come out of a yard bird's derriere. Perfect in all metaphysical and ecumenical aspects. Boiled exactly twenty minutes in common tap water here at Room 221 of the Mush Inn, Anchorage, Alaska." Charlie stood holding the eggs over his head as if presenting a flaming pudding to a princess.

All this began earlier that afternoon, just before quitting time, when Rake and Mountain Puss got into it about where the crew should eat dinner.

"Dammit Rake, I'm a hungry man," Mountain Puss had declared. "I need a steak, maybe two."

"Drink a six-pack of beer," Rake said. "That way you'll have a full stomach and be a lot smarter, too."

"The guys that eat the most should get to pick where we eat," Mountain Puss huffed.

"Better still," Quinlan said, "how about the ones who whine the most? Then the whole world would have to eat with you."

"Get real, Bob. I eat more than anybody, so I should have a say where we eat."

"Where we eat is a crew decision," Quinlan said. "Always has been."

"I'll bet I can eat more than you can," Rake said to Mountain Puss.

Mountain Puss had looked at Rake with calm amusement. "Heh, heh," he smirked. "So, the Legendary Fucking Retardski thinks he's a legend at eating, too. Is that it? I should have known. Well, I'll take that bet. Any time brother, anywhere."

Rake eyed Mountain Puss steadily. "Okay then, I propose a little contest."

After a round discussing barbecued moose, Spam, Twinkies, and cold C-rats, Rake casually suggested hard-boiled eggs. They were easy to prepare, didn't cost much, and they could do it that night. Right off, Mountain Puss agreed. He had seen Paul Newman eat forty of them in the movie, Cool Hand Luke. Eggs were one of his favorite foods, he said. Nutritious, too.

The talk in room 221 was running hot and big. Wallets got waved around. Fives, tens and twenties fell on the floor between the beds like leaves in October. In no time they became a fair pile of cash. The two groups were near equal in number, except for the two pilots who sat on the bed on Rake's side. Mountain Puss fans, however, were not deterred and quickly countered all bets. As the pile grew, Quinlan kept tally of the names and amounts bet. As COP, even though things were getting wild, I figured he felt it was better if we raised hell at the motel instead of downtown.

Kelley shoved the end of the beer bottle in my face.

"Well folks," he began, "Here's Len Swanson, referee for this evening's contest. Any last thoughts, Len, before the two contestants arrive?"

I leaned back from the microphone, thought a few seconds on why I'd been chosen for referee, then said, "I reckon you know, Matt, it's a rare day when such great talent comes together in one place. Each of these boys is known for something, the Legendary Fucking Rake for becoming a legend in his own mind. And, then there's Mountain Puss, a sexist pig widely known for trying to choose his own nickname. Either one of these gents could become immortal with a victory here tonight."

"There you have it, folks," Kelly said to his beer bottle. "The stage is set. Let's see if we can get a word with the cook, oh, wait now..."

Cheers and boos filled the room as I turned to see Mountain Puss coming in the door wearing a faded yellow bathrobe, dancing some fancy footwork, ducking his head like a prize fighter, throwing short jabs at nothing. Rod Dow and Bruce Marshall, his managers, followed along massaging Mountain Puss' shoulders. Dow carried a white towel and a bottle of red wine in his free hand. Bruce wore an Army camo shirt and a Minnesota Twins baseball cap. They quickly took their man to a far corner where they turned him around, established eye contact and talked at him direct so he wouldn't get distracted by Rake fans.

Quinlan, who had a fair amount bet on Rake, stepped to the center of the room and laughed, "Be nice now. Don't egg him on."

"No old yokes," Kelly chimed in.

Right then the door opened to another cheer, and in stepped The Legendary Fucking Rake himself, wearing a new pair of Levis and a fresh-laundered yellow BLM fire shirt, complete with BLM's blue and green triangle emblem on one shoulder and the Alaska Smokejumper round patch on the other—the one that looked like a parachuting mummy. Rake's supporters went wild, whistling, slapping their knees and stomping the floor. Dashing and in control, Rake struck a pose, flexing his muscles and holding his fists to his chest. Then, pivoting on one foot, he extended an elbow behind him, struck another pose, held it a moment, then turned and strolled back to the door. Bug-eyed, Mountain Puss threw a couple of quick jabs in the direction of The Legend.

"Let's get it on, Bro," Mountain Puss said, dancing around some more.

"Gentlemen," I said, calling the room to order, "please step forward."

Rake and Mountain Puss came to the table as Quinlan held up a fist full of money. "Seven-hundred and fifty-five dollars, cold cash," he said, waving it over his head. Another cheer went up. "Are all bets in?"

Clark Mitchell, Rake's manager, thought not. "Anybody want to put up another fifty against my man, here?" Dow and Marshall, eager to cut off what they saw as a underhanded attempt to rattle Mountain Puss, whipped out their wallets. Quinlan upped the total to eight-hundred and fifty-five.

I couldn't get the room to quiet down, so I went on anyway.

"The rules are simple," I said, nearly shouting.

"One, no betting after the eating has begun." A cheer rocked the room and people chugged on their beers.

"Two, the first man to finish his twelfth egg is the winner." More cheering and chugging.

"Three, once the eating has started, no touching the contestants by managers unless they are choking." That set them off like never before. Cat calls and bed beating showed widespread approval of the rules.

"And fourth, in case of a close finish, the decision of the judge—and that means me—will be final." Generally hostile to any form of authority, they all booed and cussed and drank more beer.

"All right, all right," Quinlan said. "Any questions?"

Mountain Puss' managers lifted the yellow bathrobe off Mountain Puss' shoulders, leaving him standing in his boxer shorts, pink-skinned and barefoot before his peers. Rake undid the top two buttons of his fire shirt and ruffled a few chest hairs. When they stepped up to the table, Rake leaned forward to look at Mountain Puss like a spider might a fly.

"The boy's have made their bets," Rake said. "What say we make a little side bet of our own?"

"Side bet?" Mountain Puss said. "Hell yeah! Whatever you say, Ratardski."

Rake studied Mountain Puss, all the time stroking his chin with his thumb and forefinger, then said, "Good... how about the loser kisses the winner's ass?"

Mountain Puss jerked back and his eyes got big. Rake supporters threw a fit, yelling and beating on each other. Mountain Puss' managers stood silently, mouthing the words, *kiss the winner's ass.* Kelly thrust the end of his beer bottle at Mountain Puss.

"Fuckin' A, Rake! Shit yeah. Right on, bro."

Quinlan turned to me and said, "What the man lacks in eloquence, he makes up for in congeniality."

Rake extended his hand for a handshake. Mountain Puss hesitated, then shook it quickly and tossed it away.

"Gentlemen, any questions?" I asked. The room quieted. "All right then. Get ready."

Mountain Puss bent over the table, his right hand just inches from his plate.

"Get set."

Rake leaned back, pulled a comb from his back pocket and began combing his sideburns and mustache.

"Go!"

Mountain Puss grabbed the first egg, chewed a few quick chews then swallowed. Then another egg and more chewing. Done messing with his comb, Rake put it away, briefly examined a broken fingernail, then picked up his first egg and casually bit off half and began chewing steadily, all the time grinning at Mountain Puss.

Having downed three eggs by the time Rake finished his first, Mountain Puss looked like the sure winner. Clark Mitchell wiped his brow, drained the last of his beer, then popped open another.

"Rake," he said. "Stop screwing around. We're way behind."

Mountain Puss snatched up his fourth egg and stuffed it in his mouth. That's when I saw what looked like a bulge behind his Adam's apple. Rake finish the first half of his second egg with the same steady pace, chewing each half, then swallowing the whole mouthful before continuing.

Mountain Puss began to dance around, snorting and all, his cheeks puffed out.

Rake's cheeks were normal. The reason, as he explained later, was that among his many and varied accomplishments in college, he had also competed in egg eating contests. Yokes are dry and quickly absorb saliva. Then they swell. Mightily! The trick is to not allow them to accumulate, so you have to swallow each bite, clearing each mouthful before taking the next.

Mountain Puss sputtered and bucked and dipped his head like a sun-struck lizard. The pupils of his eyes looked like fly specks on cue balls. Handicapped by the lack of a more broad-based education, Mountain Puss chewed on and on getting nowhere, while his mouth began, on its own, to form an open hole.

"Slow down," Dow said. "Relax. Pace yourself."

The coaching had no effect. Mountain Puss' brain was locked onto the ever expanding mass of egg that was taking up an ever increasing proportion of his skull space. Suddenly a tremor shot up his back, resulting in partially chewed egg shooting out the mouth hole and both nostrils. Rake carefully moved his plate back out of range. Cheering erupted from Rake's side of the room.

"Meechameandu," Melvin said.

Minutes later Rake picked up his twelfth egg and took a dainty bite. By that time Mountain Puss had managed to choke down only eight. Finished with his last egg, Rake burped loudly, pulled out his handkerchief, wiped his mouth and mustache, folded it formally and tucked it away. Next, he reached over and took one of Mountain Puss' eggs and began eating it, too. When finished he wet the tip of a forefinger and commenced dabbing his plate for small scraps. Mountain Puss fled into the bathroom and puked in the sink. Momentarily he was back at the table, his eyes watering and averting Rake's. Then, squaring his shoulders, he looked Rake directly in the eye and said, "All right Rake. Drop your drawers."

People elbowed in. Matt Kelly was nearly knocked over. Flash bulbs flashed. There it was, captured on film and recorded for all time, Rake's left butt cheek getting a quick kiss from Mountain Puss. Amid great cheers Mountain Puss grabbed up his robe and took out the door, half naked, managers in tow. During a brief, and to the point, interview with Kelly, Rake gave credit to the winning bettors for bearing in mind that he was, in fact, The Legendary Fucking Rake. To the rest he simply said, "*I am a winner...* and you are all *losers.*"

At that, Rake reached over, took another of Mountain Puss' eggs, took a dainty bite, then swaggered out the door.

We spent another ten days in the Anchorage area, jumping two more fires, one on the Kenai Peninsula five miles south of Cooper's Landing, and the other on a high ridge above Valdez. The first was started by a welder in his back yard and the other by kids smoking behind the Valdez High School. We contained both within the first shift with some help from the locals. I was surprised that we had jumped three fires in a row with people around. Normally jumper fires are far away from roads and towns. After the Valdez fire, Jumper 54 flew down and picked us up and flew us back to Fairbanks.

I didn't care much for getting pulled back to Fairbanks. Back to Fort Wainwright was even worse, though it was fun to be with the whole crew again. The piece from the Anchorage Daily News was tacked to the bulletin board near the Operations window. We were put on the bottom of the list, of course, and that was fine because that's the way it is with smokejumpers coming in off fires. The not-so-fine part was that I was faced with two late reports, plus another due the next day. I suppose I should have just called the DM and made up some story that I had a hard landing and my mind wasn't right, and so, I couldn't remember what happened one day to the next. But hell, knowing him, he might tell Al to pull me off the list, too. And, that was another thing. With Mort's three bad boys back in town, and all three's picture in the newspapers, Al—or even worse, me—might have to explain why. Since it was Thursday, and the weekend was coming, I figured I'd wait until Monday. Maybe I'd get on a fire by then. Maybe I wouldn't, but at least I'd have a couple more days to think about it. An hour before quitting time, Al came over from his new office in the old FAA building for a crew meeting.

Al took a chair up front, shook out a Marlboro, lit it, and inhaled a long pull, and said, "Ahh, well ah, I know it's Thursday, but I wanted a meeting today since most of you are in... and we have some important things to catch up on. First, I want to thank everyone for the good work. I'm hearing good things about your fires. The guys back here in Operations did great considering we're not set up very well yet."

Al took another drag, looked out the window for a time.

"I've been on the phone to some people... we have some R and D money that I plan to spend checking out this new plane. There are few other things in the mill but... we'll talk about those later. Again, thanks for the good work. I'm sure you've had a lot more fun these last couple weeks than I have. One more thing, everybody will be on for the weekend. Lightning is predicted up around Fort Yukon."

"Then... there's this," Al said, pulling a stack of papers out of his brief-case.

"The new DM wants each of us to sign a statement of loyalty to BLM."

A chuckle ran through the group, then flared toward anger.

"This is only serious if you want it to be," Al said, with a hint of irri-tation. "It doesn't have to be a big deal, just a signature, and then we can get on with our jobs."

"Well, I'm not signing it," Bell said. "You lay down with a pig and you start smelling like one. Just who does he think he —"

"There are two things he is," Mattlon interrupted. "One, he's your boss. And, second, he's the father of that girl you took home from the pig party."

"What?" Bell squalled. "That jerkoff's Betsy's father?"

"Yes, and she's been calling here asking for you."

"Bell," Rake said. "Oh man, this is good. You're doing the horizontal bop with Twist and Shout's daughter? Hallelujah! This is gonna be —"

"Bell," Mattlon interrupted again "You understand what this could mean?"

"It's not my fault. She's been after me ever since the party."

Al sat there thinking a minute. I supposed he was reviewing the plane hijacking in McGrath, the Red Lizard odyssey, the time Bell crashed through the roof of an outhouse on a practice jump at Campbell Field, and the brawl he and Sulinski got into down in Tok.

"If it's not your fault," Al said, "then whenever there's a disaster, why is that you are always there? That question's kind of been bothering me."

"Where else would I be? I have to be where I am, just like everybody else."

"Wherever you go, there you are," Dow said.

"Uh huh," Al said. "but this is where we are now... and we have to succeed."

"If success means signing that form, then I don't want to succeed."

"Well, I do" Al said sharply. "And so I have an assignment for you. A special assignment. See me right after we're finished here."

After the meeting I went hunting Johnny B. and found him on the sunny side of the T-Hangar playing guitar and singing some made-up song. By that time it was clear he was a music man. He played har-monica, banjo, mandolin and guitar. Lots of times he'd just be playing some chords, making up words, eyes closed, feet tappin', off in his own world.

On the ramp sat the two BLM Grumman Gooses—Jumper 46 and Jumper 47, the two BLM Dougs—Jumper 54 and Jumper 56, and the two contract Dougs, just in from hauling turkeys in Texas. Beneath each Turkey Doug engine was a pool of oil. In the cargo compartments of their tails they carried cases of it. The bottoms of their wings were streaked black. It embarrassed me a good bit, them being from Texas and all.

There was also the new ship Mattlon called a Volpar, a converted Twin Beech. The Twin Beech was a radial engine tail-dragger. This new version was a tri-geared, twin-turbine speedster with reinforced wing spars and an extended fuselage. It was white with red and black trim, sleek and fast looking. On its side were the numbers 700 WA.

I started talking as soon as Johnny B. finished playing.

"What's your thinking on this loyalty statement business?"

Johnny B. rested his harmonica on his knee, squinted into the sun, and said, "You know, I used to think that worrying just came natural to you, but I'm beginning to think you actually work at it."

"Think what you want. But there's no getting around it, the DMs got to have seen you and Mitchell and Bell's picture in the paper. You were supposed to be off the list but there you are, on the front page, still on it."

"Oh, I see. It's report time, right? And you're freaked-out about what to tell Twist and Shout."

"That's right. Hell, who knows what all he's heard."

"You're a pretty good story teller. Tell him about your cowboy relatives on Kodiak, and Mountain Puss kissing Rake's ass."

"Sure enough, Johnny B., I'll do that very thing. I'll start out by saying, And this is no shit... "

Right then Bell walked up, stopped, and stared out across the airfield.

"Howdy Don," I said. "What's goin' on?"

"These," he said, handing us each a copy of the DM's Loyalty Statement. "Al asked me to make sure everyone gets one. He knows I wouldn't refuse him. He's too good a boss for that. Said he wants us to read it over and sign it. I told him I'd take them around but didn't intend to sign it. Half the crew's pissed-off and they're not going to, either."

Johnny B. and I commenced reading.

"There's this other thing, too," Don went on, fidgeting and shuffling his feet. "Al wants me to be the jumper representative at a ceremony this coming Tuesday. The Army wants to officially welcome BLM to the base. They're gonna give some speeches and shake hands and all that shit. I didn't want to do it, but Al said it's for the jumpers, so I said I would. Then, I started thinking, I'd feel like a fool going over there by myself. So I was wondering if maybe you two would go along. You're always together anyway. I'd sure appreciate it."

"We'd be honored," Johnny B. said, grinning. "Count us in."

"Okay, I thought you'd do it. I think maybe we can have some fun."

"I do, too," Johnny B. said. "It'll show the DM that, not only does his daughter have good taste in men, but also that the jumpers take their jobs seriously."

I looked again at the paper and this is what it said:


## LOYALTY STATEMENT

I _____ , as a member of the Fairbanks team, state my loyalty to the goals and objectives of the Bureau of Land Management. As a devoted employee, I will strive, both on and off duty, to conduct myself in a manner that reflects well on myself, my crew, and the agency's long-standing commitment to professionalism.

Signed: _____

Date: _____


I felt myself getting mad. "That's him all right," I said, "like we don't have no loyalty to start with."

"It's an insult," Bell said. "And I don't take insults, especially from fat-asses like him."

"When's Al want these back?" I asked.

"By the end of next week, at the Friday meeting. Also, Al asked me to wear a clean and pressed fire shirt to the Army ceremony. Maybe you can do the same. He says it's for the jumpers. The whole thing stinks if you ask me."

"Right on," Johnny B. said, "You let us know what time and we'll be there."

The weekend came and went and Fort Yukon did get lightning but most of it was wet.

Monday morning I went to see Mort. I figured I may as well do like Johnny B. said and get it over with. Mort was right cheerful when I walked in. He was glad that I had called him, and said it was good to see me acting more professional, whatever that meant. I surprised myself and talked nonstop for ten minutes, telling him about how we caught three fires and saved a ranch and some cows; that the jumpers were happy with their relocation to the T-Hangar, and that Mattlon was an extraordinary boss. All of which was true, except for the relocation part.

"Yes indeed," Mort said, tapping his desk with the eraser end of a pencil. "But you know, a chain is only as strong as its weakest link. It's best if we identify our weak links as quickly as possible, fix them, then move on to other less weak links." Mort took a deep breath, then chuckled at some private joke.

"I reckon your right," I said, wondering how it was that it was always the weak links that saw fit to preach about the weak-link concept.

Mort rattled on a while about teamwork, helicopter technology, and a more balanced program. I mostly ignored him. But then when the conversation turned to the Native Claims Settlement Act and the building of the Alaska Pipeline, his enthusiasm was so that my ears perked up.

"This is the largest construction project in history," Mort said. "And the Fairbanks District is sitting right in the middle of it. Washington's made it clear. The pipeline is number one. Every day letters arrive from Texas, New York, Saudi Arabia, around the world. The oil companies are coming. So, do you see now why I want to get these petty problems out of the way?"

I didn't believe that last part, not for a minute. Even if the government's end of the pipeline deal had fallen into Mort's lap, and even if he did believe helicopters were the future of Alaska fire, there was no excuse for him seeing the jumpers like he did.

"Tell me about your fire on Kodiak," Mort said, leaning forward, his eyes keen.

After a cautious recap, the man that was turning my first season in Alaska into a nightmare, slid back his chair and sighed.

"I've called for a arson investigator from Washington, D.C. to check it out. A Mr. Fentori. He'll be here in a couple weeks. I plan to start recovering some of the money spent on these fires. That one was man-caused, was it not?"

That made me plain sick. Having grown up and worked on a ranch, I knew how hard it was to hold on to one.

"Uh no, I don't believe it was."

"Had to be," Mort said. "Lightning's almost unheard of down there."

I sat staring at Mort and thinking of the rancher and his wife and their life on the Terror River. I thought, too, whether I had been tricked.

Smokejumpers hardly ever leave a fire without knowing exactly how it started. It would be in the fire report. Had Mort seen it? Had he led me into a trap?

"It does lightning on Kodiak," I said. "We even saw some," I lied.

"You saw lightning?" Mort said. "Well then, the investigator can confirm it."

"I reckon I best be on my way," I said, standing up.

"Len, listen a minute. As I said before, I want to help your crew be more effective. You must have a few problems you haven't told me about."

"We've got a few" I said, wanting to tell him off. "Like no running water, no electricity, and no toilets. If we had a few portable toilets people wouldn't have to walk all the way to the FAA building. And maybe you could arrange to have a pipe over so we'd have water to wash up with after PT."


When I got to the T-Hangar I went straight to Rakowski.

"Rake of the Legendary type," I said. "We have to talk."

"It better be urgent. Otherwise you'll have to make an appointment."

I asked Rake if he had submitted the fire report from Terror River.

"Fire reports? I don't do those things until they make me. By then they're usually so pissed-off I get to stay late and log a couple extra oats. Every hour of overtime you miss, you know, is an hour that can never be made up."

I explained about the fire investigator.

"So, Twist and Shout wants to bring the Lower 48 and its laws to Alaska," Rake said. "The cost of that fire would ruin them."

"Do the report now. Say it was lightning. I'll call the ranch and tell them to say the same. No one will ever know the difference. I'll pass it along to the crew, too."

Rake grinned. "Lightning it was. Hit a tree up canyon from the rock outcropping. Consider it done... but next time get an appointment."

Hardly able to believe what I was doing, I went straight to a nearby phone booth and called the Anchorage Daily News and asked to speak to the editor who was Jennifer's uncle. I got the ranch number and dialed radio phone service.

"Hello, Over," I said. "Hello, Over," came the rancher's scratchy response.

"I'll make this quick," I said. "You don't know me and you don't need to. I was one of the smokejumpers on your fire. Over."

"Copy, you were on our fire. Over."

"I think BLM might send a fire investigator down there. I know the fire was an accident, an honest mistake. But if they see it as negligent they could bill you for the expense. If the investigator contacts you, tell him the fire was caused by lightning. That it hit a tree up the canyon from the rock outcropping. That's how it's written up here. Make sure everyone there agrees on it — your two cowhands, everyone. Over."

"Well," the scratchy voice said. "You sure on this? Over."

"Very sure. You have to trust me. I was raised on a ranch. I know what it takes to keep one, and you don't deserve to be steamrolled by some bureaucrat. Over."

"Can you give me your name? Over."

I thought a minute. "I better not. The less anyone knows about this the better. But I was the one that helped your wife move stuff to the river. Over."

"I copy. Thanks for the call, I really appreciate it. Over."

I went back to the T-Hangar and told Rake, barely able to believe what I had done.

Besides his troubles with Mattlon, Bell was fit to be tied about the next day's ceremony with the Army. Over the phone he had discussed the details with Mort. Mort wanted everything to be just so. Mort said that, as a gesture of good will, the Army had given him the honor of lighting the fuse on the cannon. And, in the same spirit, he would pass that honor on to us.

"So, I get to light off the cannon," Bell said. "I hope everything goes all right."

"Hey," the McGrath All-Star said with a big smile, "what possibly could go wrong?" He liked saying that because he liked being a smart aleck.

"We've got to be over there by 10:00," Bell said. "The Army's letting Mort speak first."

The next morning we walked over to the parade grounds together. Nearly a hundred people had taken up seats in neatly arranged rows of folding chairs. Army officers sat in the front row, along with a few upper level management people from the District Office. The remaining seats were filled with other DO managers and various Army personnel. A few came from Roadside — the fire engine folks, a few from Helitac, plus a few pilots. We were assigned side-row seats up front, I suspect so Mort could keep an eye on us.

Mort mounted the portable stage, then stepped over to the podium. The group quieted.

"Ladies and gentlemen, men, men, men," Mort turned and glared at us.

"Hah, hecklers," he said, doing a little twisting but no shouting.

Bell sat petrified. Mort readdressed the microphone.

"Commander Phinney, inny, inny, inny." Mort wheeled around, checking behind him.

"Always a heckler somewhere, ere, ere, ere," Mort said, flabbergasted.

"It's an echo," Johnny B. whispered.

"Officers of Fort Wainwright, ight, ight, ight," rattled around the buildings that surrounded the parade grounds. Mort got all the way to "members of my staff, aff, aff, aff," before he recognized the problem.

"Honored guests, and firefighters, iters, iters, iters, Welcome to this ceremony, ony, ony, ony."

Mort carried on for ten minutes stating and restating the obvious, both the Army and the BLM had a mission, both were dedicated servants "on the battlefield of public service." Both agencies had longstanding histories of honor and great class, ass, ass, ass. By the time he finally sat down, he had established two things. First, that he was dumb as a box of rocks, and second, that he possessed sufficient arrogance to demonstrate that clearly.

Commander Phinney took the podium, cut to the chase, welcomed BLM and stated his hope for a successful working relationship at Fort Wainwright. His troops, he claimed, also welcomed the firefighters, an assertion which most of the BLM people knew to be untrue. We knew how the Army viewed the unshaven longhairs who drove around in beater cars, drank profusely at the O Club, and acted extra friendly to officer wives and girlfriends. Phinney's assertion was akin to suggesting a farmer is pleased to find snakes in his chicken house.

Mort took the stage again. He and the Commander stood side by side. They were to shake hands as the cannon was fired. By that action, their bond of shared missions would be symbolized and sealed. Bell stood up. An Army regular handed him a metal device with a small flame at the end, then stepped back. Bell took his position beside the cannon, a WW II model with an eight-foot barrel and five-inch bore. It was mounted on rubber wheels. Bell held the flame to the fuse. Fizzing to life, the fuse made a quick flash, then hit the charge.

There have been moments in the history of the world that have changed it forever. Great and small ones alike that have transformed it and set it upon a new course. Such as Marie Antoinette's saying, "Let them eat cake," or when General Custer commanded his troops to, "Take no prisoners," right on down to Richard Nixon saying, "I am not a crook." And so it was for the Alaska Smokejumpers that morning when the cannon roared its fury at the US Army - BLM welcoming ceremony.

First, a pencil shaped trajectory shot out over the crowd, followed by a rolling fury of gray smoke. Chairs toppled over backwards. Men scrambled to their feet, women screamed. An enormous cloud of feathers floated down around them like snow. Two pillow cases and a naked rubber chicken lay smoking in the grass. I was mortified. Johnny B. howled. Mort looked like he was about to explode. Commander Phinney swiped at feathers on his uniform, cursing and demanding order. The last time I saw Bell he was in a dead run, his arms swinging side to side, headed for the high and lonesome.

# 6

**B**oth Doug loads that jumped the Fort Greeley Fire had rolled from Fairbanks. The wind was calm and the jump went smoothly, with all the cargo and jumpers landing in the clearing. Rake had jumped first man, first load, and so would be fire boss. But Rake wanted nothing to do with a fire on military land and asked Quinlan if he'd take it. Bob agreed. By noon the fire was forty acres. A D-7 Caterpillar bulldozer was delivered on a low-bed and began pushing fireline up the right flank on the west side. Both crews talked about the winds that often blew out of Isabelle Pass, fifty miles south. By 5:00 that afternoon, even with the progress we had made, the fire had grown to 70 acres. Just when both crews felt we had a chance to cut off the head, two things happened. Flames flared up in the biggest pulse yet and put up a smoke column that blotted out the sun. And, the wind hit.

"Okay let's move," Quinlan shouted down the line. In no time Kelly was on the radio telling his men to move north back down the right flank, too. Ten minutes later we were all back in the jump spot watching a wall of 60-foot flames a quarter-mile wide rage across the end of our hoselay and Kelly's catline.

"Quinlan," I said, "there must be something we can do."

"Okay, we've got a few minutes. Let's pull this hose closest to the road into the jump spot. At least save that."

Back along the hoselay, we spread out and began unscrewing hose couplings and gated Ys. I disconnected the 100-foot section closest to the road. Suddenly there came a roar. Off our flank a storm of flames whipped side to side, heading our way. The wind suddenly doubled. Instantly the fire erupted from one that was getting away and going big into one that threatened our safety. Quinlan, Rake and several others abandoned the hose lay and ran in the direction of Jarvis Creek. I started jogging back to the dirt road. The air commenced to tremble. Dust and ash from inside the burn blew one way, then the other, then started rotating in a wide circle. Then I saw it. Swaying side to side where it touched the ground, a pinkish-orange blur appearing then disappearing in a whirling fury, only to reappear again, each time closer, its black body swaying like a giant snake. Having grown up in Texas, I knew a tornado when I saw one. Out of the burn it came, leaving behind a storm of brown and gray ash to emerge on unburned tundra as a bright twelve-foot wide cylinder of fire, its outer edges a streaking blur of pink and orange fire that looked as solid as a wall. I ran looking for a sump hole, a damp depression, anything wet enough to dive in. A blast of wind knocked me down. Fighting to get up, the wind rolled me in the tundra. Holding on to fistfuls of grass I tried keeping low.

One thing was clear, I had to move. Staying as low as I could, I tried pulling myself away, grabbing handfuls of tundra to keep from flying off. The fire tornado seemed to track my every move. Suddenly a storm of sparks flew all around me, and the tundra came alive with running ground fire. I was trapped. The vortex was only thirty feet away. If I moved I'd be pulled off the ground. If I stayed put I'd burn to death.

"Oh shit," I heard myself say. All around me was chaos. Trees whipped back and forth in a mad dance of unthinkable horror. My body wanted to run, so did my mind. But my hands wouldn't let go. The most horrible thing I'd ever imagined was about to happen to me. I was going to burn to death in a forest fire.

Then, with the same wild unpredictability as it had come, the vortex drew back into the burn, retreated south a hundred feet, then swept north across the road a hundred yards, out into fresh unburned woods, sending dust, smoke and burning debris flying after it. Cargo chutes from the jump spot went flying into the brush. One, still attached to an 80-pound bundle of hose, flew 200 feet to land not far from the tornado. I turned and hightailed it out of there. Minutes later Quinlan's bunch came running up, all talking at once and high-fiving me and then each other.

"Damn, am I glad to see you boys," I said. "Did y'all see that?"

"Len," Johnny B. said, shaking my hand. "I looked around and saw this figure bent over and surrounded by fire, and that thing tracking him and thought, 'Ah damn. Who's that poor bastard?' Then I saw it was you."

Quinlan had me turn around so he could check me out.

"That was the ugliest thing I've ever seen on a fire," Quinlan said flatly. "Up here or anywhere else."

Kelly radioed Quinlan. Melvin and Mountain Puss had come out on his side of the fire. Some kind of fire vortex had hit them.

"They've been burned pretty bad," Kelly said. "I'm bringing them to the jump spot. Contact that BLM pickup and have him order a med-evac helicopter."

The pickup came and left for Fort Greeley with two firefighters in pain. Melvin's hair had been burned off part of his head and one side of his face was blistered. Mountain Puss had some burns on his face and neck and his ears were bleeding. We figured it was the same thing that got after me, but Kelly and his bunch were across the fire at least a quarter mile, so that didn't add up. Both crews packed our cargo and jump gear to Jarvis Creek, then waded across and cached it on the opposite side. We worked until 3:00 AM containing several spotfires that had jumped the creek, then made a rough camp and went down for some sleep.

Up at 6:00 A.M. we grabbed a bite to eat and made our plan. During the night the fire had reversed directions and spread north to become an 800 acre mess, two miles long and a half-mile wide. Kelly took his crew back to the west side which, given that the fire had switched directions, was now the left flank. With the extra hose the pickup man had brought from Delta, our crew set up a pump show and worked the east perimeter north and south, both ways from the dirt road. At 10:00 AM four private-contract D-8 bulldozers came banging and rattling up the dirt road.

Quinlan put Johnny B. and me to scouting for the dozers with the idea of pushing a doublewide catline along the east flank toward the Army fuel break. We walked our Cats to the south end of the fire where it had blown up the afternoon before, and tied-in with the skinner of the D-7. He'd been building line around from Kelly's side. We told him to go back and take his line north with Kelly.

I took the lead with my two Cats and Johnny B. came behind with his two, pushing and shoving trees and logs and brush ever which way. Three hundred yards south of the jump spot, at a point near Jarvis Creek, I ran onto an abandoned camp of some kind. A campfire someone thought they had put out had rekindled and burned over to a rotten log and become the fire that had put us on the run, sent Melvin and Mountain Puss to the hospital, and almost killed me. There wasn't much left, just a few burned cans and a shovel head with a charred handle. Not far from the camp I found a line of plastic flags. One had writing on it: AP Survey Crew # 11 — 5/27/73. Sta. D5176. I made a note in my mind where the camp was, then went on.

That afternoon the wind came up again and we had another blow up, same as the day before. All that work and for what? I had to admit, I'd only been on four fires in Alaska, so I didn't know all that much about how they burned. But, after the tornado and then that second day seeing it do like it did, I felt plumb spooked about our fire and the winds from Isabelle Pass. We'd already sent two to the hospital and, considering what had happened to me, it could have been one to the morgue. That afternoon, the way it jumped up and took off and chased us around, our crew was lucky it didn't have something a lot worse.

At 9:00 that evening, exhausted and discouraged, we packed up our camp on Jarvis Creek and were flown by helicopter to a solitary knob three miles north. By then the fire was estimated at 6,000 acres and had been designated a statewide emergency. A Type II Management team was on the way to Fort Greeley from Fairbanks. Twelve hand crews had been ordered.

Our lone knob stood two-hundred feet above a landscape that was mostly flat. On top was a half-acre of white birch and aspen and a nice level place to camp. As the sun swung low for its midnight dip below the horizon, leaves fluttered pleasantly as the wind and the fire calmed for the night.

Before turning in I went out to an overlook to watch the sky and think. It wasn't long until Johnny B. showed up.

"Hey Len."

"Hey Johnny B. Where's your pal, Duke?"

"He's down for the night. The fire's got him a little spooked."

"Well, I don't blame him. At least he didn't have to see a fire tornado."

Johnny B. didn't say anything for a while, so we just sat there quiet.

"I was thinking," he said, after a bit. "It's too bad that tornado didn't get you."

"Well, if that don't beat all," I said, looking to see if he was grinning. Which he was. "I suppose you'd get a big charge out of seeing me fly off on fire."

"You have to admit," he chuckled, "it would have been great. You'd have been a legend forever, sucked up in a fire tornado, spinning up in the smoke, up, up, and then gone, never seen again. No trace, no sign, nothing. Stories would be told around campfires for decades, statues would be made, poems written and songs sung. You'd be immortal."

"Well, now, I appreciate the thought, Johnny B., but if it don't wreck your story too much, I'd just soon go on living a while."

"And I hope you do," he said, grinning like a possum. "But we all have to die sometime and not many get the chance to do it in such a far-out way."

"I reckon it'd be hard for you to imagine how you'd feel chased by fire."

"Hey, pardner. A good story is a good story. And here you are, a new guy on just four fires and already racking up Old Salt points."

"I didn't come here to make no damn points, Old Salt or otherwise."

Sometimes Johnny B. liked to be contrary just for the sake of it. At least I had enough sense to figure that out. After a little bit, he went on.

"Hey Len?"

"What is it now?"

"I know you can be hardheaded and not too bright sometimes, but the good thing about you is you're easy to read. So, I know what's bugging you. It's okay. What happened yesterday would spook anyone."

I looked at him a short time and he looked right back. Kind of like two mules with their ears laid back, waiting for something to kick.

"I guess it's true. Quinlan and Bell said the same thing. I've been in a tight spot with fire a time or two before but I never actually thought I was going to end up dying in one."

"This country will surprise you," Johnny B. said. "Most people think Alaska is all ice and snow. But once the interior dries out it burns like crazy. It's different in different parts, but still you've got to watch out. In the tundra it's because of the total fuel load per acre. In the woods it's the high resin content in the trees. Most Alaska plants—especially black and white spruce—are way high in it. That's what keeps them from freezing up here. But when they're preheated the oils come to the surface, and... well, you saw what happened. That's why in places like this, with miles of black spruce, fires can burn hotter and faster than they usually do in the Lower 48. Especially with wind."

"Well thanks," I said. "I suppose it's like most things. You have to see it to believe it. Anyway, thanks for telling me. I just don't need a bunch of preaching about it is all."

The next morning Rake went to Delta, telephoned Fairbanks, then came back and told us that Melvin and Mountain Puss were in the hospital for first and second degree burns. They were on IV fluids, depressed, and the doctors wouldn't give a date for their release. After Rake's report, we felt even more spooked. Two days in a row the fire had jumped our lines and put us on the run.

"This is a good day for those dozers to finish the catline out to the fuel break," Bell said. "That way we'll have an escape route."

"Aackk," Quinlan said, "Johnny B. and Len, you take Len's two Cats and keep going like yesterday. I'll take the other two across and send them north with Kelly. Go direct where you can. If things get too hot, angle back toward Jarvis Creek."

"Another thing," Rake said. "This fire's trying to tell us something. Fuel moistures are record low, so this is also a good day to watch your ass."

Despite the serious talk about a serious situation, Quinlan was full of cheer. He was leading his men against a tough fire. One with a lot of hard work and suffering, elements he considered necessary to a proper life. By the time Rake quit saying his piece, Bob had taken up two spoons and began clicking them on his knee, tapping his foot, and singing some wild nonsense that sounded like chickens cornered by a weasel.

"Baaack, bah, back, back, baaach, bah, back, back . Oh, it's a good day for shining your shoes... and it's a good day for singing the blues.

Yes, it's a good day for being alive, yes it's a good day from morning till night.

Baaack, bah, back, back, back."

Bob stopped with a sudden snap of his spoons, and after a few moans and groans there was a halfhearted round of applause. More strategy talk followed, each playfully starting with, it's a good day. As we shouldered our PG bags and started down off the knob for our assignments, Johnny B. turned to me and said, "I just hope it's not a good day to die."

Quinlan met with Johnny B. and me and the four Cat operators. Their Cats were fueled up and ready to go. Quinlan reached in his PG bag, pulled out a radio and handed it to me.

"Keep this and monitor traffic now and then."

After making sure we understood the idea of building a catline north to the fuel break, he took the other two D-8s and headed across the burn to meet with Kelly.

By 4:00 that afternoon our Cats had pushed the line a mile north into a thick stand of black spruce mixed with whitebark birch. That slowed us down considerably. With no map and so much flat country and crooked fireline we weren't sure how much farther or which way it was to the fuel break. We decided to hold up, give the cat skinners a break, talk things over and eat some rats.

It was no big surprise when the winds from Isabelle Pass hit again, right along with a black smoke column that blotted out the sun. It had happened three days in a row yet there we were, way out in the middle of lot of dry fuel with miles of open fireline. We discussed whether or not to build a safety zone. If we had one and couldn't make it out before the fire overran us, we could come back. Still, it would involve a lot of work and the destruction of an acre of good trees—the same ones we were trying to save. Right then an air attack plane flew low over the knob, banked high into a tight turn and came on the radio, saying the fire was making a run directly at camp, and that a helicopter was needed for immediate extraction of gear.

Johnny B., the two cat-skinners, and I kept an eye on the black column. At the edge closest to us a strange rope-like coil began forming, rolling inward and upward indicating the same possible tornado activity as before. Ten minutes later a helicopter appeared just our side of the column, its navigation lights flashing red and green. It flared then sat down south of camp. Standing on top of my Cat's roll cage, we watched three men bail out the instant the copter touched down and start running. Minutes went by as each man ran to and from the ship with one or two gear bags slung off their shoulders. The fire raged in a solid wall a quarter mile beyond them. As the fire closed to within two hundred yards, the three crawled in and the Bell 205, with its doors still open, lifted off, rotated around, tilted forward then flew off west toward the Richardson Highway. Two minutes later, the fire blew up the little hill and turned what was left of our camp into a fury of death.

"We better build a safety zone," I said, realizing we should have already done it.

The two Cats began bulldozing trees back in all directions. Air Attack appeared overhead and came on the radio again.

"Forget the safety zone," the Air Attack Boss said. "Forget line building. You need to get moving. A road runs east - west a half-mile north of your location. Follow it west to the fuel break. Stage the Cats there."

Johnny B. and I climbed aboard our Cats and the skinners lifted their blades, hit the throttles, and launched us off into a tree crashing run for the road. Once there, we saw Quinlan driving an Army pickup. Pipe clinched in his teeth, he flipped a U-turn waving for us to follow.

At the fuel break, Quinlan stopped next to three Cats, the D-7 and the two D-8s he'd taken to help Kelly. The fuel break was at least 100 yards wide, and it was a big relief to be in it.

"Aackk," Quinlan said, pointing his pipe at the black smoke column. "I was worried about you boys. Park these Cats out in the middle. You should be okay there."

With that he jumped in his pickup and tore off down the fuel break in a cloud of dust.

"Man, I'm glad we made it in here," Johnny B. said.

I shot Johnny B. a quick look. "You and me both."

We moved all five Cats to the center of the fuel break and parked them about twenty yards apart in case one caught on fire it wouldn't spread to the rest. With their blades lowered to the ground and facing the fire we figured if things got too hot we could crawl under them and be protected from the worst radiant heat. There were two service trucks. One a crewcab, the other a regular pickup hitched to a fuel trailer filled with 800 gallons of diesel. The drivers had gone to Fort Greeley to help bring in other equipment. We parked the crewcab and the rig with the fuel trailer off a ways from the Cats.

An hour passed. The radio traffic became more excited. The run that had taken out our camp was bumping the Richardson Highway. Three homes were threatened. Residents along the highway were being evacuated. Another hour passed; the wind calmed. Jumpers had been pulled off all line sections and were now helping hold the fire at the highway. Islands of green were being burned-out in an effort to establish the highway as part of the west flank.

Another hour passed. The Cat skinners finished servicing their dozers, then took naps, either in the service rigs or in the seats of their Cats. Johnny B. and I sat in the dirt around a little campfire, keeping an eye out, drinking coffee. Johnny B. was distracting himself by adding up his oats in his Oat book, figuring out how much overtime we were making. Jumpers call overtime Oats, and everyone carried the little BLM Handy Dandy notepad to keep track of it. Besides his Oat book he had a bigger notebook. Since Kodiak he had been spending a good amount of time writing in it.

After a while he put it away, took a sip of coffee, and said, "That's the thing about fire. You work it a few years and you see some amazing things, and you begin to think that you know how bad it can get. Then one day it shows you something you've never seen before."

"I always knew you could get hurt jumping," I said. "Maybe break a leg or your back, that kind of thing. But I never gave much thought to being burned to death. I've got family back home, and I can't say I much like the idea of them having to deal with some BLM official knocking on their door and telling them I got burned up."

Johnny B. didn't say anything to that. He was in deep thought. About what I didn't have the slightest idea.

"Anyway," I said, tired of the silence, "my Dad used to say that if a man knew where he was going to die he wouldn't go there."

Johnny B. chuckled and tossed the last of his coffee away, then banged his cup against the heel of his boot.

"That's a good thing to say but, as firemen, we have to go places that are on fire. We don't get to choose. We just have go and do the best we can. Hell, if a man knew where he was going to die, it would ruin his life. He'd be afraid to go anywhere."

I decided there wasn't much more to say about it. People died all the time from all kinds of things, hardly any they had control over. Johnny B. started making notes again. Radio traffic calmed. A strange silence spread over the area. The sky began to look funny.

Then, just like before, the wind hit. We went to the Cats and stood on top of their roll cages with the operators watching the horizon turn from yellow-gray into a pinkish-orange glow.

"When it gets here," I told the skinners, "we'll see how it is. If it gets too hot, we'll crawl in under these Cats. With the blades down we should be all right. I reckon the fuel trailer will be safe where it is."

Dust and grit began to blow across the fuel break. One of the Cat men said he had never seen fire in that country like the one we saw coming. I changed my mind and moved the fuel trailer further from the Cats. As I hustled back, an Army pickup drove up and a young soldier jumped out.

"I've come to take you in to Fort Greeley," he said.

"That's a bad idea" Johnny B. said. "Believe me, I know fire up here, and to leave this fuel break with that much fire coming, and head down a narrow road through thick black spruce, is a *very bad* idea."

"It may well be, sir, but I have my orders, and I'm ordering you to get these Cats moving."

"Who gave them to you?"

"The base Fire Control Coordinator, sir. Now, let's go. The road goes straight to the Fort and he wants you there, not here."

I figured to leave the arguing to Johnny B., and that he'd tell him that Quinlan was the fire boss, and had no intentions of taking orders from anybody but him. But Johnny B. give in right off and said, "Okay, then lets get the hell out of here."

Straight as an arrow, the gravel road ran north no more than forty-feet wide including the dirt shoulders. The Army pickup was in the lead with Johnny B. following in the crewcab, and me bringing up the rear in the pickup pulling the fuel trailer. The five Cats lined out on the right shoulder. I idled along beside the last Cat to make sure we had them all. Ten minutes after leaving the fuel break I could see it was a big mistake. We were moving too slow. But stopping the Army guy and insisting we go back didn't make sense either. Who would the Cat skinners listen to, me or the Army? Critical time would be lost. It was too late. I looked at my watch— 9:07 PM. We had forgotten to ask the Army man how far it was to the fort, and I couldn't recall how it looked from the plane. Maybe it wasn't that far.

In no time a massive band of smoke blew up and started to close off the remaining open sky to the north, higher at first, then dropping down like a great black curtain, lower and lower, until the last part of the horizon disappeared and the sky was gone. Dust and smoke began blowing in the road. Everyone turned on their lights except the last three Cats, so I figured they didn't have any. I rolled down my window and looked back at a bright orange skyline. In the notch created by the walls of black spruce that lined both sides of the road there was nothing but fire. I turned the volume up on my radio and held it out the window and listened to a chaos of people talking over each other, yelling in the background, horns honking, sirens going. Apparently the fire had jumped the highway.

Roaring along full throttle, the Cats were only making five miles an hour. The skinner in the last one sat stone still, staring straight ahead, while dust rolled off its tracks all around him. I checked my watch again— 9:20. I turned on the pickup radio and dialed up local Armed Services radio.

"Zzztt... emergency evacuation," an anxious voice said. "This is an emergency evacuation. All Fort Greeley personnel. This is a fire emergency broadcast. Get your families and report to the main gate immediately. Repeat, all personnel. Get in your cars and move your family to the main gate for further instructions. Repeat. This is a fire emergency. Fort Greeley is under emergency fire evacuation."

The radio went straight from that into the middle of a rock and roll song, *"Don't you want somebody to love? Don't you need somebody to love? Wouldn't you love somebody to love?"* Damned Army, I thought. They got a fire about to run them over, they're evacuating and scaring the hell out of people, and they still got time to listen to the top ten.

Behind us a great, red glow showed above the trees growing brighter, lighting an increasing patch of sky. Embers began streaming down onto the road. If they were falling in the road, they were falling in the woods ahead of us, and maybe even on the fuel trailer. I checked my watch again— 9:38.

"Well now, just look at this," I said to myself. "Here you've gone and got yourself into another fix, only this time with a bomb tied on your tail."

Last in line, I decided I would have to make the call. How long should I wait? I decided when I saw spotfires starting ahead of us, I'd do it. I'd pass Johnny B., pull along side the lead Cat, jump out and stop it. I would order the skinners to get in the trucks directly or be left behind. I'd make it clear, "Come with us now or stay and die." I pulled up right behind

Johnny B. I scanned the woods for spots. The smoke and dust was too thick to see very far. Just when I felt I couldn't put it off any longer, up ahead I saw what looked to be a streetlight suspended on wires, swinging violently in the wind. The fort. At the light, Johnny B. stopped. So did the Cats, but only the last three. The other two had lights so I hoped they knew where they were going. The Army guy was gone, too. When I opened my pickup door, the wind took it with such force it sprung the hinges. Running toward Johnny B.'s pickup with the dust blowing and a hot wind at my back, I was thinking things couldn't get much crazier when an Army colored semi-truck and trailer with its emergency lights flashing passed under the street light. A sixty-foot missile sat on blocks on the trailer bed with its nose up over the cab. I wanted to ask directions but when the driver saw me running and waving, he gunned his motor and roared off.

"Len," Johnny B. yelled as I ran up. "This is bad. Somebody's gonna die."

"Where's that Army guy?"

"Shit if I know. He bailed ten minutes ago."

I ran to the lead Cat.

"Where'd those other fellas go?"

The skinner pointed up the road a ways. "Looks like they crossed up there."

Sure enough, on the pavement I could see what looked like scratch marks on asphalt.

"To the left," I yelled, waving to Johnny B. and the other skinners.

In a short ways we passed a school and a playground. I wondered if we could survive in it. No! I didn't think so. Too small. Wherever we were going, though, we didn't have worlds of time to get there because we had a wall of fire 150 feet high 300 yards to our left and closing fast. Storms of sparks and embers shot out of the woods and up into great boiling black clouds, then blew out onto the more open ground of Fort Greeley. There was no doubt. We were in trouble. When that much fire hit the Fort it would blow right over where we were like a tidal wave. Johnny B.'s words about dying were still in my head, and the heat was getting so bad I had to roll up my window. I thought about calling Quinlan but there was no way with all the yelling and sirens and people cutting each other off. I had to admit it, I was out of ideas. And for a fireman in a tight spot, that's not a good feeling.

Right then a pickup with its lights on came out of a swirl of smoke.

"Follow me," the driver shouted.

He flipped a U-turn, spinning in the dirt, then went up the road to join the first two Cats. The three trailing Cats fell in behind Johnny B. leaving me to follow again. After two hundred yards the smoke and dust got so thick I could barely make out the winch on the back of the Cat I was following. It abruptly turned left onto a narrow dirt track that led straight back through a stand of tall spruce right towards the fire.

"What the hell's this guy doing?" I blurted out, pounding the steering wheel. I couldn't see the Cat any more, so I hit the gas and almost ran into it just as we passed through a chainlink gate. Inside was an area of cleared land where a couple dozen Cats, giant Euclid scrapers, graders, and other heavy equipment sat parked in rows. We stopped. I jumped out and ran to Johnny B.'s rig.

"That guy disappeared," Johnny B. yelled.

"Forget him," I said. "Round up these skinners. Get them in your rig. I'll get this fuel trailer away from here and be right back."

"We can't fucking park here," Johnny B. said, pointing to the giant rubber tires of the Euclids. "These things will burn."

"Move off a ways then, dammit. Get the skinners and do as I say."

As I got into the fuel rig to move it, the pickup man showed up again.

"Leave that here and follow me," he yelled. So I jumped out, ran to Johnny B.'s rig, and piled in with him and the skinners. Moving through the smoke, still in the direction of what looked like the whole world on fire, the pickup suddenly turned right and went along a row of graders with us close behind. When the flame front hit the edge of the equipment yard, we couldn't see anything out the left side windows but fire.

No one said a word. Then, straight ahead a low, flat rectangle of light began taking form, steadily increasing in height. The rectangle turned out to be a bay door on a large concrete building. As soon as the rectangle was tall enough we drove through it, both rigs coming to a halt as the door started back down, closing off the windblown hell outside.

We gathered up at the door to a little office and stood listening to the roar of the fire and the radio Quinlan had given me.

"Get this thing zzzzt, no, don't turn, zzzzt, back up, back up. Zzzzt... Rake, have you seen, zzzzt, Bell zzzzt... Vet clinic... gone ... ah... burned over zzzzt."

The pickup man came out of the office.

"I want to thank you boys," he said, shaking hands with me, then Johnny B. "You saved my Cats and these guys, too."

"Well," I said, "you're welcome to see it anyway you like, but you're the one that saved us. All we did was run."

"Just the same, you stayed with them, that's what I mean. Anyway, I just got off the phone with the command post, the other side of the runway. They want us to come over there."

Having been nearly killed by fire twice in near as many days, I was against leaving the safety of a concrete building and flat-out told him so. He said he knew the way and insisted the route was clear. Outside the fire still raged in the woods, but not in the equipment yard. As we drove across the base we passed through several fingers of ground fire that had run across lawns, burned up small groups of trees and set two buildings on fire. The main airstrip was a vast expanse without fire and we could see across it to a group of large aircraft hangars. Driving around the west end, another missile on a semi-truck passed us going the other way. We continued on around, then stopped at a small metal building and went inside. A group of fire officers from Fairbanks were setting up tables, pinning up maps, talking on phones. The room was solemn and strangely quiet. People were missing. All but Bell, Kelly, and Quinlan had been accounted for. A few were in the aircraft hangar next door. We shook hands again with the Cat man and his operators then headed over.

When we walked through the great open doors of the hangar with our PG bags slung over our shoulders it reminded me of a scene from a war movie I saw where a couple of ragged, worn-out soldiers had made their way back to their buddies in one piece. About half the jumpers were there. Some from Kelly's group, some from ours. Quinlan hadn't been seen or heard on the radio for over an hour. A rumor was going around that his pickup had been spotted near the main gate, on fire.

We stood around shaking our heads and telling nonstop stories of running from too much fire. Some of the jumpers were still out protecting homes on the Richardson Highway.

Safe as we were there in the hangar, I could tell every last guy had just one thought in the back of his mind. We had all seen something we thought could kill us, and we had people missing. After a few minutes of frantic talk, we settled down, grabbed some sleeping bags, a couple cubies of water, a box of sack lunches, and headed out the big doors. On the lee side of the hangar, out of the wind, we ate, then spread our sleeping bags out side by side next to a wall and settled into a contemplative silence. It was time to sleep. But no one could. Sitting up, we leaned back against the wall and tried to take in what we were seeing. The sky was black, the air heavy and hot with the tangy scent of wood smoke. Across the runway, stretching its complete length, the fire front had become a pink glow lying beneath a thick blue haze. In the distance sirens blared while streetlights swayed in the wind.

Back in Fairbanks, the jumpers from Fort Greeley discovered that a second go-round of lightning fires had stalled. Twenty-five boosters had arrived from jump bases in the Lower 48. After refurbishing our gear, Al called for a meeting to review our fire. Mountain Puss, his neck and wrists wrapped in white gauze, sat in the front ready to tell his story. He had been able to protect his face with his gloved hands. He also said that when it hit him he remembered not to breathe. It likely saved his life. I remembered the tornado that got after me, and thought that mine must have been a lot bigger. I estimated the outer perimeter at two-hundred miles an hour. If the outer edge of the tornado I saw had hit me, I was certain I would have died instantly.

During the meeting it was generally agreed that, given the Alaska jumpers' experience with the winds north of Isabelle Pass, we should have anticipated such problems and built more safety zones. The Air Attack boss who flew the fire both days of the blowups told us that when, as he put it, "the thing went big," both times he saw two counter-rotating vortexes form on each side of the column shortly after the initial blowups. Both days the flames on the leading edge, at the peak of the blowup, he estimated at 150 feet high. We asked about the fuel break, and he said it was a good thing we got out of there, that the fire had raged right over it and left the ground a brassy, burnt yellow color. He had seen such fire behavior only once before, and that was in a film about fire in Australia.

Turned out the burning pickup near the main gate was Quinlan's. He, Bell and Rake had abandoned it and waded out into the middle of a small pond about the time the fire hit the fort. Over all, considering the extreme burning conditions, and the fact that it could have been much worse, it was agreed that many good decisions had been made. The group discussed them, then decided to meet again in a week to see if anyone had anything more to add.

"Melvin's in Memorial," Al said. "I saw him yesterday. The right side of his face and neck are... burned pretty bad. There's no point seeing him now. His sister's here on some village business and checks in everyday. For now, he's got all the help he needs."

The room stayed quiet, all eyes on Big Al. Big Al was the new name the crew had given him. Somehow, without a word of discussion, agreement or accord, our boss had gone from just regular Al to Big Al.

"While you guys were out playing smokejumper, I had a serious talk with our new DM, Mr. Twixenblout. Somehow he decided to overrule the initial request for jumpers on your fire."

"Well then, he needs to be killed," Bell said.

"The guy's a piece of work all right. He's stuck on the use of helicopters for initial attack. We've had several instances where it hasn't worked out, but as long as they can beat us to most of these close-in fires, which he thinks Fort Greeley was, then he wants to use them first."

"*Close-in fires,*" Bell hissed. "What's that fat-ass know about *close-in fires?*"

"Not a lot," Big Al said, but this not about what he knows. It's about what we do. This Volpar is fast. Very fast. And if we can jump it safely we'll be able to beat helicopters to almost everything. Then we might change people's minds about close-in." Big Al held up a minute, then said, "We're going to change a few other things around here, too."

By noon the next day the place was alive with activity. Flatbed trucks had spent the morning hauling rigging tables, parachutes, cabinet sets, parachute bins, plus box after box of rigging supplies from the loft on Airport Road to a deserted Army auto shop across the parking lot about 50 yards from the T-Hangar. Personnel parachutes would still be checked across town but from then on, Alaska jumpers were going to get back into all phases of their job as smokejumpers, packing and repairing chutes, assembling all firepacks, rigging the paracargo. Quinlan, Kelly, and Marshall took hoses, mops, brooms, buckets, and boxes of detergent and washed down what was to become the new loft. Jumpers dug a shallow trench, and Gene Bartell, who was studying to be an electrician, ran Romex from the pilots' lounge into a homemade switch box in the Ready Room.

The next day eight jumpers made the first jumps ever from a Volpar. Some complained. They came into the T-Hangar grumbling about how cramped the ship was, how they felt like they were just cargo with a heartbeat, how hard it was to get out such a small door, how the prop blast had tipped them over on their heads and given them line twists. The Volpar was fast and had trouble slowing down to the speed jumpers preferred when exiting.

"Ah, shut up," The Fat Indian said to them. "It's a new ship. That's why they call it practice."

Big Al led the way. He jumped first, had gone out on his head and had twists, too, but kept quiet about it. Mattlon didn't much care for practice jumps to begin with. As he once put it, What's the point of practicing something you have to do right in the first place?

Another load went up. The jumpers working around the T-Hangar stopped to watch as the Volpar circled two miles east over Birch Hill, dropping two-man sticks into a new spot Big Al called the big spot.

Johnny B. and I were on top of the T-Hangar watching. Rake and Kasson were up there too, but hardly paid any attention to the jump. They had the suit-up dummy, a department store mannequin, up there plumb naked. After taking off the jump suit they dressed him in Levis and a yellow fire shirt, and shoved a hard hat on his head. Next, they put a PG bag on his back, and a spruce bough over his shoulder. Kasson had made a small platform trolley, then mounted the mannequin on it. The trolley was attached to a continuous cable system driven by an electric motor that pulled the platform back and forth along the outer rampart of the roof. From the ground it gave the appearance of a sentry marching back and forth. Inside the PG bag Rake put a tape recorder and an extra big speaker. Bro Ratus could not only walk the walk, he could talk the talk.

Back and forth Bro Ratus tottered with his spruce bough over his shoulder, halting briefly at the end of each run to declare some wisdom to the world. Things like, "It's dry out west." After which he would do a brisk about face, then go on his way. Back and forth, Bro Ratus went, saying, "It's a big state," or "When in doubt, rack out."

The jumpers gathered below and laughed themselves silly. While Big Al, The Fat Indian and the others, in from the second practice jump, unloaded their gear, Bro Ratus stopped and said, "How many oats do you have?"

That afternoon after work Johnny B. and I ran into Bell in the barracks.

"I got a call from Melvin's sister," he said. "Melvin wants to see me, so I was thinking maybe you'd like to come along. I don't want to go by myself."

"Big Al said Melvin had all the company he could handle," I said.

"Well, that's not what she said. Melvin wants to see some jumpers. Besides, we've got something to talk about ourselves."

We piled into the Red Lizard and took off. I thought Bell had gone too far, still running around in a government rig. Hell, he'd even put a bumper sticker on it that read: SMOKEJUMPERS ARE GOOD TO THE LAST DROP.

We had barely got up speed when Bell brought up the cannon deal.

"I told Al about it as soon as I settled down," he said. "And I knew what he was thinking, *that I was there*, and that it caused trouble, the opposite of what he wanted. The DM called him and said he thought it was me since I ran off. The base commander called too, saying he intended to get to the bottom of it. I told Al that I thought it was great, but that I didn't do it. He asked me if I had any idea who did, and I said no... which was a lie."

"Uh, uh, don't look at me like that," Johnny B. said. "I thought it was great, too, but don't go blaming me. It was really funny, though, and I'm glad I saw it."

"It was likely one of those Army guys" I said. "They understand cannons and all."

"The pillow cases had BLM stenciled on them," Bell said, all the time more frustrated. "So, that means they came from the barracks, and that makes us the number one suspects. That's what the base commander told Al."

Melvin's room was on the third floor and that's where we found him, all covered up except for his head and arms. His sister, Sarah, was adjusting his pillows when we walked in. His face was taped up on one side, along with most of his neck and both wrists.

"Hey, Melvin," Bell said. "How's it going?"

Melvin smiled, but not his normal big smile, just halfway. I figured he was under the effect of pain medicine. I couldn't help look at him without thinking it could be me lying there instead of him.

"Not too bad," Melvin said, his voice weak. "Almost got burnt up."

"So did we," Bell said. "That was a hell of a fire. We had two more bad days."

"He's doing fine," Sarah said. "The doctor thinks he can leave in a couple days. I'm taking him to a relative's house here in town. He needs to come in every day and have his bandages changed. He doesn't like it here."

"Food's no good," Melvin said. "No moose stew. No caribou steak. Not even C-rats. All they feed me is leaves."

"He means salad," Sarah said, laughing. "At home we'll make him moose stew. That will make him strong, maybe even cheer him up."

From the minute I saw her, it was all I could do to keep my eyes off Sarah. She was the perfect Indian princess with long, straight hair and a face so beautiful it made me a little dizzy.

"Johnny B.," Melvin said. "how's Duke's attitude after that fire?"

"Duke's fine. He said to say Hello. He's sorry that you got burned."

"Bell?" Melvin said, "When I get out, come see me at my cousin's place. Bring along a little bottle so we can celebrate."

A doctor came in and was surprised Melvin had a room full of visitors. He checked Melvin's chart, then asked us to leave. I don't remember much of what we talked about on the way back to the Fort. Mostly I was thinking about Sarah.

# 7

Iheard a noise and looked around and saw Johnny B. coming up the hill with his gear bag. I was up on a little dome about 150 feet high and round as a saucer. Beyond him was a small lake and ten charred acres with only a few smokes left inside. After a week at the T-Hangar Johnny B. and I had worked our way to the top of the list and got lucky with this two-manner. Our fire had started the day before and had gotten some rain. Johnny B. dropped his gear bag, sat down, and looked out over the land.

"This is the most worthless looking country I ever jumped in," I said.

"Mosquito country," Johnny B. said.

As far as you could see there was nothing but these puny little black spruce scattered across miles and miles of open tundra in a land as flat as a pool table.

"Do you have any idea where we are?" I asked.

"According to The Fat Indian we're 60 miles southeast of Ruby. Most of the time they let these fires burn, but the birds are nesting now, so that's why we're here. That river over there is the Mud River. The village of Tanana is supposed to be northeast about the same distance. We'll demobe into there, probably tomorrow."

After a few minutes Johnny B. went to digging in his PG bag. I was glad to be on another fire with Johnny B., so I hauled out a bottle of Jack Daniels and had a snort while he sat Duke on our cubitainer. It was rare to be on five fires in a row with the same jump partner, but not unheard of. I handed the bottle to Johnny B. and he took it. After a quick nip, he handed it back, smacked his lips, then took out his notebook and started writing. He'd been doing that a lot lately. I figured he was writing another poem, but I couldn't see how that country could inspire a man to do much more than get drunk. I took another drink, then another, then set the bottle where he could reach it. A half hour passed, so I just drank by myself. I was getting mad at him for sitting there, off in his own world, and me left with nothing but Duke in a place where you could see forever but couldn't see a thing worth looking at more than once. Way off up north there was a line of low hills barely poking above the horizon. Everywhere else there was nothing but flats and swamp. Besides, I was feeling the whiskey, and whiskey always made me want to talk. I took another drink and said, "You gonna sit there and write all afternoon?"

"I might," he said, then sat there grinning at me like I was some private joke.

"Have some more Jack. You don't need to write all the time."

"And you don't need to talk all the time, either," he said, putting his book away.

"Hell, I better have some or there won't be any left the way you're drinking."

He took the bottle and turned it up and drank two full swallows. I reckon he was figuring on catching up.

"I've never seen anything like it," I said, waving my hand out over the country. "East Texas is pretty mean, but this here's ridiculous."

"It wouldn't be if you were a native," Johnny B. said. "An old Athabaskan man, down river in Galena, once told me that this is where God came down through a hole in the sky and started creating the world. That makes this country not just the center of the world, but the center of all creation."

I took another drink and said, "Looks to me like he messed up, then. He should have put alligators here instead of people, because there's nothing but swamps that I can see. Their skin would be just the thing for these pesky, damned mosquitoes."

Johnny B. thought on that a while, then chuckled to himself, and said, "I suppose it was like everything else God created. It probably didn't turn out like he planned. You know, fifteen thousand years ago this country was just like the Serengeti plains in Africa, teeming with herds of giant herbivores, saber-toothed cats, and bears as big as cars. It was that way from here to Spain, all across northern Asia and Central Europe. That was when man came across the Bering land bridge."

"You think God created the earth?" I asked, smiling more than normal.

Johnny B. looked over and said, "No, not really. Do you?"

"Not like most people. My folks never went to church, didn't even get married in one. But when I got school age, they made me go to Sunday school. In the books they had lions being friends with sheep. Seemed doubtful right off."

"Maybe so," Johnny B. said, "but I know this much. Most people can't face life without God. People have worshipped everything from frogs to snakes, monkeys, fish, stone monuments, great spirits, and, in the case of those South Pacific Islanders in World War II, airplanes and parachutes. Ha, ha. Yeah, dig it. The paracargo Gods."

"Seems crazy all right. Strange what religion does to some folks."

The McGrath All-Star reached over to his PG bag, took out a bag of marijuana, rolled a fat joint, and took a long toke. He handed it to me. I don't know why, but I took it. It just seemed unfriendly not to.

"I haven't seen you with this since you almost drowned in the ice pond."

"That's because I haven't had any. They smoked it all at the Pig Party. I just found this the other day."

I sat there holding it and looking at it.

"Come on," Johnny B. said, "try it."

"All right, then. What is this anyway?"

"Same as before, Matanuska thunderfuck. Grown in the lovely Matanuska Valley by descendants of Pancho Villa."

"Well," I said, "of all places to smoke pot, this is probably the safest as far as the law's concerned."

I took it and inhaled big and, right off, got into a coughing fit.

"Not so much. Just little puffs. You took too much."

I tried again and he was right. Little puffs with some air mixed in was better. I sat there a while looking at the country and the sky and feeling like I had made a mistake. Hell, knowing the way I was, I might end up a drug addict and start robbing banks to support my habit.

Within minutes, though, I felt better than I had in some time. The scenery had gone from flat and ugly to flat and filled with all the greens I'd ever seen, streaked in gold and red and purple. Spruce trees that, not long before, had looked puny and ready to die, looked noble and majestic and pulsed with life. All the sudden, and with no warning at all, I began chuckling, at what I couldn't say.

"How does it feel?" I said. "I mean, when you get high, I mean."

"It feels like you're feeling," Johnny B. said. "Can't you tell you're stoned?"

"I can tell one thing for damned sure," I said, trying not to laugh. "I hope they don't decide to come get us right now." Then I started laughing like that was the funniest thing I ever heard.

"There, see! It's not so bad to be happy. Why do you think they call it high?"

"It's not that it's bad to be happy," I said. "Hell, I actually enjoy it. I think most people do."

We both laughed our fool heads off at that.

"You say this was grown by Pancho Villa?"

"No," Johnny B. said, "by his descendents." We thought that was funny, too.

"Somehow, it's hard to imagine Pancho Villa growing dope."

"You don't have to," Johnny B. said. "I told you they're his descendants."

"Did you know *Tom Mix* and *Pancho Villa* were friends?"

Johnny B. looked at me funny again, then said, "Tom Mix, the cowboy movie star, was friends with a Mexican bandit?"

"Listen here, Johnny B., Pancho Villa was a lot more than a Mexican bandit. He was a General and had a big army and fought for the rights of poor people. Why, he could have been president of Mexico if he wanted to."

"You know a lot about Pancho Villa?"

"Oh, hell yeah," I said. "It was in this book I read one time, Tom Mix and Pancho Villa. There's a quote in it I never forgot."

"Tom Mix," Johnny B. said, "he was the one with the tall white hat that didn't come off no matter how fast he rode."

"No, no. That was Hoot Gibson. Hoot stuck with white hats mostly. But Tom Mix didn't give a shit, he wore whatever color he wanted. He did like black chaps and rode a black horse, though."

"Did old Hoot know about that?" Johnny B. said, with a big smile.

"How the hell would I know? You must be drunker than I am. Anyway, there was this book I read."

I stopped for a moment straining to recall what I was talking about.

"Damn," I said, "I had something important to say and you got me off the subject, and now I can't hardly remember my own name."

"Duke," Johnny B. said, regarding the little monkey sitting on his PG bag. "Listen to this fool. Rambling on about Hoot and Tom and Pancho and alligators and... "

"That's it," I yelled. "Pancho Villa. The book was about Pancho Villa. Him and Tom Mix was talking about things, and the subject got around to women."

I held up a minute and thought I had lost my thought again.

"Is that the whole story?"

"The whole story about what?"

"About *Pancho Villa* and *Tom Mix* and *women*."

"Hell no, it's not," I said, suddenly remembering. "They were saying how important it was to respect women, and Pancho Villa said, and this is the part I wanted to tell you, Pancho Villa said, 'I respect women, amigo. That's why I marry them. But mostly I just like to fuck them.'"

We laughed and laughed at that. Then, I started coughing again, and between the laughing and the coughing my guts hurt so bad I could hardly breathe. I know it's strange, but at one point I could swear even Duke was laughing.

"Just imagine," I said, after we calmed down, "a couple of jackasses like us, way out here in the middle of nowhere, rolling around on a hill, laughing at shit like that."

"It's about time," Johnny B. said. "You've laughed more in the last fifteen minutes than you have all summer."

"I reckon you're right. Shit on being serious. But hell, I got problems."

"Mostly you just think you do."

I started laughing again, even though what he said didn't seem that funny.

"I haven't the slightest notion of what you're talking about," I said.

"Well, it's time you learned. Life's too short to go around dragging your ass everywhere."

Suddenly I saw an image of myself dragging my ass on the ground like a sack of sand, and took off laughing again, and so did Johnny B.

"So," I said, trying to settle down. "You think I go around like that?"

"Lately you've been dragging your whole body. Let's shoot from the hip, okay? From the day you pulled me out of that lake I've been watching you, and the message is clear."

I took another drink of Jack and handed it to Johnny B. If I was dragging my ass around I might as well have fun doing it.

"What's that supposed to mean?"

"It means that most of what happens in life is a farce, Len, so why take it so personally?"

"I didn't just pull you out of the lake because you were either going to drown or freeze to death," I said. "You were a jumper in trouble. I took it as a personal responsibility."

"That's not what I'm talking about," Johnny B. said, shaking his head. "I know what you did at the lake was not a farce. What I'm talking about is all this tugging and pulling at the world, trying to make it what you think it ought to be, or what you think you can make it be. The damned DM, the reports, your call to Kodiak, all of it. It's one of the things Duke and I like most about you, Len, but it wouldn't hurt you to have a little more faith in the mystery and the magic, man."

"You're stoned," I said, laughing. "Your talking stoned-talk in the wilderness."

"Right on," Johnny B. said, shaking his head some more. "Hell, I may as well talk to the stars."

"There aren't any up here this time of year... so I reckon you'd be wasting your time."

"Oh, really? No shit?"

We sat there a minute, me taking time to get organized in my head, and Johnny B. just shaking his and chuckling, like him and Duke had some private joke. Then, just like that, the words he'd been saying lined up in my mind, just like ducks in a shooting gallery.

"Listen here, Johnny B.," I said, "there's things in this world that are just plain wrong. And, if I was to go along with them, then I'd be wrong, too."

"I think we better talk about something else," Johnny B. said. "Man, it's funny, isn't it, how different this fire is from the one down at Fort Greeley?"

That subject threw me for a loop.

"It's funny all right," I said, after a bit. "Sometimes things don't make any sense at all. This mess with the DMs got me feeling low. Especially in country like this."

"Maybe the country in your head needs changed."

"There's times I can't get around it, no matter what. Don't you ever want to just say, Fuck it?"

"Of course. Everyone does. But it's important to know what's worth fretting about and what isn't. Take the DM for instance."

"Shit on the DM," I said.

"These managers come and go like agricultural pests," Johnny B. said. "Take the boll weevil for example."

I let out a squall and went to laughing again.

"Cotton farmers panicked in the last part of the Nineteenth Century," Johnny B. said. "They thought that the dreaded little boll weevil would spread all over the U.S. and ruin everything. People wrote songs about the boll weevil, prayed in church for God to put an end to the boll weevil, petitioned Congress to enact anti-boll weevil laws. All but the songs and the singing turned out to be a waste of time. The cold northern climate kept it in the south. Hell, by the 1930s, after all that preaching and praying and ass-kissing with Congress they finally benzene hexachlorided the little fuckers off the map."

Suddenly I saw Mort sitting on a cotton boll, fat and green. Right off I wanted a can of that stuff to spray his ass dead like the rest of them. Black Flag him, then sit back and watch him thrash around twitchin' and kickin' on his office floor.

Johnny B. grabbed his harmonica and began blowing on it and rocking around with his eyes closed and his foot tapping in the tundra.

"Well, the farmer say to de boll weevil,

I see you on the square,

Boll weevil say to de farmer, yep,

and my whole damn family's here

And the farmer, he say to de boll weevil,

why'd you pick my farm,

The weevil he just laughed and said,

we ain't goin' do much harm,

Just lookin' for hooome, just looking for a hoome.

We just need us a hooome.

Well the farmer he say to de boll weevil,

you ain't getting no home here

I'm getting me a can a benzine hex,

and spray you on your rear.

You ain't gettin' no hoooome,

you ain't getting no hoooome."

I laughed so that tears blurred my eyes. Johnny B. was having a time too.

"Let's go swimming," I said.

Next thing I knew we were running down the hill, throwing off clothes as we went. At the waters edge we didn't hold up, just dove in the ice cold lake.

I woke up too warm and looked out into too much light. My head hurt and my mouth tasted like I'd been eating ashtrays. Johnny B. had been up a while and had put Duke back on lookout. A ragged flight of Canada geese passed south of us, east to west, their long necks stretched out, their calls haunting and wild. We packed our sleeping bags and some rats down around the side of the dome to a place where the sun would shine directly on us. That way we could take off our shirts, roll out our bags, and get some sun since there wasn't a thing to do but lie around.

After a moment I said, "What time did we go off the clock yesterday?"

"I don't know, maybe we should stay on it until they come and get us."

"Well, that don't seem right... after all we didn't work all night."

"No, but we were here. And if something had happened, like the fire escaped, we'd have had to fight it, right. So, it's kind of like stand by."

"Well, it's a damned good thing we didn't have to fight no fire, I can tell you that. After smoking that thunder stuff I couldn't even slap my ass with both hands at the same time."

"I see," Johnny B. said. "I guess that half bottle of Jack didn't have anything to do with it."

"Who cares what it was. Besides feeling hung over, I sure had fun."

We built a small fire, made some coffee and ate some more C-rats, then went down to check on the fire. There were only a few small smokes left in the middle. After a couple hours we went back to our gear to follow the sun on around the dome, and wait out the day. I had this little book I had found in a dumpster at the barracks. *Confessions of a Workaholic*. And, of all things, a man named Wayne E. Oates, had written it. Johnny B. had a fit when he saw that.

"What a trip," he said, laughing. "This Oates guy must be a reformed oat hog?"

"Quinlan needs to read this," I said. "Might help him calm down some."

"The E. must stand for extra," Johnny B. said. "This is a good sign."

"Look here," I said. "He's founded the Center for Oates Studies, and here's a chapter on the positive enforcement's a workaholic needs. This is what it says, 'A positive enforcement can come from a close coworker. Coworkers can help each other by looking at the possibilities of living more sensibly and examining various sources of motivation and satisfaction. An atmosphere of banter and humor often pervades their conversations, giving way to a more balanced existence between work and the enjoyment of life.'"

"Sounds to me like he'd be in favor of us running our time straight through," Johnny B. said. "We nearly got killed on our last fire, so we should get a little extra on this one."

"I was nearly killed twice," I said. "But that doesn't mean they owe me double."

"All right," Johnny B. said. "We'll just run it straight through until tonight."

"Well, I don't think we need all that."

"Why not?"

"I don't rightly know," I said, "but I didn't grow up thinking that work was a bad thing or a good thing. It was just what everybody did. There's always things need done on a ranch, so we worked at it as soon as we could get to it. That's the way it had to be, or else we'd get behind and go broke and lose everything. I was raised to believe that doing good work was honorable, not something to cheat on."

"I don't see it as cheating," Johnny B. said. "Look, we've got a great crew because we have a lot of experienced people who keep coming back year after year. But they have to make enough money each season to do that. So, adding a few hours here and there keeps the pay good and the crew strong and happy. I've watched it over the years, and the more money we get, the stronger the crew gets, and, in the long run, fires are put out much quicker, and so with less cost."

"I just want to work hard and get paid for what it's worth," I said.

"In that case I'd have to take you off the clock all yesterday afternoon, since you were stoned, drunk, and not worth a shit."

"I reckon that'd be the right thing to do all right, but hell, if we just put down the hours we worked on this fire, we wouldn't get no overtime at all."

"Okay. How about this? Let's wait and see how things go. Then, we can decide what's right."

"Do you think they'll come today?"

"I don't know, maybe I can find out."

"One thing sure," I said. "It's a good thing they didn't show up yesterday."

Johnny B. dug into his PG bag, tossing stuff aside, a hooded sweatshirt, a wool stocking cap, a pair of dirty socks, two plastic bags of half eaten trail mix, a mud-crusted rain fly, a headlamp with a cracked lens and a smashed Snickers bar that looked like the bill of a platypus.

"You know where my radio is?"

"No, but the last time I saw you with it, you were up on top trying to get a hold of Galena.

Johnny B. went to the top of the dome and in a few minutes I heard him.

"Galena, Galena, Galena. This is the Mud fire. How do you copy?"

He did that three or four times then tried another way.

"Attention... anyone that can copy. This is Mud River jumpers broadcasting in the blind. If you read, we're ready to demobe our fire. If you're not Galena dispatch, please relay our message to them. Mud fire clear."

We read and slept a while, then moved on around the dome following the sun, reading, dozing, then moving again, eating as little as possible since our supply was running low. We smoked some more of Johnny B.'s thunder road, drank some Jack Daniels then lay around laughing at ourselves like fools. We kept at it, getting stoned, nipping the Jack, getting the munchies, watching the last of the food disappear, getting uptight about that, then getting stoned again. The entire night passed the same. Then came morning and I looked across the way and saw a bunch of trash scattered on the side of the dome.

"Well, now," I said, half hung over. "If that don't beat all. Somebody's come way out here, had a picnic, and then gone off and left their trash."

Johnny B. looked over, then back at me, and said, "Isn't it amazing how some people are? Come out here and throw shit around, not giving a damn about nature. That's not like you and me."

"Hold up, now," I said, so stoned I could hardly think. "You don't reckon that's our... ?"

"Hell no," Johnny B. said. "People come out here and eat C-rats and John Wayne crackers all the time."

That's when I figured it out. We had gone clear around the dome and run into our own mess. Imagine being that bad off. Sometimes it's hard to keep track of time in Alaska in the summer, with the sun going around and around in a big circle, and we hadn't done enough work to know the difference between day and night or next week. Besides, we had taken mind-altering drugs.

I needed to do something to straighten myself out, so I decided to walk the perimeter of the fire to check for smokes again, even though I knew there weren't any. On the way back I stopped at the lake to fill my canteens. On a grassy bench I sat down and started dipping my Army canteen cup full of water, then pouring it into a canteen. Some ran over the side and made little bubbles in the lake. Half way through my second canteen, just like that, there it was, yellow and green with dark fins and big, black eyes, nibbling at the bubbles. My heart commenced to pound. It didn't know me, and it didn't know canteens, but it knew that something moving on the surface might be food. Just then Johnny B. came by.

"Hey, come look at this. Stay low and crawl over here. It's a big pike."

"Good grief. That thing's gotta be three feet long."

I went and cut a willow pole. From my PG bag I got a roll of fiberglass tape, which is to smokejumpers what bailing wire is to farmers. Carefully stripping the tape I made several thin strands, then tied them into a ten-foot line and fixed one of the hooks I always carried in my wallet on the end. From our last can of John Wayne crackers I broke off a chunk and worked the hook into it. Eight feet off shore was an area of lily pads. I swung the cracker out over the water and as soon as it hit, it exploded in a splashy, yellow-green blur. I hauled back on the pole. The pike appeared in a rainbow of colors, then flopped back into the water and snapped the line clean. I went flying backwards and the next thing I knew I was sitting on my butt in a mud hole.

Johnny B. got to laughing so hard he could barely talk. "Damn, the way you flew back... Oh, man, that was something."

"Well," I said, still in the mud, "I'm pleased you found it entertaining."

"Oh, I did. Those were your best moves since the fire tornado."

I got to my feet, picked up my baseball cap, and looked at the line. "Son of a bitch. Broke it clean off."

"You looked like you were trying out for the Bolshoi ballet."

"I need stronger line."

"And a harpoon and a couple grenades."

Johnny B. was so tickled he could hardly talk. I just ignored him, and started tearing thicker strips of the tape, tying them together again.

"A damned fish like that needs to die," I said. "Scaly cold-blooded bastard."

Two casts later the water exploded again. I had him that time, wrestling him back and forth, up and back, around in circles, all the time closer to shore. I was about to drag him up onto the grassy bank when he bolted, taking another hook, all the line, and the tip of the pole with him. And, of course, I followed along just like before, landing on my ass for a second time. Same mud hole.

"Damn the luck," I yelled.

"Hey Twinkle Toes," Johnny B. roared. "You're supposed to keep your hands up over your head when you do a pirouette."

"Listen here, Johnny B." I said, getting mad, "I all but die fighting a sea monster and all you can do is poke fun."

"I'm telling you, Lenny," Johnny B. laughed, barely able to control himself. "Even Baryshnikov couldn't have made some of those moves."

Mad at the world in general, and one bloodthirsty Northern pike in particular, I got to my feet, disgusted.

"Ballet or not, he's gone now. And, after that ruckus, you can bet he won't be back."

Johnny B., still tickled with himself, went to the lake and started filling his own canteens. I sat a while thinking I might cut a spear. Even after Johnny B. had his canteens full, he kept pouring, making bubbles. I think he was wanting more entertainment at my expense. He kept on for at least five minutes and then said softly, "Hey, Len? Your friend's back. Come look."

Six feet offshore, under the edge of a different raft of lily pads, there he was, lurking in the shadows. You could see his broad snout and one of my lines trailing out the corner of his mouth about three feet.

"It's watching the bubbles," Johnny B. whispered.

Right then the pike thrust its side fins, glided forward, then halted at the bubbles and began nibbling at them.

"Man, this guy must be hungry," Johnny B. said.

I got down on my belly and crawled to a clump of grass near where Johnny B. knelt pouring. Parting the grass I could see the pike, breathing easy, thinking he was about to get something to eat. I thrust my hand in the water and grabbed for the line. The water exploded again, only this time in my face. All I could see was a blur of green and yellow and a gaping white mouth, lined with rows of teeth slashing within inches of my nose. I grabbed at all of it, and was suddenly juggling him out and up into the air. Teeth came and went, then came again. His tail hit me in the face. In a contest of who was to eat whom, we went at it, the fish snapping its teeth and me batting it higher and higher into the air, hoping to knock it on land. Johnny B. made a wild swing with his canteen cup and hit me on the wrist, and I yowled, missed a stroke and the pike flipped end over end back into the water.

"That son-of-a-bitchin', yellow-eyed fucker," I yelled. "Tried to take my face off."

"Man," Johnny B. said, "the minute you put your hand in the water he went for it. He's never seen anything he couldn't eat."

"That mindless reptilian throwback," I yelled. "I'll kill it if its the last thing I ever do."

"Sorry I clobbered you," Johnny B. said. "I was trying to help."

"High-eyed, scaly, no-good... What I wouldn't give for a shotgun."

"I found a half-grown duck in one once," Johnny B. said.

Coming off an adrenaline blast, I grabbed my PG bag and took a big swig of Jack.

"I don't rightly care for fish like that," I said, handing him the bottle. "If he'd gotten my hand in his mouth he would have ripped the flesh clean off."

Johnny B. went back to pouring bubbles on the water.

"You're wasting your time," I said. "After that he'll be gone for sure."

"The magic, Len. Like I told you, you have to have some faith in the magic."

I sat and watched Johnny B., thinking about that big mouth and all those teeth.

"I'll be seeing those teeth for years," I said. "Rows of them, curving all which ways and angled back. Even across the roof of its mouth there's nothing but teeth."

I tipped up the bottle and glugged down some more Jack. Johnny B. continued to dribble his canteen.

"He might come back," Johnny B. said.

"No creature, no matter how dumb would come back now. Even if he did, what could we do?"

"Hunger's a powerful motivator," Johnny B. said softly.

I watched Johnny B. pouring the water, amused and thinking his persistence a waste of time. Minutes passed.

"Psst," Johnny B. signaled with his free hand. "Guess who's back?"

I was reaching for the bottle of Jack again when I saw my Woodsman's Pal in the side pocket of my PG bag. Crawling again to the grassy shore, I clutched my Woody Pal tight in my right hand. Peering through the grass I saw the pike exactly as before, under the same raft of lily pads, line still trailing out its mouth. Johnny B. continued making bubbles. With a single thrust of its fins, the pike shot straight for us. Holding on tight to a clump of grass with my left hand, and gripping my Woody Pal in the other, I lunged forward swinging it as hard as I could. The blade sliced through the water and into the pike's back. I'd cut its spinal cord right behind its head. As the fish fluttered helplessly I rammed two fingers into its gills and flung it onto the bank where it lay quivering in the afternoon sun, its great mouth gasping, eyes wide open.

First thing the next morning I ratted through what was left of our food.

"This is the last of it," I said. "Besides that trail mix and extra garbage in your PG bag, and what's left of the pike, this is all that stands between us and cannibalism."

"If you were a rookie," Johnny B. said, "I'd wash you out right now. If we have to, we can boil the rest of the fish in our Army canteen cups. Jumpers up here call it Poor Man's Lobster. That'll do us a couple more days."

"They're bound to come tomorrow," I said. "They know we've only got three days food. The Jack Daniels is gone, too."

The day passed and we tracked our second time around the dome, following the sun like hands on a big clock—this time picking up our trash. After a dinner of boiled pike and stale trail mix, Johnny B. walked up and sat down on top of the dome again. I looked though my binoculars and saw him sitting alone up there, elbows resting on his knees, silhouetted against a blue and pink sky, staring out at the big world. Just before the sun went down he started writing in his notebook. After a time he put it away and made his trek back to camp. It was midnight but we couldn't sleep, so we lay on our sleeping bags just looking up into the deep blue starless sky.

"Hey look," I said, pointing. "There's a satellite."

We watched as the tiny light blinked across the sky towards the southwest, then disappeared.

"It just entered the shadow of the earth," Johnny B. said. "For that satellite the sun just went down. For it and part of the earth, too. Did you ever think that somewhere on the planet the sun is constantly setting? That it's been doing that since the beginning? Same for sunrises. The simultaneous beginning and ending of what we call day and night. Right now the sun is sinking into the Gulf of Mexico along the west coast of Cuba and the Yucatan Peninsula, while somewhere in China, a young woman sits on a bluff above the sea, playing her flute as the sun rises up out of the Pacific. The beginning and the end... the eternal moment."

We lay there for a minute in the quiet, looking at the sky. That was a lot of information to think about at one time. Especially since I was convinced that smoking the pot had permanently wrecked my brain.

Standing at the end of the Tanana airstrip, we watched as the Bell 205 left the ground, rotated forward, then sailed off in a wide arc out over the Yukon River headed for Galena. A BLM man from the village told us our plane would not be in until the next day. In the meantime we could stay the night in the Russian Orthodox church. We took up our packs and headed in the direction he had pointed. A light rain began to fall.

The church was a weathered log building with a roof made of corrugated aluminum. It stood on a high bank of the Yukon, facing the great gray river, which at that point was a quarter mile wide. The rain started coming down hard just as we got to it.

Inside it was dark and quiet. In a corner the BLM man had a rough desk on which sat a lamp, a map of the Tanana area, notes on local lightning fires, and a handheld radio with a homemade wire antennae that ran out a window to a tree. Near the desk sat a case of C-rations. The church's main room had a wood stove in a corner. Firelight flickered through stove's cracks, and the sweet smell of wood smoke hung pleasant in the air. Windows let in scant gray light to reveal several rows of pews. Statues of saints stood near the alter. Two candles cast a dim glow on a painting of Jesus kneeling in robes, somewhere in the wilderness, his face turned up toward a stream of light.

Rain blew in off the Yukon and tapped against the windows, the radio hissed softly. It was beginning to storm outside but the church was warm and snug. While Johnny B. was looking at the Tanana map, I sat in the last row of pews eating a cold can of beef stew, feeling thankful for another special moment. After eating we went outside and sat in the woodshed and watched the river. Johnny B. took out his harmonica and began playing, tapping his foot, eyes closed. After a bit he started to sing.

> Hey, hey there big river,
> What can a low man say?
> Hey there good flowin' river,
> Gimme some peace, I pray, pray, pray.
> Just a little peace, I pray, pray, pray
>
> From the hills I gather courage,
> visions of the day
> and dreams for the night time
> to carry my soul away, way, way,
> Yeah Lord, carry my soul away.

# 8

Stretched out in one of the bat caves in the Ready Room, I listened to the rain. It had rained for two days. Bat caves were what the jumpers called the spaces created by the newly constructed dexion shelves. They were intended for storing jump gear, but many had been hijacked for bat-caving instead. Each one had its own chicken bag and served as a good hunker spot on rainy days. Burlap bag curtains hung on wires and could be pulled closed to shut out the world. It was cold in the hangar and, with most of the chutes rigged and checked, there was little to do. So some of us took refuge in our chicken bags to read, sleep or whatever it took to escape our present predicament.

I couldn't do either, so I lay there and wondered about the strange nature of my life and a season stopped dead by rain all across the Interior. The place felt like a morgue. Worse than that, the jumpers were grumpy about some of their fires, having been demobed too quick and replaced by helitac or EFF crews. Two of their fires later escaped and had gone big. Mort had kept to his idea of letting the helicopters man close-in fires. Most of the fires jumped had been demobed as quickly as relief crews could be hired. Even on fires they could have put in one or two more days, the jumpers had been pulled off. In one case they hadn't even finished gathering their cargo when local dispatch radioed and wanted to know when they would be ready to demobe.

Getting pulled off fires, brought into town, then put on straight time, riled the crew to the point of wanting to kill Mort. They wouldn't have to wait long for their chance. At roll call it had been announced that he was coming over the next day for an afternoon meeting. A cartoon on the bulletin board showed a helicopter flying behind a jumpship with a big butterfly net, catching jumpers halfway to the ground. Above it was a paper cutout of a fish. The paper was yellow office stuff with green lines. Johnny B. had taped three pieces together and drawn it full size with green spots, snaggle teeth, and big, silly-looking eyes. Underneath he wrote: World's Record Pike taken with Woodman's Pal.

The next morning the sun came out and cheered us up. The only people in the bat caves were those who stayed out late and came home drunk. With no regard for them, Mountain Puss set up some saw horses and marked a few boards. Bell began sawing on them. Still wearing one bandage, Mountain Puss had been taken off injured-reserve and put on the jump list. Keep A Goin' Construction was the name of his new company, and its stated goal was to make the T-Hangar more fit for human habitation.

"Dammit it, Bell," Mountain Puss said, "you're ruining good lumber."

Bell paid no attention and went right on sawing, filling the Ready Room with the sound of fighting cats and sawdust. An electric arc flashed. Boards clattered off sawhorses, and people yelled as the skill saw went flipping across the floor.

"Yowww," Bell yelled. "That was great. I sawed the cord in half."

"That arc to your crotch was great, too," Rake said.

"I know," Bell said, shaking his head. "I saw it, I already hurt there, too."

"Aackk," Quinlan said, as he charged out the Ops door, "what's going on out here? I ask a group of grown men to do a simple job and what do I get? A group of simple men trying to do a grownup's job. And, Don Bell... You *are* always there."

"Hey Quinlan," Bell said. "You know who the first carpenter was?"

"No, but I know who some of the worst are."

"It was Eve. She made Adam's banana stand."

Big Al walked into the Ready Room, stopped just long enough to see Bell in the middle of chaos, then sat down at the center table, leaned back and put his feet up on it.

"Quinlan," Big Al said, "tack this memo on the bulletin board."

This is what the memo said:

July 6, 1973
All Department Heads
Vehicle Accountability

It has come to my attention that a red BLM carryall is being used for other than official purposes. Although it is not clear who the employee is, it is also clear that soon they will be found out. Anyone knowing anything about this matter would be well advised to come forth. Misuse of government property, in some cases, can be viewed serious enough to warrant criminal charges.

Mort Twixtenblout
Manager, Fairbanks District

Quinlan tacked up the memo, then whipped out a pen and put "ly" at the end of the word serious. "Damn the illiterate," he muttered. "Wouldn't know an adverb from an aardvark."

Keep A Goin' Construction got back to work. Bell took up a hand saw. Hammers pounded. Nails bent and were pulled out. Bat-cavers cussed. Quinlan was right, if there was one thing these jumpers weren't good at, it was carpentering. Nonetheless, by three o'clock two new suit-up racks stood at one end of the Ready Room. Tony, a Mexican smokejumper from Silver City, New Mexico, named them Hernando and Lupe. By four another section of dexion bat-caves had been finished and an old pop machine set up in a corner. The boys hung two orange and white cargo chutes from their apexes and tied their suspension lines tight to the tops of the dexion shelves. The high, dark recesses of the hangar were gone, veiled by colorful, light-gathering chutes that moved easily in the air.

At 4:30, Mort walked in. Big Al took him around, then out to see a couple jump planes. Back inside, Mort wandered into Operations were he took his time looking over the aircraft availability chart and jump list. At 5:00, The Fat Indian came on the new intercom:

"All jumpers report to the Ready Room. Crew meeting."

Big Al and Mort sat in folding chairs near the Ops window as the crew filed in and took their seats.

"Ahh, well, okay," Al began. "Just a few things, then I'll turn this over to our District Manager."

No one said a word. At the far end of the runway, a PB4Y retardant plane was running up its engines for takeoff.

"If you guys have any fire reports to complete, talk to Cleermont. We need to keep them up to date. Also, after jumping the Volpar, I'd like you to fill out an evaluation form. Cleermont has those, too. Nothing too elaborate, just some observations about your exits, getting out the door, your body and opening positions."

Big Al usually called Cleermont The Fat Indian like we all did, but with Mort there it was good he didn't. The Fat Indian wasn't really fat anyway, just a little thick in the middle. No one called him the Fat Indian without tolerable respect for fear he would kick their ass. As a member of the Flathead tribe that lived around Flathead Lake, Montana, he was an all-Conference halfback playing football his senior year at the University in Missoula. Sometimes we called him Jim or Cleermont, but mostly The Fat Indian.

The four big engines of a PB4Y-2 retardant plane roared from the end of the runway. On it came, louder and louder, then deafening. Past the T-Hangar it lifted off in a window-rattling, air trembling celebration of the harmonics of radial engine power. The sound moved off in the distance and quiet returned to the room.

"That's all I've got," Big Al said. "So, I guess it's time. Fellas, this is Mort Twixtenblout, our new DM. He's here to take a look at our operation and say a few words. Mort?"

Mort stood up, nodded to Big Al, then the rest of us.

"Gentlemen," Mort said, after clearing his throat. "This is quite a place you have. I can see that you're a very interesting group. A special group. You are the Alaska smokejumpers. No other smokejumpers can make that claim."

Mort paused. The crew glanced around at each other.

"Alaska is a special place. It's fires are difficult in ways not encountered in other regions. Not only are the fires different, the people are different, too. Let me give you an example. Just the other day I spoke to a native elder in Alatnuk. I asked him if didn't he think we should allow some of these fires to burn, especially those caused by lightning?" Mort paused again. "And, do you know what that man said?"

From the back of the room, a native accent muttered softly, *"You're too white."* Those close enough to hear tried not to laugh. A few failed and faked a coughing fit. Some chuckled. Big Al turned a whiter shade of pale.

"That man spoke right up and, to my surprise, said, 'No! Fire's better put out.'"

Another suppressed silence.

"Fire's better put out," Mort repeated. "So I asked him about all the lightning fires that burned before we came and started putting them out. And the man looked at me and said, 'There was no lightning here before the white man came.'"

The room exploded. Mort smiled big, pleased at making such a strong impression.

"Well, that may be," Mort went on as the room quieted. "but there is plenty now. And when it starts fires, we'll be the ones to put them out. We'll be the ones to get the job done. Because that's who we are."

Mort paused again, as if waiting for applause, then went on again after it was clear there wasn't going to be any.

"But first let me say that a good firefighter, a good secretary, any good employee is only as good as their loyalty. The Bureau is our employer, and I feel it's my responsibility to make sure everyone understands to whom their loyalty is owed. That's why we have the Loyalty Statement, and that's why I want them signed by the end of the week. Thank you."

A strained silence followed. Mort sat down and Big Al asked if anyone had any questions. No one did. The meeting ended. As the crew filed out of the Ready Room, Big Al pulled me aside and said that Mort wanted a word with me. On the small deck outside the pilot's trailer house-lounge, we shook hands like it was the first time we'd met, then sat down.

"You've got a nice place here," Mort started in. "I'm glad it's worked out."

"It's all right," I said. "But what makes it is the people, not the place. It was right depressing at first. A few guys just came back from Vietnam and getting put back on a... "

"Good for them," he said, "I just wanted to see you a minute and check if you might have anything for me. Something to report, I mean."

I pushed my ball cap back off my forehead, looked out across the runways, and shook my head. "Not really. As you know we've been busy. We had some good fires, some a little rough. Even had a few injuries. But this crew is serious about firefighting. I'm proud to be —"

"Did you take pride in the cannon incident?" Mort interrupted again.

I didn't see that coming. So, I just sat there looking at the airfield and thinking. When I knew I couldn't wait any longer, I looked at Mort and grinned. "It's pretty clear that the Army did it. They know all about cannons and..."

"You know damned well it wasn't the Army," Mort said with a fierce look in his eyes. "So, Len. Let me shoot straight here. It was one of you three or someone on this crew, and you can't tell me they haven't talked about it. Also, I've asked about the red carryall and no one's said a word. You can't tell me people here don't know about that, either. Just to be clear, I will find out, not only who it is, but also why and who is covering it up. If criminal charges are filed, you could be an accessory to the fact. But that will all come in time, don't you think?"

I felt heat in my face. "If you've come here to say something useful, then say it."

"What I'm saying is useful," Mort said. "You're just too hardheaded to see it."

"I might be," I said. "But the jumpers aren't in charge of vehicles. We got plenty to do besides keeping track of who's driving BLM rigs... and I'd think you would have, too."

"Humph," Mort said, glaring at me. "I'm a hands-on manager and hands-on managers keep an eye on..."

"When in doubt, rack out!" came a voice across the parking lot.

I looked over and it was just as it sounded. Someone had thrown the switch on Bro Ratus, and there he was in his fire shirt and helmet, on top of the T-Hangar with a spruce bough over his shoulder.

*"What on Earth?"* Mort said.

"Ah," I said, "that's Bro Ratus. He helps us keep focused and stay positive."

"How many oats do you have?" Bro Ratus called out, turning a one-eighty.

"A dummy on the roof," Mort said. "Ha! How appropriate."

"Sure enough. Bro Ratus is famous among smokejumpers. Next to Big Ernie, he's about the most well-known. He and Virgil."

"Big Ernie, Bro Ratus, what in God's name?

"It's hot and dry out west," Bro Ratus said.

We sat watching, me glad that Bro Ratus had changed the subject, Mort struggling to remember what he had been talking about.

"Anyway," he finally said, "I've got to go. The arson investigator called yesterday. When I mentioned the Kodiak fire, he said someone from the jumpers had called and wanted to talk with him about the Fort Greeley fire."

I looked across the airfield again, wondering how much Mort already knew.

"So what? He's an investigator, and you wanted one."

"He wouldn't give me the jumper's name. Said it's best to keep names out of it."

I didn't know what to believe. Maybe he had a name, maybe he didn't.

"I guess that'd be his business," I said.

"Wherever you go, there you are," Bro Ratus said.

Mort lurched side to side, tapping his fat fingers on his knees.

"For now, it might be," Mort went on, "But just so you know. I didn't get him up here to investigate the Army or the pipeline project. The official report says the fire was started by an unexploded ordnance. It doesn't need investigated, and I would like to know why anyone here might be saying anything different. I've told that to Al Mattlon, and I'm telling you, too. One last thing... I also have the final say on all end-of-season performance ratings, some of which might contain a no-rehire. Do you understand what I'm saying?"

We sat there staring at one another like a mongoose does a cobra, and I thought to myself, I might ought to stomp this bastard right now and end my misery. But instead, I said, "Well, sir, I reckon I do. But if a BLM fire inspector wants to talk to me, and me being a man about to sign a loyalty statement to the BLM, you can bet I'll do it. Now, if you'll kindly excuse me, it's quitting time."

The next morning at roll call there was a new memo on the bulletin board.

### rumor control - rumor control - rumor control - rumor control

July 14, 1973
Rumor Control Headquarters

EL OTRO — Riding The Crest Of Civilization.
WELCOME TO OIL CITY

Once again the T-Hangar is abuzz with the lusty cries of Overtime, Hazard Pay, and Good Deals. Our fire season is off to an ambiguous start, but remember in the game of life, there are winners and there are losers, and at different times you're bound to be both. In times of defeat we tend to forget our triumphs. Or, as that famous social commentator, religious sage, and bisexual advocate, Mohammad Ralph Louie used to say, "There are those who fuck and those who get fucked." With that in mind, let us strive to watch ourselves this summer. Or as the sophists of classical Greece put it, Shut-up and deal. Best remember, we are under BLM and military influence here. That reminds me of a little story:

A very free and small bird was flying along minding his own business and then a freezing rain came. He decided to keep his mouth closed and then it froze shut. He decided to keep his eyes open and they froze open. The dreadful rain iced up his wings and he began falling to the ground. He lay on the ground wounded and thought, Oh lord, I'm going to die. But just then a moose came by and shit on his head. The warmth of moose shit thawed out our little friend. He lifted his head triumphantly and began to chirp and sing. He was happy to be alive.

Unfortunately a big wolf heard the singing bird and came over and gobbled him up feathers and all. And so, as you can see, there are three lessons to be learned in the face of our current difficulties here on Fort Wainwright. 1. Being shit upon is not necessarily bad. 2. Rising above the shit is not necessarily good. And 3. If you do manage get above the shit, don't sing about it.

~The Black Hand


After all the times I'd seen Johnny B. writing in his notebook, I had no doubt who wrote it. When I asked him, he denied it, just like I figured. Anyway, it didn't matter. It was funny and the jumpers thought it was great, especially when viewed alongside those from the DM.

That afternoon Melvin called Bell, and said he wanted us to join him and his sister, Sarah, for a barbecue after work. Johnny B. and I took off in my pickup, bought some beer and chips and drove to the Chena River Campground on the west side of town. Stands of white-bark birch and tall white spruce surrounded open areas of lawn that had nice views up and down the river. There was a pole structure with a shake roof, cement floor, a barbecue and some tables. The Red Lizard was parked next to it. Melvin stood in a cloud of smoke, cooking caribou steaks. Sarah had brought a pot of chili and some salad. Once we finished dinner we sat around the campfire drinking beer and talking about the main course.

"Gwich'in means people of the caribou," Sarah said. "It's been that way as long as the elders can remember. The caribou are the center of our lives, both culturally and economically. Spiritually we believe that every caribou has a bit of the human heart in it, and every human has a part of the caribou's heart. That way we always have some knowledge of what the caribou are thinking and feeling. It's the same for the caribou, they have a similar knowledge of us. So you see, at times, hunting them is easy, at others it's difficult. In all hunting the animals are respected. Except for the bear, not one is respected more than the caribou."

Sarah spoke looking people right in the eye, and that made it double hard to concentrate on what she was saying. Her long black hair fell off her shoulders and down around her breasts. With her dark eyes, finely shaped lips and ears poking out a little through her hair, she was as beautiful a woman as I'd ever seen. She spoke with a slight native accent, her English better than most, mine for sure.

"Our people depend on hunting," Sarah went on. "We get 75 percent of our calories, as well as clothes, tools, and other necessities from caribou. It's been that way for at least 10,000 years. The total Porcupine herd is around 130,000."

Sarah stopped to sip her beer.

"Is that why you came to Fairbanks?" I asked.

"Well," Sarah said, "that's why I stayed. I came here originally to keep track of Melvin while he was in the hospital. In the meantime something's come up and the village wants me to stay and see what I can find out about this talk of drilling for oil on the coastal plain."

"I've heard the oil people refer to the struggle over drilling rights in the Arctic National Wildlife Range as An-War. Have you heard that?"

"Oh yes, of course. But they never say it to our faces. That leaked out to some big newspaper on the East coast. We don't approve of that kind of language. It doesn't fit the way our people think of the land."

"You think you can stop the oil companies?" I said. "They have powerful friends in Washington."

"At this point, who knows?" Sarah said. "What we do know is that we must try."

"You can do it," Bell said. "You know what you're doing is right."

Johnny B. hadn't said a word the whole time. He was too busy watching Sarah, agreeing with everything she said. No doubt he thought she was pretty, too, but then maybe he was keeping quiet on account he might say something to reveal he was the head of Rumor Control.

"I think you can, too," I said.

"Thank you," Sarah said, smiling. "The Gwich'in most closely associated with the Porcupine herd live in Alatnuk, Fort Yukon, and Chalkyitsik in Alaska, and in Old Crow, Fort McPherson, Inuvik, and Aklavik in Northwest Canada. Our village and Old Crow are the most centrally located to the herd, and so have the greatest responsibility. About 8,000 of us live in the northern villages, here and in the Yukon and Northwest Territories. They feel the same. We're all related. We understand our duty."

"Any idea where you might start?" I asked.

"For the caribou the heart of it is their primary calving grounds. If they're disturbed they'll have to move to less ideal areas, there'll be less feed, and the bears will kill more calves. Thirty to forty thousands are born each year. This wild nursery must remain intact. Someday we hope to change the current designation of wildlife range to wildlife refuge. That would give greater protection."

I took a sip of beer. I could see I was getting way behind Bell and Melvin. But I figured I better not try to keep up or Sarah might think I was just there to get drunk.

"You've got a big problem, then," I said. "I grew up in Texas, and the oil companies didn't pay any attention to the land or what people thought. They just came in and drilled and pumped and moved on, leaving a mess. Money talks, and they got a lot of it."

"Yes," Sarah said. "We know that. They're spending millions of dollars on television ads in the Lower 48, coming to the villages and paying for large feasts, attempting to convince the people to accept the things that will come with drilling. But we want to keep our traditional ways, and at the same time, teach the world in a good way, too."

Some of this I already knew from reading the Fairbanks Daily News Miner. Everywhere in Fairbanks the rush was on to build the Alaska Pipeline.

"Has BLM been to your village and talked with your people?" I asked.

"Just last week, your District Manager came. He has a funny name. He was there for the big dinner and slide show put on by the oil companies. He seemed interested in helping us. I'm going to Anchorage to speak with our state representatives. After that, I want to meet with him again."

An airliner on final into Fairbanks International passed low over the campground, so we quit talking for a while. Bell and Melvin and Johnny B. went to the horseshoe pit for a game of shoes. Sarah asked if I'd like to take a walk by the river. As we were walking I mentioned that she might watch out when dealing with the District Manager.

"Melvin says that you're friends. That you had a meeting at the T-Hangar."

I nearly choked when I heard that. "*Friends?* Good lord, no. I'm no friend to him. We had a couple meetings is all."

"Umm," Sarah said, "how were they?"

I stopped and took a minute to look out over the river. Little surface swirls reflected the blue and white sky.

"Sarah... I don't believe it's right to run down a man just because I don't like him. You meet him. See what you think. Maybe we can talk about it then."

"Fair enough," Sarah smiled. "What about you? Melvin says you're part Indian."

"My great grandmother was full Choctaw, married my great grandfather in 1880, five years before they moved from Louisiana to West Texas."

"I knew it. I could see it in your cheek bones."

"Well, I don't reckon there's much left in me now. That was nearly a hundred years ago."

Sarah smiled and looked the prettiest she had all night.

"Marrying an Indian back then was almost unheard of. They must have been in love."

"Well, I wouldn't know about that. What I do know is that he joined the Union Army and fought in the Civil War with the First Arkansas Infantry at the battle of Prairie D'Ane. That's where he was wounded. He eventually died from it. That was after they had moved to Texas. She had six kids, my grandfather being the youngest. She had a time of it alone. Then, my great grandfather's two brothers came out to help her. They fought for the South where most of my family's from, but he was for the North. At any rate it was good she got help."

"You know your family history," Sarah said. "That's important. I'd like to hear more about it sometime. Do you remember your great grandmother's name?"

"Oh yes, it was Teneya. I've got some letters from back then and, even though it wasn't popular to marry Indians, my family loved her a good deal."

"Then, here's to Teneya." Sarah smiled and lifting her beer to mine. "We Indians have to stick together, you know."

The next two days were clear and warm. The rain had been mostly in a triangle between Fairbanks, Nenana, and Delta. The rest of the state was dry and lightning was predicted. Rod Dow formed a group he called T-Hangar Comforts, and they had a number of projects going. Some wash tables had been set up on the east side of the T-Hangar, and there was a hose with cold water, some dish pans and paper towels to wash up with. Not far from the wash tables, Dow had tacked a Copenhagen can to the wall and put a sign beside it that read, Snoose Locker. Quite a few jumpers had the habit of chewing snoose. A good percentage chose to ignore that fact by not buying enough and thinking that when they ran out, they'd quit. Instead, they'd bum from other more realistic chewers, making up all kinds of excuses why they didn't have any. With the Snoose Locker, you could borrow from the community can and then, when you were packing, as they called it, you were expected to return an equal amount. Dow claimed it was a social experiment.

While all that was going on, Johnny B. had gone to Dow with an idea of his own. Johnny B. and I weren't official members of T-Hangar Comforts, but Dow said we could try the idea and, depending on its success, we might be considered later on. Johnny B. insisted on keeping it a secret so we worked in an abandoned warehouse the other side of the pilots' lounge. On a run to the dump, Johnny B. had found a four-foot diameter wooden cable spool and brought it back and hid it in the warehouse.

It was damp and musty in there, but Johnny B. was inspired. After taking it apart, we cut and measured and refit it back together in a way that formed a crude rocking chair. We tried it and it rocked nice enough. At quitting time Johnny B. and I were cleaning up our mess when I looked out a window and saw, of all people, Miles Morgan. He was snooping around, peeking in windows and taking pictures. After what happened at the Pig Party, I was hoping we'd never see him again.

The next morning at roll call, Johnny B. unveiled the I-Hear-You-Walkin-Chair, said it was a gift on behalf of T-Hangar Comforts.

"Behold, the I-Hear-You-Walkin-Chair," the McGrath All-Star said.

The crew clapped and carried on.

"Because of the nature of our job," Johnny B. told them, "and due to certain life problems, and even the movements of planets, there are times when a person needs refuge from the storm. And, as such, the I-Hear-You-Walkin-Chair is dedicated to the principle of safe haven. Whether it's getting a bad deal fire, going on injured-reserve, or the plain ole' depression of Fort Wainwright, if a person needs to, he is welcome to sit here, do some rocking and summon his inner strength, knowing he will not be bothered or judged. No talking, no hassling, no work assignments. However, to assure the person that they are not alone in their hour of need, it will be permissible to look them quickly in the eye and simply say, 'I hear you walkin.'"

Mitchell and Quinlan, both squad leaders, had immediate objections. At best, they claimed, it was some kind of Rumor Control conspiracy; at worst, a prelude to collectivism and anarchy. Paying them no mind, and impressed by the latest innovative notion of T-Hangar Comforts, the crew filed out of the Ready Room for morning PT, leaving them with their first opportunity to try it for themselves.

The following day a tape player, an old refrigerator, and three beat up corrugated garbage cans were set up in the Ready Room. There were other improvements, too. Three portable toilets were delivered and positioned near the back of the hangar. They were funny looking space-age plastic things, and the jumpers, right off, started calling them Astro Crappers.

It was good that the weather had changed since the rain had caused a run of downtown drinking that landed a few in jail. Almost every morning at roll call, we'd get a call from the Fairbanks police, and someone would have to go down and bail them out. Yesterday the jailbird was a pilot of one of the Texas Turkey Dougs.

The most fun of all, though, was that the Volpar practice jumps started again, and I got in on a couple. The door was half the size of a Doug door and hard to clear, and so I went out and ended up on my head the first time like most people did. Don't worry about it, Big Al would say, We can only get better. I could tell he was set on making the Volpar work as an initial attack ship. During the test jumps he had Pops Johnson go through fire records and check the distances to fires and the times it had taken to get there and put jumpers on the ground.

That afternoon we rolled a load to a fire in the Forty Mile country, and sent one to Galena to stand by. Lightning was predicted out west. Although we figured we were about to get into another bust, there wasn't much to do for work with all the chutes packed and cargo rigged. So the Bros mostly lolled around, played cards, or holed-up in bat caves and stuff. A group headed-up by Mat Kelley held their first meeting. Mat was studying Transcendental Mediation, TM as he called it. The purpose was to get the members to focus their minds and their thoughts, and maybe someday be able to lift themselves off the ground. I don't think anyone really believed it but still, for a smokejumper, it could be handy on pack-outs.

Trouble was, some of the crew thought it foolish and formed a second group, and called it MT for Mental Trauma. While Kelly's guys would meet in a back corner of the T-Hangar and sit in a circle of silence with their eyes closed, concentrating on their mantras, vowing never to reveal them, the MT group would gather in the other corner, form a circle of its own, then laugh and shout their mantras at each other. Things like Boing, Boing, Boing, or Wainwright, Wainwright, Wainwright, or Ribbit, Ribbit, Ribbit.

# 9

Jumper 54 made a low pass over four acres of fire spreading active-
ly in tundra and scattered stands of black spruce at the east end of
a mile-long unnamed lake west of Mooseheart Mountain. Bell
stood in the door shouting back and forth with the spotter while the rest
of the crew checked out the scene. The lake was shaped like a fat pear with
a slough running into its southeast corner on the skinny end. Dense stands
of black spruce ringed the rest of the lake. We would jump next to the
slough. Things went bad right off. The wind kept changing and, after four
confusing streamer passes, the jump spot was moved closer to the lake.
Bell, Rake, and Quinlan were in the first stick. Out the door, Bell was in
good position for the spot when suddenly he blew backwards over a
patch of spruce with some fire in it. From the plane we saw him disappear
in the smoke. Rake and Quinlan made the spot, but the jump was held up
until word came that they had found Bell and pulled him clear. His chute
burned.

The jump spot was moved to a swampy area near where the slough
met the lake. On the last cargo pass the pump kit wedged in the door.
When it finally cleared, it splashed down 50 yards out in the lake. Kasson
and Quinlan pulled off their boots and shirts and swam for it. They came
back dog-paddling with the partly submerged pump kit and cargo chute
in tow.

After gathering cargo, Bell lined out the crew. Kelly would stay
behind and try to get the Mark III pump running. Bell would take the first
half of the load and burnout from where the slough emptied into the lake,
up the slough to the east in an effort to keep the fire south of it. Quinlan
and the second half would work south up the right flank, turn the corner
and head east.

The tundra tussocks were tall, with deep holes between them, all of it
covered by matted dry grass. These Boone and Crocket tussocks, as we
called them, made walking tough, constantly sinking into the bog holes
between them. Flames burned five to six feet high and hot. Johnny B. and
I worked the left flank with Bell's bunch. We both had backpack piss-

pumps and took the lead. By knocking down the biggest part of the flames, the rest could move up behind us with spruce boughs to beat out what was left. Piss-pumps weigh forty pounds when full, and hauling them around was no rose garden. Nor was standing in smoke beating flames, but we kept after it. We were up against a tough fire. Besides our normal push, there was now the issue of Big Al. If catching fires made him look good, then that made our difficulties more tolerable.

My eyes burned. My lungs, too. Hot, bitter smoke rolled up in our faces and drove us back off the line, choking and coughing. Once when the smoke was too heavy, I moved off the line and lay down in the tundra and put my face down into a dark, swampy hole between tussocks, smelled the rich stink of rotting vegetation, and felt its cool moisture comforting my lungs. I pressed my face against the cool, wet moss and wished I could disappear down into the earth and get some rest.

Back in the smoke, I returned to the head of the line and, crouching low, pumped the trombone of the piss-pump at what looked like an endless wall of flames. Back along the line, Rake and the others stood shoulder to shoulder slamming their spruce boughs, or burlap bags partly filled with wet moss, at the somewhat cooler perimeter. With steady beating the flames would slowly disappear, then burst to life again, only to be knocked down by the next jumper in line. Bringing up the rear, Mountain Puss acted as dragman, sweeping the last of the embers back into the black and patrolling back and forth making sure flare-ups didn't pop up behind us.

At 10:00 PM Bell went scouting. By then the head was about a quarter-mile wide. At its hottest point flames averaged ten feet high and the heat zone was 30 to 40 feet deep—not something a man could escape through. At 11:00 the wind from the east picked up, then switched north. This put heat and heavy smoke against the slough. Bell returned at midnight. Due to increased fire activity along the slough, plus the general condition of the fire, Bell called a quick meeting.

"I hate to say it," Bell began. "But we need to back off and make sure it holds at the slough. If we lose that, none of this will matter anyway. Quinlan agrees. He's pulling back, too."

After a mile walk across the burn and slogging through the slough, we got to the lake where the others were busy gathering the last of the cargo and the 1000 feet of hose initially used to work the right flank. The fire had blown up completely. All our work had been for nothing. Jump gear and cargo was stacked in two big piles at the lake's edge. It was 4:00 AM, and the sun was a red sphere in a gray haze along the eastern horizon. We went down for some sleep.

Three hours later, around a smoky campfire, our beaten and exhausted crew ate rats, and talked about what had gone wrong.

"Nothing went wrong," Bell said. "We did our best. We didn't lose it because we never had it in the first place. The wind was too much, that's all. I called Tanana and asked for a helicopter. They can replace us with a couple EFF crews. Don't feel bad. We did all right."

The crew agreed. So much effort, though. Most times it worked. This time it hadn't. We continued to eat and make small talk.

"Hey Bell," Rake said, "Tell us about your big date with Betsy Tits-in-Blouse."

Bell glared at Rake. "Would you quit calling her that? Things are bad enough already without you making up stupid names."

"I heard you took her to the Fossil Creek cabin last weekend. I hear there's a lot of bones around there. Did you jump hers?"

"I don't want to talk about it," Bell snorted. "I'm starting to feel about women the way a chicken farmer feels about coyotes."

"More likely the way chickens do," Quinlan said. "Is it not the coyote that makes the chicken's life interesting?"

"They don't make mine interesting, they make it crazy."

"Sans coyote," Quinlan explained, "a chicken's life would be little more than scratching in the dirt, picking shit, a little crowing and some egg laying. No! Every chicken needs a coyote."

"Or a fox," Rake said. "Like Sweet Betsy."

Bell's radio squelched, then a squeaky female voice said, "Mooseheart fire, Tanana dispatch."

Bell grumbled something about chickens, pulled his radio out of its holster, stared at it a second, then said, "Chickenheart—I mean *Mooseheart*, go ahead."

"Regarding your request for a helicopter, Fairbanks says none are available."

Bell's free hand flew into the air like he wanted to hit something.

"Are you saying that between Tanana and Fairbanks and Delta, there's not one single helicopter? We got a big problem here and we need one."

"Stand by. I'll check again," the squeaky voice said.

"Stand by she says. Shit! What does she think we're doing? We're surrounded by fire. What else can we do but *stand by*?"

Shortly the squeaky dispatcher was back.

"Fairbanks says there are only two helicopters not working fires, and they're keeping them for initial attack."

Bell followed every word, mumbling them to himself, "two helicopters, not working... " Then back on the radio.

"Let me get this straight. They're holding two helicopters *in case* they get a fire, and we're here *in the middle* of one that's more than we can handle, and they can't spare us one? Is that it?" That was followed off the air by, "Incompetent morons, running things from dispatch while we're out here *standing by,* and they have to keep their piece-of-shit helicopters in town in case it catches on fire!"

"They said you have a lake if it gets too bad," the squeaky voice said.

Bell — off the radio. "A lake, ha, ha. They said there's a lake. Slimy, pig-eyed, worms."

Bell — on the radio. "Listen a minute, now. Just do this. At 0900 call Al Mattlon's office. Tell him the jumpers at Mooseheart need a damned helicopter. Immediately! Will you do that?"

Squeaky dispatcher said she would and signed off with, "You have a nice day."

Bell's eyes turned to ice as the words bounced around in his head.

*"Have a nice day,"* he hissed, ready to kill something. "Imagine saying shit like that to someone surrounded by fire. Maybe I don't feel like having a *nice day.*

"Did you have a nice day at Fossil Creek?" Rake said.

Bell shoved his radio back in its holster, poured a cup of coffee, took a sip and a deep breath.

"Hell no! Fossil Creek was a total disaster, just like this damned fire."

"Really?" Rake said. "You take the sexiest babe in Fairbanks to a remote cabin for two days, just you and her. And, you expect us to believe it was a disaster?"

"Believe what you want. But that's how it was. Not at first, though." Bell took another a sip of coffee to calm his nerves, then looked out across the burn like he wished he was somewhere else.

"It started out good. We had a great drive out there. Found the cabin and took a hike. That part was good. Everything was going all right. We drank some wine and had a quiet dinner with a nice fire in the wood stove. After a while it started to rain. She got undressed and climbed on the bed, naked. She lay there in the candlelight with the rain coming down real nice."

"Did you take any photos?" Rake asked.

"Hell no, I didn't take any photos, Rake! What's wrong with you? Even if I did, you'd be the last person on earth I'd show them to."

"I don't mind being last," Rake said. "It'd be exciting just to wait."

"Well, you'd be wasting your time because there aren't any."

"Rain on the roof, candlelight, a naked Betsy in bed. Doesn't sound like a disaster to me."

"Well, it was," Bell said. "And you're not getting to hear anymore about it."

"What?" Rake howled. "You give us the all the stuff right up to the good part and then quit?"

"The rest of it's not important, and you don't need to know it."

"I think we should be the judge of that. We don't hide stuff from you."

Bell refilled the fruit can that served as his coffee cup, then went to pacing back and forth. The whole group went quiet. He just might do it. At times, Bell's love of storytelling would reach a point where it overran standard limits of caution.

Bell took a deep breath then exhaled slowly. Johnny B. shot me a knowing glance.

Bell took another deep breath. "It was raining, like I said, and... she was there on the bed, so I stoked the fire one last time, brought in some firewood, then made sure the door was locked. I brushed my teeth, rinsed them, then wiped my mouth off with a towel. After that I went to the bed and got undressed. That's when she sat up and started kissing me all over, and that got me going, so when I reached over to blow out the candle I knocked it over and splashed hot candle wax on... on... on my dick."

The group went berserk. Rake laughed so hard he fell off his cubitaineer. Button-eyed Duke fell forward to the edge of the campfire and was quickly rescued by Kasson, who was howling like a madman. Quinlan sat stoned-faced. By the time the laughing eased up, Bell was cursing the fact that he should have known better than to reveal a personal tragedy to a bunch of callous smokejumpers.

"On the old peckeroo?" Rake squalled, "I saw you were walking funny, but thought it was because of that time you cut the cord on the Skilsaw."

The crew was still laughing.

"I was hopping around in the dark, yelling, trying to wipe myself off with one hand, and trying to find a flashlight with the other. Shit! I knew I shouldn't have told you. It was an *accident*, just one of those things that happens sometimes."

"Aackk," Quinlan said. "Indeed! Why, almost every week you hear of someone spilling hot wax on their genitals."

"Not *every week*," Bell cried. "I didn't say every week. I said sometimes. And I know what you're thinking. You think it was my fault.

Hell, the whole thing wouldn't have happened if she'd stayed lying in the bed."

Quinlan waved campfire smoke away from his face, leaned back and said, "Like Al said in the meeting, 'If it's not your fault, then why are you always there?'"

Bell stood a moment staring at Quinlan, then waved his hand in disgust. "That's a strange sort of logic if you ask me. Blaming people for something just because they're there."

Bell told us to get some more sleep. There were more fires, maybe we would jump one that afternoon. Too tired to care one way or the other, I strung up a cargo chute hootch and fell inside, barely able to pull off my water-logged boots before I was out. Sometime later I heard shouting. I opened the flap of my hootch to a fairly strong wind and a world that lay under the shadow of a great smoke column. In minutes everyone was up and tearing down hootches and packing gear to a stretch of shoreline near where the slough entered the lake. Bell stood on a small rise watching the head of the fire.

"Len," Bell said, never taking his eyes off the fire. "Get the Mark III ready. Check to see how much fuel's left. We need to wet down the area around camp. Save a couple gallons in case we need it later."

"You think it'll reach camp?" I asked.

"It might. First it took off and made a big run along the south side of the lake. Then, at the other end, it turned and ran north along the shore. Now it's turned east and coming back on the other side."

After setting up the pump, Johnny B. and I covered the gear pile with sheets of visqueen, then stretched two cargo chutes over the pile and wet them down. Kasson and Quinlan stretched the hose out in a line to wet down a perimeter east of camp. Ash began sifting down like light snow. The area we needed to protect was about the size of two baseball diamonds, longer along the lake shore and angled off towards the slough. We put lateral hoses around the perimeter. I would man the one closest to the lake, Dow would take the second, and Quinlan the third. Bell called a meeting at the gear pile.

"Okay. Everybody's here, right?" he said as he made a quick head count. "Here's the plan. Don't anybody go wandering off. If we have to make a stand we'll do it here."

A half hour later the wind picked up even stronger. We could hear the roar of the fire gaining strength. Along the north side of the lake, flames raged above the black spruce right down to the water's edge. At noon two other columns appeared on the east side of the fire beyond our previous night's effort. The interior was reburning. Fields of black tussocks became fields of shimmering orange. Bell paced the shoreline back and forth casting glances at the approaching fire and talking on his radio to Tanana.

A small smoke appeared in the tundra beyond the hoselay. In minutes it was a spotfire the size of a pool table with Johnny B. and me in hot pursuit. Seconds later the spotfire had been transformed into a steaming puddle of muck. Two more started out beyond the reach of our hoselay. We wondered if it might have been better to allow the spotfire nearest camp to burn. The initial spot may have been easier to hold out of camp than a collective run made by multiple spots pushed by the head, or worse the head catching up to the spots and all it of coming at once.

Ten minutes later the head rounded the corner of the lake. Multiple spots were taking off. A fixed wing aircraft roared over, then pulled up in a steep climb angling off toward the opposite end of the lake.

"Mooseheart fire, Air Attack 21."

Bell grabbed his radio. "Air Attack, Mooseheart. Go."

"We see you there by the slough. Helicopter 68 Juliet is ten out. The head's making a run for your camp. The rest of the fire's reburning. If I didn't know better, I'd say this fire is out to get you guys. How on that?"

"Thanks for showing up," Bell said. "We need to get everyone out. Two loads should do it. Take them to Mooseheart Mountain. We can wait there, then come back for the gear later."

The crew lined out behind the wet perimeter, spruce boughs and burlap bags in hand. Air Attack continued to circle.

"Mooseheart, helicopter 68 Juliet on red."

"68 Juliet, go!"

"I'm five out. Are you ready for extraction?"

"Affirmative. We're ready. Our camp's at the east end of the lake, by the slough."

"Copy that, we have you in sight."

"Everybody, listen up," Bell yelled. "When the copter gets here, we'll load eight at a time. The first load will be Shearer, Wilbur, Kelly, Bates, Dow, Rohrbach, Harlo, and Grendahl. Get to the helispot with your PG bags."

In the distance the familiar slap of Bell 205 rotors could be heard mixed in with the roar of the fire. Then, low on the horizon, moving toward us under the smoke column, we saw it. On final into camp 68 Juliet began its flare for landing. The rotor wash fanned the close-in spotfires into waves of running ground fire. The ship kept on coming. Just as it was about to enter in-ground effect, it turned, rotated forward and flew away. Seconds later the pilot came on the radio.

"Hey guys, I'm real sorry but we're too late. It's just too crazy down there."

Word spread around the T-Hangar that the Mooseheart jumpers had been surrounded by fire after being refused a helicopter. Big Al was in dispatch calling on the radio. There was no response. Helicopter 68 Juliet was holding in Manley Hot Springs. Air Attack 21 had reported where he had last seen us. They had returned to the area one time and tried to raise Bell on the radio. Records indicated three radios had been taken from the plane when we jumped, two besides Bell's. Individual radios could fail and, for various and strange reasons, often did, but not three. Most of the crew was out on fires, but those in the Ready Room waited nervously for news. A few rigged chutes in the loft. The whole bunch was in a tense and ornery mood.

When the fire hit camp, we took to the lake, but left the pump running. Waist deep in water, Johnny B. kept a steady stream on the gear pile and saved it from catching fire. Most of our food and replaceable gear burned. It was a sight, us there in the water, soaked to the bone, cold as hell, watching something most people never get to see—that much fire that close. By that I mean they don't without dying right afterwards.

Next morning the Mooseheart crew demobed into Fairbanks with a nasty assortment of partly burned gear and bad attitudes. The base was nearly jumped out, with only Mitchell and The Fat Indian running things. Four others were taking care of paracargo and packing chutes. Melvin had taken charge of paracargo and it was good to see him off injured-reserve and back in the T-Hangar.

Big Al phoned Ops and called a meeting. Two hours later he sat in the Ready Room, slumped in a chair, running his fingers through his hair, waiting for us to settle down.

"Sorry about the Mooseheart deal," Big Al said. "Besides some crazy burning conditions, I know you made a good effort. There was some, ah... mix-up between Tanana and the District Office. Somehow Tanana was told that the state wouldn't release a helicopter. I checked with state dispatch and they never got the request. I'm checking into it. Seems like someone in the DO got their wires crossed."

Bell shuffled his feet, hissed, mumbled a few cuss words, then let fly.

"Tanana told us the state was holding the helicopters on stand by for new fires, and that we should *have a nice day*. Imagine that. Me, stuck with a crew in the middle of fire, and a dispatcher telling me what kind of a day to have."

Big Al explained that she was new, just trying to do her job—that he was checking into it.

"But Al, that's the point," Bell said, "she didn't do it. We're on the fire, not her, and not these nitwits in town, either. Who's going to run these fires anyway, us or them?"

"I said, I'm checking into it." Big Al slumped further in his chair. "I know the screw-up was on this end. I know that things go best when people in the field... call the shots. That's the way it's always been, and that's the way I intend to keep it."

Sitting there, slouched in his chair, Big Al was no big image of leadership, great, strong or otherwise. But he was there in that same honest way he always was. Every time. That's how I saw it anyway. Sometimes we had problems with Big Al, but we still trusted him. We respected him. He was always sticking up for us whether it was with the Army, the outstations, or the new DM. Another thing he always did was let us have our say without cutting us off. And I believe that's why the crew knew when it was time to let up on him and move on. Whether it was by design or default, I couldn't tell for sure, but Big Al Mattlon appeared to hold to a management style that valued involvement rather than dictating, honesty more than pretense, and patience instead of haste.

"This will take time," he said after a contemplative pull on his cigarette. "Just remember, slow is smooth, and smooth is fast. Anyway, that's enough for now. Take a couple hours. Go to the barracks, clean up, then get back over here."

It was a good meeting but didn't do much to change the way we felt about how we'd been treated. The crew had suffered from the new initial attack idea, both at Fort Greeley and Mooseheart as well as several other fires. What Big Al could do was none too clear. I knew he'd try, but I'd seen jumpers screwed over before, and all we did was go ahead and accept it with the understanding that what we did was more important than what people did to us.

We showered at the barracks and returned to the T-Hangar to get fire-ready. But something had happened to the high spirits we usually had after a fire. I don't know what it was, but in place of the normal kidding and laughing and carrying on, there was a sadness to it that was unmistakable.

To make matters worse, Miles Morgan was prowling around again, taking pictures and acting friendly. Johnny B. and I went up on the roof to hide out. Alone, except for Bro Ratus. But he was unplugged and staring off towards the Alaska Range, keeping his views to himself. Looking down we watched Miles cross the parking lot and go into one of the new Astro Crappers. We laughed at that and wondered what he would think of the graffiti written in it.

Stuff like:

Imagination is more important than knowledge. Knowledge is limited.

Imagination encircles the world. ~   Renowned   physicist   Albert
Einstein

Imagination sucks        ~Unknown ex-physics student Rolf Snooder

Confidently pursue your dreams. Live the life you've imagined.
~Thoreau

DOW 4 - 7

Other Enlightened Observations:

| | |
|---|---|
| To do is to be | John Paul Sartre |
| To be is to do | J. S. Mill |
| To be or not to be | William Shakespeare |
| Do be do be do | Frank Sinatra |

"That jerkoff's in there," Johnny B. said, "taking photos and making notes."

"I hope he passes out from the fumes," I said.

Right then we heard the racket. It was Mountain Puss on a forklift. We couldn't understand where he was going in such a hurry, but then he cut the engine back and rolled up to the Astro Crapper with Miles in it. A scratchy, scraping sound came from beneath the floor and the Astro Crapper rocked violently a couple times, then jumped up off the ground.

"Hey," Miles screamed, "there's someone in here. Hey, hey."

Miles pushed on the door but it only opened a few inches before it hit the lift rack. I reckon he could see it was a forklift but not the driver. "Hey," he yelled again.

The Astro Crapper went sailing across the parking lot, rocking back and forth this way and that, and all the time Mile's hand waving out the door. After stopping in front of the fuel shed, the forklift revved its motor, and the Astro Crapper began rising, higher and higher, as did the volume of Miles yelling and beating on the door. When Mountain Puss had him high enough the motor slowed down and the Astro Crapper lurched forward and back a couple times, then dropped a few inches and came to rest on top of the fuel shed. But Mountain Puss wasn't done yet. He pulled the forks back to the edge of the Astro Crapper and started rocking it on purpose, back and forth, back and forth. Then the rocking stopped and, in no time, the forklift was roaring back in the direction it had come. Miles threw open the door shaking his fist, only to see himself at the edge of a ten-foot drop-off. Grabbing the sides, he screamed and almost fell out.

Some Mooseheart jumpers down by the big bay door went to laughing and hooting and imitating Miles' pleas for help. After a bit they went back inside, paying him no mind. Miles spent a good fifteen minutes in the Astro Crapper before an Army private came by and went to fetch a ladder. On the ground, Miles stomped around, looking at himself, and wiping himself off. After he helped the Army man put the ladder back where it belonged, he jumped in his BLM car, spun its wheels in the dirt, and took off.

Two hours later I was in back of the old warehouse where Johnny B. and I made the I-Hear-You-Walkin' Chair, greasing my boots. That's when I saw Miles' car coming back. Nothing could have surprised me more than seeing him again, especially that day. He got out and disappeared between the building where he and the Army guy had put the ladder. I went flying over there, careful he didn't see me, and when I peeked around a corner, there he was, looking in a window right next to where they had leaned the ladder. He went to fiddling with the window and finally got it open. Once he was inside I sneaked over and peeked in.

In the dim, gray light let in by a couple dirty windows, there it was, the mud-splattered Red Lizard. Miles was taking pictures of it from every angle a man could think of. He opened the door and took what looked like a letter off the seat and put it in his pocket. His last photo was of the SMOKEJUMPERS ARE GOOD TO THE LAST DROP bumper sticker.

I turned off the Steese Highway and drove west on Farmer's Loop Road six miles, then took a left down a little dirt track about a mile to the end. I found the trail just like she said I would, pretty well used and soft underfoot with moss. After a hundred yards or so I saw the cabin. It was made of logs and sat in a tall stand of White spruce next to an acre pond. Truth told, I felt a might nervous. I didn't really know Sarah that well, but she had called and asked me to dinner. There was no way I'd say no.

The cabin was old and had an open-sided, shed-roofed porch with water jugs, a chainsaw and some tools lying around. Two pair of snow-shoes and some cross-country skis hung on the wall. A shed out back had smoke coming from the stovepipe. The cabin door was made of heavy planks with bolts and big iron hinges. I knocked.

"If you're Len, come on in."

I pushed open the door. "That'd be me, all right. Thanks for asking me to dinner. I brought us a bottle of wine. I hope you like wine."

Sarah was standing at the sink with her back to me, washing something.

"I do," Sarah said, turning and smiling, "but a little later."

The cabin was tidy and smelled like wood smoke. It had a loft where the bed was, and down below there wasn't room for much more than a sink, some counters and cabinets, a wood stove, a table and four chairs. A tall book shelf took up one corner. There were windows on each wall and they let in a little light. Sarah was playing James Taylor on a cassette player, and he was singing about fire and rain and summer days he thought would never end.

I put the wine on the table. Sarah came over and put her hand out, and I shook. I didn't know what else to do with it. I wanted to kiss it, but hell, nobody does that these days, and I didn't want to look like a fool.

"I'm glad you came."

"Yeah, me, too. Thanks again for the invite."

We just both stood there looking at each other, right in the eyes.

"You sure you wouldn't care for some wine?"

"A little later," Sarah said again. "After dinner I thought we'd sauna. I've got the fire going and it's not a good idea to drink alcohol before sauna."

The idea of taking a sauna with Sarah was not something I had not thought of, and it made me even more nervous. Saunas in Alaska were common. Most times people went naked. We had one downstairs in the basement of the barracks, and one in McGrath, too. I had taken some, and liked them, but that was with smokejumpers. I couldn't image doing that with Sarah.

"It's good to see Melvin back on the jump list," I said. "He's a good man to have on fires."

"I know. He's glad, too, especially the way it's worked out with him back on the same load with Don Bell. He thinks Don's his brother."

I wondered if she knew about Bell and the Red Lizard, and how Melvin would take it when Bell got fired.

"A lot the crew feels that way," I said, "I mean like we're brothers. It's not just here, but everywhere in smokejumping."

"Melvin told me the two of you helped save a woman and her baby from a bad fire on Kodiak. He said you were very kind to her."

"We sort of teamed up on that," I said. "No telling what would have happened if we hadn't got there when we did."

"Len, would you mind cutting up these vegetables for a salad."

I didn't mind at all. It was nice to be there, close to her, doing anything.

"I made some caribou spaghetti, I hope you like it."

"Speaking of caribou, how did your meetings in Anchorage go?"

"Okay. I'm learning as I go. It wasn't my choice to get involved like this. But the people seem to think I'm the one to represent them. They chose me out of 300 people that were nominated. I'd like to become a lawyer, but I doubt I'll get the chance anytime soon."

"You must be proud they chose you."

"I wouldn't say proud," Sarah said. "Pride's not something we admire much. More like honored, I think is the way it would be put in English."

"Well, it's clear they made a good choice."

"The elders and spiritual leaders of the entire Gwich'in nation, all fifteen villages and the residents scattered over several million acres, have begun meeting about this idea of drilling on the coastal plain. I've visited most of them."

"Well," I said, "it makes me proud to know you, Sarah. It's going to be a struggle."

"That's one way to look at it, but struggles are not new to my people. Fifty years ago they were stone age hunters, and the transition hasn't been easy. Besides, how else do we come to know who we are without what you call struggle?"

I was glad to hear that. The jumpers talked that same way at times. They liked to say things like, When the going gets tough, the tough get going, or No pain, no gain.

"President Kennedy said one time that 'Adversity is the abrasive that gives a sharp edge to courage.' Is it like that for you?"

# The Smokejumpers

"It's a wise thing to say," Sarah said. "We all need courage. Without courage, all other virtues are meaningless."

"I reckon so. But sometimes things like courage and pain leave me sort of confused."

"You're pretty serious, aren't you? It's important not to take yourself too seriously, you know. It's a habit of your culture. My people look at it as more like a game to be played than a fight to be won. Being too serious makes it impossible for the joy of every day to sing in your heart."

I thought about Mort and the fire investigator and Miles and the Red Lizard, and had a hard time seeing how you could find much to sing about in that.

"That's why Melvin loves Don Bell so much," Sarah said. "He plays at life, he makes a game of it."

"That may be, but it's not because he plans it that way. Things don't always work out."

"But," Sarah smiled, "when things do work out, they're a lot more fun. Is the salad ready?"

I stirred the salad with a couple big forks and we sat down to eat. Sarah said a caribou blessing, thanking it for its wild and sacred ways, and for making good spaghetti sauce.

The dinner was perfect. Sarah lit a candle so, right off, I thought of Bell and what the jumpers were now calling the Fossil Creek Incident. Anyway, I enjoyed dinner, except for feeling nervous about the sauna. We finished and did the dishes. Sarah changed the music to Bonnie Raitt and Bonnie began singing, *"I'm takin' my time, so please don't rush me."*

We sat a while and I was thinking maybe I should just go home. I could tell her I was on the first load, which I was, and needed some rest, which I did. But, I didn't. I was in too good a mood. Visiting there with her, off in the woods in a little cabin, felt like the best thing I'd done in a long time.

"Are you ready for sauna?"

I wasn't exactly what you'd call ready, but I wasn't gonna' say no to that, either.

"I didn't bring a bathing suit."

Sarah looked at me funny, then said, "You can use a towel."

We went out back to the little shed with the smoking stovepipe and went in a small dressing room and she handed me a towel. I took my shirt off. She did, too. She wasn't wearing a bra. By the time I got down to my pants, she was down to hers. So, I held up. What happened next couldn't

171

have surprised me more than if lightning had struck the sauna, because she went right on and took hers off. I tried not to look as she went inside. I could see her through this little window, putting wood in the stove. I took my pants off and wrapped the towel around me tight and went in. We sat on the high bench where it was hottest, just quiet with me looking straight ahead, not knowing what to say.

'Tell me about yourself," Sarah said. "Where you were raised, and your family."

I thought about that a minute.

"I grew up on a ranch in North Central Texas, about a hundred miles north of Abilene. Dad and Mother, and my brother, Larry, still live there. We raised cattle and hay. We had horses, too. Both to ride and a big working team of Percherons, named Dick and Tom. We didn't have a tractor until 1950. I can still remember it sitting in the barn when it was new. It was blue and shiny and I didn't like it because people talked like it would take the place of Dick and Tom.

Sarah was beginning to sweat, I could see that out to the side. I could see her legs, too, and part of her breasts. That made concentrating on my story a problem.

"Let me tell you a little story about my Dad. He was part Choctaw, like I told you. He had a temper. It was mostly me and Larry that brought it on. Well anyway, we had this rooster that my brother and I hated. It was always after us and pecking at our legs. So, one day when the folks were gone, we cut our arms and made a blood ceremony to kill it. Dad kept dynamite in a shed and we went and got a stick and cut it in half and put in the cap and fuse like we'd seen him do. Then we cornered the rooster in the hen house, threw a canvas over him, then put him in a gunny sack. We didn't know how much dynamite it took to kill a full-grown chicken so we used the whole half stick. We didn't know how much fuse to use, either, so we cut it a foot long to make sure we had time to get away. We got the rooster out of the sack, cussed it some, and taped the dynamite to its back so that the fuse would burn close to its tail. Out in the yard I held the rooster and Larry lit the fuse. But it didn't burn fast enough and the rooster ran around in circles squawking. Pretty soon it got lined out and took off and flew up and landed square on the peak of the barn. It no sooner landed than there come this big explosion of feathers and shingles flying ever which way.

Right then Dad and Mother drove up in the yard. They had seen the whole thing. Dad jumped out of the car yelling, 'What in the hell have you boys gone and done now?'"

"'Dad,'" Larry called out. "Did you see that? It was the amazing exploding chicken phenomenon."

Sarah and I had a good laugh.

"See there," Sarah said, still amused, "you're much better company when you laugh."

I hadn't told that story in a while, and the laughing made me relax some. For a few minutes it did. Then, Sarah got down off the high bench and stood in front of the wood stove pouring water on herself, naked as the day she was born, just standing there with her long, black hair wet down her back, washing under her arms and between her legs. She turned, put her foot up on the bench I had mine on and washed her legs just as natural as if she'd known me a hundred years. I didn't say a word and I know she knew I was looking at her.

"Will you wash my back?"

I just kept quiet and nodded. She handed me this sponge that looked like it had grown in the ocean. After turning her back to me, I started in high on her neck, then down some, seeing how beautiful her brown skin was, then down to her waist, then up again, letting the sponge go, and using my bare hands. She reached around and took them in hers and pulled them around and put them on her breasts, and I kept right on washing. After a while she turned to me and I stood up and kissed her full on the lips. That's when my towel fell to the floor.

# 10

I dropped my pack at the top of the small rise. Bands of yellow and orange clouds lay along the northern horizon above the dark rim of the earth. To the west toward the coast, rain fell in gray curtains. From somewhere in the flats below came the wup, up, up, up wing beat of the Nighthawk. Such a place, I thought. The peace and serenity of early evening in the bush.

The McGrath All-Star came up the hill with his pack and dropped it beside mine.

"Were getting boned," Johnny B. said. "It'll take days to walk around this thing."

"Weeks is more like it," I said. "Just before Hairface put us out, he said it was 10,000 acres. That's roughly three miles by six miles, which likely means fifty miles of fireline if you count all the fingers. And I'll bet a dollar to a donut there's not one smoke on the whole damn thing."

"Big Ernie must be pissed-off," Johnny B. said.

"I don't doubt it a bit," I said. "Especially at you."

"At me? Hell, things are fine with me."

"Is that a fact?"

"You mean the fires?"

"Johnny B., sometimes you aggravate the piss out of me. You know damned well what I mean; the chicken feathers in the cannon, the Rumor Control memos, the Black Hand. I can't imagine what all you've done."

"So you think it's me?"

"Why, it's got you written all over it. We haven't heard the last of it, either."

"I had nothing to do with the cannon deal. As for the rest, believe whatever you like."

"Bell's already in enough hot water without you making things worse."

"I told you, I didn't do it. Anyway, it's done. Right now I'm more concerned about how to deal with this fire. Hairface said it got a lot of rain but McGrath wants it checked anyway."

"Well, then, we're plumb screwed," I said. "If we start right now and do ten miles a day, we'll be done two days after the food runs out. I don't see why we can't get a regular fire for once."

"Duke's got a better idea," Johnny B. said. " He thinks we should split up. If we each walk ten miles a day we'll only have half as far."

"Duke's as crazy as you are then," I said. "What if something happens like a fall, a sprained ankle or a bear attack? Besides, we can't walk ten miles a day in this tundra. You have to look every time you step and you can't walk a straight line in tussocks. Every step takes purpose, every place you step is different. Twenty-five miles maybe we can do, fifty will kill us."

"That's why we should split up. Come on, Len. Think positive. We'll pace ourselves, sleep when we need to, eat less. It'll be interesting."

Against better judgment, I finally agreed. I'd go north, Johnny B. south. We'd call each other on the radio twice a day, at 9:00 AM and 9:00 PM, or when something extra good or bad happened. Not that it would matter. If we got bear-mauled it would be too late to do anything but say goodbye. We decided we'd each pack a pulaski, two burlap bags, a plastic tarp, some EFF cord, Bandaids, seven C-rats, and two quarts of water. Before we parted we ate again. When we were finished, we stashed the remaining gear, walked out to the fire's edge, shook hands, then turned and faced what looked like an endless run of open fireline without fire.

To my way of thinking, the plan was crazy. Especially the sleeping part. If it rained things would, sure enough, be interesting. Here and there occasional strips of black spruce cut across the plain. A man could hole up in one and build a fire.

The hours passed slowly with nothing but the crunching of my boots on dry tundra. Some places it was easier walking in the burn where I could step between tussocks better. Then again, sometimes outside the burn had small tussocks, even some open places of caribou moss. It was best to keep to the edge of the burn in case of smokes, which only added to the silliness, since it was clear the fire had been rained dead out.

Although a plain, the land was not all flat. Low ridges, a few plateaus, and long drifts of higher ground were separated by broad swales, flat bottoms and swamp. Nowhere did the high ground rise more than two-hundred feet above the rest. On the first high point, I stopped to see what I was up against.

The fire edge ran down a gentle incline, became ragged in a wet bottom, then angled up again onto a plateau where it disappeared, then reappeared further on, more to the left on another broad run of open country.

I had been walking for six hours and judged that I'd made four, maybe five miles. Stopping for a break, I took out my first rat, Chicken, Boned, Cooked in Water. I thought to myself, even the chickens were boned on this fire. As I ate I noticed the various plants at my feet; bear berry, Labrador tea, arctic lupine, cottongrass, blueberry, and others I didn't know. Summer in the Alaska Interior is brief. In ten weeks plants emerge from under eight months of snow, grow, blossom and seed. Pink, yellow, purple, and blue flowers no bigger than the head of a thumb tack set on stems only two inches tall. Thinking of Sarah, I carefully I picked a tiny bouquet, then pressed it between the pages of my Oat book.

I decided to walk all night. Sleeping midday would be more comfortable than dealing with the cool night without a sleeping bag. I dropped down and crossed a small, flat-bottomed valley and came upon a five acre pond. Out on the horizon the sun had dropped from sight, leaving the Northern sky pale red and violet with a few yellow clouds. The pond, surrounded by a dark tree line, mirrored the same sky. Alone and in silence I stood there, given over to sudden and unexpected beauty.

A wolf howled. A low moan that built, floated in the air, held some, then trailed off to silence again. I strained to see. The wolf was close, maybe right across the pond. A second wolf howled. Higher pitched and closer. I looked to see if any trees were big enough to climb. Prospects looked grim. Even if you could get up one, it would likely fall over before you got high enough a wolf couldn't jump up and grab you. Wolves, I thought. They each howled again. Another silence. I read once that wolves howl when they get separated, or when they sense an intruder in their territory, or to unite the pack before a hunt. I gave up the idea of walking all night, gathered up some firewood and kindled a fire.

An hour passed. No more howls. Maybe they were gone. Maybe they were hiding in the trees, watching me with yellow eyes, licking their black lips. It was 3:00 AM. I shook out my rain tarp, rolled up in it and tucked my sweatshirt under my head  But I couldn't sleep so I lay there thinking about Sarah. The morning after the sauna I woke early and spent some time just watching her breathe. She had her back to me and her hair was fanned out on the bed, black and long. It had been a fine evening, with the music and the spaghetti, and Lord knows, what all went on in the sauna. Just when I'd met a woman I could spend some time with we had to have a fire bust. I had no idea when I'd see Fairbanks again. I had all those thoughts, then finally went to sleep.

I dreamed my fear dream again. The one where I'm on the first load, standing by at a jump base somewhere and the siren goes off, and I can't find some part of my jump gear, the next thing I know the first load is on the plane with the engines running, ready to go, waiting. I've lost some part of my gear and I'm not fire ready. I have failed again.

Three hours later I woke up stiff and cold and a little sick, but got right up, packed my gear and started walking. For the next two hours I trudged along without stopping. On a rocky ledge I ate another rat, Spaghetti and Meat Balls—Spags and Balls the jumpers called them. I backed it up with a can of fruit cocktail. After eating I took a moment for a good look around.

Up ahead something wasn't right. A hundred yards off the fireline, there was a pyramid shaped mound about a 200 feet high. When I got closer, I was surprised that it was covered with spruce, some of them real tall. I held up at the edge of it, not believing what I was seeing, then went in. The spongy tundra, right off, went to moss covered ground where two-foot diameter white spruce lofted overhead while their massive roots snaked about in big moss-covered lumps. Light streamed through the trees, and where it hit the ground, cold misty steam rose up from decaying logs. Near the top of the cone there was a crater with a tiny stream flowing out. Having broke out one side, it ran down and made a little pond that was filled with sunlight and pretty green water. I found out later that what I had come across was a pingo, an oddity in lands of permafrost. If a spring produces enough flow to keep the water from freezing in winter, the saturated perimeter freezes and thaws and lifts the land higher and higher until a pyramid is formed. The soil in a pingo is deep, making for tall trees, plant succession, and its own individual nutrient cycles. A pingo is a little world all its own.

I found a nice place and sat down for a quick snack of John Wayne crackers and grape jam. There were several red squirrel seed mounds. The pingo was a small paradise in the middle of a barren landscape. When I finished eating, I shouldered my PG bag and had only gone 50 feet when I came across a game trail, bigger than a squirrel run, but smaller than moose would make. It led back into the heart of the pingo to a vertical embankment. At the bottom, something had dug a den. The hole was big enough for a man to squeeze into, but too small for a bear. Down on my hands and knees, I looked in and waited for my eyes to adjust. The den had a rotten, wild stink to it. I couldn't see a thing, just pitch black. Then it was there, the face of a wolf, perfectly still, looking straight at me. Did it know I could see it? It never moved or made a sound. I pulled back, got to my feet, then stepped away, my heart pounding. Two hundred yards out, I turned to look one more time. Inside the pingo, I thought to myself, there was a heartbeat, maybe more than one. I thought of the den and the darkness and stink and those haunting yellow eyes that I would not soon forget.

I radioed Johnny B.

"Johnny B., this is your hero, Len Swanson. Come up on red."

There was no answer, then, "What's up?"

"Not much, how's it going?"

"Fine. I walked all night. I'm tired."

"There's wolves over here. I heard them howl, and then saw one."

"Cool. Did you pet it? They like to be petted, you know."

"Doesn't everybody? How are your legs holding up?"

"They're getting sore, but I'll make it."

"Hey," I said, "I'm getting tired of being over here all by myself. Why don't you recite me one of your poems?"

Another silence. I thought of asking again.

"Why don't you recite one?" Johnny B. said.

More silence.

"Because, the only ones I know are the ones my mother read to me when I was a child... things like The Owl and the Pussy Cat, and The Owl and the Pussy Cat don't quite fit this country, that's why."

"Okay then, how about this," he said, chuckling. "Let's do one together. And since it's your idea, you name it."

I held up. "All right. How about Lone Wolves?"

"*Lone Wolves?* No, no, no. Much too pedestrian, as in flat and lacking imagination."

"Don't be running down pedestrians, Johnny B. Pedestrians is what we are. And wandering around in flat country like this doesn't call for much imagination, either."

"Oh, I get it. You're uptight about our hiking program. I guess we better do a poem then, give it some special meaning, maybe even a little magic. I'll tell you what. I'll do a line, then you finish it. I'll start. We'll call it Unknown Country."

"Unknown Country," I mumbled, knowing I may as well argue with a fence post.

"We are all explorers... " Johnny B. began.

After a little, I said ". . . in unknown country."

"Each setting out... " Johnny B. continued.

"Ah... " I hesitated, "to walk around a fire that's dead."

"on a journey alone..."

". . . except for some yellow-eyed and black-lipped wolves..."

"... but still the paths are many, the destinations obscure..."

"... Especially when you don't know where you're going..."

"... in search of meaning and purpose..."

"... the likes of which no sane man could explain..."

"... Only now can I see that the journey has been..."

"... a total waste of time... "

"... It is a journey made standing still..."

"... by two jackasses and a stuffed... "

A faint radio transmission walked on my line.

"Unknown country... this is lost jumpers, repeat lost jumpers. How do you copy?"

"Lost jumpers, this is unknown country," I said. "You're weak but readable."

"No time to talk — battery low. Write this down."

I grabbed my Oat book and a pen. "Okay, ready to copy."

"Helicopter 68 Juliet, set down, canyon bottom. Christmas Mountain. East of Shaktoolik. Need fuel. Coordinates - Latitude, 64 33 37. Longitude, 160 33 28. Relay to BLM."

In a steady downpour, Helicopter 68 Juliet landed on the helipad east of the McGrath station and cut its engines. We unloaded as the big main rotor slowed to a stop. Rake, Kasson, Dow, and Klingel, the crew from the missing helicopter, off-loaded their gear, along with Johnny B. and me. After being rescued by a fuel drop, 68 Juliet had stopped on its way to McGrath and picked us up. Once inside the ship and strapped in good, I looked around, smiling at all the jumpers, and there right in the middle of them, was none other than Miles "Big M — little organ," Morgan. I about fainted when I saw him.

In McGrath Dispatch we were met by a few BLM overhead, shaking hands and expressing relief at having found 68 Juliet. Our rained-out fire had been put in monitor status. It's just like them, I thought, having us jump and do all that walking for nothing, when we could have been fighting a real fire.

One of the turkey Dougs was in McGrath standing by with a load of jumpers. Several others jumpers were hanging out in the tent frames behind dispatch, waiting to fill out another load or be demobed back to Fairbanks. Rake came in and sat down by the wood stove and told us how 68 Juliet got lost.

"We jumped around noon Friday," Rake began. "That afternoon Big M coptered in. We couldn't believe it. Said he wanted to check on our fire, our performance, things like that. Said he'd stay until the fire was finished, then demobe with us. Shit! We had the fire contained by midnight and finished mopping up in the rain the next morning. The third day 68 Juliet picked us up. I was riding right seat, up front. Ten miles north of the fire we came to a fog bank near the coast. The pilot decided to fly over it since we barely had enough fuel to make Koyuk."

Rake and the pilot were talking about the fuel situation in Koyuk when they came to an opening in the fog. Beneath it there was nothing but blue. Somehow the pilot had flown out over Norton Sound. Immediately he checked his Loran then pulled a hard right and headed east toward the coast north of Ungalik. No sooner had they leveled out than the ten minute warning light flashed on. They had ten minutes fuel and showed fifteen miles out to sea. The Bell 205 cruises at 100 mph, which is roughly 1.65 miles per minute in a dead calm. It would be close. With no survival gear, to go into the sea would be certain death. The pilot radioed over and over but no one answered. They came to another opening and could see the coastline. The two-minute warning light came on. Three minutes later the copter sat in a small meadow at the entrance to a narrow valley off the Shaktoolik River, three miles south of Christmas Mountain. It was on Christmas Mountain that Klingel and Kasson had heard our poem.

That's when I hiked back to the pingo and was able to raise McGrath on the radio. Three 55- gallon barrels of Jet A were flown to the lost ship by a Jet Ranger out of Nome.

A mob of jumpers took three tables in the back of Joe's Roadhouse, and commenced to yelling for drinks.

"You should have been with us," Kasson grinned. "We nearly killed Big M. The fire was pretty straight forward. Then, out of nowhere, he shows up with a clipboard and a list of questions. He said the District Office sent him out to check on jumper performance. *Fucking insane!* The next day it rained and there wasn't much left, just a little mop-up. The second night in camp... tell them, Melvin, how you fixed Big M up with that stuff you made."

Melvin, normally not a talker, but loosened up by two quick beers, rocked back in his chair and started right in.

"Well, funny thing. At the campfire he saw my Copenhagen can and wanted to try it. Said he used to chew it. I had two cans. Some of my people, especially old ones, use Iqmik. They mix conk ashes with Copenhagen, then pour in a little whiskey. That's the way they get conked. I gave Big M that can instead of the one he saw. He took too much."

Sarah explained to me later that there's a fungus conk that grows on birch trees in interior Alaska, and that these plants contain alkaloids that pack a big wallop. Native Athabaskans have long known that if you burn the conks in a can, then ingest the ash, it can produce a euphoric state along with a fearless attitude and a sharp increase in energy.

"An hour later, Melvin said, happily, "Big M started running around camp picking up sticks and beating on trees, ripping up tundra and throwing it around. I knew he was a Meechameandu... and that proved it."

"You should have seen him," Kasson laughed. "It was worse than the Pig Party. He was all amped-up about performance and the state office and how much he loved women with big tits.

"Around midnight, he was out in the woods taking a dump," Kasson went on. "We heard this horrific cry and saw him running for camp, holding his pants up. In camp he tripped and hit his head on the woodpile, and was knocked unconscious with his drawers still down around his knees."

The whole bunch went wild, laughing and cussing Miles.

"After determining he wasn't dead," Kasson said, "we had to decide what to do with him. So we got a cargo chute and wrapped it around him and left him there all night."

"That Big M guy," Melvin said, smiling big. "He made a real good performance."

As the night at Joe's wore on, jump stories flowed at a rate consistent with the falling level in Hairface's bottle of Crown Royal. By eleven Melvin lay passed out, face down on the table, snoring. At one point I found myself outside Joe's back door, standing in a patch of fireweed, laughing to myself and weaving back and forth until I accidentally pissed on my boots and pant leg.

Back inside, the subject of the Loyalty Statement came up.

"Loyalty," Bell snarled. "I don't need to hear about it."

The crew let fly with a storm of cussing and raving and nobody listening to anyone else. Dow slapped his hands down flat on the table to quiet things, then leaned forward and said something no one expected.

"Listen up a damned minute. I've already talked to Rake and some of the guys. I'm going to sign it." Stunned, we all wondered if Dow was also conked. The recent transfer from McCall was as big a rebel as any, naturally suspicious of authority, and usually quick to question things like Mort's Loyalty Statement. As a good firefighter, and the self-appointed head of T-Hangar Comforts, he had also gained considerable respect among the crew.

"And I'll tell you why," Dow went on. "Whether we like it or not, this is a matter of loyalty. And so, I'm signing it because Big Al's asked us to. We don't call him Big Al for nothing. His loyalty has always been to us, even if it meant risking his job. So, it's only right that we owe ours to him. If we can take the pressure off him, like he keeps it off of us, then I say, let's do it. Pass the word around. This isn't about the DM or BLM, it's about Big Al."

The group kept quiet. It was true. Big Al had stuck his neck out time after time, not taking Bell, Rake, and Johnny B. off the list. He was working on the cannon deal plus other run-ins with the Army, like the illegal cooking in the barracks that set off fire alarms, or the case of Dow burning donuts on the barracks lawn in his old Chevy, White Trash, and most recently when Weird Bill Harlo gave the finger to a jogging soldier that turned out to be the base commander.

"Now that makes sense," Hairface insisted. "The boss takes care of you, now you can take care of the boss."

"Damned rights," I said. "If this is for Big Al, count me in."

"Me too," Rake said. Others shook their head in agreement. We were all drunk as skunks. Dow lifted his beer in the air and said, "And the sooner we get it done the better."

Just after 3 A.M. we filed out of Joe's and lit out for camp. Melvin was in bad shape so Bell had to haul him in Joe's wheelbarrow. The trail ran through woods of paper birch and tall spruce, and we staggered along, laughing and coaching Bell over the big roots that cut across it. Off toward the river a bunch of sled dogs commenced to yapping their fool heads off. Orange and red clouds created an alpenglow that turned the paper birch trunks gray and pink out in the open and a soft, baby blue in the shadows. Fifty yards short of the tent frames, Bell rammed the wheelbarrow's front tire against a spruce root and dumped Melvin in a mud puddle.

Two days later the sky above McGrath cleared and one load rolled to a fire north of Galena, and my load was dispatched to a fire reported near Pilot's Station. We couldn't find it and returned to Aniak to stand by. We ended up spending the night sleeping in an old warehouse owned by the Lower Kuskokwim Air Service. I guess it was too late for McGrath to get us rooms at the Aniak Lodge, so we were left with a dusty concrete floor and the chicken bags we carried on the plane. There were no mattresses. There was no heat. The crew woke up stiff and grumpy. After phoning

Fairbanks dispatch, Hairface told the crew we were to return to McGrath and hold there.

"Boned again," Johnny B. said as we loaded our gear back in the Doug. "Stuck in the McGrath vortex. Anytime you're within a hundred miles you can feel the pull. Next thing you know you're sitting on your ass in the rain, logging straight eights."

"Aackk, malcontent," Quinlan said. "Here you are getting paid to fly around, eating for free, sleeping free. This is smokejumping, not Outward Bound."

Johnny B. just looked at Quinlan and scowled and tossed his gear bag up to where I was standing in the door. I tossed it on to the next guy in line, and soon we were loaded up. The Doug was a turkey Doug, and a leaker that had already blown one engine. On board we had just settled down with some sprawled out in their chicken bags, eager for a snooze, when pilot talk and toggle snapping were heard up front. Then, the captain said real clear to the co-pilot, "They're dead." Hairface appeared in the door of the cockpit.

"Don't get too comfortable," he said. "Our batteries are dead."

The crew off-loaded and began to haggle with Hairface for a hot breakfast at Aniak Lodge. He and Quinlan ignored us and headed for the air service office, leaving us to gripe to ourselves. The man running the place said that the only auxiliary power unit in Aniak hadn't run for a month, but if we felt up to it, we could try to get it going. Hairface and Quinlan went into a shop next door to check it out.

The captain walked up, "Somebody get that forklift," he said, pointing. "And a letdown rope."

I climbed back into the Doug and got mine. Kasson fired up the forklift and came sputtering over, tipping this way and that in the loose gravel. The rest of us stood back and watched as the co-pilot climbed a stepladder he'd placed under the right engine. We had no idea what was going on. When he got to the propeller—to our amazement—he began wrapping the letdown rope around the propeller hub. The ten-inch diameter hub stuck out a foot in front of the propeller, and the co-pilot wound wrap after wrap of the tubular nylon around the thing like a person would wind a cord on a old-fashioned lawn mower. The captain slid his cockpit window open and talked with the co-pilot.

"This is sure enough crazy," I said.

"I'm just glad it's your letdown rope and not mine," Johnny B. said.

The co-pilot climbed down and tied the rope to the hitch of the forklift. The captain flipped a couple switches and gave a thumbs up. The crew backed away. The forklift began bucking side to side, wheels spinning. The rope tightened, the propeller began to turn, the rope flew off and whipped into the air and landed on the ground beside the forklift. The propeller stopped.

"We need more speed," the captain yelled. "Get that pickup."

While the co-pilot wound the rope again, Rake tied it to the pickup bumper. The pickup started out, the prop began turning again. The pickup's rear wheels spun, the rope flew, and the prop stopped just like before.

"We need more weight," shouted the captain. "You guys, pile in the back."

With six jumpers in the back and the rope pulled tight, the pickup moved forward without spinning. The propeller began to turn slowly, then kicked into a spin as the engine backfired, then roared to life in a cloud of blue smoke. We all cheered and high-fived. Hairface and Quinlan came out of the shop. Although horrified, they were clearly impressed. In ten minutes the batteries were up and the left engine cranked over until it roared to life just like the first. Having forgotten our empty stomachs, we climbed on board and took off, as happy as gophers in soft dirt.

After landing in McGrath we changed over to Jumper 54, and the turkey Doug flew back to Fairbanks for new batteries. Gene Hobbs took over as our new spotter. He and the replacement Doug had come from Fairbanks and had been busy on one fire run after another. Not long after getting our gear switched we got a fire call. Coming in low, the Doug dropped its left wing and flew in a wide circle above a forty acre fire that had received some rain.

After a quick look we climbed to jump altitude. Gene strapped on a standard backpack spotter's chute. The Doug pulled on final for our first streamer run. Gene bent over to grab a handful of streamers out of the spotter's kit. There was a blur. A loud bang shook the plane. Gene was gone. Yelling came from the cockpit as the plane yawed right, left and the nose dipped forward. The faltering Doug shuttered, roared, then regained a more stable attitude. Dow and Johnny B., the two closest to the door, rushed to look out. A few others did the same, causing the pilots to yell all the more. Moving bodies had shifted the center of gravity too far to the rear and the pilots had enough trouble as it was.

"Get forward, get forward," Kasson shouted, waving wildly.

As soon as the plane leveled out the co-pilot came shoving back through the jumpers. He was none too happy. As the Doug circled all eyes pressed against the windows. A lone white canopy drifted over a vast, green plain. The Doug winged in tighter and when we flew past at a hundred yards we saw Hobbs hanging in his harness, arms dangling, head bent forward, chin to his chest.

My first thought was, Gene Hobbs has just been killed. From a lighthearted crew, suited up for a routine fire jump, we now faced the likelihood that our spotter, friend, and fellow jumper was dead. Like the jumper death I had seen before, I found myself struck by the same grim presence of tragedy. And just like then, I was having trouble knowing how to react. Was Gene really dead? Was the plane seriously damaged? Should we jump before it came apart?

"Everyone!" Kasson yelled. "Get forward of the wing. Sit down. Keep calm. Tell the pilot to radio McGrath for a helicopter. Open a firepack, get out the sleeping bags. Get the trauma kit ready to kick."

Kasson and Johnny B. checked the door. Gene's backpack chute had come out of its container, caught the turbulence of the open door, flew out, and opened alongside the fuselage halfway back to the tail. Flying backwards, the right side of his body had slammed the aft part of the door opening and ripped away part of the fuselage. He then spun to the left and struck the forward part of the door opening with his right leg, after which he was sucked out and fell away under the plane. The door through which we normally jumped clean and clear was a mess of mangled metal, especially the lower rear corner where the static lines end up during exits. Two pieces stuck out into the slipstream like great knifes, causing an unnerving howling and banging in the plane. Kasson and Johnny B. tried bending some of the worst pieces in closer to the fuselage. The rest of us could do nothing but watch.

Gene hit the ground blowing backwards. The chute faltered a second then caught a gust and jerked his limp body across the tundra ten feet before it collapsed and came to rest in a light breeze. Jumper 54 came around and made a low pass as near as possible. The only sign of movement was the wind rippling across the chute.

Kasson stood back from the door.

"Anybody here with skydiving experience? Anyone done a jump and pull?"

No one had. To clear the door would require a running exit, then the presence of mind to fall away under the tail, wait a few seconds then pull the emergency chute handle and hope it opened since there would be no backup if it didn't.

"Okay then, I'll do it," Kasson said. "Johnny B., hold a sleeping bag against the edge of the door so that the static line won't get cut." The idea was that the static line would be cushioned from the jagged metal long enough for the main chute to be pulled from its deployment bag. If it cut, then Kasson would still have his reserve. The captain had turned the ship over to his co-pilot and was now approaching the door.

"It's too risky," he yelled. "With the spotter gone, I'm in charge. No one jumps."

Kasson looked at him, disgusted. *"Fuck too risky.* Gene could be dying."

"He's probably already dead," the captain snarled. "What do you want to do, take the whole load down? From now on, you'll do as I say."

Kasson and Johnny B. looped a letdown rope around the banging debris, snugged it as tight as they could against the fuselage, then ran the rest of the rope back and forth across the opening to prevent anyone from falling out. Jumper 54 made one final low pass, then pulled up for McGrath, leaving Gene Hobbs alone in a big empty land, under a big empty sky.

Two hours later, the helicopter was back in McGrath where a Lear jet was waiting on the ramp with its engines running. Miraculously, Hobbs was alive. Jack Anusewitz, a former Army Medic and booster from the North Cascades Smokejumer Base, had headed up the rescue. Jumpers stood by to help with the body transfer. Minutes after the jet departed, a helitac crew took off for Gene's fire. For the rest of the day I kept hearing something Anusewitz had said during the transfer, something I couldn't get out of my mind, "By the time we got to him, his face, his neck, his hands, everything was solid black with mosquitoes."

That afternoon, while walking to the standby shack, I was stopped on the road by the station foreman. When he rolled down his pickup window, I stepped up to the door and saw a pistol in a leather holster sitting on the seat.

"Have you seen that dog lately?"

"I reckon by *that dog*, you mean Ripcord."

"That black mutt. I don't know his name."

"What do y'all want with him?"

"I'm going to shoot him."

I looked at him a moment. "I'd give that some serious thought if I were you. He belongs to a woman in town. Ask the cook. She'll tell you."

"Well, she should keep him home, then. He causes trouble around the station. When the helicopters land, he runs out to the pad and barks and runs in circles."

"So what? I don't hear of a whole lot of helicopters wrecked by dog. You can't just shoot a good dog for no reason."

"I do what I'm told, and I've been told to shoot him."

The pickup rattled off down the road, and I ran to the standby shack and found Johnny B. playing Go Fish with Danny.

"Hey," I said, tugging at Johnny B.'s shirt sleeve, "there's gonna be trouble."

After a quick talk, we went back and told the boy that the game was over, and that he should go back to the cookhouse until lunch. The way we figured it, it was just another way for the McGrath overhead to get our goat. They knew we liked the dog. The dog and the boy were about all there was to keep us from going nuts in McGrath.

"Screw it," I said to Johnny B. "I'll be damned if I'm gonna just sit by and let him kill Ripcord."

I grabbed a radio out of the plane and told Hairface that Johnny B. and I were going down to the station to clear up the dog problem. Hairface protested that we should stay out of it, but I wouldn't listen and was off down the road with Johnny B. right behind me. In dispatch we went straight into the Area Manager's office and began to make a case for the dog, explaining that it belonged to some local, and that it would only worsen feelings between the community and BLM. So what if the dog barked and ran in circles. It couldn't interfere with a landing because if it got too close the rotor wash would blow it into the brush. The man behind the desk got fed up, said it was none of our business, then told us to leave, concluding that if he needed any suggestions on how to run McGrath, he would let us know.

On the road back, I saw the foreman's pickup coming, and flagged him down.

"You're making a mistake," I said. "Give us a day or two to find the owner. The cook knows who it is."

The foreman looked down the road and not at me.

"I don't make the rules around here," he grumbled.

"Don't you shoot that dog. I'm telling you, don't you dare shoot him."

The foreman dropped the pickup in gear and drove off. We were almost back to the standby shack when we heard it stop. Ripcord came out of the woods wagging his tail, happy like he always was. A shot rang out and the dog flew sideways and flopped over kicking his its hind legs. I started to run, but Johnny B. tackled me, and in no time Quinlan and Kasson had piled on.

I spent the rest of the day alone in the plane, sick. Just before quitting time the Station Foreman came to the standby shack. Hairface and

Quinlan were playing cribbage. He walked right in and said that from then on, the boy would not be allowed around the jumpers. Said that the boy's mother wanted it that way.

At dinner I went into the kitchen and asked her about it. She had said no such thing, and that they had no right putting restrictions on her son. She said she would talk to the Area Manager and get to the bottom of it.

That night Bell, Johnny B., Rake, and most all our load walked into Joe's eager to put the day behind us. Seconds after we cleared the arctic entryway, I saw the foreman sitting with some ground pounders at a corner table. They looked at us like we were skunks showing up at a lawn party. While the rest took seats at the bar, I walked casually over to their table, and without a word dove across it, grabbed the foreman by the neck, knocked the table over, and ended up in a pile in the corner. One of his buddies started kicking me. Bell grabbed him and ran his head into the jukebox. Soon the corner was a mass of people fighting. Joe came wading in, yelling for us to quit. Non-fighting jumpers stopped the fighting ones and walked us outside. Quinlan was talking a blue streak. The foreman and his friends left. Once they were gone, Joe invited us back in, set me down and gave me an ass-chewing, then bought me a drink. By midnight we were all drunk.

The next morning at breakfast no one said much. The boy, who usually ate with us, was missing. At lunch Hairface came in and told me Big Al wanted me to call him ASAP. I went into the back of the kitchen, dialed his number on a wall phone, and stood there knowing I was in trouble. The phone rang several times.

"Jumpers," Big Al said.

"Al, this Len Swanson in McGrath."

After a small but uncomfortable silence, Big Al said, "What the hell's going on down there?"

"It's a long story," I groaned, "but I can explain it all when I get back."

"Yeah well," Big Al said, "you might be able to explain it to me... but who'll explain it to the DM. They called him, not me. To put it bluntly, you're in deep shit."

"I may well be, Al, but it was finally just too damn—"

"Listen Len," Big Al interrupted. "I haven't got time now. We're in a fire bust up here. The assholes and elbows kind. Hobbs is in rough shape. This is exactly the kind of crap we don't need... okay? If you can't stay out of trouble down there, then I'm going to have to ask you to come back to Fairbanks... and ah... and turn in your gear."

# 11

After three more days in McGrath we were sent back to Fairbanks. The fire bust was still on, but with us going to the bottom of a jump list, and twenty more boosters from the Lower 48, there wasn't much chance we'd get a jump before it ended. Held hostage in McGrath for a week caused us to miss a least two fire jumps, go to the bottom of a big list, and me to nearly get fired. Still, it was a good deal compared to what we'd been through. The T-Hangar was full of activity with jumpers just in off fires, all kinds of cargo rigging, chute packing, and the general good feelings of busy jumpers. In the Ready Room first-load jumpers checked the list, bugged Operations with questions and fussed with their gear on the speed racks. Someone had taken a tin can and some string and made a phone out of it. The string ran from the window near Operations straight up to a cupola on top of the hangar where Sam Houston—a former Army medic—had started collecting and organizing medical equipment. If you needed to talk to the cupola, all you had to do was pull the string tight and talk. When you were finished, you just hung the can on a nail. Everyone loved the thing, especially the down-south jumpers.

Right in the middle of the Ready Room hustle and bustle, Big Al sat in the I-Hear-You-Walkin'-Chair, rocking back and forth. He glanced at me when I passed by. I wasn't sure what to do, but I nodded to him just like he was anyone else and said, I hear you walkin'. Right after lunch I was called to his office over in the FAA building for a talk. I did most all the talking, though. Sometimes he'd shake his head, disgusted, but I couldn't tell if it was because of McGrath or because of me. He looked like his normal self, thin and pale. But that little spark he had in his eyes at the first of the season was gone. Rumor had it that he'd been staying out nights, gambling and drinking downtown at a place called Sam's. It was one of the new gambling parlors that had sprung up with the arrival of thousands of construction workers to build the Alaska Pipeline. I thought maybe Big Al was hung over. Whatever it was, he just sat there listening and staring out a window until I finished.

"Well ah, yeah," Big Al said, taking a deep breath, shaking his head. "Maybe it'll blow over. Maybe it won't. A word of advice. Try not to let yourself get mixed up in shit like this again. The DMs watching everything we do. That's enough for now. Let's get back to work."

Walking back across the ramp to the T-Hangar, I ran into Don Bell.

"Hey Don. What's up?"

"These damned things," he said, holding up a manila folder. "This is all Dow's idea. He says I should deliver the Loyalty Statements to Al myself, and that'll show him that I'm not always just involved in disasters. They don't mean shit to me but I went ahead and signed one anyway, and now here I am taking them to the boss. *Dow!* Hell, Al won't be fooled. He's too smart to think I'd do something like this on my own."

Back in the Ready Room, The Fat Indian waved me over to Ops, and then handed me a half dozen notes. All but two were from the fire investigator, a man named Fentori. He was wondering why I hadn't returned his calls. The note with the most recent date had a different phone number.

One of the other notes was from Mort and it said:

I hear you were on a fire with Don Bell. When you get in, give me a call.

The last note, and the only one I was glad to get, was from Sarah:

7-25-73   Glad you're back. Call me — 774-2256

After a long shower, I put on a pair of clean Levis and a new shirt then dialed the fire investigator in Washington. I knew it was too late for him to be at work, but at least I could say I'd tried to call.

"Hello, Bill Fentori, how can I help you?"

I thought to myself, how about helping me disappear, then said, "Mr. Fentori, this is Len Swanson in Fairbanks."

"At last. I was beginning to think you didn't get my notes."

"I been in the bush. Sorry it's so late."

"That's fine. I'm not in Washington, I'm in Anchorage, same time as you."

"What? You're in Alaska?"

"Yes, I arrived two days ago. Yesterday I met with Mr. Deering, of the Kodiak ranch. He assured me their fire was caused by lightning. I've called his wife and she says she saw it hit in the woods and then the smoke. Proving otherwise would be difficult, you know, their word against ours, and so, for now at least, I've decided to write that one off."

"Well," I said, "I'm glad to hear that."

"But the Fort Greeley fire. When we spoke on the phone you said you thought it was started by a survey crew. What makes you say that?"

I waited a minute thinking what I might be about to say, and about what Big Al had said about keeping out of trouble.

"I reckon I may as well tell you. I found a campfire. It was clear what happened."

"But how do you know they were surveyors?"

"Ah... I found some flagging. It had writing on it."

"Like what kind of writing?"

"Like, AP survey crew, the name of the lead surveyor, the station number and date."

"And you think AP stands for Alaska pipeline?"

"Well, it's in the pipeline corridor."

"Can you remember the crew and station number?"

"I don't have to. I've got the flagging in my room."

"Copy it down and call me back," Fentori said. "In the meantime, I'll do some checking. If it was, in fact, a pipeline crew, then I need to get up there and take a look."

"Mr. Fentori," I said. "Just one more thing, if you don't mind."

"What's that?"

"There's some funny stuff going on up here. I've been told not to talk to you. So it would be best to keep my name out of it."

There was a long silence.

"Someone told you not to talk with me?"

"That's a fact. And I'm not saying who, so don't ask."

"But... but how do I contact you without using your name?"

"Call the jumpshack. Leave a message for Len, a number and time to call, that's all."


I picked up Sarah and drove to The Blue Marlin, a pizza parlor in the basement of a building on College Road that had flooded when the Chena River overran its banks in 1964. Cement steps led down a narrow cement stairwell filled with the smell of hot cheese, salami and tomato sauce. I asked for a table in the back because I didn't want any smokejumpers coming around like they always did when they saw another jumper with a pretty girl. Sarah ordered a large combo pizza and a pitcher of Prince Brau, a new Alaska beer. I poured Sarah's frosted glass full until it spilled over onto the table and made a mess. Once the waitress had cleaned it up, I made a toast to seeing her again. We clinked glasses.

"Good to see you again, Miss Sheenjek. You look pretty as ever."

Sarah sipped her beer and smiled, "Well, thank you, Mr. Swanson. And how have you been?"

"Oh, I been all right, I reckon. I only had one fire while I was gone, and it was a bad deal with Johnny B. Our load got stuck in McGrath standing by and missed out on things up here. I suppose you heard we had an accident."

We talked about Gene and I told her most of what I knew, but not the part about his broken neck and short memory. She'd already seen Melvin and Mountain Puss laid up in a hospital, so I figured she didn't need any more of that kind of thing.

"How are your meetings going?" I said, changing the subject.

"Some were good, I'd say even hopeful," she said, reaching across the table to take my hand. "A couple not so good. It's made me suspicious of the whole process. But the government people in Anchorage seem to be listening. That's because we have native representatives living there who work with the legislature in Juneau."

"Have you met with the new District Manager yet?"

"I have! And when I spoke about the caribou, it was clear he didn't understand. I think he's just a dumb guy with a job that's a lot bigger than he is."

"I don't reckon he's qualified for much... maybe a crash test dummy."

We had a laugh over that.

"Remember how you said you didn't want to talk about him before I met him?" Sarah said. "Well it wouldn't have mattered. His problem is he's not just stupid, he's too arrogant to be able to tell he's stupid. It's common with a lot of bureaucrats. He says he wants to come to the village again and talk with the elders. I told him that would be good. Especially now that we have total Gwich'in involvement with the proposed U.S.-Canada Porcupine Caribou Agreement. It's our goal to encourage greater cooperation between the two sides. We're urging our people in Canada to adopt a new model of conservation—a bio-cultural reserve or caribou commons. It would include the entire range of the Porcupine herd in both countries. We need firm protection for the calving and post-calving grounds, plus other critical wildlife habitat. It would also be dedicated to meeting the subsistence needs of the Gwich'in and Inupiat Eskimo cultures. A World Heritage listing may be possible later. When I went through all this with him, he just sat there and stared, without asking a single question. When you can't grasp something, how can you ask about it? So, that's how it's going. At least with him."

"I'm glad I didn't waste any time trying to convince you of that at the river. It's better you found out for yourself."

"The good news is we're coming together, the Canadians, too, on the commons idea. The land has the capacity to serve us forever if it's managed for the long-term. Any fool can take something and ruin it. But taking care is what matters. Who will stand up and explain to future generations why we let the caribou die?"

"There's no such thing as long-term for oil companies. Down home they take the land when and where they want it and leave the explaining to the jackrabbits and coyotes."

"Yes," Sarah said, nodding her head sadly. "They're trying to stop every effort to increase protection of our land. But there are more laws now. This is public land or native land, it belongs to the people, not a few companies. There's more at stake here than just caribou and oil, too. It's the way we, and by that I mean all Americans, feel about who we are. How would it feel, in our hearts, to know that we are a people willing to set something aside for the sake of others? How would it feel to recognize that we don't have to have it all, that we are responsible enough, and strong enough, to leave some for the caribou, the wolf, the bear, and the snowy owl."

When Sarah talked about her people, the land, and the animals that way, I couldn't help but think she was the most beautiful woman in the world. I was trying to pay attention, but the truth was, I was thinking about making love to her again. Having nothing to say, I leaned over and tried to kiss her on the cheek.

"This manager of yours," Sarah went on, pulling her head back and giving me a mean look. "He's going to be a hard one."

"Well," I said, flustered that I'd missed a kiss, "it's good you know it. He's only out to promote his own interests. And you're right, he's none too bright."

"One more thing ," Sarah said. "Something odd has been going on up in the Range."

"What do you mean?"

"We're having fires where we hardly had them before. It started a month ago."

"Well, I hear these last few years have been real dry, and fires are burning hotter than usual this year, that's a fact."

"Do you know that BLM has a new policy of not taking action on some? That's the case with these I'm talking about."

"Did the DM tell you that?"

"In so many words. I just wondered if you knew anything about it. Melvin told me he sends you notes, that you talk with him on the phone, even meet with him. He still thinks you're friends."

I nearly choked as I sat my glass down, shaking my head. "I don't know where he got that notion. I met with him a couple times and that's all. It had nothing to do with oil, letting fires burn, or friendships of any kind."

"Melvin says that's why he invited you to the cannon shooting with the Army."

"Sarah, that's not true at all. I went because Bell asked me to. The DM didn't even know I was going to be there. I'm no friend to him. If anything, it's the direct opposite."

"You think you'll meet with him again?"

"I don't want to, that's for damned sure. No good comes from it. But he's fixin' to call one. There was a note when I got back to call him in the morning. So, I guess that's what I'll do. He claims he wants to help the jumpers but his real aim is to dig up dirt, write reports and get us fired."

"Len," Sarah said, leaning closer, not having heard a word I said. "Do something for me, will you? I'd like to know as much about him and this new let-burn policy as possible. The University of Alaska in Anchorage has analyzed caribou density maps. When you overlay them on the maps showing were oil companies want to drill, two-thirds of it's the same. Two fires are still burning in a major migration route. The rain put the rest out."

"And you think the oil companies started them?"

"Why not? It would be easy enough. They fly around in helicopters. All they'd have to do is let a campfire go here and there or drop something out that would start a fire. Who would know?"

I refilled my glass and took a long drink. Sarah sat there waiting for me to agree with her. And me being me, I went ahead and did.

"So," I said, feeling the beer, life's general goodness, and the pleasure of looking at a beautiful woman, "if the calving grounds burn, the caribou will move and... "

"If it burns enough, they will. They'll have to. Caribou moss can take decades to return to productive feed. Caribou exist on a thin margin. Any disturbance can be critically disruptive."

"I don't believe they'd do such a thing."

"It doesn't matter what you believe. What matters is that we have an agreement with BLM to suppress all the fires in that area until this is settled. That's the policy issue I mentioned."

"I reckon if he's changed the fire policy up there, he sure as hell won't tell me about it."

"Maybe not," Sarah said, winking. "But you know, he talks a lot. Get him on the subject and let him go. If he's responsible for those two fires not being suppressed, it could give us a good deal of leverage, don't you see?"

From double agent to triple agent, I thought. What in the world did I ever do to get myself in such a mess?

"Sarah," I said after another big drink, "you need to understand, I'm not the spying type."

Sarah winked again, and smiled sweet and sneaky-like.

"Well," I finally said. "I reckon I'll see what I can find out. I'll likely be busy jumping fires, though. That's what I came here for, not to be some kind of smokejumping James Bond."

The next morning another memo appeared on the bulletin board by the Operations window.

**rumor control - rumor control - rumor control - rumor control**

Public Service Announcement #1
July 31, 1973

## THE ALASKA SMOKEJUMPERS
## THE NEXT BEST THING TO UNEMPLOYMENT

"The really efficient laborer will be found not to crowd his day with work, but will saunter to his task surrounded by a wide halo of ease and leisure."

~Mohammad R. "Ralph" Louie

Is this job tightening up or what? That's a good question. Rumor Control sources indicate that, indeed it is. Always on the watch for that which would destroy the Alaska Smokejumpers, Rumor Control operatives suspect subversion may have played a role in the recent Mooseheart fire fiasco. Certain individuals (code name WIMPS, for weasels in management positions) are lurking in our midst, posing as our friends, while all the time spouting ingratiating, yet oblivious platitudes about how to fit a gnat's ass over a doorknob.

In the meantime, the good deals just keep rolling in with the pipeline project and its rude incursions both downtown and on the Fort. Alnoka is a loose and thus fascinating organization. Watch closely and pick up on the good deals as they flow from the National Honey Pot. Such as free donuts and coffee 24 hours a day at Building 1514 across the street from the east end of the ramp. Wear a Pipeline ball cap for endless freebies—they're not checking. Talk some pipeline trash, make sure it's legit. Also free bus rides to town every half-hour, pickup at Murphy Hall. Free movies nightly in basement under Admin. building across from FAA building. Hats not required.

—-About the Town—-

The point you must keep in mind when going to town is this; That you are what's happening, not Fairbanks. Mellow out and take 'em like they fall, 'cause you're too good a person to get messed up down there; good deals will be coming your way.

—-Good Deals—-

There are still some good places to eat in Fairbanks and, in Rumor Control approved restaurants, the prices haven't gone up that much. On Two Street (Watch out for the holy rollers and the pimps—part of the new pipeline crowd) the Firelight Room (next to Tommy's) offers a lot to eat for a decent price in a nice setting. Order a sandwich and get everything you get with a dinner. A big relish tray, crackers, good salad, sandwich, fries or baked potato and a little loaf of bread, all for $3.50. For $4.50 order a dinner and you pay too much. The people are nice there and can really dig your trip. On down Two Street the Tiki Cove is still pumping out Asian cuisine for around five bucks a shot. They have a nice bar and it's a good place to take a lady.

The El Sombrero has only jacked up their prices $.50 for a filling, honky-style Mexican meal = $4.50. They are next to Foodland. On south Cushman, Jake's, The Other Place and Mom's are good spots. This is the word from Jim Kasson, an honest man. Then again, if you're in the mood for some real good eatin', get yourself together and head down to Sweet's Bar B Que, and get your wallet out, 'cause you're going to pay for it. Order a combo in the $5.00 size and you get a plate of ribs, cornbread, black-eyed peas and filled up. Beer is $2.00.

Whatever you do, don't go to McDonald's, DQ, (Banana splits $2.50) Kentucky Fried, Uncles, or any other dives. If all else fails you can always go to the Arctic Pancake House and do O.K. Open 24 hrs a day.

For those of you illegally cooking in the barracks, you can buy food at Market Basket and Safeway. Foodland is too high. The little markets are nice and the people are local owners and friendly, like Lindy's out on College Road, and Whole Earth sells "natural foods" with some good buys—but watch out, the woman smokes Pall Mall straights.

On buying booze, check around. Seven bucks a case is a good deal for most beers. Gold Hill Liquor is cheap, but a longs way to drive. Don't let looking for sales become a way of life. The drinking situation makes no sense at all on a per night cost basis. You can go to the Howling Dog in Ester, across from the famed Malamute Saloon, and for a cheap price you could come back with more than you bargained for. This year's Rumor Control Drinking Establishment Award goes to the Boatel with fifty-cent draft beer, a dart board, and a nice view of a ten acre gravel pit.

—-Health and Safety Alert—-

Like to party, Honey? Wanta party with me? Be careful on this one. It'll cost you $40 dollars PLUS. The Black Hand knows. Just remember. Everybody is a person, and there are some truly nice ladies in town. Be nice and be cool. The man is watching.

*STATE HEALTH CLINIC across the street from the High School on Airport Road can solve a lot of your problems, and they are friendly. Don't be shy.

~The Black Hand

Right after PT I called Mort. He was out of his office so I left a message that I was on the third load and couldn't meet with him. A few jumpers were in off fires and we had rolled two loads late the night before while I was at the Blue Marlin with Sarah. With luck I'd get out that day and be gone and leave all my troubles in Fairbanks where they belonged. Everywhere you looked jumpers were busy making firepacks, rolling streamers on the new roller Johnny B. and I made, loading airplanes and filling out fire reports. It was our policy that, unless we were over-whelmed, Alaska jumpers would do all the work, so a few boosters were sitting on the sunny side of the T-Hangar greasing boots, reading and writing letters. Four or five were shooting hoops under the new basketball backboard in paracargo. I went to rigging parachutes over in the new loft. Johnny B. was rigging on the table next to mine.

"Where'd you go last night," Johnny B. said, as he untangled suspension lines.

"I went out."

"I know that. I saw you leave. Maybe you better tell me about it."

"I don't reckon you need to know everything."

"Maybe not but you've been acting strange, worse than strange, even."

"I got a few problems, but I can't see that telling you will help."

"No, but it can't make them worse, right? Come on, where'd you go?"

"Figure it out for yourself," I said. "You always think you know more about me than I do."

"Okay, how about... you took Sarah to dinner."

I strapped down the risers on my chute and didn't answer. Bob Dylan was on the radio singing about a girlfriend who had become a rolling stone and caused him a bunch of trouble, and it was hard to think about that and Johnny B.'s pestering, and, at the same time, make sure I was packing a parachute right.

"I knew it," he said. "You had moose-eyes for her, both in the hospital and at the campground. Where'd you sneak off to?"

"Look who's talking sneaky, "I said, "That Black Hand fella's sneaky as they come, him and that Mohammad Ralph Louie."

"Where'd you go, Lenny?"

"To the Blue Marlin, dammit. Now, does that make you feel any better?"

"You can't imagine," Johnny B. grinned. "Where'd you go after that?"

Well, now that beat all. Once Johnny B. made up his mind to hound me, he never let up.

"I've never seen such a stubborn bastard," I said. "Pay attention and pack that damned chute. Who knows, you might have to jump it yourself."

"Oh, I'm not that crazy," he chuckled. "I never jump my own chutes."

"Well, you might have to one day and it'd serve you right if you did."

I didn't want to talk anymore, so I kept quiet. I needed time to think. I needed to get out of Fairbanks, even if I did have a pretty girl.

"Let's go out tonight," Johnny B. said. "Tanana Grass is playing at the Howling Dog. Let's go out there and listen to some bluegrass."

"I'm not making no plans for tonight. We'll probably jump anyway."

"If we don't, then let's go. What do you say?"

"I told you. I'm not making plans. Now shut up and get to work on that chute."

Two loads were held on stand by for lunch, so feeling sleepy after spending a night with Sarah, I went to the barracks for a nap. On my door there was a note to call Bill Fentori.

"Hello," he answered, "Bill Fentori here."

"Inspector Fentori, this is Len Swanson."

Mr. Fentori explained that he was an Arson Investigator, not an inspector.

"I was hoping you'd call," he said. "I'm in Fairbanks. I need to go to Fort Greeley and see your campfire, take some notes and photographs."

"I reckon that won't be possible. I'll likely jump today, tomorrow for sure."

"Look, Len, I'm talking to you because of what you told me. I need to proceed with this investigation. If not, I need to get back to Washington. If you want I'll talk to your District Manager and have you put on hold for a day."

I froze right there. The world of fire inspectors and Mort and oil companies had me trapped.

No! No! Don't do that. I asked you to keep my name out of it, and that's the way it has to be."

"Even with the *District Manager*?

"Especially him," I said. "And I'm in no position to argue about it, either."

There was pause, and for a moment I thought the phone had gone dead.

"All right," he finally said, "then we'll go tonight, right after you get off work."

I thought a minute. I was screwed. He would take only so much of me and my secret ways. I wanted to see Sarah again if we didn't jump, but now instead of that, I was facing an all night, five-hundred mile drive that was sure to do nothing but lead to more trouble.

"Len, you have to realize that this is probably nothing I can build a case on. The evidence is over a month old. People, no doubt, tromped all over that fire mopping it up. So let's go and get it over with, then you can return to your normal routine and so can I."

"I reckon you're right," I said, against all sense. "Meet me at the flag-pole outside the main gate to Fort Wainwright at six o'clock. If I'm not there by six thirty you'll know I jumped a fire or been held on stand by."

"Six at the flagpole, Fentori said. "See you then."

I went back to work and spent the rest of the afternoon wishing for a fire call more than I had in my whole life. At three they rolled one load east toward Canada. That moved me up to the second load. At five we gathered in the Ready Room for a crew meeting. Johnny B. and The Fat Indian made a dash for the I-Hear-You-Walkin'-Chair. Johnny B. got there first, but The Fat Indian ran him off and took it himself.

Big Al welcomed the down-south boosters, talked about all the good work the crew had done, then asked Quinlan for an update on Gene Hobbs. Al had sent Bob to Anchorage for a few days to look after him. Gene's wife had flown up from Moscow, Idaho. Quinlan stood before the group, and told us that Gene was flat on his back inside a large stainless steel wheel with his body parts pulled in different directions. A metal plate had been screwed into his skull to hold his head still.

"Gene looks like a mummy," Quinlan said. "His head's bandaged with just holes for his eyes, nose, and mouth. He's lost a lot of his long-term memory. Some short-term, too. He knows he's a smokejumper though, and he said to tell you guys hello."

The preliminary investigation had been completed. The emergency back pack chute Gene was wearing had been tossed in and out of several aircraft during the previous week of the fire bust. Jarring the chute had most likely caused a condition called pin creep. Tightly compressed parachutes are held together by elastic flaps that are secured by metal eyelets drawn tightly over small metal cones. The cones have holes in them through which the pins of the ripcord are placed to hold the eyelets on. Chutes are checked frequently to ensure that the pins have not slipped. During a week of repeated fire runs, late night missions, plus different spotters moving gear from plane to plane, the chute had probably escaped inspection. As Gene bent down to get streamers from the spotters kit, the stress on the tightly packed canopy was the final move needed to pull the pins out, releasing the flaps. First out was the spring loaded pilot chute, followed by the canopy off the pack tray filling with air and exploding out the door. Judging from his body mass and the damage to the door of Jumper 54, it was estimated that Gene had accelerated — in only five feet — from 0 to 70 mph. He had been pulled off his feet and slammed into the aft part of the door, his helmet and right shoulder striking its upper left corner and knocking him out. As his body spun out the door, his right foot hit the forward part of the door opening, breaking his right leg. Doctors speculated that being unconscious may have saved his life since a limp body offers less resistance; that it may have helped both with the initial impact and when he landed. After Gene was outside the plane the canopy caught on the horizontal stabilizer of the tail. As he fell away the chute pulled free and opened with only a few tears. Hanging in his harness, adrift over Alaska, an unconscious Gene Hobbs had a broken leg, a broken arm, a broken collar bone, some messed up internal organs, and a broken neck. Jack Anusewitz, the former Army Medic, was credited with saving his life. One vertebra in Gene's neck was broken ninety percent through. Careful handling by Jack and the rescuers kept the vertebra together, and that made the difference. Quinlan finished up with a few questions, then Big Al thanked him and continued the meeting.

The Volpar had beaten several helicopters to close-in fires. The reason, Al claimed, was its 200 mph cruising speed. Mitchell went over what he called the new physical training standards. Although we regularly did PT, or some version of it, we weren't as strict as bases in the Lower 48. And we didn't do it every day. That's how it was when I first showed up. But now, Mitchell said we had to do PT every day, for a full hour, right after roll call, even if we were hung over. That brought on complaints about tightening up, lack of trust, and the coming ruination of Alaska smoke-jumping. Kasson got pissed-off and, after reviewing the number of times he'd nearly been killed in Vietnam, warned the squad leaders that if they started badgering him about PT, he'd kick their asses. I couldn't see how it was going to work out. One reason was Big Al himself. He was no lover of PT, and did it less than anyone. Al believed everyone was born with just so many heartbeats, and if you did too much exercise, you'd just use them up faster and die sooner. Mitchell said that we had to run at least a mile and a half, do at least 7 overhand pull ups, 25 push-ups, and 45 sit-ups daily—Minimum! The rest of the time we could do whatever exercises we wanted as long as we kept at it. Everyday, regular work days, weekend stand by, at all outstations, in Alaska, or wherever. The only excuses were if you'd just come in off a tough fire, were on crutches, in the hospital, or dead. In those cases, you could skip a day.

The crew went on grumbling and griping about the new PT standards, but it was near quitting time, so I ducked out the back and took off one minute before six in order to get away from Johnny B. There was no way I was going to tell him about Fort Greeley.

We crossed Minto Flats flying west. The Doug's engines throttled back to cruising speed and most of the crew was already asleep on the floor in chicken bags. I looked out the window as I had done all the way from Fairbanks. The Tanana River ran in braided channels that flashed silver in the morning sun. Thirty miles to the south the Wood River Buttes lay low and flat in a broad plain of oxbow rivers. Beyond them stood the Alaska Range, a wall of ice and snow towering 20,000 feet above the rest of the country. I felt something flying over Alaska that I didn't feel any other place, not even in Texas. It wasn't just the beauty, either. It was the scale; big and grand, empty and wide-open. On most days visibility was two hundred miles. On both the eastern and western horizons, I could see the curvature of the earth. There were good feelings in that, but that morning it only made me feel worse. That's the trouble when you go and get yourself into a mess.

I had barely made it back from Fort Greeley in time for the fire call. Bell was in the barracks and told me we had one, so I jumped in my pickup and headed over. I was already road-foundered from my all-night run with Mr. Fentori. We'd gone straight to Army headquarters and got right in with his badge and some papers. But, when we got out to the burn, the road was filled with burned spruce fallen ever which way. We had no chainsaw, so we took off walking. The country looked different too, but I could see the little knoll we'd camped on and that helped navigate some. It was midnight by the time we got to the jump spot. I told Inspector Fentori how the fire blew up and the tornado got after me. A half-hour later we found the campfire. I showed him the line of ashes left by the burned root. He took pictures and notes and made measurements. By the time we left it was nearly 2:00 AM., and we had to walk back through all those downed trees. By the time we got to the car I was tired, but Inspector Fentori was completely worn out. We stopped for coffee and some breakfast at an all-night place in Delta. He was ruined after that and I had to drive since he couldn't keep awake. I didn't get any sleep at all. But that wasn't the worst of it.

When I showed up for the fire call, Miles Morgan was there waiting in the T-Hangar parking lot. He walked right up to my pickup and started in.

"The District Manager wants you in his office, now."

"I haven't got time. We're going on a fire."

"You just came in off one," Miles objected, not knowing what he was talking about. "You'll have to wait and go on the next one. Tell them you're sick."

"Look," I said, getting mad, "don't go telling me what to do. I'm on the jump list and we've got a fire to jump, and that's what I'm going to do. Tell the DM I'm sorry but fires come first."

Miles wheeled around and grabbed a manila folder out of his car.

"Go ahead. Jump a fire," he said. "But when you get back, I'd advise you not to talk with the fire investigator. If you do, I'll have no choice but to show these to the District Manager."

He opened the folder. "Don't think you can steal them, either. I have duplicates."

I filed through the photos. There we were at the Pig Party, drunk, Big Al down in the mud with Teeny, Mitchell buck naked with a can of beer in one hand and a joint in the other. He even had some of the Red Lizard he took the day he found it in the warehouse. There was this letter, too. Just then the siren went off and Miles glanced over at the T-Hangar, so I slipped it in my back pocket.

"You no-count, worthless— "

"It's like I said," Miles interrupted, grabbing the folder, "you talk to the investigator and I show these to the DM."

Miles got in his car and drove off, leaving me mad enough to eat rocks. What he had would ruin the crew. What would they think if they found out I had been in on secret meetings with Mort and had allowed the photos to fall into his hands? Once the state office got wind of it some people would be fired, starting with me. Not in a million years would the crew understand why I'd caused such a mess just so I could talk to some BLM outsider from Washington. Fired or not, with the crew I would be finished.

"Okay everybody," Hairface yelled from the cockpit. "Fifteen out."

I took off my harness and set it near my reserve, then dug into my gear bag. After I put on my jump jacket, pants and harness, Johnny B. helped me with my main chute and reserve, then knelt at my feet and began speaking out loud, going through the buddy check:

"Left boot strap under heel. Right boot strap under heel.

Leg pocket tie-straps, tight and tied.

Left leg strap snapped. Right leg strap snapped."

Johnny B. got to his feet and continued.

"Chest strap through buckle, tail tucked.

"Lower left reserve snap—check. Lower right reserve snap—check.

"Left upper reserve snap closed, safety pin in and bent. Right upper reserve snap closed."

"Door coming open," Hairface shouted as he pulled it in and swung it towards the hell hole in the tail. The sweet smell of smoke rushed into the plane as we rounded the head, bouncing in turbulent air.

Johnny B. continued the check, unsnapping the reserve inspection cover.

"Right and left reserve pins in place, safety thread unbroken and sealed.

Cover snapped shut. Reserve knife blade pointed away from body.

Left capewell seated, one, two," he said as he clicked both the closing fitting and the protective outer cap. "Right capewell fitting seated, one, two."

Taking the static line hook in his hand Johnny B. opened and closed it, noting the travel of the clip and the snap when it closed.

"Static line hook good," he said as he tucked it back under my reserve knife.

Following the static line around my left shoulder he checked the static line stows.

"Line stows good." Then facing me, he asked. "Helmet, gloves, let-down rope?"

"Got 'em."

"Okay Len. You're good.

I knew that all the time he was checking my gear he was thinking I'd gone and snuck off with Sarah again. But he didn't say anything and I was glad of it.

The Peace River fire burned thirty-five miles west of Granite Mountain in typical Seward Peninsula rolling hills, tundra, and grasslands. Bell was first man and would be fire boss. I watched as the fire appeared under the trailing edge of the wing, its tail and flanks burning moderately, its head a solid wall of orange rising up into a gray smoke column.

"First stick," Hairface shouted. "Hook up."

Bell and Rake hooked up. Dow and Shearer got ready as second stick. Johnny B. and I would follow them. The plane turned final. Hairface had his head out in the slipstream with his beard blowing ever which way. Then, head back in again, he talked into his head set. The plane yawed left.

"Get ready," he shouted, looking up at Bell and Rake.

Down came the slap, and they disappeared into the roar of the slipstream, falling along the fuselage, as Hairface pulled in their deployment bags. I watched as they drifted in the great space above the fire. The second stick got ready. Dow cleared the door with Shearer right behind. Instantly there was a loud bang as something slammed the side of the plane, then rumbled off.

"Shearer had a bad exit," Hairface yelled. On the next pass Jumper 56 leveled its big broad wings and pulled on final. "Get in the door."

I stepped forward, grabbed both sides, planted my left foot on the threshold, looked down quickly, then back to the end of the wing.

"Get ready." I felt Johnny B. pushing slightly on my main.

Seconds later I watched the big tail of the plane pass above me, then disappear. My chute opened. Johnny B.'s did the same. Instantly the chaos of jump were gone, replaced by the sudden silence. I checked my position, then took a look around. To the south, Norton Sound extended out to the Bering Sea. Straight west, a hundred miles, I could see the end of the Seward Peninsula and more of the Bering Sea. Across it stretched a barely visible, thin, gray line — the coast of Siberia.

Turning into the wind at 400 feet I watched the smoke swirl across the burn. My landing would be backwards and fast. The forward speed of the FS-10 was ten mph, and the wind was gusting to twenty. The ground came rushing up. I hit and went flying like a rag doll, jerked off my feet and onto my back. In seconds Dow was on my canopy, knocking it down.

The rest of the load came down with jumpers running to deflate chutes before they dragged someone off. Rakowski yelled that Shearer was okay, then something about him acting more ringy than normal. I found Pat sitting on a clump of coral moss, rubbing his head.

*"Real smart,"* he said. "My static line was under my arm when I when out, so I got a good close look at the side of the plane. Those high-speed rivets are pretty interesting, you know. It was like slow motion. In each panel between the rivets I saw a part of my life — a crying baby, a mean little kid with a wooden sword, my wrecked '57 Nash Rambler, my first fire jump. It was all there. Ha, ha. A two-second movie of my life."

Pat showed me the yellow stains under the arm of his jump jacket. Usually the static line runs from the static line cable straight to the back of the chute so that when the jumper clears the door the pull comes straight off his back. With the line under his arm, it spun him around and slammed him against the plane, then banged him down the side.

"I thought it tore my arm off," Pat chuckled. "It was like I was on the end of a big rubber band, kabang, kabang, yaaahhh. If that isn't bad enough, now Rakowski's going around saying I'm ringy. Imagine hearing that from him."

On the first cargo pass two chutes came out, the first attached to four cases of rats, the second to a single sideband radio — our only contact with the outside world. One opened, the other did not. While the nearly indestructible C-rats sailed down like a feather, the wooden case that contained the radio streamered-in and hit the ground in an explosion of wood splinters, glass and smoke that blew tubes and batteries fifty feet.

Quinlan took seven up the right flank working in off the river, while Bell and the rest of us headed up the left side in a typical split-and-beat strategy. Wind driven, the fire's resistance to control was high at first. But by midnight the wind had died down and the head slowed into a run of snaky fingers hidden in heavy smoke. Our crew broke for a quick rat, then turned the corner and started across. By 3:00 AM there was hardly a quarter-mile of open perimeter between us and Quinlan's bunch. In the back of everyone's mind was the simple understanding that until the fire was stopped our lives would stay miserable. Smokejumpers don't normally get support from outside forces. On difficult fires the story is simple; the sooner we catch it, the sooner the hard work ends. If we fail to contain a fire in the first burning period, usually the first day and night, then we will be stuck with a day, maybe two, of extended attack and all the effort that goes with it. While this is true for most wildland initial attack crews, it's especially true with smokejumpers.

Once we saw Quinlan's crew across the head, we shifted our bodies into high gear and our brains into low. On and on we beat until our arms ached and the bottoms of our burlap bags blew out and we had to tie knots in them to hold the wet moss that provided the weight needed to the beat out the flames. It was time to dig deep and every one knew it. From time to time different ones stepped back from the heat and smoke to kneel down and find cleaner air nearer the ground. Every last one of us was racked with fatigue, coughing and spitting, eyes burning from smoke and sweat, sucking in ash, our heads splitting from oxygen-depleted blood. No one complained. Despite the misery, I couldn't help but think about Mort and Miles, the photos, and the threat they posed to a crew. Men like Rake and Kasson and Marshall, fresh from the war in Vietnam. Or Mountain Puss and Melvin with scars on their hands and necks, back on the line. How different it would be to just have to endure the hardship of the fire. I had done it many times and always got through it. But now there was this gnawing in my gut that had been there since I stood outside the T-Hangar and watched Miles drive away. For what we did, and who we were, to go unappreciated by those who had never seen it, and likely couldn't do it themselves, made me plain sad.

Ahead, through the smoke, I saw the leaders of Quinlan's group, beating faster and harder the closer they came. Our guys did the same. With the last few feet beat out, we joined up in a flurry of flying burlap and hooting and hollering, high-fiving, and carrying on like kids.

"Aackk! What have you girls been doing?" Quinlan said, his shirt soaked with sweat.

"Well, well," Rake said, "if it's not Burlap Bob and the right-flank Butt Snorts."

Quinlan took a long drink from his canteen, "For a while I thought we were going to have to put this whole thing out by ourselves."

"Shit!" Rake said, "If we'd as much river as you did we'd been around it by midnight."

"Nothing feels better than catching a tough fire," Bob said.

"Better than prancing around annoying people?" Rake laughed.

Others jumped on Quinlan, calling him names like Chicken Legs, Stewing Chicken, and Mother Duck.

"Aackk," Quinlan replied. "Chihuahuas, nipping at the heels of the noble lion."

# 12

Sitting alone on a knoll, I looked out over a green land of rolling hills and windblown grass. To the west, the black scar of our 1000 acre fire ran south, fanning out into a ragged half-mile head. We had flown a long ways. We had made our jumps. We had put our heads and hearts together and had caught a tough fire. Still, I couldn't get over the way I felt. I couldn't decide whether I didn't care anymore or that, if I did, I was too mentally worn out to do much about it.

I took the letter I had stolen from Miles out of my pocket and read it again.

To My Rocket Man
Fossil Creek Cabin

A quick note while you're sleeping. Great idea to come to this BLM cabin. So, so magical. From the time I saw you at the party with the burned pig's head, lighting those rockets, I knew you were special. And, now, oh my gosh. I've never known anyone like you, so gentle and giving in all the ways that count for a woman. Too bad about last night, the candle I mean, and the little rocket man with the funny helmet. I was glad to kiss him and make him feel better. And now that he's on injured reserve, I'll be waiting so we can get him back on my jump list. Hugs and kisses from your favorite redhead,

Betsy

I didn't see any profit in tearing the letter up since Miles claimed he had copies, just like with the pictures. I heard something and turned around and here come Johnny B. trudging up the hill. He flopped down, took Duke out of his PG bag, and set him between us but closer to me. Duke looked right at me with his yellow button eyes, he wanted some answers.

"Nice fire, huh?" I said.

Johnny B. sat there, elbows resting on his knees, rubbing his head.

"What is it, Len? Something's wrong. Duke thinks you're about to crack up."

"Oh, no. It's nothing important. I'm just tired is all. Hard night, huh?"

"Hard but good," Johnny B. said, still rubbing his head. "Are you going to tell us or just keep dragging your ass around like usual?"

I knew that was coming.

"I reckon you won't take no for an answer," I finally said. "I just feel bad about a couple things, that's all. Last time I felt this bad was when one of our Redding jumpers got killed."

"I remember that," Johnny B. said. "What was his name, Tom something, right?"

I didn't feel like talking about Tom, either, but I thought if I did it might throw Johnny B. off.

"Tom Remington," I said. "You sure you want to hear this?"

"I'd like to, yeah. You were there, right?"

Johnny B. got some John Wayne crackers out of his PG bag and was fixing to eat them with some C-rat peanut butter.

"It was three years ago, 1970, on the Big Bar Ranger District of the Shasta-Trinity. We had this hot little two-acre lightning fire near the top of a steep ridge covered with big Doug fir and pine, and mixed hardwoods—the Oak Fire is what they finally named it. Tom was twenty-six. We called him Remmie for short. We had a sixteen-man load on 51 Zulu, the Redding Doug. The last time I saw Tom alive, he was waiting behind me in the plane, ready to go. I jumped number twelve, third man, fourth stick. Not long after I landed the Doug made a cargo pass. A couple minutes later I heard a jumper coming through the woods yelling if I'd seen where the chainsaw landed. I asked what was the matter. It's Remmie he said, and I think he's dead. He was kind of crying and talking at the same time. I couldn't believe it, so I ran across the hill and come on four or five guys gathered under a big madrone."

I stopped for a while, looked over at Johnny B., and let the images come back. It was the first time I'd seen a dead smokejumper.

"I got there just as our fire boss was turning his face to the sun," I said, going on with my story. "His eyes were wide open, pupils real big, you know, and... they made no reaction to the light. None at all. His eyes were dead, which meant he was, too. But they laid him down in the madrone leaves and pumped his heart and traded off breathing for him anyway. They did that for nearly an hour, then the helicopter came."

"Shitty deal," Johnny B. said.

"The jumpers on the plane saw the whole thing. He went out third man with too much static line pulled off the rubber bands on the back of his main. When he started for the door part of his static line blew out and he stepped on it, tripped, and fell on his belly. He should have quit right there, that was his big mistake. But he reached up and grabbed the sides of the door and pulled himself forward, still on his belly, head first. With his head out in the slipstream it caught the extra static line and blew a loop out in front of his head so that it caught on the hinge of his face mask. By the time he got to the end of his static line he was falling head down in a dive with the line running from the chute around the front of his helmet then straight back to plane. The debag and his head were jerked violently together. It tore his helmet off. The chute opened with him dangling under it, his head slumped forward almost to his reserve. His spinal cord was completely separated at the base of his neck. He felt no pain, just a flash, then darkness. You can't die faster. His heart never beat another beat. There was this long gash on his cheek where the face mask cut it and the blood ran out just a few inches. His pupils looked like black marbles, and that jagged cut down his face... you don't forget. I've dreamed it more times than I can count. Terrible as it was though, when I flew off that mountain just before dark, even though I'd decided I had to quit smoke-jumping, I took from that place a greater love for life than I ever had before."

"But you didn't quit," Johnny B. said.

"I'll tell you what, Johnny B., it was a damn sad deal. I understood I could break a leg or a back or an arm, but I never seriously thought I could get killed. I just couldn't image putting my folks through something like that. Half the crew said they were going to quit, too."

Johnny B. went on eating his crackers, keeping quiet, not saying anything.

"Like I said, it was a sad deal. Remmie was getting married in two weeks. His best man jumped in the stick with him. He saw right off that Tom was hurt and yelled for the other jumper in the stick to go for the spot and get help, and that he would follow Tom. He did. But when they came into the trees Tom's buddy hung up over a hundred feet in the top of this big fir, while Tom sailed down between several big ones and landed in a small clearing. His chute caught in the madrone and set him down on his butt in a bed of leaves, sitting upright, hanging on his risers. Remmie had the softest landing of any of us."

I stopped, pulled up a grass stem, put it in my mouth, and looked out over the country.

"Well," Johnny B. said, "your friend, Tom, he died doing what he loved."

"He did," I said softly. "And that matters, doesn't it?"

"Of course it does," Johnny B. said. "Any life worth living is one worth dying for."

"I reckon so. I know that's the way we talked about it after the accident."

"So why didn't you quit?"

"It was the investigation. Back in the loft, they laid out all his gear and the chute on a packing table. For two days only our base manager, our loft foreman, and some big wigs from the Regional Office were allowed to look at it. Then, they finally said we could go in, too. Right off, one of our regular jumpers picked up a magnifying glass that was on the table, and went to looking at the static line. He called us over. Just a few feet from where the static line attached on to the deployment bag was this faint pattern of crosshatches, the same a face mask would make. Someone got a helmet and laid it on the marks and they matched perfectly. That's when they decided they had to find Tom's helmet. They found it three hundred yards downhill from the jump spot. After they brought it in they found yellow fibers wedged in the corner of the mask that matched those on the static line. That proved what happened. Once I saw that, I knew it was because of a bad exit and poor body position. With it being a freak accident, I felt better about staying on. We all did. All except his best man... he quit anyway."

We sat a moment looking at the country and the beautiful day. For some reason, telling the story made me feel better. It also had thrown Johnny B. off the subject of me and my ass dragging. After a while, looking in the direction of the sun, I saw a faint shimmer across the burn. Thin lines of silvery light were moving over the black tussocks.

"It's the spiders," Johnny B. said. "When a fire comes they go under the tussocks, crawl down the stalk and hide where the air's cool and damp. After the fire dies out they crawl on top of the tussocks and wait for the wind. When it blows hard enough they spin a strand of web, and when it gets long enough they let go and drift away wherever the wind takes them."

We kept quiet a while, then I said, "Sounds a lot like smokejumpers to me."

It was the third day of our fire. Thirty six hours had passed since the last smoke, and besides lying around wondering why we hadn't had a flyover, we were a few rats short of running out of food. To make things worse, we didn't have shade. The trees were too puny to hold up a cargo chute, so we had to sit in the sun. Each day passed the same, calm and clear in the morning, windy and clear in the afternoon, then calm again in the evening when the sun swung low and the mosquitoes came out in swarms.

Bell hiked to the knoll and tried calling in the blind on his radio. It was too far to Galena for a hand-held but he thought maybe a plane might hear him. None did. Even though the single-sideband radio had augured-in and looked like someone had beat on it with a hammer, Quinlan had got it to where it made strange noises. Up on the knoll he spent hours calling over and over while Dow and Shearer held up the antenna with two skinny willow poles.

"Galena, Galena, Galena," Quinlan squalled. "Peace River jumpers. Do you copy?"

The only thing he heard back was outer space noises, whistling, crackling and hissing with occasional growls that he took for human language.

"Any station. This is Fire #5051, broadcasting in the blind. Sixteen jumpers, Peace River, west of Granite Mountain. Three days. Low on food. Anybody copy?"

That night we sat in camp eating a few grayling, some blueberries, and the last C-rats. The whiskey had been finished the night before, so there went our favorite evening entertainment. Firewood was also a problem. There were just sticks from dwarf willow thickets along the river. It was going to be another long night after another long day, our food gone, not enough wood for a decent campfire, no booze. The crew talked and told stories, Johnny B. was reading a new book, *The Strange Last Voyage of Donald Crowhurst*. Duke sat on a cubitainer. Even he was bored.

Kasson pulled out a plastic bag of powdered imitation orange drink called Tang. He poured about a fourth of it into an empty canteen, then added equal parts of water and Everclear.

"Not that again," Quinlan said. "Is that all you can think to do, drink grain alcohol?"

"What, no Orangu*tang*?" Kasson smiled. "Beats the hell out of sitting on a hill yelling at a piece of junk. Try some. This shit's 190 proof. If everyone had this instead of whiskey we could party for three more days."

Jim Kasson had come to Alaska straight from Vietnam. Over there he was known as Killer Kasson. As a CIA agent, he had trained secret forces in the mountains of Laos. Forces that the US claim didn't exist, even to the point of abandoning them when things went sour. Kasson never talked much about it. But when he went to drinking at night in the barracks, sometimes the stuff he yelled was its own telling. Word was he had left the agency knowing things it didn't want him to know; that he had prepared two duplicate packets of information and given them to his brother. He then told those that didn't like him that, if he were to die suspiciously, an unidentified person would present one packet to the U.S. Justice Department and the other to the New York Times.

"Fastest and cheapest blast you can get," Kasson said. "Kills the bugs in your guts and the spooks in your head."

Kasson held his canteen towards me. I took a swig.

"Ahhh, damn," I said, as Orangutang went down my throat cold then hot, then really hot, like I imagined sugar-flavored gasoline might do.

"Whewee!" I exhaled, sticking my tongue out to cool it off. "It ain't all that bad, I guess."

"It might kill the bugs," Rake said, "but what about these damned mosquitoes?"

"Well," Quinlan said, "after sucking 190 proof blood, they should be easier to kill."

Mosquitoes can be bad on Alaska fires, but I had no idea they could get that bad. It would have helped to have had a smoky campfire, but we didn't have one, smoky or otherwise. Campfires can be a lot of company and also help keep mosquitoes away. As it was, we just sat there in clouds of them and stayed bored. Each man had at least 200 buzzing in a big bubble around his head. No matter how much Army bug dope I put on, they pressed in and bumped my face every few seconds. If you talked, you sucked one in every minute or so. They floated dead in the coffee and hot chocolate until we drank them, because there was too many to fish out, especially with fingers coated with bug dope.

Quinlan took the two spoons he carried in his PG bag, and began tapping them on his knee. Johnny B. got out his mouth harp and joined in. In no time he was singing.

Once upon a time there was an engineer
Drove his locomotive both far and near
Had a little monkey that sat on a stool
Watchin' everything that the engineer do
One day the engineer went for a bite to eat
Left the monkey sittin' on the engineer's seat

Monkey pulled the throttle, locomotive jumped the gun
Made ninety miles an hour on the mainline run

Johnny B. blew in between the singing and Quinlan was tapping spoons and grinning like a possum in a corn crib.

Big locomotive is makin' good time
Big locomotive comin' down the line
Old locomotive number ninety-nine
Left the engineer with a worried mind

Engineer rang the dispatcher on the phone
Told him all about how his locomotive was gone
Get on the wire, we got trouble tonight
'Cause the monkey's got the mainline sewed up tight

Switch operator got the message in time
Had a north bound limited on the same line
Open the switch, gonna put him in the hole
'Cause the monkey's got the locomotive under control

Big locomotive comin' down the line
Big locomotive comin' right on time
Big locomotive number ninety-nine
Left the engineer with a worried mind
Yeahhhh... left the engineer with a worried mind.

The jumpers cheered and clapped. All but Bell.

"God ah mighty," Bell said, swinging at mosquitoes. "I don't know what's worse, that music or these stupid bugs."

"Aackk," Quinlan said, "quit sniveling about the mosquitoes. They could be worse."

"I'm not sniveling," Bell snapped. "And don't go lecturing about worse. I know worst. Like on the coast that time."

"Pray tell, my man," Quinlan said, "Exactly how bad is worst?"

"Don't go calling me *your man*, either," Bell snapped. "I'm not your man or anybody else's."

"It's just a figure of speech," Quinlan said. "Meant to gain accord, build good cheer, calm the beast, and..."

"I don't care what it is, I don't need it. I like to talk like a smokejumper. Maybe you should do the same."

"I see," Quinlan said. "Then, just how bad were the little bastards on the fucking coast?"

*"The worst,"* Bell said, his voice now low and dark. *"The absolute worst.* That fire in '71 out on the coast. Remember that, Rake?"

"South of Unalakleet?"

"Yes, *south of Unalakleet,*" Bell hissed, as if he hated everything south of Unalakleet.

"Yeah," Mountain Puss said. "No shit. They were bad. Bit me right through my Levis. I had to put bug dope on my ass to take a shit, but they still bit me on the balls."

As if seeing a vision, Bell put his hands up like a holy roller preacher. His eyes got big. The mosquitoes on the coast south of Unalakleet were back. Right there in our camp.

"Clouds of them," he said. "They came at us as soon as we hit the ground. One got inside my helmet and bit me on the lip before I knew what was going on." Bell made a squeaky sound, then let fly, "Sneaky little bastards. Hanging around all the time. Buzzing, buzzing, always buzzing. Acting like they know what they're doing. Poking their noses at you. They were the strongest I'd ever seen, too. They'd come up under the helicopter, get in behind you, out of the wind, and hang on trying to bite. The helicopter couldn't even blow them away."

That did it. Don Bell was fighting mad.

"Pesky, chickenshit cowards! Hiding there, out of the wind, trying to bite you everywhere. Then, when the helicopter powered-up, they'd hang on as long as they could, crouching low, trembling in the prop blast, until they finally got blown off into the brush or sucked in the engine. Ha, ha, ha."

Once we quit laughing at Bell, Mountain Man said, "It was really bad, man. We were literally bug-fucked."

"Wait a minute," Quinlan protested. "Literally bug-fucked? You mean to say you were actually being fucked by insects?"

"Oh, up yours, Quinlan," Mountain puss groaned.

"That casts doubt on the whole story," Quinlan said. "My, how the weak crumble in the face of adversity."

"You're one to talk," Bell said. "You weren't even..."

"Aackk," Quinlan interrupted, "glorious is the moment of torment. So very Tartarean. Just as the Greeks well understood, 'Tis punishment for all the wickedness and evil doing of..."

"Fuck evil and wickedness," Kasson blared out, throwing his empty Orangutang canteen aside. "Fuck it all. The Greeks, the geeks, the gooks, and all the war mongering brass sitting on their asses, sipping champagne and eating caviar and watching from the tops of their big hotels in Saigon, while our troops are out in the fucking jungle dying, day after day after day, to take the same fucking hill for the tenth fucking time. *For no reason.*"

The crew looked at Kasson, stunned.

"Hey Jim," Rake said. "Easy, now. Take it easy, buddy. It's gonna be all... "

" I don't give a shit. Nobody gives a shit. You come home and all you hear is people bitching about the war. Fuck it."

"Forget them," Rake said. "Forget all that stuff. You know as well as I do that, when it comes to Vietnam, there are only two kinds of people... those who were there, and those who weren't."

A long silence hung over camp.

"I'm sorry," Kasson finally said, reaching for the Everclear. "I'm sorry I blew up. I apologize."

The next day about noon we heard a smokejumper aircraft on Bell's radio. Everybody in camp cheered. At first we thought it was talking to us, but in no time it was clear it wasn't. It was headed for Granite Mountain to pickup a load of jumpers. They said there was a fire bust going on and some jumpers were out of communication.

"Out of communication?" Bell yelled at his radio. "What do you mean *out of communication*? Answer your radio, you idiot. We're not out of communication, you are."

"Aackk," Quinlan said, "Irksome children. Now I see why lions eat their young."

"We can hear you," Bell yelled. "We're on the Peace River fire. Look at the spotter's report. We been here four days. We're out of food. We're out of coffee. Kasson's drinking Orangutang. We need demobed."

After trying several times to reach the jumpship, Bell threw his radio down and stomped it.

"Bell hasn't been right lately," Rake laughed. "Not since he roasted his gopher at Fossil Creek."

Our fifth day passed like the others, only with more worry. Kasson and Rake spent most of it talking on the knoll, alone. Bell said they were talking about Vietnam. We caught a few more grayling, baked them in campfire coals or boiled them in goodie cans. We found a few more patches of blueberries but most weren't ripe yet. The batteries in the sideband had gone dead. That evening Kasson and Rake went hunting and Kasson ground-sluiced two spruce hens with the sawed-off Winchester Model 12 he broke down and carried in his leg pocket. We cut them up and roasted them on the fire. They tasted good, a little ashy, and ended up making us more hungry than ever.

"E hoggis mortiem," Rake said, belching. "Big pig gets most."

By midmorning of the sixth day the crew was bored and starved and downright disgusted. Something had gone wrong. Quinlan had one of the WAC charts that pilots and spotters use in his PG bag and went to studying it. He figured it was thirty miles to Granite Mountain. That's a long walk in tundra and, although it was higher ground, it wasn't all that much higher. It would be easy to miss. Sometimes BLM sometimes cached fuel barrels at the airstrip. With fires in the area, maybe there would be a staging area. Quinlan estimated he could make it in two days.

That afternoon the wind blew in from the coast steady and strong. I walked out to a firepack that we hadn't yet brought to camp, hoping against hope to find a missed C-rat. When I lifted it up, a gust caught the cargo chute, jerked the firepack against my legs and knocked me down. The chute took off with the firepack bouncing behind, files, first aid kits and EFF cord flying ever which way. I dove on the firepack and hung on as it hopped across the tundra then stopped. The bunch in camp cheered.

As we cussed the fact that the last C-rats were gone, Kasson and Melvin dragged the firepack and chute into camp, then stood around pointing at different things, scratching their heads. In no time they had pulled the internal packframe out of the firepack, cut the fiberglass tape that bound its corners and mashed the heavy cardboard flat. Another firepack was gutted for a second pack frame. The two pack frames were placed side by side, then lashed together with F'er cord then slipped inside the flattened firepack so as to create a semi-rigid structure inside a cardboard platform. They cut holes with their Buck knifes and lashed the cardboard firmly to the pack frames. After attaching the cargo chute, Dow stood on it while Melvin got down on his hands and knees on the platform. When Dow shook out the chute, it snapped open, and launched Melvin into a ten-foot jump. Half way through it, he fell off backwards and landed on his head.

"A tundra sled," Melvin said, laughing and staggering to his feet. "Like in that movie I didn't see one time with my brother."

After capturing the tundra sled, Kasson tied a cargo strap to the two front corners forming a six-foot loop. With it, a man could stand on the platform and lean back holding on to the strap. That fixed two design problems; first it gave the pilot a means of holding on and balancing, and second it enabled him to pull back and lift the nose to keep it from digging into the tundra. At the same time, Dow ran to his hootch and got his main, a 32 foot circular T-10, and tied it on in place of the 24-foot cargo chute.

"Now we're getting somewhere," Kasson crowed. "This is like replacing a Ford tractor with a Ferrari."

The steering lines of Dow's chute were quickly taped to the risers. The driver or pilot, most likely in that order, would be too busy hanging on to concern himself with steering. After a short briefing, Kasson secured another loop to the front of the flight platform. It extended forward ten feet to where it was tied to thirty feet of letdown rope which was then tied to the risers of Dow's main. By now these flight engineers had the attention of the crew, and it gathered around to comment on the value of such a contraption.

"That's government property you're tearing up," Quinlan said.

"Get real, Bob," Kasson said. "We're conducting aerodynamic research with parachutes. We could be on to something big here."

Quinlan turned to the crew. "Behold the rationale of the sheep-killing dog. Next you'll be putting in for research and development bonus pay."

"Len," Kasson yelled. "Come on. You discovered it, so you get the honor of testing the latest model of the tundra sled."

"Aackk," Quinlan said. "Don't take him. He's one of the working jumpers. Take Rakowski instead."

"Shut up or we'll glass tape you to it and let it go towards the river," Rake said.

"Get over here, Swanson," Kasson waved. "Now you know what John Glenn felt like. That's it. Now look. Stand here. Hold on to the loop, lean back like this. Be ready when it starts. There you go. Perfect."

Melvin ran up with a coil of F'er cord, cut a long piece, then tied one end to the skirt of the main and the other to a belt loop on my Levis.

"Now," Melvin, said, eyes shining, "if you fall—not saying you will—but when you do, you'll pull the main down so the wind can't take it away."

"Will that be before he's killed or afterward?" Quinlan asked.

"Probably about the same time," Kasson said. "Think of it this way. We're out of food, right? If this thing works, Len can ride it to Granite Mountain and get help."

"As a squad leader, it's my job to supervise in critical situations."

"And you have," Kasson laughed. "You've supervised the whole thing, and look how well it's turned out."

"Aackk, rebellious ingrates," Quinlan said. "We have no medical gear, no contact with the outside world. Orangutang has damaged your brain. I can't bear to watch."

I planted both feet firmly on the platform, then leaned back to test the loop. Kasson handed me a pair of goggles and a hardhat with a chin strap. The wind gusted. Silver waves rippled in the green grass. I was ready. Dow and Kasson marched out to where the main lay rolled up and pulled it apart, still holding the skirt low. Melvin made a last minute inspection of the knots and overall rigging. The McGrath All-Star yelled, "It's been nice knowing you." Then, with a thumbs up from Project Director Kasson and former tundra sled Test Pilot, Melvin Sheenjek, Kasson and Dow lifted the skirt of the big orange and white T-10 to the wind. Filling instantly, it shot up thirty feet, whipped side to side, then yanked the tundra sled into full flight.

I don't know how I managed to hang on. Like a big kangaroo, I went fifteen feet in my first jump. Project leaders and casual spectators went to yelling. The cardboard platform tore off, rocking back and forth on its rear corners, me leaning back, holding up the nose, barreling over tussocks like I was driving a Roman chariot. I went with it. I had no choice. I sure as hell wasn't jumping off. About then it began to sink in that the maximum speed of a tundra sled had not yet been established. Aside from that, I found the whole thing to be downright wonderful. So much so that I began laughing out loud. Behind me I could imagine the crew leaping around and carrying on. In no time I had covered two hundred yards and was wondering how far I would, or should, go. Maybe I should go for it. Granite Mountain was, in a general sort of way, straight ahead. My, I thought, how impressed would they be to look up and see such a sight coming? A master in command of the wind, a winged god, akin to nothing they'd ever seen. My story would spread to the halls of jump bases everywhere, and be told around campfires for years to come.

No. A quarter-mile was one thing, thirty would be suicide. I could fall, break something and die for lack of help. Right then, though, I just wanted to ride and laugh and enjoy being at one with the wind, the sky, and maybe even myself.

Up ahead I saw a low strip of brush and settled on it as the place to bail off. I figured it would be the fastest roll I'd ever done, the feet together, go with it, take-it-like-a-man kind. Turned out there was more rolling to it than I expected. After flying for a while, I rolled for what felt like five minutes, and ended up in a pile, goggles knocked catty whompus, and the hard hat plumb off. With Melvin's F'er cord having killed the canopy, I found myself lying on the sweet, good earth, wiping tears from my eyes, laughing at nothing but the sky.

A few minutes later the crew came running up with Quinlan in the lead.

"Lenny," Quinlan said, trying not to laugh, "you're alive. And in one piece. We didn't see the crash, but the sight of you flying away with the wind, I mean, Ben Hur never made a more stirring impression."

Late that evening I was back on the knoll by myself, thinking about things. The wind had quit. As hard as it was to be hungry, without shade, out of the loop, and missing a bust again, the worst part was not having any idea how we ended up forgotten by the jumpers. If we were lost in the woods, at least we'd have firewood and poles to put up a cargo chute and build a decent camp. As it was, our hootches, barely held up by thin sticks and firepack boxes, blew down every afternoon. And, while we did manage to catch a few fish every day, boiled fish and green berries did little to diminish our constant craving for food.

Still, I was feeling better than I had in some time. It was the ride that did it. The ride and the laughing and the way the crew had had such a time with it. A lot of the crap I'd been worrying about was shaken clean out of my head by the tundra sled.

Below the knoll I watched Quinlan, Rake, Mountain Puss, and a few others looking for firewood along the river. I could hear the snapping of willow branches and some grumbling about why sharp sticks were hard to fit into burlap bags. With their rough clothes, old crusher hats and bandanas tied around their heads, they looked like peasant women, all bent over with big, brown bundles slung over their backs, cackling back and forth, gathering wood for their village.

I felt a sudden, warm feeling. Our he-man smokejumpers had become old ladies in a faraway land, working for a common good, players in an act as ancient and basic as humanity itself. In that low, golden light of early evening, in a place of rolling green hills, far from the rest of the world, I could see that no matter how hard we worked at being strong and brave, there was a threshold to human fragility beyond which notions of heroism and courage simply became meaningless. In our present situation we were just ordinary people, doing our best to get through another day.

Across a little hogback someone came walking, silhouetted against the sun. Dropping down into the shadows I could see it was Kasson, shotgun cradled in his right arm, carrying two more spruce hens. Moments later he was on the knoll with me.

"Hey, the great white hunter returns."

"I got them with one shot. My last number eight. All I've got left is four slugs."

Kasson sat down and started picking one of the spruce hens. I started in on the other one.

"I'll gut them at the river," he said. "It's not much, but they're fat and make good stew."

"Too bad we don't have anything to add to it," I said, pulling feathers.

"I've survived on a lot less."

I wondered if he meant in the war. I'd never heard him talk about it to anyone except guys like Rake and Marshall and Doc Houston. Sometimes in the barracks at night they would get in a room and lay out the maps Houston had, and go over them, talking for hours.

"In the war?" I asked.

"Yeah, in the war. I've got movies of the Lao hill fighters eating at this crude wooden table, and if you look close you can see things wiggling in their rice bowls. We ate snakes, lizards, grubs, worms, you name it. They're tough, those guys, food didn't matter as long as they had a chance to kill Viet Cong."

"So, they were good soldiers?"

"They were great soldiers. They lived their whole lives in those mountains. Every step they took was up or down, so they could move a lot faster than most. They were small and tough and endured things I couldn't have, if not for them. But the VC are tough, too. And determined. No one can deny that. When they heard that the kill ratio between our forces and theirs was ten to one, instead of getting discouraged, they said as long as it was that they'd eventually win. For them it's all or nothing. They're in it together, the men and the women doing the ground fighting, the supplies, and most of all, their commanders. While most of our generals sit on their asses in fancy hotels in Saigon, theirs are eating rice and bugs and fighting right with them."

"Well," I said, hesitating a moment, "I wasn't there, but I sure thank you for what you did."

"Yeah," Kasson said, looking at the horizon. "Nobody knows how fucked up it is over there. The bullshit piled up so fast in Nam not even the birds escaped. There were these... I guess some people call them misunderstandings. And, so now we're stuck in something that could turn out to be a lot bigger than we are."

Kasson held up a minute, thinking about something.

"Anyway," he finally said. "Thanks for saying thanks. It means a lot to me. It really does."

"You think they'll come tomorrow?"

"Well, tomorrow's a week. I'm thinking there's more wrong here than jumpers being busy."

"What do you mean?"

"I don't know, but something. I spent two years with the CIA and you get a nose for things. Things like that guy Miles. The minute I saw him at the Pig Party I knew he was trouble. Then, when he flew into our fire and started taking notes and shit, that proved it."

"I remember in McGrath when Melvin told about him getting conked," I said.

Kasson grinned. "I don't know what's in that stuff, but it sure fucked up his fire research, raving about the state office, and how much he loved women with big tits. By the next morning he looked worse than these spruce hens."

I laughed at how Miles always got messed up when he got around jumpers.

"Well, you've got him pegged," I said. "He's out to do harm, that's a fact."

"My training taught me how to read people," Kasson said. "It's like anything else. Once you see it, it comes easy. I can tell when something's bothering people. They act strange, you know what I'm saying?"

I glanced at Kasson and wondered if he meant like when someone was dragging their ass.

"I reckon so. Although, truth told, I'm not the best at noticing people's feelings."

"There's more to it than feelings. I can watch people, even at a distance, even when I can't hear what they're saying, and I can tell when there's tension. The body language, eye contact, each is different, especially when they're hiding something."

I looked down at my spruce hen, saw it picked nearly clean and felt kind of sorry for it.

"Like the other day when you were talking with Mort on the pilot's deck."

I looked at Kasson. He was looking me right in the eye.

"I was on the roof with Bro Ratus and saw you over on the deck and decided to plug in Bro Ratus, and watch his reaction."

"Oh, yeah," I said. "That really fired him up when he heard Bro Ratus."

"He's up to something," Kasson said. "He's got Miles spying on us. He's fucking with Big Al. My guess is he's fucking with you, too."

I looked off the knoll at the crew gathering firewood. Quinlan was singing about a dancing pig that lived in Cincinnati. Bell was cussing and swatting mosquitoes. I took off my ball cap and ran my fingers through my hair.

"Jim," I said, pulling my cap back on, "I guess I may as well tell you, I'm in a heap of trouble."

"It'd help if you'd look me in the eye, Len."

"The whole crew is," I said, turning to him. "You have to promise this won't go any further than this knoll?"

"Bullshit! I did enough of that in the war. Either you trust me or you don't."

I just sat there and stared at him. He just stared back.

"All right, hell, I may as well start at the beginning," I said. "It was right after Bonanza Creek. Mort called me to his office. Said he was new, and that he wanted someone to report directly to him about the crew's needs and things like that so he could help us do a better job. I didn't want any part of it, but he sort of threatened me, so I decided I best give it a try. Then the season started and we got busy. After the Terror River fire he called another meeting, and I told him everything was going good, that we had a great crew and all. That's when I learned that he wanted a fire investigator, this Mr. Fentori, to go to Kodiak and investigate the ranch so BLM could collect the suppression costs. That didn't set right with me, so I called the ranch and told Mr. Deering to claim it was lightning, and how Rake was writing it up that way in the fire report. Then we had the Fort Greeley fire, and I found the campfire that started it. That's when I looked up Mr. Fentori's phone number in the BLM Washington office and called him and told him I thought the campfire belonged to a crew surveying the pipeline, but I didn't tell him who I was, only that it looked like a man-caused fire, and since he had come all the way to Alaska, he should check that out, too."

I reached over, took my canteen out of my PG bag, took a long drink.

"The investigator must have called Mort and told him some jumper wanted to talk to him about the Greeley deal. That's what Mort wanted to know when we met on the pilot's deck, if it was me? I didn't admit to anything. By that time I'd had it with his sorry ass. He's got some big thing for this pipeline deal. Says Washington doesn't want nothing holding it up. He got mad and threatened me again. Said it was the Bureau's role to assist in the pipeline, not get in the way. That meeting on the deck didn't go well. Now the investigator's in Fairbanks and the real shit's going to hit the fan."

"What kind of real shit?"

"Just before we left for this fire, Miles came to the T-Hangar, met me outside and showed me some photos he had of us at the Pig Party, Big Al down in the mud, people smoking weed. That kind of real shit."

"And that's it?"

"It's all pretty clear. Mort doesn't want me talking with the fire investigator, Miles is working for him, and so he's blackmailed me with the photos. Said he had duplicates. Said if I talked with the investigator, he'll show them to Mort. Then the siren blew and we took off."

"That was the morning we left?"

"It was!"

"How long will the investigator be in Fairbanks?"

"He said about a week."

"A week," Kasson said softly, the two of us still eye to eye. "Interesting."

"What do you mean?"

"I mean you could be the reason we're still here. As long as you're here, you can't talk with the investigator, right?"

"That's crazy. First off, Mort doesn't know for sure that it's me. And, even if he did, he's got no say about when jumpers demobe."

"Maybe yes, maybe no. But you can bet he knows it's you. You're the only one that mentioned you'd seen that campfire."

"That's not true, Jim. The only one I told about the campfire was the investigator. And I told him to keep my name out of it. Maybe he didn't. At any rate, if that's the case I'm in more trouble than I thought."

"Yeah you are," Kasson said, "and now, so is the crew."

"Problem is," I went on, "I already met with him. We went to Greeley the night before we came on this fire. Miles has us by the ass with those photos. Hell, for all I know he's already given them to Mort."

"Not a chance. Once he does that, he'll lose the power they represent. And that's the power to achieve Mort's goal of making sure you don't talk with the investigator. No, he'll hold them and wait for his next move."

"Well," I said after a bit, "it's a hell of a mess all right, but I'm glad I told you."

Kasson cut the feet off his spruce hen, then said, "Yeah, me too, but don't say anything about this to anyone else, not even Johnny B. I need time to think."

By midmorning of our eighth day, the crew was worse off than ever. Only Quinlan remained cheerful, playing spoons and singing songs. That afternoon Rake suddenly shouted, "Hey, hey. Listen up."

Off to the west, the faint but distinct whop, whop, whop of a Bell 205 helicopter could be heard pounding its way through the air.

"Yeah baby," someone yelled. Others joined in, "Here they come. It's about damned time. Maybe they've got food."

"Get this trash picked up," Quinlan yelled, "or it'll blow all over the place."

The crew began securing the camp. The whop, whop, grew louder until a black speck appeared above the horizon. Everyone cheered and high-fived. At last our ordeal was over. Gathered up, we watched the speck grow bigger and louder. Bell tried calling on his radio, but the battery was dead. Then, we saw it, heading straight for us. A few headed out to their hootches and started taking them down. The ship closed to within a quarter mile, its pounding rotors familiar to all jumpers waiting for pickup in the bush. We began to wave and yell. The helicopter flew straight over the top of us at 300 feet and went right on without the least sign it had any intention of stopping.

"Stop, come back," Bell yelled into a radio with a dead battery. The sound of the helicopter grew fainter and fainter until previously restrained tensions erupted in a fury of cussing and condemnation that included everything from blind pilots and worthless radios to comments about Quinlan's choice of songs. Bell threw his radio down and stomped it for the second time.

"Aackk," Quinlan said, in an effort to restore order, "Imprecation and scurrility will not serve us well in this dark hour of the soul."

The next morning as the crew sat around the campfire complaining about the weirdness of the previous day, Mountain Puss spent it gathering up rocks on a stretch of riverbank, then took them to a sandy beach and arranged them into words. Two hours later a different helicopter came and landed in a flat close to camp. As it lifted off with the first eight bound for Granite Mountain, I looked out the window at the beach and read FUCK BLM.

# 13

As we walked into the T-Hangar the next day, Kasson yelled out, "Honey, I'm home."

"Big deal," The Fat Indian said, "You guys jump a fire, milk it for nine days, then come back in here thinking you're heroes."

Kasson laughed. "Hey, at least we weren't missing out on a fire bust."

The Fat Indian explained that the list had rolled three times since we left. They were using the Volpar to jump a lot of fires. He had spotted six loads himself. Most of the action was north between Galena and Dahl Creek. A few had popped up east of McGrath. All told, fifty-three fires had been jumped. All had been caught.

The afternoon of our demobe we were flown to Galena where we spent two hours in the cookhouse eating like pigs. After a night there we flew back to Fairbanks. Quinlan had called Big Al. By that time Al knew what had happened but not a lot about why. Somehow our fire had fallen through the cracks. Central dispatch in Fairbanks had no clue. Galena dispatch, without direction from Fairbanks, would not have known to send a detection ship to check on us.

Next day it showered some but mostly just around Fairbanks in the hills. After roll call the Peace River jumpers settled into a slow day at the T-Hangar, grumbling that they had missed the entire bust, most likely the last of the season. A few worked on their gear, greasing boots and repacking PG bags. Those who had spent a night gambling at Sam's or carousing in the bars on Second Street crawled up into the bat caves, pulled the burlap curtains closed and tried to sleep.

I went to the loft and called the District Office. I talked to Miles and set up a meeting with him at the T-Hangar that afternoon. I couldn't imagine why Kasson wanted one, but I did what he said anyway. Next I dialed Fentori's number in Washington. I was hoping he'd say there wasn't enough evidence to say the Greeley Fire had been started by the survey crew, but that's not the way it went. He was definite. He was sure he could prove his case. Whether he would try depended on things he didn't want to talk about—at least not with me. On the other hand, he had decided to drop the Terror River investigation altogether. He also told me the DM had asked questions about the jumper that had provided the information, and that he had told Mort that as long as the investigation was still in progress he didn't want to say any more about it. For now, he said, my part was over, but at some point I would have to make a written statement. He knew where I was if he needed me.

At 10:30 Big Al came into the Ready Room, called for a meeting, then went to the bulletin board to check on the latest. A new Rumor Control memo had been pinned to it.

### RUMOR CONTROL "OLD SALT" SELF-TEST

It has come to the attention of the Rumor Control Staff that there's a need to set some standards pertaining to "Old Salt" jumper status. A meeting was held at an undisclosed location, on an undisclosed date, to determine guidelines and standards by which "still wet behind the ears" jumpers can mark their progress towards Old Salt bragging rights. Here, for the first time anywhere, are the criteria hammered out by the staff at said undisclosed location.

It was decided that attainment of Old Salt status should not be based on age, but on an accumulation of Alaska plus Lower 48 experience with certain experiences mandatory, and others of an optional nature. Ten mandatory (life-enhancing) experiences were designated by the committee as prerequisites which must be met. These ten are stated in Section 1. Optional (character building) experiences are listed in Section 2. Each experience in Section 2 is given a number value between 1 and 5. In addition to meeting all ten mandatory requirements, a score of 55 must be attained in Section 2 if one is to attain genuine Old Salt fame.

SECTION 1. MANDATORY ( Life-enhancing ) PREREQUISITES

1. Minimum of 100 BLM or Forest Service jumps with at least 20 in Alaska (including Canada).

2. Must have jumped a fire out of a Grumman Goose.

3. Must have jumped out of at least five different types of aircraft. (1 bonus point may be gained for each type of aircraft in excess of five, and may be applied to points earned in Section 2.)

4.  Must have jumped and lost at least one initial attack fire that went to project size. To fulfill this requirement you must have been fire boss.

5.  Must have been "gobbled over" at least once where you lost gear or had to "run for it."

6.  Must have had at least one problem bear encounter on a fire.

7.  Must have caught a salmon on a fire. (Len Swanson's World Record Northern Pike Taken With Woodsman's Pal, satisfies this requirement, and brings him two bonus points that may be applied to Section 2.)

8.  Must have been miss-plotted or forgotten on a fire and run out of food, and been forced to rely on your skills as a woodsman to survive.

9.  Must have urinated in the Yukon River.

10. Must have demobed from a fire by Grumman Goose off a river or lake.

SECTION 2. OPTIONAL ( Character Building ) EXPERIENCES
*55 points must be achieved

1.  Flying in an aircraft that lost an engine  (5 points)

2.  Emergency helicopter landing  (4 points)

3.  Emergency reserve deployment (5 points) — (if it didn't open, disregard)

4.  Ripped static line cable out of jumpship  (3 points)

5.  Been airsick on jumper or paracargo run (2 points – 1 extra point if puked on spotter)

6.  Jumped flat-pack chute  (5 points)

7.  Spotted or had water/ice landing (must have been at least three feet deep - 3 points)

8.  Hung up over 100 feet  (5 points)

9. Snow landing  (minus 2 points)

10. One point for each jump base you boosted AND jumped a fire.

11. Jumped in Canada  (2 points)

12. Demobed fire by riverboat  (2 points)

13. Demobed by Alaska Railroad  (4 points)

14. Packed out a minimum of six miles across tundra, Fifteen miles on solid ground (4 points)

15. *Beard (2 points), Mustache (1 point), Goatee (O points)  * Hairface can claim 1 bonus point for two beards on one face.

16. White Boots at least 5 years old (2 points)

17. Buck knife at least 5 years old  (2 points)

18. Chew snoose (3 points), smoke pipe (2 points), roll your own (1 point)

19. Crusty hat (2 points), crusty Filson vest (2 points)

20. Have eaten Muktuk and/or seal oil (2 points — 4 points if you liked it — Remember this is the honor system)

21. Had sexual adventure with native Alaskan (3 points), (5 points if on government time)  *(3 bonus points for You-Know-Who for having sex with the Chief of the Northway Tribe)

22. Had at least 700 hour overtime season (4 points), 1000 hr. overtime season (6 points)

23. Broken $1000 net on one paycheck (3 points)

24. Sworn at least once that you were not coming back to jumping next year.  (2 points)

25. Gone out into the real world, got a real job, then gave up and came back to jumping (5 points)

That's it. Good luck on becoming an Old Salt. Questionable claims will be critically reviewed by the committee at undisclosed location.

PS:  In the meantime Rumor Control applauds the new PT program. This is what we like to see in our organization. A strong body makes a strong mind, etc, blah, blah, blah. Good job everybody.

~The Black Hand

Big Al left the bulletin board and ducked into Operations, shaking his head. As the crew pulled up chairs and gathered around the two long tables in the Ready Room, I took Kasson aside and told him Miles was coming at 2:00. The bat-cave people stayed put, opening their curtains but holding on to prime rainy-day real estate.

After a few minutes Big Al came out and sat up front, and like always, took out a cigarette, lit it, then stared out a window.

"Ahhh, well, ah," he began, "I'm still trying to figure out what happened on the Peace River. The original spotter's report is on file here, and a copy was sent to dispatch... so that's not it. I talked with them. They have it in their log that you were placed on the action board, Bell + 15, along with your fire number. When the problem was brought to their attention they discovered that the tag was no longer there. Maybe it fell on the floor and the janitor. . . ah, accidentally swept it up. With your tag not on the board, they had no reason to check the spotter's report. Beyond that, they have no idea what happened. They had a lot of fires, a lot of people coming and going, all-night shifts. I called Galena, but they only track jumpers who IA out of there. I doubt we'll ever get to the bottom of it."

Kasson glanced at me and grinned.

"But this much I can say, it won't happen again." Big Al took a drag and blew a couple unhurried smoke rings. "Fairbanks is setting up a double record system where each out station will be notified of jumpers in their zone of responsibility. Fairbanks will contact them at 6:00 PM every day to update the status of each crew. All I can say is that... I'm sorry. So is dispatch. Like I said, it won't happen again."

"Something's not right here," Rake said. "First we get screwed by not being allowed to IA the Fort Greeley fire while it was small enough that we could have caught it before it blew up and burned Mountain Puss and Melvin and 20,000 acres of Fort Greeley, then we get bent over on the Mooseheart deal for the same kind of ivory tower bullshit."

"Yeah," Dow said. "No shit! Every time we turn around, it's some new thing like these oil dripping, dead-battery, low-bidder, flying time bomb Turkey Dougs, being jacked around in McGrath, cheated out of standby time, killing the dog. I'm with Rake, something fishy's going on."

Big Al took it all in, nodding slightly now and then, frowning, slumping further down into his chair, his cigarette ash growing long.

"I know, I know," he finally said. "Believe me, I'm not happy about a lot of this, either. But things take time. I'm a smokejumper base manager, not a magician."

The room quieted. Big Al waited for someone to say something. No one did.

"What about the Volpar?" Quinlan finally asked, changing the subject.

"Well," Big Al said, sitting up straighter, "so far I like it. Even though it only carries eight, it's fast. I talked them into running patrol flights during the bust, and we beat the helicopters to several fires. Dispatch is impressed. They've agreed to some test runs out of here. The way I've calculated it... even starting out at the same time from the same airport, we can beat them to anything farther out than 60 miles. And that's why we're going to this new six-minute getaway time."

"Six-minute what?" Bell said.

"Siren to wheels-up in six minutes. The pilots say they can do it. And, if you have your gear on the speed racks ready to go, so can you. The bad part is that there's not enough room in the Volpar to suit-up in-flight, so you'll have to fly suited-up."

"Great," Bell snorted. "So now we have to fly in our jump gear, hotter than hell, weighted down with all that shit, just to prove that we can get to fires faster than helicopters. Is that it?"

"That's it exactly," Big Al said. "On patrol flights we'll remain unsuited for now and see how it goes. On a regular fire run the eighth man will fly unsuited and check everyone just before the jump, then suit-up himself and be checked by his jump partner. We're calling him the monkey. He'll be last on the plane. After picking up the tail stand, he'll crawl in, store the tail stand in the hell hole, make sure the door's secured and the safety chain's hooked."

"Another monkey?" Johnny B. piped up. "Duke's not gonna like this."

"I don't particularly like it, either," Big Al said. "But we've got to show these people what we can do, or we might be looking for other work. It's as simple as that."

"Let them look for *other work*," Bell huffed. "If they'd come on fires they'd already know what we can do."

Shrugging his shoulders, Big Al looked at the group calmly for a long moment then said, "But they won't. It's not how they see their role. And frankly, just so you know, I'm tired of having to listen to everyone bitch about it all the time."

After a short uncomfortable silence, Bell said, "But Al... that's your job."

Directly after the meeting broke up, Big Al told me he needed to see me in his office. On our walk across the west ramp to the FAA building, neither one of us said a thing. I was sure he was going to give me an ass-chewing at least, maybe even a suspension notice. At the door to his office he glanced at me and said, "Just so you know, this wasn't my idea."

Big Al opened the door and, as soon as I stepped in, shut it behind me and was gone. There, behind Big Al's desk, sat Mort Twixtenblout, Fairbanks Area District Manager, fondling some photographs with his puffy, fat fingers. I froze a moment, a lamb done led to slaughter. Good lord, I thought, Miles went ahead and did it. It's all over now but the yelling and the firing.

"Mr. Swanson," Mort smiled, sitting the photos aside. "I asked your base manager to bring you here since you seem to have trouble responding to my requests for meetings."

I just smiled back, thinking it amazing how some people's denial of reality was, in fact, the only reality they knew.

"I told you before, I came to Alaska to jump fires. If I wanted a job attending meetings I'd kept the one I had in the Lower 48."

"Well," Mort said, "like them or not, meetings are an important part of our job... that is, of course, if we expect to *keep our jobs*."

I don't know why, but right then I saw myself back on the Seward Peninsula, riding the tundra sled, sailing along, laughing and feeling so good about life I couldn't help myself. That was smokejumping. Getting browbeat by a jackass was not, and so I decided I wasn't putting up with any more crap from Mort.

"A smokejumper's job is to catch fires and it's plain as day that we're good at it. So, I reckon we'll be keeping *our jobs*."

Mort shook his head, disgusted. "You just came off of one, how was it?"

"It was hard. Fairbanks forgot about us. We spent a week stranded without food. Other than that, it was a great."

"Yes, I'm sure it was," Mort said. "Mr. Fentori, the investigator was here. He wanted to talk to you."

"Me?"

"Yes, you! It's clear you're the one he refers to as the jumper."

I knew right then Mort was lying. Mr. Fentori already knew how to get a hold of me.

"That a fact?" I said. "I reckon you're free to think what you like."

"Just so we understand each other here," Mort said. "He's gone now, so let that be the end of it. Do I make myself clear?"

"Clear as mud," I said, standing up. "Now, can I go?"

"Hell no, you can't go," Mort said, grabbing the photos. "Your fire boss on that Seward Peninsula fire was Don Bell, isn't that right?"

Well, I thought, there it is. Mort knew we were on a fire on the Seward.

"He was," I said, "and he did a good job. Bell's a good fireman."

"He's also in a lot of trouble," Mort said, tossing the photos across the desk.

There in the old warehouse was the Red Lizard covered with mud. Several shots had been taken. A close-up showed the inverted green triangle BLM insignia. Another showed the SMOKEJUMPERS ARE GOOD TO THE LAST DROP bumper sticker.

"That," Mort nearly yelled, "is the vehicle I've been looking for. It was hidden in a building next to your parachute loft. This Don Bell, this so-called *good fireman* of yours, is the one that's been driving it. Misuse of government property is a serious offense, and in this case it's serious enough to warrant criminal charges."

Mort stared at me waiting for a response. I handed the photos back, wondering if he had any idea what had been going on between Bell and his daughter. The trip to the Fossil Creek cabin was, no doubt, made in the Red Lizard, and there were likely things that went on in the front seat that would be hard for him not to see as a misuse of government property.

"Jumper's drive government rigs all the time," I said.

"That's official duty. This is not!"

"Well... sometimes it's hard to tell the difference."

"Obviously, for some of you it is, but not for me. He drove it to your smokejumper party out on Chena Hot Springs Road, that much I know."

Yes, I thought, and he drove it home, too, with sweet Betsy all over him.

"Why," I said. "I just can't imagine Don Bell doing a thing like that."

"And here's another thing," Mort huffed, grabbing some papers and shoving them at me.

"Who the hell is this Black Hand guy and his pal Mohammad Ralph Louie?"

To my surprise there was a copy of the Rumor Control bulletin that had appeared in the Ready Room two weeks prior. The one entitled:

EL OTRO  —  Riding The Crest Of Civilization.
WELCOME TO OIL CITY

I looked over its major concerns: overtime, hazard pay, winners and losers, Mohammad Ralph Louie, a bird shit on by a moose. Then the signature, The Black Hand.

"Well," I said, "it claims here that he's a famous social commentator and bisexual advocate."

"I suppose you think this is all very funny," Mort snarled, *"I do not!* Black Hand, my ass. It's one thing to have fun, it's quite another to run down the oil industry, Fairbanks, the Army and the BLM. It's totally unprofessional, and I'm going to find out who's behind it, too."

"Well," I said again, "we don't have any Mohammads on the crew, but we do have a Ralph, and a Louie, if that's any help."

Mort jerked the Rumor Control Bulletin away from me, then said, "Go on. Get out. I'm tired of trying to reason with you."

I went to the door, then turned, "Mind if I ask you a question?"

"What is it?"

"Why did you call me over here?"

Busy stuffing photos and papers back in the folder, he mumbled something under his breath, looked up, got red in face, then blurted out, "Just who do you think you're working for, young man?"

"Truth told," I said, "I'm working for myself mostly. I know I get all the money when the checks come. Besides that, I work for the American taxpayer, and I intend to do the job they pay me to do."

That flabbergasted Mort, and he said, real mean-like, "You know, if you don't like the way we do things here, you can always leave."

"Well, I reckon I could," I said, "but the way I see it, that same option's open to you."

That ruined our talk and, in a fit of twisting and shouting, he ran me out of Big Al's office.

I went looking for Bell and found him packing cargo chutes in a back corner of the T-Hangar. I told him that the DM had photos of the Red Lizard, that he had to give it up, that Mort was out to press legal charges and get him fired.

"Who told you that?" Bell said, unimpressed.

"Listen, I know this sounds crazy, but I just came from Big Al's office and a talk with Mort. He showed me the photos. He knows where it is. He's got a folder on you."

"That's ridiculous," Bell laughed. "Why would he show them to you and not me?"

"I can't explain it right now. Just trust me. Don't go near it, I'm telling you. If this guy finds out about you and Betsy and the Red Lizard, he'll fire you sure."

Bell informed me that Mort's timing was off, that he already had plans with Betsy for another trip to Fossil Creek, that she had insisted on it, that there would be no candles allowed near the bed. He concluded his reasoning with, "And the Red Lizard's the only ride I've got."

I shook my head. "Borrow White Trash from Dow, or some other bro rig. The Trout or The Stallion, or hell, just take my pickup. You have to understand, Don, this isn't just about you. The rumors are true. This guy's dead serious about putting an end to smokejumping up here."

"Let him try. Go ahead and worry if you want to, I don't need to hear about it."

Bell went back to rigging chutes and I went to sit in the I-Hear-You-Walkin' Chair. Operations put two loads on for lunch stand by, so I got up and rechecked my gear on Lupe, one of our two new speed racks. The first eight jumpers' gear was hung on pegs for fast suit-up on Hernando, the second eight on Lupe. My gear was okay so I went out to my pickup to eat a sack lunch. That's when I saw the Rumor Control flag for the first time, flying high on a pole above the EMT cupola on top of the T-Hangar. About four feet square, it was all white with a two-toned chocolate chip cookie in the middle surrounded by crumbs. Under the cookie were the words: *That's The Way It Crumbles*. I knew right off it was the work of The Black Hand.

While I was in my camper eating lunch, I got an idea. As soon as I finished, I went to the building where the Red Lizard was hid and found a way in through a side door that was covered with an old canvas. I lifted the hood, pulled off the distributor cap, slipped the timing rotor off the timing shaft, put it in my pocket then snapped the cap back in place.

At 2:00 o'clock I met Miles in the parking lot. Together we climbed the interior stairs above paracargo that led to the top of the T-Hangar. Hurrying across the flat expanse of the roof, we passed Bro Ratus draped in a yellow rain slicker. I stopped to salute the Rumor Control *That's the Way it Crumbles* flag, then we ducked in the EMT cupola. Inside, the air was cool and heavy with the tangy with the smell of Ben-Gay, Heat, and other sore-muscle medicine. Rows of shelves were stocked with cartons of bandages, bottles of iodine and jars of aspirin and anti-inflammatory pills. Three pairs of crutches leaned in a corner. On the wall nearest the desk was tacked a paper that read Major Trauma. Under the title it listed hypodermic needles, Demerol—a pain killing narcotic—Dextran, an artificial blood supplement, then rubber tubes and special splints. Next to the Major Trauma paper hung the tin can telephone that connected to Ops.

"What's all this medical stuff doing up here?" Miles said.

"There's no place for it down below. Doc Sam was an Army medic in Vietnam. He's starting an EMT program and getting this stuff organized. We could sure... "

Just then the door opened and Kasson stepped in.

"So, you made it," he said, looking at Miles. "I didn't think you'd come."

As we pulled up chairs, Miles shot me a hard look and said, "What's he doing here?"

"Ask him," I said. "He called the meeting."

Miles looked Kasson over then frowned. "I remember you. You were the one with the gun."

"And you were the one with the notebook and the camera."

"I was on an assignment. What about it?"

"I know about your photos. Len told me. He also told me you threatened to give them to the DM if he talked with a certain BLM official. So, I guess, first off, I'd like to know why you think it's Len he wants to talk to?"

"That's none of your business."

"Well it is now because as long as you think it's Len you can hold those photos over our heads. That's blackmail, and blackmail's why I wanted to see you."

"Call it what you like," Miles said, his face red, hands beginning to shake.

Kasson stared fiercely at Miles. "For the record, let's call it chickenshit. The way I see it, you'll use them as long as they serve your purpose, then you'll turn them over at the end of the season anyway, right?"

"You drink too much," Miles said. "I could see that on the fire, a drunk with a gun. Besides, like I told you, this is none of your business."

I sat there listening. To my mind, Kasson was just wasting his time. Then, he smiled, reached inside his jacket and said, "Maybe these will give you a clearer picture of what kind of business we're talking about here."

Two packets of photos appeared. He handed one to me and the other to Miles. Miles took one look then croaked like a bullfrog. There they were, photos of a madman somewhere in a smokejumper camp, staggering around with a canteen of orange liquid, his shirt torn, looking like he'd just seen the devil. One was particularly bad with him sprawled out unconscious near a wood pile with his pants down around his knees, his white butt covered with mosquitoes.

"You're a lot of fun when you're conked," Kasson chuckled.

Miles commenced to cussing. "Conked? You poisoned me. It wasn't my fault. I wasn't on duty, and you... "

"Sure you were," Kasson said. "Don't you remember, we were stranded, the helicopter was out of fuel, so we ran our time straight through. The time slips have been turned in and approved and you've already been paid. Besides that, you twisted little shit, we definitely weren't on duty at the Pig Party, but that defense doesn't seem to be available to us. But who knows, maybe the DM will cut you some slack since you're his favorite brownnoser."

"You won't get away with this."

"That depends ," Kasson said. "You keep your photos and nobody's hurt. Give them to the DM and we all are."

"I'll make you a deal," Miles said. "I'll give you mine and you give me yours."

"I'll make you a better one," Kasson said. "I have copies of these in a sealed envelope with the state office's address on it. There's a letter, too. It has all the important stuff in it, the fire, the date, your name and position description. Keep your fucking photos and that envelope goes nowhere. Turn them in, and you can kiss your pissant career goodbye."

After dinner at the Tiki Cove, the McGrath All-Star and I sat with our beers, sneaking glances at the pretty waitresses. I would've rather been with Sarah, but she called the day before we came off the Peace River fire to tell me she was going Anchorage for a few days. Just my luck.

"Hey Len. The sad sack routine's about to kill me. Is it the DM again? Talk to me, man."

I downed my beer, sat the glass on the table, then fingered the rim, thinking.

"Hell, it's way beyond that now. But telling you won't help."

"Hey Lenny, it's me. Johnny B., your old jump partner, and you know what a piss-poor liar you are. So fess up. It started on the Peace River, and now, back here in town, you're worse than ever, keeping to your ass-dragging, shifty-eyed ways."

"You're one to talk," I said. "This thing with the DM has done got out of hand. I reckon I should just go on and go crazy and get it over with."

"Crazy is just what you need," Johnny B. said, taking a pull on his beer.

"All that Black Hand shit's not helping, either. Him and his sidekick, Mohammad Ralph Louie."

"Hey," Johnny B. said. "Desperate times, desperate measures. Besides, you're the one that said I should do some writing, remember?"

"I do. But I don't see any profit in making trouble with it."

"Speaking of trouble, where's that girl of yours?"

"You mean Sarah?

"She must be out of town."

"What makes you say that?"

"Because if she wasn't you'd be with her, not moping around with me."

I stood up. "Let's get out of here, I need to do some serious drinking. That'll do me more good than sitting around arguing with you."

Outside, Second Street was a regular zoo of early-stage pipeline people. In two short months downtown Fairbanks had gone from zero to weird and was still spinning its wheels. Three topless bars, The Flame Lounge, Sneak Preview, and Rosie's had sprung up like mushrooms in the midst of the more traditional dives like the Chena Bar and the Savoy. Girls strutted the sidewalks in miniskirts and halter tops. Even college girls, some guys said, were up here to make some quick cash. Hell, when you can dance your way through college half-naked, I reckon it makes more sense than getting a student loan.

In a parking lot a group of Georgia Island singers, all women, was lined up behind a black preacher, who stood holding a microphone, speaking directly to the girls, "Sisters," he was saying. "I see you there, walking with the devil, holding hands with the devil, giving your bodies to the devil. Come and stand with us, and feel the glory of the Lord's love for all his children." "Hallelujah" the singers whooped, rattling tambourines and bursting forth with a jazzed up version of "Rock My Soul." On the next corner three men stood with a trombone, a clarinet and a saxophone, jamming. They had a hat upside down on the sidewalk. Two cops wearing dark glasses sat in a patrol car in an adjacent parking lot taking in the whole scene.

"Come on," Johnny B. said. "I know just the place." A few minutes later we were two blocks over on Fourth Street, walking along looking into the empty store windows of abandoned businesses and shops.

"Where the hell are you going," I said. "I need a drink, not a tour of skid row."

Johnny B. stepped into a small entryway and pushed a buzzer mounted near the door.

"Oh no you don't," I said. "I'm not interested..."

"Just relax, it's not that kind of thing."

We waited, me pacing back and forth, mumbling to myself about Johnny B.'s state of mind. Two or three minutes passed. Just when I decided I couldn't stand it any longer, a voice on the other side of the door said, "Yes?"

"Al Mattlon," Johnny B. said softly through the door.

Keys jingled and the knob turned and the man invited us in. I had no idea what was going on. Locking the door behind us, the man led the way down a dim, narrow hall to another door.

"What is this?" I muttered, "Rumor Control Headquarters?"

Johnny B. waved a finger, warning me to keep still. Another door was unlocked, then locked again as we were escorted deeper into I didn't know what. Another door and the same. Then, a heavy wood door with carved panels depicting caribou, moose, and wolves. The man fit the key into its slot, pushed the door open, stepped aside and said, "Welcome to Sam's."

For me it was like I'd gone from a gray, overcast day in Texas to a bright spring morning in Ireland. A great run of green carpet covered the floor. Six dark brown antique card tables were surrounded by the same kind of chairs. The walls were blue-green and held fancy framed oil paintings of women, each showing a good bit of cleavage, and all lit by track lighting. Close to where we had come in, a brass-rail bar ran from corner to corner, stocked with rows of liquor, and backed by two big, long mirrors whose beveled edges cast prisms of rainbow light. Opposite the bar, a clawfoot pool table sat glowing like an emerald under a crystal chandelier. From speakers hidden somewhere, Waylon Jennings was singing about lovable losers, no account boozers, and how a man could easily loose all his money and mess up his life by hanging out in a Honky Tonk named Green Gables.

"This beats all," I said. "So this is Sam's. I've been hankering to see it."

"This is it," Johnny B. said. "That's why all the locked doors. If the cops come, Sam's people have time to stall them and hide the tables, then it's just a regular bar. The cops know anyway. Sam pays them off. Look, there's Big Al and the boys."

Sure enough, Dow, Shearer, Mountain Puss, and Big Al sat with their cocktails and piles of chips, staring businesslike at blackjack cards. Doc Houston, Mitchell, Kasson and The Fat Indian sat at the next table, flirting with the dealer. The place was about a third full. Rake, Hairface, and Master Bates stood at the bar.

"It's all free," Johnny B. said. "The drinks, the food, everything. There's even a sauna and shower room. And, if you want a steak, just tell the bartender. He'll barbecue you one on that grill over there. The only way to spend money here is to gamble.

"You got any Irish Whiskey?" I said, shaking hands with the barman.

"Bushmills okay?"

"That'll do just fine. Make it a double."

Johnny B. ordered a Margarita on the rocks, no salt, then laughed. "This must be heaven for a cheap bastard like you."

"How long's this place been open?"

"About two months. Maybe the pipeline's not so bad after all, eh?"

I sipped my Bushmills and licked my lips then sipped it again.

"So we got in here because of Al?"

"Uh-huh," Johnny B. said, smiling. "This is Big Al's second home. All you do is knock, wait, and then mention his name."

"He must win a lot."

"Yeah right," Johnny B. said, giving me a hopeless look. "He does some nights, but mostly he just drinks and loses like everybody else."

I sat at the bar thinking how much I liked scotch and watching the jumpers play hand after hand, calling for more cocktails, piles of chips steadily going down. Happy when they won and jolly even when they didn't, they were evidently having a good time. All except Big Al. He just played on and on, chain smoking, now and then sharing a comment with Shearer, but otherwise showing little emotion, like his mind was off somewhere else.

The dealers were all women, all young, and all beautiful. On the walls a few feet behind them, the women in the oil paintings sat upright and pert, just like the dealers at their tables. Positioned near the middle of a semicircle, they dealt from chairs higher than those of the players. There was something else. They all wore strapless, low-cut, tight dresses that pressed their breasts up into smooth round mounds that showed their cleavage. As they leaned over to ask about different bets, the mounds loomed bigger. The visual connection between the dealers and the women in the paintings was clear evidence that Sam was no dummy.

I slurped down the last of my drink, and tapped the bar for a second.

"The guy's a genius," I said, turning to Johnny B.

"What guy?"

"This fella, Sam. He's got these guys looking like salmon jumping at a waterfall."

"Now that you mention it," Johnny B. laughed, "they do have that need-to-spawn look."

"It ain't right," I said. "First off, Sam gives them free drinks, then he decoys them to the tables with the ladies. After that they don't care what's happening so long as they can keep talking to them. Next thing they know they're drunk and too horny to think straight, and that's when they lose."

"Sometimes they don't," Johnny B. said.

"The way they run this place, you know most everyone's losing. What it comes down to is, we're here drinking up the bro's money, and they don't even know it. Way I figure it, that can't be right."

Johnny B. shook his head, aggravated. "Relax Swanson. It's gambling. Sometimes you win, sometimes you don't. It has nothing to do with right and wrong."

"They work too hard for their money just to have Sam cheat them out of it."

Well then," Johnny B. said, "why don't you just saddle up to the table there and suggest they give up their evil gambling, boozing and sexually perverted ways?"

"You know damn well I won't do that. It just makes these free drinks taste sort of different, that's all."

"If it makes you feel any better, then get your ass off that barstool, and get over there and do some gambling of your own. Then, the bros can be drinking on you. Make a damned contribution."

"I don't reckon I will. I'm not very clever at cards."

"Doesn't matter," Johnny B. said. "If you win, good. If you lose, you're helping support the bros. It's a win-win deal."

"I swear, Johnny B., you come up with some of the sorriest logic I've ever heard."

"Okay, how about this, then. Keep track of how much you drink tonight and pay them back in the morning at roll call."

"Good lord," I said. "Can't you, just for once, not be so damned contrary?"

Johnny B. shook his head, looked at himself in the mirror for a time, and then said, "Some people just can't help themselves, I guess. Come on, Grandma, grab your free drink and let's shoot some free pool."

We shot pool and got drunk. The action at the card tables got loud. Losing or winning, the blackjack jumpers were having a time of it, laughing, carrying on, and enjoying themselves. That cactus juice Johnny B. was drinking had him as loco as I'd ever seen him, dancing around with his pool stick, singing made-up songs to one end like it was a microphone. I was drunk, too, but not like Johnny B. There was this big bowl of candy sitting on a coffee table and it was filled with little Tootsie Rolls, bubble gum, Hershey Kisses, and butterscotch drops. As we were filling our pockets, Big Al came over and asked if he could borrow a hundred dollars. Johnny B. didn't have it, but I did and gave it to him right off.

By the time they escorted us down the hall and out onto the street, we were in a lot different condition than when we went in. Neither of us knew for sure where we'd left my pickup, so we wandered on back to the Tiki Cove and found it parked right in front. We took off for Trainor Gate. But when we got there it was locked. It was usually open, but lately the Army had taken to locking it, we figured because they knew jumpers used it late at night as the most direct way home. Johnny B. went to raving. "Fuck it. Take the damned railroad tracks," he said, plumb delirious about the Army. "It's only a hundred yards."

"Hell yes," I said. "It's encouraging to see you with a good idea for once."

It was more like four hundred yards but, if you went back a ways to F street, you could drive up on the road crossing and get on them, and the pickup tires fit nicely outside the tracks. So we did that. It was bumpy as hell, though, and I could hear stuff bouncing around in my pickup camper and glove compartment. It was slow going, but in no time we passed the gate and only had about a hundred yards to go to where we could get off by the railroad bridge. Everything was going fine except for my dishes and glasses and cups crashing around in the back. I tried to go slow but it didn't matter what speed we went, the jarring was right severe at any speed.

"There's not many trains come on these tracks, is there?" I shouted, above the racket.

"Not too many," Johnny B. yelled. "Four or five a week. Mostly at night. They bring coal for the power plant. But they don't go very fast."

Right then I saw a white car with red and blue lights flashing come along the road and slow down, then stop. A man jumped out and ran toward us yelling something and waving, so naturally I stopped, too. Another man followed. Military Police. Guns pointed in our direction. I rolled down my window, all the time deciding on a plan to act normal.

"Good evening, Sir," the first MP said.

"You done left your lights blinking," I said, trying to be helpful.

"Do you mind telling me what you're doing driving on a railroad track?"

"Well," I said, "we're headed home is all, and this is the short way."

"It's against the law to drive on railroad tracks," the first MP said as they put away their guns.

"Bullshit," The McGrath All-Star shouted. "I've never heard of such a law. Show me in the vehicle code."

"May I see your driver's license, Sir," the MP said, ignoring Johnny B.

242

I got out my wallet and was looking for it when Johnny B. jumped out of the pickup and stumbled around to the front and stood in the headlights and commenced to yell.

"You think this Fort Wainwright's a big fucking deal, don't you?"

That made the MPs jump back and draw their guns again.

*"Well, it's not,"* Johnny B. went on. "The fort's a joke, the whole damned Army's a joke. Chainlink fences everywhere, people marching around, helicopters flying at night shooting at wrecked cars, dropping bombs in swamps... "

Johnny B. was staggering this way and that, tripping over the rails, making a bad impression, so I got out, took hold of him, walked him back around, and put him in the pickup.

"Now you listen to me, Johnny B.," I said. "You stay in here and keep still. If you get out again I'll knock you in the head."

I went around the front of the pickup and apologized to the MPs. While I was trying to think of something to say that might offset the ruckus Johnny B. made, I noticed that the head MP had 82nd Airborne wings pinned to his uniform.

"I'm real sorry about this officer," I said. "But my friend here, he's not right tonight. He had a bad day, and now he's drunk and this is not really normal for him. I see you were airborne, so you can understand. He had a malfunction today on his main, and he fell a long ways with a streamer and barely got his reserve out before he hit a tree and slid down the side with his chute breaking off branches. The chute caught the top just before he augered-in on his butt. Spent the whole afternoon walking around in circles at the T-Hangar, and he's not been right since. As airborne, I know you'll understand."

The airborne MP stood back, squared his shoulders, nodded quickly.

"Yes, Sir. I know exactly. Same thing happened to a friend of mine two years ago."

"I'm sorry about this railroad track traveling, too," I said. "I was just trying to get him home and to bed before he hurt himself. The gate was closed, so we went this way. It's my fault, really. I let him drink too much."

The airborne MP went to the pickup and looked in.

"Is that right, sir?" he asked Johnny B., "You had a total malfunction?"

"Totally total," Johnny B. moaned, acting serious. "Spinning like... the ground... around and up and up and over and around, ohhh Yes, sir... I'll never jump again."

That's all he said, and I was glad he quit before he ruined it.

"Well, sir, the MP said, "I'll let you go this time. Now get this pickup off the tracks. Don't try this again. We'll follow you to the barracks. Maybe he'll be better tomorrow. Terrible thing, sir, a malfunction like that."

# 14

When Johnny B. and I walked in the Ready Room the next morning, I saw a few jumpers gathered around someone in the I-Hear-You-Walkin' Chair. Moving closer I could see it was Big Al, passed-out, his hair messed up, and a few dollars poking out of a shirt pocket. Pat Shearer was kneeling beside him.

"Hey, Al. Wake up. It's Pat. It's time to go to work."

Quinlan arrived with a wash pan of water and a hand towel, and began wiping Al's face.

"This is new," Quinlan said. "Started about two weeks ago. Instead of going home, he comes here."

I watched as Al began to come around, and remembered him the night before at the card table. If I was dealing with the DM's underhanded style, likely Big Al was dealing with a whole lot more. Pat had Al drink some water, then poured him a cup of coffee from Quinlan's thermos. Ten minutes later, Al was on his feet, combing his hair, and getting ready for the morning briefing at the FAA building. That afternoon, just before quitting time, he came up to me.

"Len, ahhh, well, ah? Did you lend me a hundred dollars last night?"

"I did, there at Sam's. But you don't need to pay me now."

Big Al took out his wallet and handed me five twenties. "Don't do it again," he said. "No matter how much I ask, if I'm drinking, just tell me no, you told me not to. I'd appreciate it."

The next three days passed quietly with warm sun. Most all the jumpers were still out on fires. A few had come into McGrath and Galena and were held there for standby. Johnny B. and I were relieved that we hadn't heard anything from the Army about our attempt to destroy my camper on their railroad tracks. Some dishes had fallen out of the cupboards and broken and the front end of my pickup rattled a good deal more but other than that, we were lucky we didn't end up in the brig.

Besides good weather and good luck, there was one other thing that made the slow days more agreeable, Betsy Twixtenblout. Most days she had lunch on the pilot's deck with Bell. She'd walk right into the Ready

Room and say 'Where's my Rocket Man?' When she wasn't around Rake and a few of the Bros called him Rocket Person, which he hated, but didn't complain about, remembering what had happened to Mountain Puss. Bell would likely not have taken to the name Rocket Puss.

I wondered if Betsy knew that Bell had lost the Rocket Man letter, and that Miles had it and might have given a copy to her father. I couldn't resist the thought of Mort reading it. I could see his mouth hardening into a toothy derangement, his eyes bugging, jumping to his feet, twisting and shouting. Maybe he'd be thinking about the SMOKEJUMPERS ARE GOOD TO THE LAST DROP bumper sticker, too.

"Crew meeting, five minutes," The Fat Indian announced on the PA. At morning roll call we had been warned. Big Al didn't know the specifics, but apparently the DM wanted another chance to talk with the crew. Right after Mort walked in, Johnny B. showed him the I-Hear-You-Walkin' Chair, gesturing like he was a salesman in an expensive furniture showroom. Johnny B. was explaining the chair's role in helping maintain crew morale when Mort suddenly shook his head, scowled and walked off.

A few minutes later, Big Al called the meeting to order. I looked around for Bell and saw him hiding behind the dexion shelves.

"Ahhh, well, I don't have a lot," Big Al said. "We're getting a lot of good reports from the field, most all the fires are nearly out, so we should be seeing some people back in here in the next couple days. Thanks for getting all the chutes rigged and paracargo back in order. There's a few rumors about a down-south booster, Region Six mostly. With this warming, though, there's bound to be holdovers, especially out west. We'll just have to wait and see. Anyone have any questions?"

Nobody wanted to say anything with Mort there, so the room stayed quiet. Since Big Al had started the meetings, contrary opinions, petty complaints, overt criticisms, and general crew hardheadedness had—at times—weighed heavily on him. But then, too, they were the direct result of a level of trust he had built with us. The DM was no part of that.

"All right, good," Big Al said, half to the crew, half to himself. "We've got the DM here with us again, and he'd like to have a word with you."

Mort stood and faced the crew.

"Thanks Al," Mort said, followed by a quick exhale from his nostrils. "It's good to be here. Here with you, here close to your work. I've taken time out of my schedule to come and talk about something very important to me... performance. Performance, quality performance, has always been my goal. Performance is of great importance in our lives, both personal and professional. It's so common to our everyday information flow that we tend to assume we know what it means. The Funk and Wagnell's Dictionary defines performance as, 'operating or functioning, with regard to effectiveness, as of a machine.' But we're not machines. We are humans. Let me assure you, I will insist upon that here in Alaska."

Mort paused, allowing time for this wisdom to sink in. Big Al stared at the floor. No one moved.

"The reputation of your crew as regards fire fighting is something you should be proud of. Your reputation, and by that I mean performance when it comes to your personal behavior, however, is a different matter. Your drunkenness, your gambling, this flaunting of authority is what I'm talking about. You all carry knives. Some have guns. You drink and gamble in the barracks. It's only a matter of time until knife fights will break out. And, as you know, one thing leads... "

"Armed and hammered," Rake said.

The crew burst out laughing. Al laughed a little, too. Mort did not.

"You're grown men," Mort said, as the room quieted, "so I'm telling you this for your own good. My staff will be working with your people to see that you address this problem. Thank you."

The next morning at roll call, a color photo was found tacked to the bulletin board. It was taken in front of the barracks, where I had Johnny B. flat on his back, down on the lawn, sitting on top of him, wielding my Woodsman's Pal. Johnny B. had on his dark glasses, and there was a big blood stain on his white t-shirt, an empty wine bottle in one hand and his buck knife in the other. The jumpers whooped and hollered when they saw it. Big Al never said a word. Later in the day a half dozen photo copies appeared in the FAA building, even one in the District Office.

The next afternoon I saw Dow gassing White Trash around the parking lot, towing the Red Lizard, while Bell sat at the wheel cussing, grinding gears, and beating on the steering wheel. Stopping in a cloud of dust, the two got out and opened the hood.

"Must be out of gas," Dow said.

"It's got gas," Bell said, exasperated. "If it didn't, why would it be running out of that thing there."

"That thing," Dow said, "is the carburetor, maybe the float's stuck."

"I don't care what it is," Bell said, "it wouldn't have gas running out of it if it was out of gas."

Little did they know that the Red Lizard's timing rotor was only 40 feet away in the glove compartment of my pickup. Bell grabbed a long-handle screwdriver out of the Red Lizard and began to beat on various things under the hood, including the battery. Sparks snapped. Fire and black smoke boiled out of the motor well.

"Shit," Bell yelled. "Get a fire extinguisher."

Dow pulled out his knife, cut the tow rope, then jumped in White Trash and spun gravel at the Red Lizard. Bell threw handfuls of dirt. The insulation under the hood caught fire. Jumpers ran up and joined in throwing dirt. I ran for the T-Hangar, trying to remember where I'd seen a fire extinguisher. Just as I got there, Quinlan came running out with one. Moments later the front half of the Red Lizard disappeared in a storm of white dust that turned the black smoke gray. Quinlan looked at Bell. "Aackk, it's true," he said. "You are always there."

The Legendary Fucking Rake and Mountain Puss came with a water hose and sprayed the Red Lizard until it looked new, except for under the hood. After making sure the insulation and wires were no longer smoking, they pushed it back into the hide-out building, then scattered, agreeing that the whole thing never happened.

Just before quitting time two loads were put on stand by. I was on the first, and normally would have been happy about that, but Sarah had called. She was back from Anchorage and asked if I'd like to come that evening for dinner and a sauna. I won't say it's outright superstition, but smokejumpers—no matter the base—have this thing about messing with the jump list. When your turn comes, you take it, climbing on a plane for a patrol flight, going out the door to a fire, or accepting an assignment to the Lower 48. To smokejumpers the list is sacred. To mess with it is risky. I took myself off one time to go to the airport and pick up a girlfriend. The first man on the second load moved up to last man, first load. They jumped an airplane crash that afternoon in the Brooks Range in a big wind. The jumper that replaced me drifted up a ridge and slammed into a tree and compound fractured his femur and wound up unconscious, hanging upside down in his suspension lines. When he came to he said he knew his leg was broken because when he looked up, he saw his leg bent over so far he could read the brand name on the bottom of the sole of his boot. The fire came racing up the hill and a couple jumpers pulled him down and dragged him away just in time. His chute burned. His leg didn't mend right. He never jumped again.

So I didn't want to go off the list. If we got a fire call that evening I would miss it and no longer be part of the crew I'd been with all summer. But I hadn't seen Sarah in two weeks and needed a sauna pretty bad, so I told Operations to take me off until morning. Right after work I headed for the barracks and a shower, then picked up a pizza and a bottle of wine, and I tore off to her place.

When I got there I saw smoke coming from the sauna and knew I had made the right decision. As much as I didn't like the idea of missing a fire, it sure was good to get off the fort and away from smokejumpers for a time. We are like brothers and call each other Bros, but there's also this thing called Broverload, and I had a bad case of it.

As soon as I stepped in the door Sarah took the pizza and wine and put them on the table. We kissed and hugged and kissed some more. In no time she had my shirt tail out and hers off, and the next thing I knew we were on the bed rolling all over each other. I can tell you this, there wasn't a thing wrong with Sarah's body. Round and firm and proud, her breasts poked up even when she was on her back. With a smooth, flat stomach, and a waist and set of hips that curved every which way, and all of it covered with the most beautiful brown skin, Sarah's body was a fine example of nature's excellence in the feminine form. When we had finished, we lay on the bed a while just looking at the ceiling and smelling the pizza, not saying much.

I heard an airplane fly over and, from the sound it made, knew it was a Volpar. It was headed west so it was on its way to a fire. I had made my choice and was glad. I had much rather been with Sarah right then, lying naked and snug in the little cabin, than cramped in an airplane all suited up in my jump gear, headed for a fire and a night of hard work, sweat, and smoke.

"It's good to see you again," I said. "It's been a while."

"Only two weeks. Did you have a good time?"

I didn't know how to answer that, and to tell the truth, I wasn't all that comfortable with us lying there naked talking about regular life.

"Well," I finally said, "I guess you could call it good. But it was more different than good."

"I don't understand."

"They lost us, dispatch did. On a fire on the Seward Peninsula. For nine days."

"Lost you? How did that happen?

"They don't know. Somehow our fire location tag got lost. They had lots of fires, nobody even noticed we were missing. Dispatch claims we fell through the cracks."

"Wait a minute," Sarah said, rolling up onto an elbow and tapping my chest with her finger. "They had it at one time, because I saw the tag for your fire on the action board. I was at the District Office on business, and afterward I went to dispatch to see when you and Melvin were coming home. They told me at the T-Hangar you were with Bell."

"You saw our fire tag on the action board?"

"Yes! It was in the upper right-hand corner with Bell + 15 , the date and a fire number written on it. I wrote it down so when I checked back later I could tell them the number."

"Well, if that don't beat all."

"Your DM was there, too, studying the board," Sarah went on. "We talked a little, and he asked me if I knew Don Bell. I told him he was a friend of my brother's. There was no one in dispatch at the time except Mort, so I went to find someone to ask about when you might be coming off the fire. When I got back only two dispatchers were there, one on the phone, the other on the radio, so I didn't want to bother them. I checked the board again. The tag was gone. I thought they'd removed it. I got tired of waiting and decided to call later, but then left for Anchorage and forgot all about it."

"What the devil? Are you saying you saw our magnetic tag on the board when Mort was there, and when you came back the tag was gone, and so was Mort?"

"Yes, he was there when I left and gone when I came back. Just like your tag."

That no good skunk, I thought. Maybe Kasson was right. Mort didn't want me to talk to Fentori. Then, too, there was the SMOKEJUMPERS ARE GOOD TO THE LAST DROP deal. Whatever it was, it was too rotten to believe.

"That pizza smells good," I said. "Let's get up and eat."

Sarah put the pizza in the sauna to warm it up while we waited in the cabin, talking.

"I hope you get to meet my father someday," Sarah said.

She didn't have anything on but a long-waisted shirt, loose buttoned up the front. I wondered what her father would think of the way we'd been carrying on. Melvin had to know about it.

"That'd be fine with me," I said. "I'd like to meet your whole family."

"When I was a little girl my father took me with him on his trap lines," Sarah said. "He treated me just like my two brothers. He wanted us to see the country and get to know it in the same way he had when he was young."

"Well," I said, "your Dad sure enough sounds like a good man. Have you told him about me?"

Sarah laughed, and when she did she leaned forward and I could see inside her shirt.

"I did. I told him you were shy and had an Indian great-grandmother, and that you liked to peek at women's breasts when you thought they wouldn't notice."

That was the thing about Sarah and Melvin. They spoke their minds. I liked that in both of them, but especially her.

"You're hard to keep from looking at, Sarah. I hope it doesn't seem rude."

"It's not rude, Len, it's nature. You were taught not to trust it, and I was taught that you have to. As Melvin would say, 'You're too white.' Come on, I'm ready for some pizza."

While eating we talked about the Anchorage meetings. Natives had come from across the border in Canada and were in favor of the caribou commons idea.

"The Gwich'in voice is being heard. Our goal is to reframe the debate from a dispute about environment versus oil to one that centers on our ability to continue living off the land."

"Well, I wish you luck," I said. "Fact is, there's a big world out there that doesn't know a caribou from a catfish. And most of them don't care to learn, either."

"Len," Sarah said, reaching over and touching my hand, "I know that. And we may not be able to do much to change it. But we have a legal relationship with the U.S. government, based on our uninterrupted use of this land for thousands of years, plus two centuries of court decisions and international treaties that protect our way of life. Canada has it, too."

"Some folks back home call people like you Do Gooders."

"They're right. We are doing good, and we're not quitting. We're ready to travel the world with our story. We're going to become the voice the caribou doesn't have."

The pizza was gone, and nearly all the wine. Although I was listening, I was still distracted about what was inside Sarah's shirt.

"Have you seen any more fires up where the caribou drop their calves?"

"Yes," Sarah said. "I'm glad you asked. But not in the calving grounds. My father and a cousin flew up there two weeks ago, into one of the main valleys the caribou come through during migration. They found seven fires. Five had been rained out. Two were still smoldering. One is over 10,000 acres, and only thirty miles north of our village."

"They don't think it was lightning?"

"My father doesn't. Large fires that far north are almost unheard of. Usually there's too much rain. I'm going to talk to the DM about it. We don't care if some burn. But no more this year. Caribou moss can take a hundred years to grow back after a fire. Too big a loss in one area is a problem."

I sat at a window of Volpar 700 Whiskey Alpha, studying the rivet patterns in the wing and wondering what our fire would be like. I couldn't believe I was back on the first load again, back with Johnny B., Bell, and my old crew. The plane I'd heard the night before at Sarah's was my load all right, but they couldn't find the fire and came back on a dry run. The only change in our old load was The Fat Indian. Cleermont was sick of running Operations and put himself on first load. He claimed he needed to get on a fire so he could get some rest. He came on as the monkey.

Our fire was reported at fifteen acres, wind-driven, five miles south of Lake Minchumina, moving north towards the lake and several cabins owned by Alaska businessmen and politicians. On the phone to the Governor, the locals had demanded fast action. Big Al and dispatch had agreed on two loads, a Volpar and a Doug. A Bell 205 helicopter with four helitac people had been sent to the airstrip at Lake Minchumina where it would stand by to evacuate locals if needed.

Lake Minchumina sat like a blue opal in a vast lowlands thirty miles north of Denali National Park. There was an airstrip near the lake's east end. Most of the cabins were along the three-mile south shoreline, closest to the fire. To the south, the dark green channel of the Herron River meandered through low hills. Beyond the river, the Foraker, Herron, and Straightaway glaciers lay frozen below the 12,000 foot, ten-mile wide, Wickersham Ice Wall. Denali, the tallest mountain in North America, loomed high above it all. As the morning sun painted the lowlands different shades of green, yellow and gold, the snowy, high canyons of the Alaska Range remained veiled in shadows of blue and gray.

Up front two jumpers looked through the cockpit windshield at a towering smoke column. Bell was first man, first load, and so would he in charge again. The Volpar dropped its nose, cut power, and began a steady descent. Big Al came crawling back through the jumpers, then took up his position at the door.

"Guard your reserves," he yelled. After making sure we all had a forearm over our reserves, Al grabbed the door, jerked it open, swung it around behind him and secured it to the safety chain. A sudden roar filled the plane, wind tussled hair, last minute gear checks were made. Nearly everyone thinks it takes a lot of nerve to be a smokejumper. Mostly it's just skill, good gear, and following procedures. But at times they're right. Those moments when you first see the smoke, smell it in the plane, brace yourself against the rough bouncing of the plane, feel the tightness in your gut, all the time knowing full-well that you will jump—that's when it takes a fair amount of something special.

Al leaned out into the 110 mph slipstream and looked forward under the wing, his hair blowing, his shirt rippling against his body; even the skin on his face and neck were rippling. Back inside he pulled Bell to him and started pointing, shouting in his ear. The fire had made its initial run into the curve of a slough, jumped it and formed the current head. Given the winds out of the Alaska Range, the head would widen as it moved north. Lake Minchumina lay directly in its path. The tail and rear flanks had burned into areas of muskeg and little sloughs and were holding. The head was two hundred yards wide, putting up a wall of 20-foot flames running freely in tundra and stringers of black spruce.

After circling at 500 feet, 700 WA leveled its wings, poured on the power and climbed to jump altitude—1500 feet. After a quick yelling session it was decided that we would violate a main rule in jumper initial attack. As a rule, we jump at the tail, secure it, then divide the crew and flank up both side towards the head. But, this time, because property and possibly lives were threatened, we would try a more aggressive plan— jump at different spots along the mid-perimeter, leave the rear portion for later, and try to contain the head the first night. Al pointed out a knoll that would be the jump spot for the Volpar load. The Doug load would drop eight directly across the fire from us, and the other eight further up, closer to the head. As fire boss, Bell would command our flank, and Quinlan would take charge of theirs. Our group would work from the jump spot across a grassy flat of small sloughs toward a big ridge to the north. If the wind carried fire across the rear-flank sloughs there was some potential that it could hook around behind us.

Watch your escape routes," Big Al shouted to the entire load.

The first set of streamers fluttered yellow, blue and red in the bright sunlight, then settled down not far from the knoll.

"First two?" Big Al yelled. "Are you ready?"

Bell and Melvin nodded.

"Get in the door."

"Three-hundred yards drift. Stay wide of the fire. Any questions?"

Bell and Melvin shook their heads, no.

"I'll carry you long... Okay, we're turning final."

Thrusting his head back out into the slipstream, Big Al tucked his chin in and said something into his handheld microphone. The plane yawed right.

"Get ready."

The Volpar cut power. Down came the slap and Bell cleared the door with Melvin right behind. We made a wide circle and watched as the first stick made the knoll. Big Al called for two more. I got in the door and Johnny B. moved in behind me. Al put us out with clockwork precision, just like Bell and Melvin, but my feet went flying up and as the tail moved away, I saw I was tumbling all the way over backwards. The horizon appeared in a quick upside-down blur just before my chute opened hard and spun me around under a coil of line twists three feet tall. The twists in my risers were so tight they forced my head forward and down to where I couldn't look up to check my canopy. Around and around I went seeing the smoke column, Johnny B. under canopy, the Alaska Range, Lake Minchumina, then Johnny B. again, around and around like that. At least I wasn't falling faster than Johnny B., so I knew I had a good canopy, not that I deserved one. The twists had barely cleared when the ground came rushing up. Even though I was mad and had missed the spot, I had to get ready to land.

For the next five hours our load worked north across a flat of tall dry grass, beating out perimeter flames with spruce boughs and burlap bags. With the flames knocked down, the interior cooled quickly enough that we could move forward with fair confidence that the line would hold. At four o'clock we came to a slough of swift water four feet below the level of the land, eight to ten feet wide, and too deep to see the bottom. After walking a good ways, looking for a place to cross, we gave up and took a break to figure things out.

"There must be places we can jump it," Bell said. No one offered any objections. The edge of the far bank was hidden by tall, dry grass that curled down over it. Beneath the rim was a vertical wall of gray mud. The penalty for failure would be to fall backwards into the water.

"All we need is one guy to make it," Bell said. "Then he can help the rest."

"You're the Rocket Man," Rake said, "fire-up your afterburner and go for it."

Bell looked at Rake a second, then turned and threw his PG bag, hard-hat and radio across. He got back thirty feet, spit in his hands, then rubbed them together. The crew cheered. Bell charged the slough and launched himself into an arm-flailing, leg-kicking maneuver that landed him directly on the far edge. Grabbing handfuls of grass, he slid down into the water up to his knees. The bros went from cheering to laughing.

Bell cussed, then commenced to laugh himself, which made the slipping worse.

Right off The Fat Indian tossed his PG bag and stuff across. The Fat Indian wasn't actually fat, just round in the middle. As a former all-conference halfback at the University of Montana, Jim Cleermont could outsprint anyone on the crew. Like Bell's jump, Cleermont's wasn't pretty, but it did land him high enough to gain the other side. Quickly, The Fat Indian got to his feet, grabbed Bell and pulled him up. Melvin, a less athletic, no-conference-at-all Indian, made a graceless lunge and landed two feet short in a big splash. The Fat Indian hung on to Bell's legs while Bell crawled down, grabbed Melvin and pulled him up. The rest took the same approach, jumping just far enough to be rescued.

Wet, muddy, and covered with ash, we pressed on. After working a half-mile of hot, tall-grass perimeter, we came to another slough, this one too wide even for The Fat Indian. Throwing our packs across, we each jumped in and dog paddled across. Silently we slogged on towards the head, beating out flames, covered with mud and ash, like a bunch of surly pigs.

For the next hour we kept pushing north and west, crossing two more sloughs, maybe the same ones for all we knew. As night came on, the fire calmed some. We figured it was about 600 acres. The head was no longer a running flame front. At the top of a small rise, we held up to look over the surrounding country and evaluate our options. Five miles to the north lay the thin gray line of Lake Minchumina. Behind us was a grassy plain, beyond which the Alaska Range stood in pink alpenglow against a dark blue sky.

"Let's take a minute and eat," Bell said, dropping his PG bag.

We ate cans of Pork and Beans, Chicken Boned, Ham, Water Added, Spags and Balls.

"It's eleven now," Bell said, glancing at his pocket watch. "Depending on what we run into, we could make the head in four or five hours. Quinlan and his load are right across from us. They've got more trees, so it's good they have more people. Problem is, I don't think we'll have a chance to catch it unless we push all night. What do you guys think?"

No one answered. Sometimes it's best to return to the jump spot, catch some sleep, get more food, then hit the line in the morning with renewed energy. But, with the jump spot so far back and across four sloughs, going back didn't make much sense, really.

"We've got to push on," Bell said. "It won't be much fun, but if we expect to keep this thing from running on Minchumina tomorrow, I don't see we have much choice."

"In the middle of the road of life," Johnny B. said, "I woke in a dark wood, where the true way was wholly lost."

Bell stared a Johnny B. a few seconds, then said, "What do you mean *wholly* lost? People don't get *wholly* lost, they just get lost."

"It was the true way that was wholly lost," Johnny B. said.

"Look, when you're lost, you're lost. So why not just leave it at that.

"Dante believed that the journey begins right here," Johnny B. went on. "Right beneath your feet. There's no other place and no other time. For all that you've done and all that you are, life still refuses to grant you—and will always refuse to grant you—immunity from the difficulty of the moment. Becoming aware of this, according to Dante, is what you need to do when you find yourself in a dark wood."

"Well fuck him then," Bell scoffed. "It's obvious he didn't spend much time enjoying the outdoors. I've woke in dark woods hundreds of times and never felt like that once."

"It's the hero's journey," Johnny B. insisted. "Dante and Virgil. Virgil tells him they can eventually get to heaven, but first they have to pass through hell."

"You smoke too much dope," Bell said, scraping his spoon in the bottom of a can of cold hash. "If you don't watch out you'll end up as fucked-up as Dante and his weird friend."

"Whatever," said Johnny B. "All I know is I'd rather be here with you guys, right now, doing what we're doing, than anywhere else."

"I wish I wasn't," Melvin said. "Even McGrath was better than this. I wish I was home. If I was home I'd be sleeping with Jenny under her blankets. That'd be better than choking on smoke and jumping in water and..."

"Uh, oh," The Fat Indian said, pointing. "Look there."

A mile back a curl of blue smoke drifted above a small flicker of fire.

"A damned flare-up," Bell said. "Right on the line, too."

We all knew we'd come a long way without checking the line behind us. But with the sloughs and all, we'd taken a chance. Someone would have to go back or all our work would be wasted.

"I'll go," Johnny B. said, reaching for his PG bag. "This is what Dante was talking about, Bell."

"I'll go too," I said.

"Thanks," Bell said. "You and Virgil should be able to get it. When you're finished, check the line back to the jump spot. Wait there. First thing in the morning I'm going to try to get that copter for a recon. I'll have them pick you up. Bring a couple cubies of water and two cases of rats."

Going back meant crossing the sloughs again. There wasn't much to say. From time to time we came upon pockets of coals close to the line and scuffed them out with our boots. Exhausted, we halted at each slough, slung our packs across and jumped in, too tired to do much else. Finally reaching the fire, we took up our burlap bags and in twenty minutes had it knocked down except for a five-foot section which we heaped grass on, then stood around stripped to the waist, warming up and drying out. After making sure the slopover was out, we turned to face the great mountains and the long walk back to the jump spot.

Feeling something hit me in the back, I rolled over and there was Duke, the firefighting monkey, lying on his back, covered with ash and mud, staring at the sky, his eyes like yellow marbles on a tar baby. It made me think how Duke had once belonged to the boy riding his bicycle in Israel, the one who died in Johnny B.'s arms. I had given a fair amount of thought to that. And the way I figured it, Johnny B. had kept the little monkey, given it a name, and even given it a life as a way of doing a little something to help compensate for the one the boy in Israel never got to live.

"Duke thinks it's time to get your ass up and get to work," Johnny B. said.

"I reckon he would. So why aren't you out rustling up firewood so we can make coffee?"

"Man, Len, you look bad. You look like the Million Dollar Man built on a 500 dollar, pay-as-you-go-plan."

"I appreciate you pointing that out, Johnny B., but you don't look all that good yourself."

I pulled the cargo chute off, dreading the thought of putting on ash-caked pants, wet socks and boots as hard as concrete. As soon as we were dressed we set out making trip after trip to retrieve parachutes, firepack boxes, and cubitainers of water. By eight o'clock we had all the gear piled on top of the small rise. In a sandy place scoured out by winter wind, we made a campfire, heated water for coffee and ate a couple rats.

Two hours later helicopter 44 Sierra approached from the direction of Minchumina, made a low pass, then came back and landed not far from our gear. The plan was to ferry us and two firepacks filled with food and water up to Bell's bunch. On the flight out I sat up front next to the pilot and asked if we could take a quick look at the head.

During the night the forward perimeter of the fire had bumped a large wet meadow on Bell's side, and a crescent-shaped lake between Mitchell and Quinlan on their side. The head, however, had advanced up a long incline of scattered black spruce, then, in the last few hours, moved up onto the top of a broad treeless ridge covered with caribou moss. The ridge was bounded on each side by a creek. The creeks formed a giant upside-down wishbone, with the fire burning in the middle toward a bluff that dropped off steeply into a flat where the creeks ran together.

We found Bell and the first load held up where the fire had bumped the meadow on our side. On the ground, I asked the pilot to wait, then ran to get Bell while Johnny B. off-loaded the firepacks.

"Come on, Don," I said, "you've got to see this."

While Bell climbed into the seat behind the pilot, I asked him to fly over and pick up Mitchell and Quinlan so they could see, too. We circled the ridge, pointing and exchanging ideas. In ten minutes we were on the ground again. The copter shut down and we held a quick meeting. The main fire, pushed by afternoon winds out of the Alaska Range, would reach the end of the ridge sometime during the heat-of-the-day burning period. Most likely it would spot down off the ridge into the flat at the confluence of the creeks. If allowed to burn on its own, that much fire would jump the creeks. From then on, there would be nothing between it and Minchumina except four miles of thick spruce.

"We have to hold it at the creeks," Bell said.

"Maybe the copter can make some bucket drops," Mitchell added.

"That would help," I said. "But what about this? If we time it right, we can fire out along the creeks on both sides so that we reach the junction about the time the fire reaches the top of the end of the ridge. If we time it right, our fire will be sucked upslope into the main fire and pull most of the flying debris back into it. In the meantime we can be working the spot-fires."

Bell turned to the pilot. "Do you think you can talk them into letting you do some bucket work out here later on?"

"I don't see why not," the pilot said. "We've got things squared away back there, and the helitac foreman is dying to help out."

Mitchell, Quinlan, the pilot and I crawled back into 44 Sierra, flew to the knoll jump spot and got all the fusees out of the firepacks. We flew to the other jump spots and did the same.

By noon both the right and left flanks were tied into ponds and sloughs, the crescent lake, and the two creeks. The head was confined to burning toward the top of the long ridge. The plan was to begin firing as soon as the wind picked up or at two o'clock, which ever was judged best. We would light along each creek so that our burnout would run upslope onto the ridge and join the main burn as it moved down toward the creeks. Timing was crucial. We had to be at the confluence of the creeks at the same time the fire reached the end of the ridge. That was our thinking anyway. If we wound up with something different, like way too much fire, we had the creeks to jump in.

The wind started at 1:00. By 2:00 smoke boiled on top of the ridge and rolled along the perimeter that slopped down off the sides. Bell radioed Mitchell to start firing. Rake, Johnny B., and I started on our side. Bell and the rest moved along behind us, watching for spots.

Based on our recon we estimated we had a total of about a mile to reach the confluence. The fire had become a running fury on top of the ridge. Large copper-colored columns of smoke rolled up, tucking in on themselves, sucking in more oxygen. The sun became an orange ball, then red, then violet. The land and the sky darkened. A great roar filled the air.

Fearing that we'd underestimated the burning conditions, I wondered what the residents of Lake Minchumina were thinking now. Whatever they thought, we were too far into our plan to change it. The woods were dry, there would be spotfires. At the speed of a normal walk we kept lighting and moving forward. Up ahead spotfires appeared on the side slopes of the ridge. The creek began its turn to the left as we approached the end of the ridge and the flat adjacent to the confluence. Mitchell and those lighting on his side were nowhere in sight.

A helicopter came whopping out from around the point of the ridge with a full bucket of water. As 44 Sierra flew passed, the helitac foreman waved and gave me the thumbs up.

"Let's not burn any more for a while," I said to Rake and Johnny B. "Mitchell's bunch was supposed to be in sight by now. Why don't you two head on around and see if you can hurry them up. I'll stay and light the rest when I see you coming back."

When the main fire crested the end of the ridge, 300 yards away, it began pulling into itself with enough force to keep the head from throwing spots across the creek. That was all well and good. But higher, out of the main column, little branches and spruce cones trailed thin streamers of smoke as they fell farther out into the woods.

Bell came up and got on the radio trying to reach Mitchell. Helicopter 44 Sierra flew by again and circled a spotfire out a ways under the shadow of the smoke column. Moments later it dumped its bucket then flew off in a line for the crescent lake. High on the ridge, a storm of flames tore at the black skeletons of spruce trees, their limbs waving wildly. Ground fire ran back and forth below the ridge, at times pulsing downslope, then rushing back up but steadily eating its way toward us.

"Yahoo," Rake yelled as he and Johnny B. came back through the smoke. "Burn baby. Burn."

"Where's Mitchell," I shouted.

"We didn't see him," Rake shouted back.

"Bell," I said. Bell waved me off, still talking on the radio.

I dropped my PG bag then waded into the main creek and started across.

"Bell!" I yelled from the middle of the creek, "Radio Mitchell. I don't want to light this until we know where he is."

"What do you think I'm doing," Bell said. "I can't get him or Quinlan either one. The copter can't either, but the pilot says he thinks they're back about a quarter-mile and coming."

"We've still got time to let the ridge burn off some more," I told Rake and Johnny B. "Y'all should go back. Keep going until you see Mitchell, then burn back together. We'll need everyone here so we can fire this out all at once."

I watched and waited. Helicopter 44 Sierra dropped another bucket. The timing that was so critical to our plan was slipping away minute by minute. The burnout at the confluence had to be lit while the fire on the ridge and upper slopes had enough draft to pull our fire into it so that they met at least halfway, far enough from the creeks not to spot across too much. Five long minutes passed. I took a smashed, half-melted Snickers bar out of the top flap of my PG bag, tore off most of the wrapper, wiped the spruce needles off, then ate what was left, paper and all, washing it down with warm water from my canteen.

"Oh, brother," I said to myself. "Come on you guys, come on."

Bell had disappeared somewhere. Several smokes were coming up out in the woods. We needed to be out there, working with the helicopter, hitting them while they were small.

Just then Mitchell, Rake, the McGrath All-Star, and two other jumpers came through the smoke looking like ghosts in a Viking movie. With spruce boughs in one hand and burlaps bags tied around their waists, the only part of their get-up missing was horns on their helmets. Removing his hard hat and wiping his forehead with the back of his wrist, Mitchell walked up and started talking.

"We left the last two-hundred yards until we tied in with you," he said. "The rest of my crew's working a spotfire, but I don't know if they can hold it. It won't matter anyway if we can't hold this. Retardant's on the way from Fairbanks. There's also supposed be a second Bell 205 coming."

"Let's light her off," I said. "You guys go back, light this way. We'll do the same. When we meet up back here we'll get with the helicopter and decide what spots to work first."

Johnny B., Rake, and I hurried back along the creek to the point where we had last fired-out, and began mass-firing. Mitchell's bunch already had a lot of fire. Hopefully what we were about to create wouldn't make things too much worse. By the time we met at the creek junction, the roar of the combined fires was so loud everyone had to yell. Drawn from the bottom, our burnouts rushed upslope and slammed into the main fire sending tongues of flame a hundred feet high up into a great rolling black and gray smoke column. The whole upper half of the ridge was now raging at full strength.

The firing crew waded into the creek. I waited until last, wanting to make sure that we had everyone with us. Five minutes later we joined up on the far bank, then fought our way through thick brush and out into the woods before stopping to talk things over.

"If we have to," I said, out of breath, "we can take to the water like at Mooseheart."

A Bell 205 roared over and began to turn, its large rotors slapping at the air. Out of the smoke, its gray shape appeared fifty feet above the trees, its navigation lights blinking red and green, a strobe light flashing under its belly. When it reached us, it turned sideways. Bell leaned out the open door holding a package in his arms, his hair and shirt sleeves blowing in the rotor wash. He tossed the package out, then pointed out into the woods ahead of the ship just as it lowered its nose and rotated forward.

Inside a burlap bag was a cardboard box with ham sandwiches, bags of potato chips, two six-packs of Coke, and a large bag of smoked salmon. On the box someone had written: Thank You — The people of Lake Minchumina. Then, beneath that: Pump, Hose, Fuel, Where I'm pointing. Radio for Swanson.

"They maybe sent this before they saw the smoke column," Melvin said, tearing into the bag of salmon. "Anyway, too late now. May as well eat."

"We'll eat later," Mitchell said. "Let's get this pump and hose going, or all this will be for naught."

"For not what?" Melvin wanted to know.

"For naught, as in for nothing."

"Well," Melvin shrugged, "it's not for nothing to get smoked salmon. Want some?"

As we crammed the food into our PG bags, Mitchell said, "Rake, you and I'll scout for spots."

A hissing sound came from out in the woods in the direction Bell had pointed. By the time we got to it, the spotfire was the size of a volleyball court, burning hot, half in open tundra, the rest in thick spruce. The pump and hose had been dropped off fifty yards beyond the spotfire in a small opening. I pulled my radio from its holster.

"Bell, this is Swanson."

"Bell."

"Don, we've got the pump. We'll work this side of the creek. What about the other side?"

"Quinlan's guys are moving up. They should be in there any time. He's got a radio so you can work with him. He doesn't have a pump but he can use yours when you're finished with it. Retardant is ten minutes out. When they get here, I'll turn them over to you. Talk on air-to-ground, channel five."

In one trip four of us packed the pump kit, 600 feet of inch and a half nylon hose and two five gallon cans of premix to the creek. While Melvin set up the pump, Johnny B. and I rolled out hose. Rake and Mitchell continued gridding the area, knocking down small spotfires.

In the distance I heard the roar of a large aircraft coming in low from the north.

"Swanson, Tanker 122. Come up on air-to-ground."

"Tanker 122, Swanson. Go."

"We're coming up on your fire. Are you there where the creeks run together?"

"That's affirmative, on this spotfire west of the main creek."

"Copy. That looks like your priority for now... that one about 100 yards out?"

"Copy. That's it. Shoot us some mud."

"Yes, sir. Let's try to box it in along the creeks. How on that?"

"That'd be just dandy. While you're circling, give us a good look for spotfires. It's pretty smoky down here."

"Well, it's hard to see under the column, but we don't see anything major at the moment. There are several across the creek from you, though. Is your area clear?"

"Copy, we're moving out."

We headed for the small rise where the pump had been dropped off.

The roar of the plane moved out somewhere beyond the smoke column, then muffled as it went behind the ridge, then roared again as it came around the other side. Seconds later we heard something big and powerful coming, a high-pitched whine, a dark shadow rushing through the smoke. Then, suddenly, a brilliant flash of wings and the release a 1000 gallons of pink fire retardant that hit right on target, lining one side of our area, including most of the biggest spotfire.

"On the money 122," I said. "Y'all do good work."

"We aim to please," The pilot said. "But you're the ones doing all the work. We're just up here riding around having fun."

The second drop tied the corner of the first drop to the main creek. Within minutes our bunch was back on the line and taking advantage of the retardant. Melvin started the pump and Johnny B. began wetting the perimeter. Back at the junction I did a quick recon. The main fire was holding.

# 15

Fifteen minutes after the retardant drop, Quinlan and his crew met with Bell, Rake and me.

"Aackk," Quinlan said. "This little weenie roast has you boys scared, doesn't it?"

He said that as soon as he was close enough for us all to hear. I reckon it had been hard on him not having anybody but his own bunch to rile up.

"Hark!" Rake said. "It's the General Patton of smokejumping."

"General Annoyance, is more like it," Bell said.

Quinlan shook hands with us, then took out his pipe and lit it.

"Well," Quinlan grinned from inside a cloud of blue smoke, "it's a good thing you got on these spotfires. Sorry we couldn't make it sooner."

"Well, we haven't got it yet," Bell said. "Here's the plan. Big Al wants me to phone the jumpshack, so I've got to go into Minchumina. Don't ask why, because I don't know. Quinlan, take your bunch across the creek and work those spots. While I'm in there I'll pick up another pump, some hose and fuel."

An hour later Bell was back. The helicopter circled, then landed in a dry meadow on Quinlan's side of the creek where a pump kit, ten bundles of hose, fuel, water and rats were off-loaded. We gathered up the pump show on our side, then lugged everything a hundred yards downstream and set it up again.

That evening, as the sun swung low to the horizon, the sky turned from gray into a high ceiling of streaked yellow and orange. The air was alive with the drone of hardworking pumps and the shouting of people finding and working spots. After topping off Quinlan's pump with fuel, I walked out on a sandbar and sat down on a drift log to take a good look at the smoky, black ridge.

We had taken chances. The results bordered on a miracle. A handful of jumpers, along with some timely help from the helicopters, several well-placed retardant drops, and people working their guts out, had contained a fire that had serious potential to go big. For all the reasons people give for becoming smokejumpers, and all those they give for coming back year after year, most of them have to do with what we had just accomplished. For the time being, our fire had been stopped. It was a fine thing. And, fine things are often better left to the moment to which they belong. Most all wildland fire fighters feel the same. We have seen them and we have lived them. And that is enough.

At 10:00 that evening Bell called for a meeting with Quinlan, Mitchell, and me by the dry meadow. I thought I had arrived first, but then saw Bell sitting off by himself, writing in his Oat book. Ten minutes later Mitchell and Quinlan came trudging up, then began filling their canteens from a cubitainer. Bell got to his feet, picked up his PG bag, and made his way over to us.

"Which one of you wants to take over this fire" he said, disgusted.

"Why?" Quinlan asked. "You need some sleep?"

"No more than anyone else."

"What is it, then?"

"I talked with Al. Fairbanks wants us off this fire, first thing in the morning."

"What the hell?" Mitchell said. "That won't work. It's not controlled yet. Even after people get in here, the transition will take at least a day."

"I told him that," Bell said. "I told him we had lots of spots, that the whole back end where he dropped us was still uncontained."

"They must be out of jumpers," Quinlan said.

"They're not," Bell said. "Two loads came in since we jumped. He said he'd explain later. They're bringing in EFF crews. Two are already at the airstrip."

"That's fine," Mitchell went on, " but we can't leave before we get them in here on these spots and along the line. Besides, if they don't need us, why not keep us here and let us work it. The Minchumina airport's just ten minutes away if they need us."

"Al said it was out of his hands. If they lose the fire, then they can answer for it. He told me just to do it. To bring everyone off."

"I don't rightly give a damn who answers for what," I said. "We can't leave. All this thing needs is tomorrow's wind and it will roll again.

"Well," Quinlan said, "If the boss says we have to leave, then we have to leave."

"Well, I'm not going to be the one to tell the crew," Bell said. "You want this fire, it's yours. From here on out, I don't want any part of it."

"I'll take the fire, and I'll tell them, too," Quinlan said. "But let's wait until morning. It'll be easier on them once they've had some rest."

By midnight the entire area lay under a blanket of blue smoke. The ridge had been reduced to a giant blackness that thrust upwards into a smoky gray twilight. The creeks ran by swift and cold while the earth calmed around us. At 1:00 AM Quinlan radioed that a Bell 205 was on the way from Minchumina to pick us up and return us to our respective jump spots.

Gathered on the jump spot the next morning, we ate rations straight from the can, and finished off the sandwiches and smoked salmon sent by the Minchumina people. A thick haze lay over the fire, permeated with the tangy scent of burnt spruce resin. Pockets of smoke drifted low along the southern muskeg perimeter. It was coffee and jump story time. Tales of individual fire fights brought on their usual measure of laughter and good cheer. Spirits were up. But not mine. I sat at the edge of the group, eating alone, waiting for Quinlan to call. Bell spoke up.

"Ah, good to see everyone this morning. You guy's get some sleep?"

"Some more than others," The Fat Indian said, nodding toward a firepack with two boots stuck out the end. "The Legendary Fucking one has decided to sleep in."

"Get your ass up, Rake," Bell said, picking up a can of Peaches—Sliced, Water Added—and throwing it at Rake's cardboard hootch.

"I've got a problem," Rake groaned.

"No," Bell said. "You don't have a problem, you are a problem."

"Mr. Midnight's got me wedged in here. Come, take a look."

Bell went over to the firepack, grabbed one side, flipped it over and started it rolling downhill. Rake's cussing was muffled by the speeding firepack as it crashed into a small clump of black spruce. Bell laughed and yelled, "What's Mr. Midnight think of that?"

The crew hooted, laughed and slapped their knees.

"That was good," Bell smiled. "I don't feel so pissed-off now."

"Face it, Bell," Rake chuckled, climbing up the knoll. "You've been pissed-off ever since you hot-waxed your unit at Fossil Creek."

"I'm not facing anything," Bell said. "And I don't need to hear any-more about it, either."

Right then the call came. "Bell, Mitchell, this is Quinlan."

Bell took his radio out. "Bell, go ahead."

A few seconds later Mitchell answered the same.

"This is Quinlan with a message for all jumpers on this fire. It's time to pack up. Fairbanks has sent word. We have to demobe immediately. Bell and Mitchell will explain as much as we know. We'll be flown straight to Nenana, no stop in Minchumina. With twenty-four jumpers and gear we should be able to do it in three loads. We'll go in the order we jumped, Bell's group first. Mine last."

On the knoll Bell explained what Big Al had told him, and how Quinlan was now in charge. After the initial shock, our crew went into a fit of rage. We were getting pulled off the fire too soon. It had happened before. Transition was critical. This was bullshit. It was the helicopter-with-the-butterfly-net deal in the cartoon in the Ready Room, and on and on.

An hour later our demobe started. The flight took 45 minutes. When we landed in Nenana we were met by the drivers of a stake bed truck from the Fairbanks warehouse and a school bus from transportation. The stake bed carried eight 55-gallon drums of Jet A for the helicopters, and would haul our gear bags back. The bus was for us. Shortly after the first half of Quinlan's group landed Mitchell took up a collection, jumped in the stake bed and lit out for Moocher's Bar. He returned with three cases of ice-cold Olympia beer.

"Three cases?" The Fat Indian grumbled. "That's just three beers a piece."

"It's enough for now," Mitchell said. "We're in official travel status. This is just a little consolation for catching a tough fire and then getting screwed."

"I like dat, Oly," Melvin said, popping a can and emptying it in one long swig.

By the time the last helicopter arrived with the final load it was mid-afternoon, and the first two loads had finished all three cases and were, even by jumper standards, well on their way to getting smashed.

"Okay, we see your beers," Pat Shearer said, "now where's ours?"

"These guys drank it all," Mitchell said, burping loudly.

Shearer and Mountain Puss took off to Moocher's for two more cases.

Kelly walked over to Bell and handed him a note:

Don, I'd said I'd take over this fire—that's what I'm doing. I'm not coming in. Without someone here that knows the situation and how to conduct the transition, it's as good as lost. So I'm staying. Tell Al I'm prepared to let the chips fall where they may. We did too much good work to let it go. You guys have a good time in Fairbanks.                    ~Q

Bell went straight to Mitchell and gave him the note. While the crew gathered around the stake bed, loading gear bags and firepacks, four fuel drums were loaded into the helicopter. As it ran up power for takeoff, the crew hunkered behind the stake bed to avoid the dust. Off the ground and heading for Minchumina, the sound of the helicopter faded in the distance. Once things quieted Mitchell conducted a quick roll call to make sure we had everyone. We did. All but three.

When we got to the T-Hangar Big Al was waiting. Mitchell showed him Quinlan's note. After hearing that Bell and Melvin had gotten back on the helicopter and returned to the fire, he called for a meeting in a back corner of the hangar. As the crew gathered around, he stood at the big bay doors, looking out across the runway as an air tanker lifted off en route to Minchumina. I figured he was trying to decide what to do about an obvious case of insubordination, that he knew he should be furious, that enough was enough. But I wrong. He was proud. And we could tell. Quinlan's decision had, no doubt, been made as a matter of conscience. Bell's the same, after reading the note. Melvin, as usual, did what Bell did. Whatever their reasons, in each case, they had acted out of a sense of loyalty. By their actions, they had both provided hope that the fire might still be caught, and, at the same time, allowed for the impression that it had been demobed as ordered.

"Ahh, well," Big Al said, opening the meeting. "I know you're not too thrilled with this. I also know you deserve some answers. I've talked to dispatch and the District Manager. Here's the deal. It was his call. He sees jumpers as initial attack and that's all. I'm working with some fire staff to convince him otherwise. He doesn't understand these fuels. He doesn't understand how spots hold for days. He doesn't understand the importance of leaving us in place until the replacement crews are oriented to the particulars of how it burned before they got there, and what we've figured out about what it might do next. I tried to tell him, me and some of the other fire people. But his mind was made up."

"Screw his mind," Cleermont said. "What about the other fires where jumpers are still out?"

"They're way out," Big Al said. "Not close to an airstrip or highway."

"But they're not near a lake with a lot of cabins and homes, either," Cleermont said. "It was a wonder we stopped that thing in the first place. It took everything we had. There are spots all over the place."

Plumb disgusted, the jumpers let fly with several comments regarding bullshit, dumb asses, top-down micro-managing sons-a-bitches and other stuff Big Al had heard lots of times.

"I know, I know," Big Al said, raising his hand for quiet. "And now they've been rolling retardant for three hours. I don't like it any better than you do."

I couldn't keep still any longer.

"Al," I said. "This's the worst thing that can happen to a good crew. It's against everything we believe in."

Mattlon ran his fingers through his hair, shaking his head. "Don't you think I know that?"

"We'll," I said, trying not to get mad, "we've got to do something. We just can't sit around and pretend that... "

"Nobody's pretending anything, Len. And, as far as doing something goes—and this applies to everyone—you just keep doing your jobs. In the meantime, give me room to do mine."

Normally upbeat and humming with good cheer, the mood in the Ready Room the next morning was strained, to say the least. Storytelling jumpers in off other fires and the dispirited troops from Minchumina made a strange and uncomfortable mix. The only funny thing that happened was a song two friends sang right after roll call. It was written by Tony, the Mexican from Silver City who named the speed racks Lupe and Hernando, and his fair-skinned Texas amigo, Winko. Winko had married Tony's first wife after she and Tony divorced. Tony and Winko were buddies, jumping together out of Boise, Idaho for several years, so they didn't have a problem being related that way. Their song was called *My Name Is Tony*, and was based on the western tune *My Name is Lisa*. They sang it to standing side by side with big smiles, arms over each other's shoulders. Like this:

My name is To-ny... my name's not Wink-o

My skin is brown-o... my skin's not pink-o

You used to love me... but now you love him

As if a Tex-as man... is better than a Mex-i-can

While we laughed at Tony and Winko's song, Big Al got on the intercom and called for another meeting.

"Ahh, well, just some news here before we start our day," he began. "This is mainly for you guys in off the Minchumina fire. I got a call early this morning from Quinlan. He's taken command as fire boss. Bell's line boss. Melvin's at the airstrip working as some kind of liaison between the EFF crews and the people of Minchumina. A spot blew out yesterday afternoon in the area of the creeks and burned another 15 acres. I talked with Birkey at Air Attack, and he told me they dropped $35,000 worth of retardant knocking it down. Beside their problems with spots, there's a mile of perimeter at the tail that's still unmanned. According to Bob, they're putting a crew on that today. Bottom line is... thanks to the work you did, along with our people still out there, it looks like they may hold it."

Big Al paused, waiting for someone to speak. No one did.

"So that's it," he sighed. "I expect they'll be rolling more mud this afternoon. Don't let it get you down. In a way you're still out there."

The meeting adjourned after a brief review of the other fires, then we dressed down for PT. The McGrath All-Star and I went running together. At the east end of the runway, we crossed a big lawn and did a couple laps around a soccer field, then took to the trail through the woods along the Chena River. The trail was more interesting than the asphalt, chainlink desolation of Fort Wainwright, so we ran the river, jumping logs and downed trees. At one point the trail crossed a sandy beach.

"Hey," I yelled, "let's go for a swim."

After stripping down, we dove in and swam out into a part of the river that was full of morning sunlight, whooping and laughing because the water was so cold. I rolled over on my back and kicked against the current. Water splashed up like diamonds.

"Last time we were in the water together was at Bonanza Creek," Johnny B. laughed.

"No no. The last time was at that lake with the big pike, and we were stoned."

"Oh, that's right. Bonanza Creek was when you saved me and became a hero."

"I might should have let you drowned, for all the trouble you've been."

"Well, you didn't," Johnny B. said, "so quit crowing about it. You don't always have to be bitching about something."

"What the hell are you talking about?"

"I saw you this morning. It was all you could do to keep your mouth shut."

"Shit on that," I said, the heat of my body gone to an icy cold that drove me to shore as fast as I could swim.

On shore I was drying off with my t-shirt when Johnny B. come along and wallowed up on the bank like a sick catfish.

"You're not the only one pissed-off, you know," Johnny B. said.

"All that work," I said. "Beating all night, crossing those damned sloughs, then having to go back and cross them again, working the slopover, then the next day, the big burnout, actually catching the head and all those spots. That was ours. We caught it, and we deserved to stay there and hold it. But no! We get it shoved up our butts and are supposed to roll over and pretend it ain't a problem. If there was ever a time to raise hell about something, then this is it."

Johnny B. was fit to be tied. I could tell by the way he stared across the river while I was talking instead of paying attention. Then he went to hissing like a snake and said, "Maybe you're wrong, Len. Maybe you're right. Whatever the case, what makes you think it has to be a Len Swanson-to-the-rescue problem? It's a crew problem. So let the crew deal with it. Big Al asked us to let him do his job. Have a little faith, man. Enjoy life."

"Enjoy life, hell," I said. "Is that all you can think about, *enjoying life*?"

"What's wrong with enjoying life?"

"It doesn't take much ambition is all."

"And just what do you intend to do with it?"

"I'll enjoy it if it's good. But when it's wrong, I'll fight it, by God. I'll fight the hell out of it."

Johnny B. looked at me and shook his head.

"Len," he said, pausing to give me time to settle down. "We had this bulldog across the street where I grew up as a kid, and it liked to chase cars and bark and bite at the wheels. My Dad hated it. So he got in his pickup one day and went around the block, stopped, and tied a rag onto the wheel, then drove by the bulldog's house real slow. The dog ran out, barking like always, raced in, and grabbed the rag."

Johnny B. stopped, grinned, and looked at me for a minute.

"So what?"

"Here's what," Johnny B. said. "That dog was too hardheaded to let go of the rag, so it beat him against the road, wham, wham, wham. When he finally turned it loose all he could do was run in circles and bite at himself. He lived the rest of his life with a skinned head and walked sideways like a crab, but apparently he learned something because he never chased cars again."

"Well, I'm glad he turned out to be a good dog," I said. "Listen, Johnny B., it's not just Minchumina. You don't know the half of it."

"Well, it's not like I haven't asked. As entertaining as you are, Len, I'm getting tired of trying to figure you out. This much I know, though. You wish you'd gone back to the fire like they did."

"I do... and I still have a mind to. The way I see it I don't have a rats-ass chance of getting hired back here next year anyway, so I may as well do what's right."

"I imagine you will," Johnny B. said as we put on our running shoes, "but if hardheadedness gets any credit, you'll probably end up getting a promotion."

We sat there staring at the river a little more, no one saying anything. Finally, I couldn't take it any longer.

"I got a call last night from a fire investigator," I said. "He claims he wants go after the oil company for the fire fighting costs of the Fort Greeley fire. He says I'll have to fill out a report on it."

"No shit?"

*"No shit!"*

"And you don't want to, right?"

"I do and I don't. That's the trouble."

"It has to do with that DM, doesn't it?"

"It's even worse than that. It's all kinds of shit."

"Sounds like something The Black Hand might be interested in?"

"Black Hand my ass. You and that Mohammad Ralph Louie business have only made things worse."

"Yeah right. You go farting around in all kinds of intrigue, and then have the nerve to mouth off when I do it in a playful way."

"I'm not doing any such thing. I'm just explaining that I've got a problem."

"No Len," Johnny B. said, "that's not what you're doing. You're insisting that I agree with all your right and wrong bullshit. So, go ahead, chase cars all your life, see if I give a shit. Fuck it! I'm tired of trying to be your friend."

At that, he got up and took to the trail by himself, mad. I got to my feet, mad too. I picked up a rock and threw it as far as I could out in the river. The splash created circles of light that got bigger and bigger as they drifted downstream.

I hid out that afternoon on top of the T-Hangar with Bro Ratus. At least I could talk to him without arguing. Bro Ratus kept a positive attitude, and that's what I was looking for. He hadn't been plugged in for a while, but I could tell he knew what was going on, standing there with his spruce bough over his shoulder, looking out across the runways towards Lake Minchumina. Johnny B. had avoided me since the run. I felt bad but didn't know what to do about it, him being so stubborn and all. Sarah was gone again, too. This time to Dawson, over in the Yukon Territory. I was ready for some more pizza and wine, and another sauna or two, but when it came to that I could see I was going to have to get in line behind the entire Porcupine caribou herd.

I was sitting there feeling sorry for myself when I looked over towards the FAA building and saw Big Al moseying across the aircraft ramp towards the T-Hangar. He was wearing his usual Levis, plaid cowboy shirt, and Wellington boots. He didn't wear much else. He had his head down. I reckon he walked that way because he liked to think when he walked. Word was he was still gambling and drinking a lot. Besides that, there was no doubt about it, Big Al Mattlon was a different kind of boss. His loyalty to the crew was plain as day. He was gutsy, naturally intuitive and smart. Most important, he was willing to risk his own neck for ours. He had done it time after time. And he was doing it again with Quinlan, Bell and Melvin, and the Minchumina demobe. But there was more to it than that. What made him truly extraordinary was the times he allowed us to see him vulnerable, whether down rolling in the mud with Tienharra at the Pig Party, or slumped hung over in the I-Hear-You-Walkin' Chair in the Ready Room. When you got right down to it, the way we felt about Big Al wasn't just because he was a good boss, it was because he was one of us.

Not far from the T-Hangar Big Al stopped and stared at the ground. I couldn't tell what he'd seen, but when he knelt down I saw it was an ant hill made in a crack in the concrete. He knelt there looking at ants, and I had to wonder what could be so interesting about a bunch of ants. Maybe he wished our crew was like them, always working, not pissed-off and bitching all the time. After a couple minutes, he got to his feet and entered the T-Hangar. He went right into Operations, got on the PA system and announced another crew meeting. By then everyone knew the story of the Minchumina demobe, so I figured the meeting was another attempt to calm us down.

The McGrath All-Star was sitting in the I-Hear-You-Walkin' Chair with Duke on his lap. Matt Kelly stood and faced the group. To our surprise, Matt was going to conduct the meeting. Recently he had given himself a nickname, Blue Leader. Things had not been going well for Blue

Leader and his group of TM guys, the Transcendental Meditators. Too much fighting with MT, the Mental Trauma bunch, and then with the fires and everything, levitating practice had been called off. If Omar Sharif had come to the T-Hangar straight from the Dr. Zhivago movie, he and Matt Kelly would have been twins. Broad shouldered, handsome, over six feet, Matt was a bright star in the evening sky of peculiar individuals. Funny and genuine, one on one, Matt would look people straight in the eye, talk softly and proceed to tell them some of the strangest things they'd ever heard. Things like, "When I was a boy growing up in Africa, this old Zulu Chief and I went to the moon together."

"Big Al asked me to start the meeting," Kelly began. "So...  for some of the things that have you upset these days, you might look at it this way. If you keep on doing what you're doing, you're going to keep on getting what you've got."

The room stayed quiet a second, then Rake said, "Thank you, Swami Rama Lama Ding Dong."

The group laughed. Kelly blinked a few times, smiled, then said, "We have a guest here with us today. And we want all our guests to feel safe and welcome here in our workplace."

Out of the corner of my eye, I saw someone edging forward along the wall. It was none other than Miles, "Big M—little organ," Morgan, carrying a briefcase and a stack of papers. Placing his briefcase on the floor beneath the bulletin board, he began handing out four different sets of forms, all the while talking.

"Our District Manager has asked me to acquaint you with the new paper work. Aside from his interest in improving performance, Mr. Twixtenblout sees problems with accountability as well. Which brings up Form 55, the new time sheet."

Shuffling papers, the jumpers grumbled instant opposition.

"Form 55 incorporates the new policy regarding justification of overtime on fires. Time slips from the Minchumina fire show crew times running from 8:00 AM, your starting time on July 28th, and running straight through until 2:00 AM on July 30th for a total of 42 hours with no breaks."

"They show that because that's what we worked," Mitchell said. "We had to in order to catch the fire. We made our move when conditions...  "

The door to Operations opened and Mattlon stepped out, whispered something to The Fat Indian, then left.

"... allowed us a chance to catch it the first night. We had to. Otherwise it would have been too late."

"It's unsafe to work that many hours without rest," Miles said.

"Of course it is!" Mitchell said, shaking his head. "That's why we only do it when we have to. In the long run keeping fires small means less total danger than when they go big and have to be worked for days, sometimes even weeks."

"You could still have taken a few breaks," Miles said. "Which should be off the clock."

"How would you know," I said. "How many nights have you spent on a fire?"

"At least one I know of," Kasson said. "It's the only time I ever saw a man dig fireline with his head." Angry comments about the conking of Miles Morgan on the Shaktoolik River filled the room. Sweat beaded on Miles' forehead.

"We were miles from our gear," I said. "It was 2:00 in the morning. What were we supposed to do, abandon the line, hike all the way back to the jump spots, sleep, then hike all the way back out there? You don't know what the hell you're talking about."

"There's no reason to be rude," Miles said.

I jumped up. "And there's no call for you to come here and insult us, either."

"All right, all right," The Fat Indian said, waving for me to sit down. Then he turned to Miles, "A few more minutes, that's it. You need to run this by Al."

Nervous as a long-tailed cat in a room full of rocking chairs, Miles glanced down at Form 55. "In the future written justifications will be required for all shifts over 19 hours the first day, and 16 each day there-after. Each will be subject to approval by fire staff."

In my mind I saw an image of hell with Miles going down a red esca-lator into a cave glowing with fire.

"Big M," Rake said, "there're a lot of comedians out of work these days. Maybe you should consider another career."

"I may not be funny," Miles said, "but I can add and subtract. For those of you on fires out west, you can't add an hour every time you go from Alaska time to Bering time, and then add another one when you come back. By that method, one of you got 26 hours in one day. And another thing. Once your fire's controlled, you have to start showing cof-fee breaks."

"That's enough," The Fat Indian barked. "Thanks for coming. See you later."

The next morning another Rumor Control memo appeared on the Bulletin Board.

## rumor control - rumor control - rumor control - rumor control

August 3, 1973
Rumor Control Headquarters

Rumor Control has recently become aware of a serious development in the bureaucratic end of Alaska good-deal smokejumping. That is to say an insidious portion of BLM management preoccupied with the rote and mechanical accounting of the time worked by the jumpers, may be acquiring unseemly powers and deputations out of keeping with the jumpers' primary purpose — putting out fires. Our secret correspondent, whose name cannot be revealed in the current atmosphere because it would endanger his life, has revealed that alarming changes are in the works over at Fire Control. For example, the premature pulling of jumpers off the Lake Minchumina fire; a decision not made on the ground, but by some ivory-tower weenie-types in Fairbanks. Meanwhile, the government has spent $55,000 on fire retardant while the community of Lake Minchumina remains in peril, all unnecessary had the jumpers been left in place.

Timekeeping appears, to some, to be consummately significant. That is to say, more important than fire suppression itself. This shift in viewpoint is the result of those who find it necessary to spend large amounts of time completing what has become a steady stream of forms which are collected and kept in the possession of an increasing number of people. This form mania represents a most ineffectual method of making a record of whatever information is now deemed necessary — basic stuff that anyone can see by just standing around and watching.

Rumor Control suspects something else may be in the wind. For example, the aforementioned, but unnamed, source unwittingly discovered a strange, intricate grid under one of the District Office Xerox machines — an unusual array of numbers which seem much like a secret test scoring system. Upon careful examination the grid has turned out to be exactly that. What has been revealed is nothing less than a scoring of various jumper's ability to enter certain information into the proper spaces on forms. The resultant test scores are designed to reveal personal (and thus sacred) information regarding an individual's general aptitude for lying, personal inclination to cheat the government, disposition toward deceiving bean counters, and resistance to being trained to do paperwork. And so, don't panic. Be alert. Be vigilant. As Mohammad Ralph Louie—a personal friend of mine—once said, "It's never too late to fuck up your life."

~The Black Hand

# 16

On August 5th Quinlan, Bell, and Melvin came in from the Minchumina fire. August 5th is a day all smokejumpers remember. On that day in 1949, on the Mann Gulch fire in the Helena National Forest, twelve Missoula, Montana smokejumpers and a fire guard burned to death. They ran for their lives up a steep, hot hillside during a sudden wind that spread fire quickly below them. Thirteen white stone crosses, surrounded by tall grass and burned snags, still stand on that silent hillside, high above the Missouri River, marking where they fell. Three jumpers, Wag Dodge, Bob Sallee, and Walt Rumsey barely escaped.

The Ready Room was full of commotion with two groups of jumpers just in from Galena, unpacking gear bags and telling stories. As for me, I had taken to the I-Hear-You-Walkin' Chair, mostly so I could be left alone and think, but also so I could be close enough to hear what the Minchumina jumpers had to say. I'd been keeping to myself ever since my falling out with Johnny B. at the river. We were still jump partners, and him getting mad only made me feel worse about everything. He was the one person I could always lean on, and now he didn't even want to even say "I hear you walkin'." Bell and Quinlan and Melvin were in the Operations office talking with Big Al. It was quiet at first and I thought things were serious but before long I heard them laughing. Someone tapped me on the shoulder and when I looked around I was surprised to see Sarah standing there, smiling. I got up and we went outside and over to the deck outside the pilots lounge.

"Good to see you again, Sarah."

"I know. "It's good to see you. Melvin's here too, isn't he?"

"He is. He's in there with Don Bell talking with the boss.

"He called me yesterday and said they were coming."

"How was Canada?"

"Canada was a lot of meetings. Difficult meetings, but we're getting things moving in the right direction."

"Things haven't been much fun here either," I said, "especially without you."

"I know," Sarah said again. "But I can't sit around waiting for you. You never know where you're going or when you're coming back. But that's the good part, isn't it?"

"What are your caribou friends up to these days?"

Sarah laughed. "The last time my father checked, they were still on their summer range. But they'll be moving south soon. That's their way. They're a lot like smokejumpers."

I laughed at that. "Well, I wish them luck then. Tell me more about your work."

"Our work requires patience and shared leadership. That comes naturally to me because my culture requires it. I consult with the elders. And that means humility and living by the examples they set. In the case of Canada, they're our people, too. We share the same history and we share the same caribou. So, I was over there working on the caribou commons idea. We want to educate people about the consequences of their actions. And that includes the outside world."

I sat there listening but distracted by the fact that every time I saw her she was more beautiful.

"Well, it's noble work," I finally said, "and there's a big need for that kind of thing."

"The caribou commons would include the entire range of the Porcupine herd both here and in Canada. It could also lead to a World Heritage listing, or being established as a Biosphere Reserve. Both could be done by the U.N. It's important. I know you understand. It's your great-grandmother helping you to see the world the Indian way."

"How long will you be in town?"

"I'm not sure. Other than a trip to Juneau in a couple weeks, I don't see going anywhere for a while."

"What's in Juneau?"

"Politics!" Sarah said. "And politicians. Indigenous peoples are a minority with little perceived power. So, my work has to be broad-based and boundary crossing. To be heard we must find allies wherever and however we can."

"Your work makes mine seem trifling."

"We each need to do what we can, when we can. Comparing isn't important."

"Hey Swanson," Rake yelled from the bay doors of the T-Hangar. "Get over here. Someone wants to see you in Operations."

"I reckon I better go. Can I see you tonight?"

"Come by around six. Maybe we can go to the Howling Dog."

I headed for the hangar; Sarah walked with me. She wanted to see Melvin. When I got to the Ops window I was surprised to see, of all people, Mort and some other guy, both of them wearing suits.

"Well, well, here's Len," Mort said, extending his hand. I shook it. Not that I wanted to, but because I was taught not to be rude. "Senator, meet Len Swanson," Mort said, sweet as pie. "Len, this is Senator Ted Jensen."

After we shook hands, I turned to Sarah. "Sarah, you know Mort already. This here's Senator Jensen."

"Senator Jensen, Sarah Sheenjek, nice to meet you," Sarah said, shaking hands.

"Sheenjek," the Senator said, cocking his head. "You wouldn't happen to know Melvin Sheenjek?"

"Of course, Melvin's my brother."

"We'll then, it's a pleasure to meet you, too, Miss Sheenjek. I was just telling Mort here how the jumpers and the other firefighters saved our Lake Minchumina community. And your brother! He was the one who managed the staging area at the airstrip, and helped set up all the water pumps and hoses. Brought a hose clear around my cabin. Didn't need them in the end, but your brother's work with our people was, indeed, heroic."

Right then Melvin came up and Sarah gave him a hug, which he got embarrassed about.

"Melvin," Sarah said. "Are you a hero?"

"No!" Melvin said. "I don't think so. Sometimes I wished I wasn't out there. But, then, everything got better and we had spot fires and we turned them off."

"Well," the Senator said, "you're a hero to me, Melvin. And to Lake Minchumina, too."

Everything seemed just dandy the way we were all talking. But then The Fat Indian came to the Operations window and said, "Len, our District Manager wants you to suit-up and show the Senator how our jump gear works. Can you do that?"

I went to my gear where it hung on Lupe, and started suiting up, talking as I did, telling the Senator how each piece went on, the jump jacket, the jump pants, the harness and all. I didn't care for it. Especially since it was Mort's idea, and he was trying to show off the jumpers for his own benefit after all the sneaky stuff he'd done running us down. I put on my main, my reserve, even my helmet, and stood there ready for more questions.

"What's this cross strap for," Mort said, pointing to the strap that's sewn down the outside of one leg of the jump pants, then passes under your boot like a stirrup and then up the inside where it crosses over about six inches below the crotch, and then down the inside, under the other boot and up the outside of the opposite leg.

"That's for when you're coming down in trees and you straddle a branch. It hits the strap... instead of here," I said, indicating my crotch. "The strap transfers the shock to the bottom of your boots."

I didn't like talking about things like that in front of Sarah, and was plumb fed up with Mort using me like a suit-up dummy.

"Let's show the Senator," Mort said. "Stand with your legs apart, and he'll kick you and see how it works."

By that time some jumpers had gathered around, looking and grinning. I could hardly stand it, but I didn't see any way to say no. Mort had singled me out, planned the whole thing, and I was trapped. So I spread my legs and Senator Jensen, who was clearly enjoying being the center of attention, lined up and kicked me square in the crotch. It about lifted me off the ground. He did it twice. After Mort had taken the second photo he said he was going to send it in to the BLM monthly newsletter so that it could be published nationwide.

In a dim corner of the Skyways Lounge, we were sprawled on the floor with our heads resting on our PG bags, trying to sleep. I was under a table by myself. We had arrived at Seattle-Tacoma International Airport at 2:00 AM. At first we waited at a flight service station that was open all night, but had to move to the lounge because, according to Quinlan, our COP (Chief of Party), there had been a change in plans. Quinlan found a pretty waitress and instantly charmed her, explaining that we were firefighters who had been up all night and would not likely get any sleep before parachuting into wildfires in the morning, and would she be so gracious as to allow us to take up some floor space in her fine establishment.

Dark red and soft, the carpet was a good deal compared to sitting in the plastic chairs with fixed arms and backs or lying on the linoleum floor under bright fluorescent lights like at the flight service station. I looked across rows of reclining smokejumpers and watched yellow flames flicker in the fireplace. Rain fell outside the big windows facing the runways. During our five hour flight south across the Alaska Range, then down the coastal waterway, I had looked out the window as the light of a northern summer disappeared behind us. Stars began to appear. Moonlight reflected in a silver band over the Pacific. Small clouds cast moon shadows on the snowy slopes of Vancouver Island. Then there was Seattle, shimmering at the edge of Puget Sound, its outlying districts separated by areas of dark water that outline the city at night. I thought about the people as we flew in over the city, millions of them, most asleep in bed, some dreaming, some making love, the precious beauty of it all.

We had left Fairbanks four hours after dispatch had called for a down-south booster. I didn't even have time to see Sarah, so I called her cabin and left a message with Melvin, who stayed behind. His father had called from Alatnuk, and said that he wanted him to quit for the season and come home. The last time I had seen Melvin was at the T-Hangar, standing by the bulletin board with Mort, just after I'd been kicked twice in the crotch by a career politician.

Sarah and I had gone dancing at the Howling Dog that night. Bell and Betsy were there, too, dancing and carrying on. Sarah and I danced and talked with them and had a few drinks but left early. Bell had borrowed White Trash from Dow, so the problem of the Red Lizard, and by that I mean his possession of it, had ended—at least for the time being. The Red Lizard remained parked in the old warehouse, its' distributor rotor in my pickup's glove box, its' the wiring burned out, looking like it had been bombed.

Sarah and I had spent the next three nights together. That took some kinks out of me for sure. But now I was gone and she was in Fairbanks. Just as she was going to be around, I up and took off.

Looking over the rows of resting jumpers, I saw Johnny B. He looked asleep. We still hadn't talked and I figured he might be bothered by me taking up with Sarah without telling him much about it. Maybe he was hoping to do that and I beat him to it. Lots of jumpers had had the same girlfriend at different times—not Sarah, but others. There weren't all that many in Fairbanks to start with, so it was necessary to be polite about it.

Lightning had moved in over Eastern Oregon in its typical summer pattern. The La Grande base was out of jumpers. The sixteen in our group were on our way to boost them. Lying there, staring at the fireplace, even though I already missed Sarah, I knew there was no other option for me. A trip south was the next step in a complete Alaska smokejumper summer. It was my first, and likely my last. Mort would make sure of that. It just burned me up the way he had come to the Ready Room, been overly friendly to the Senator, and, in the end, right in front of Sarah and all the jumpers, gotten me kicked in the crotch — *twice.* When the newsletter came to the T-Hangar, there I was on the front page, six inches off the ground, arms flapped out like a penguin, head rolled back, looking like a fool.

Just then a woman in a Forest Service uniform came to Quinlan and said, "There's been another change. La Grande's been boosted by McCall. We're sending you to Winthrop as soon as we can arrange another charter."

The woman had no way to haul our gear from the first flight service to the one that would fly us. So, for the next two hours, we made two round-trips of about a mile each, to the second flight service, in a misty rain, lugging our 100 pound jump gear bags, then the big cardboard boxes filled with extra mains and reserves and rigger's kits. This place was a double-wide trailer with more stiff-back chairs, no carpet, and no room to lie down. By 6:00 A.M. we were loaded and ready to fly. An hour later I woke to the drone of twin turbines, snowcapped Glacier Peak, the Entiat Mountains, and the bright silver reach of Lake Chelan. The earth moved slowly beneath the plane. Bell slept in a seat across the aisle. Quinlan was reading the morning edition of the Seattle Post Intelligencer.

The Methow Valley lay in hazy blue shadows with rolling hills at it's edge, higher mountains to the west, and rugged crags north towards Canada. Farm fields covered the valley floor, some green, some yellow, different triangles, rectangles, and squares of alfalfa, oats, and pasture. The Methow River was lined with cottonwood trees, and ran south to north, winding across farms and ranches. Houses, barns, and sheds stood bright white, old and new, weathered and run-down. In the distance, just a little south of the small town of Winthrop, I could see an airstrip, a large red quonset building, a smaller silver one, and an office building—the North Cascades Smokejumper Base.

On the ground we were met by Will Landy, the base foreman. Will was known in the smokejumper world as The Old Bull, and was believed to be one of the toughest jumpers, ever. He had us put our gear in the red quonset, which served as their parachute loft, Ready Room, and sewing room, all in one.

"Breakfast will be in an hour," Will said. "We didn't know we were getting you until a few minutes ago."

The Old Bull went on to tell us that the bust was likely over, that most of the regulars had come in off fires that night. There would be an orientation after breakfast, but for now we could kick back on the lawn and wait. Sixteen of us gathered up on an area near the office. Most of our regular bunch was there, Rake, Bell, Dow, Mitchell, Kasson, Master Bates, Mountain Puss and the rest.

The rich chlorophyll of fresh-mowed alfalfa combined with the sweet scent of dry grass and the cottonwood trees and damp lawn in the cool morning air. Fairbanks has nice enough weather in the three months of summer but nothing like the day to day complete summer of the American West in early August. We lay down on the cool grass, and before long most were asleep.

"HUP, one, HUP, two, HUP, three, HUP, four."

Smokejumpers yelling and doing jumping jacks attacked my sleepy dream like a horde of Mongols. I woke, lifted up on an elbow, and stared. Right there before us, not eight feet away, twenty Winthrop jumpers had lined up in rows and were exercising, shouting out the counts, every last one dressed in black Can't Bust 'Em jeans, white t-shirts, and logger boots. By comparison, we lay ever which way, dressed in Levis of all shades, Army kakis, plaid shirts, and what all. They had a uniform. They liked having one. They were tough, and they liked that, too. Next to them we looked like extras on a movie dedicated to fur trappers, destitute cowboys, and cheap bastards.

Throughout the small, odd world of smokejumping NCSB jumpers had the reputation—and apparently cultivated it—of projecting themselves as the genuine article. After all, Winthrop was where smokejumping was born. The first experimental jumps were made here in 1939. After that came thirty-some years of tradition based on the military management style popular after World War II. The way the NCSB jumpers saw it, most all the other jump bases were Johnny-come-latelies. This was especially true when it came to Alaska, the last base to form, and the one notorious for being home to those who couldn't cut it or fit in the Lower 48.

From four-count jumping jacks, they went to push ups, shouting just the same, then back to jumping jacks, all the time shouting, "Love it. Love it. Want more of it."

It was clear. These men, jumping up and down in arrow-straight rows, all dressed alike, were not just welcoming us, but putting us on notice that this is what NCSB smokejumpers were, and what any worth-a-shit smokejumper ought to be.

"Get some. Love it. Yeah! Yeah! Want it, do it," various ones whooped.

For the next twenty minutes they did one exercise after another, breaking into sweats, always loving it, looking straight ahead, right over us, like we weren't there. Without warning they stopped, chuckled to themselves and fell at ease.

Matt Kelly got slowly to his feet, turned to them and smiled.

"Wow!" Kelly said in a calm, sincere voice. "You guys must be sexually frustrated."

That caused some chuckling in our group and some grunting objections in theirs.

"That's okay, though. I'm Blue Leader. I instruct Transcendental Mediation. I can teach you ways to cope with the psychic injuries associated with being over-sexed and under appreciated."

The Alaskans laughed. The welcoming committee stiffened. As the laughing died down, the Winthrop guys lit out on their morning run.

Winthrop had this old wash house with some showers, sinks, and a washing machine. Having been up all night, sleeping in airplanes and on floors, we needed to spruce up. Some shaved, a few hopped in the shower. A steel triangle rang out the call to breakfast. Across a big lawn sat a ranch-style cookhouse surrounded by beds of petunias and snapdragons and a few old elm trees. Inside, rows of tables were separated by a center aisle. Photos from every year, all the way back to the beginning, covered the walls—the crew suited up, front row kneeling, two or three rows standing, holding their helmets—the year written below. On the tables sat plates of bacon and ham and scrambled eggs and pancakes and biscuits hot from the oven. At each plate was a quart of cold milk. Black coffee steamed from white pitchers. Honey, jam, and syrup containers were spaced for easy reach, all of it served home style by local cooks. After the war-like welcoming committee, the cookhouse of the North Cascades Smokejumper Base was a haven of warmth and good cheer.

"You boys eat now," a large, pink woman said. "Sit anyplace you want. Don't be bashful. There's plenty to go around." For many of us, she was the Mom we hadn't seen in a long time.

The clomping of heavy boots and screeching of chairs was followed by the respectful quieting down of hungry smokejumpers. Everyone was polite to the cooks—even to each other. Once seated, I took a moment to look around and thought, "My, my, this place has class." Two thin, parallel green lines ran around the rims of each white plate, cup, and saucer, along with the badge emblem of the United States Forest Service. This was the Forest Service of old; an outfit steeped in tradition and pride.

After breakfast we were told that we would not be put on the jump list until we'd finished orientation, which meant a trip to the woods to climb what The Old Bull called, "The big trees we have down here."

So off we went in a truck, the bunch of us, headed for the woods. Except when I was a kid, I never cared much for climbing trees. Next to packouts I saw climbing to retrieve parachutes and cargo as the next most miserable thing a jumper had to do. Also dangerous. I strapped the four-inch-gaff climbing spurs on my boots and secured them to my calves. Then I buckled on the harness, made sure I had my Fanno saw and hard-hat and started up a four-foot diameter Ponderosa pine. When a tree's that big, it's hard at first to get a throw that advances the rope up the tree. You have to pull yourself in close and at the same time whip a loop up and around, attempting to lift the rope, and all the time hoping your spurs don't slip out. If they do, you have to pinch the rope tight in front of you to keep from sliding down the trunk. Whatever you do, you almost always get a skinned nose and your hardhat knocked crooked.

"Is this high enough?" I asked, looking down from sixty feet. The trunk was clear of limbs the first fifty feet, and after performing three limb-overs to prove I had the technique down, I saw no reason to go higher.

"All the way to the top," an NCSB squad leader said, clearly glad about it.

So that's how it is, I thought. I felt like telling the guy to lump it, but then I remembered what Big Al told me before I left Alaska, "Don't go down there and cause a bunch of trouble," he had said. "You've got enough people pissed-off up here. Just keep your mouth shut and you'll do fine. Remember, the crew comes first."

So on I went. By then it wasn't the rope flipping that was hard, it was the one after another limb-overs. When you have your main climbing rope around a tree and come to a limb that's too big to saw off, you have to use a second short belt. The short belt is attached to the main rope. You move it above the limb, then fix it back to your harness, undo the main rope, then go on up to the next limb, using the short belt then come to another limb, and do it all over again. It was hot and I was sweat soaked. I had spider webs and bark dust in my eyes, and my gloves were part full of scratchy bark pieces and my wrists were skinned up like my nose from all the limbs and stuff. Besides that, my legs were tired. I'd stop and lock them once in a while, and try to lean back and relax, but they begin to hurt in that position, too, so I'd go on, trying not to get mad.

A half hour later I was way up in the ponderosa, where it was about two-feet thick. From that point on I decided to free-climb without spurs and rope. Sitting on a limb, I slowly unbuckled each spur and tied it off to a branch. Dropping your climbing spurs would make it impossible to get down without considerable help. The embarrassment would be ruinous. Some jumper would have to climb to the lowest point I could free-climb and bring me another pair.

Still, I made sure of my moves and headed on up. At a diameter of about six inches, I held up and looked out over the forest. Four other Alaskans had attained similar perches, Kasson, Quinlan, Blue Leader, and Johnny B. I waved and they hollered back, all except Johnny B.

Back at the base, right after lunch, The Old Bull started our orientation by handing out a single sheet of paper.

## NORTH CASCADE SMOKEJUMPER
## MINIMUM STANDARDS FOR SMALL FIRE SUPPRESSION

1. The final fireline will be at least 18 inches wide, down to mineral soil and free from all burnable material.

2. All trees will be limbed as high as possible, and all small trees inside the fireline will be removed.

3. The area inside the fireline will be spaded and cold-trailed with bare hands regardless of whether dry or wet mop-up is used.

4. All lightning struck trees will be carefully checked for evidence of fire. If in doubt, climb and check tree or fall it. With rare exceptions, all lightning trees will be felled.

5. All grass fires will be completely lined.

Things like that, on and on. A whole page about the proper method for just about every possible decision an on-the-ground jumper would have to make. Such details didn't sit right with me. I'd been kicked off a fire by management, stranded on a fire by management, kicked in the crotch by management, photographed and shamed before the entire country on the front page of a BLM newsletter by management. Treated like out-of-area jumpers was one thing, but treated like we were kids with no sense was a bridge too far. The room was quiet. Most were still reading.

"Y'all have lots of reburns?" I asked.

The Old Bull looked me over like he wasn't used to questions like that. Just as he was seen as one of the toughest jumpers in history, he was also seen as one of the most rigid in his views as well.

"Almost never," The Old Bull said. "And we don't want any, either."

"You almost never have reburns, but you made up this paper anyway?"

"Every base has a reburn now and then," The Old Bull said, shaking his head. "You know that. This is new. Something we want to try."

I did know that. I also knew that reburns were extremely rare. But the nature of fire, with its ability to hide pockets of coals in tree roots and under big rocks made them a sure thing over time. What I didn't know was that anyone thought they could prevent them with a bunch of rules.

"Well," I said, "I was raised on a ranch, and my Dad used to say that it was important to be able to tell the difference between imaginary problems and real ones."

Quinlan shifted in his chair and give me the stink-eye, then said to The Old Bull, "Don't mind him, Will. We'll do what needs to be done."

The Old Bull liked that, and finished the meeting saying we could take the rest of the day and hang out in the barracks and get some rest, and that he would put us on the list first thing the next morning.

The silver Quonset hut was cool inside with creaky wood floors, a lounge and TV area, and little rooms with two jumpers assigned to each. As jump partners, Johnny B. and I were put in one together. Without saying a word we went in, lay down and tried to sleep. Not long afterwards we heard the first siren. Twenty minutes later we heard the second. Next came a knock on our door.

"Get up boys," Quinlan said. "We need to get our gear ready."

In the Ready Room a bunch of Winthrop jumpers were looking at a map and the jump list.

"We got a fire," The Old Bull said. "On the Okanagan. They may need help."

"Is that where the first plane went?" Mitchell asked.

"No. That was a load to boost La Grande. They've picked up more fires."

Hell, I thought to myself. That's where we were going in the first place. Now we're stuck here and getting passed up on the list. But I just kept laying out my gear and didn't say a word. Quinlan had already give me an ass-chewing about my input on the minimum standards, making it clear that some jump bases did things differently than we did on our ranch in Texas.

By the time the jumpship was back from the Okanagan fire another call had come for a Doug load to the Pasayten Wilderness. That put us on the next load. They dropped all sixteen on the Pasayten, and by the time the plane got back we had a request for a fire on the Colville.

As we took off I watched the ground fall away beneath the plane and thought to myself, this is the best and the worst of it. Instead of sleeping in the cool barracks and getting a good night's rest, we were on our way to a fire on a hot August afternoon and what was likely to be a hell of a lot of misery and hard work. Our flight was nearly two hours, way up into the northeast corner of Washington on the Colville National Forest, so we did manage to get some sleep.

"Fifteen out," The Old Bull yelled from the open door of the Doug.

Johnny B. and I went to checking each other, him first, then me. We did it just like always, by the numbers, every time, exactly the same. When he was done, he said the usual, "Helmet, gloves and letdown rope?" And I answered, "Got 'em," and he said, "Okay, you're good to go." Then he added, "You still hanging on to that rag tied to the car wheel?"

I nearly fell over. Imagine bringing up a smart aleck thing like that during a buddy check. I just stood there looking out the door, but instead of seeing a forest and a fire, I was seeing a bull dog beat over and over against a road, flipping end of over end and biting itself, then running off.

At ten acres, our fire was burning in second-growth mixed conifers and logging slash. The entire perimeter was active ground fire with ten-foot flames at the head, flaring to twenty. By any measure it was a hot and nasty deal on steep ground. But it was a fire, and in smokejumping you take your turn in the door as it comes. Two sticks later ours did.

"Drift's about three hundred yards," The Old Bull said. "Do you see the spot?"

The spot was west of the fire a couple hundred yards, about half the size of a football field and surrounded on three sides by great tall Douglas firs. The best way in was from the direction of the fire, but no one would attempt an approach that took you out over that much fire. I was listening to what The Old Bull was saying, but also thinking about Johnny B. and what he'd said about the rag deal. As the Doug pulled on final, I turned to him and yelled, "I reckon I don't know otherwise. Thanks for asking anyway."

I turned back to the door. At least now if I died or burned up or something, Johnny B. would realize I wasn't as stubborn as he thought. I placed my left foot at the edge of the threshold so that the toe of my boot stuck out over it, grabbed the sides of the door, and shoved my head out into the slipstream. I loved to do that, especially in a Doug, with its big engines hanging out on its wings, thundering with power. Never have I felt more alive than when standing in the door of a jump ship ready to go; the earth below suddenly especially beautiful, the moment especially grand, life especially precious.

I could feel Johnny B.'s hands on the back of my main as he steadied himself. When the slap came, I lunged hard, cleared the door, bent forward at the waist, looked down to be sure my boots were together, tucked my arms in close over my reserve, rotated back, and watched the big tail pass overhead. Five seconds later I was swinging silently under canopy. After calling to Johnny B., I started steering. In Alaska the most thrilling part of the jump was the exit and fall from the plane. But down south, it was the last 300 feet dropping into big timber. Already I could see the scary depths between the tops of trees and the ground. Dark shadows lay across the jump spot, defining the space into which I somehow had to find a way. A jumper was holding up a signal streamer indicating light wind from the west. At five hundred feet, a breeze began to push me so that I needed to crowd the spot closer and not drift too far out over the trees. At three hundred feet the wind slacked, but I was still in danger of missing the spot. Johnny B. was higher and in better position. I could see that if I came in like I wanted I might hog the space he needed for a safe approach. So I held off, gave him room and hoped for a tail wind. It didn't come. Within seconds I was down near the tops of great trees at the edge of the clearing. Nothing gets your attention like sinking down into the tops of tall timber. I gave up on the main spot and looked around desperately for an alternate. There was one off to the side but it was filled with rocks. When I turned back, my canopy oscillated wildly and my body crashed sideways into the top of a dead red fir. Next thing I knew I was tumbling end over end in a freefall of green blurs, limbs crashing, and all kinds of crap and corruption. I reckon I fell forty or fifty feet like that. Once you start falling you forget about spots and start thinking—to the extent that you can think at all—about when your chute will hang up. Every jumper knows it takes time. When canopies cap the tops of trees the fall is short, only twenty feet or so. But when you don't, and the canopy is pulled down into the mess of broken branches and collapses, away you go and the questions come, Is the canopy too small to catch on anything? If it does catch, will the branch or branches be strong enough to hold? Will one break off and spear through my jump suit? That's the way it was with me. There was a lot of crashing and up was no different from down. Would I fall through it all, then into the open space below and hit the ground with nothing to slow me down but a torn up ball of nylon? Just as that appeared to be my fate, there came a terrible jerk and my body swung violently against the trunk of a big Douglas fir. Broken limbs and branches fell around me. I looked up. My canopy was hanging down half way with the skirt caught on a stub of a four inch diameter limb I'd broken off. I looked down. I was hung up about 80 feet.

I went right to work—mad as hell—cussing and checking for loose lines around my neck, certain that I had almost died. I found three and I tied them up in loop knots out of the way. I unsnapped my reserve and PG bag on the right side and let them hang left. Next I took the end of my letdown rope out of my right leg pocket and ran it twice through the two D-rings sewn into the front of my jump pants. After tying off the rope to my tight riser, in this case the left one, I grabbed the tight riser with my left hand and, pulling as hard as I could, lifted myself while pulling the slack out of my rope with my right. Next I ran the rope under my right leg, brought it around, and tied it to the rope I had tied to the tight riser. With the safety knot secured, I had two free hands. I released the loose riser's capewell fitting from my harness, not a matter of much exertion since all my weight hung on the tight riser. Then came the critical part of every letdown—releasing the tight riser. The release had to be smooth. If it was sudden and strong, the limb could break and away I'd go. I took a firm grip with my left hand on the tight riser and lifted myself a few inches. Then, while supporting my body, my jump gear and PG bag with one arm, I reached across my chest with my right hand and released the capewell fitting. A jangle rang out as the riser popped loose. I bounced on the stretch of the letdown rope, but everything held.

Hanging on my rope, I made one last check for loose lines, then reached down, took the rest of my letdown rope out of my leg pocket and let it drop free, unraveling birdnest knots as it fell. After untying the safety knot, I let rope play through the D-rings and rappelled down. Hell, I'd only been in the state of Washington one day and I'd already been in the top of two big trees.

By the time I got to the ground Johnny B. and a Winthrop jumper named Dale were there to make sure I was okay and help me out of my gear.

Before dark three more loads had jumped the Colville fire; one from Redmond, Oregon, the second all the way from Redding, California, and the last from NCSB with the rest of our Alaska crew. Our first load had dropped to the bottom, split up and began cutting line up each flank. When the Redmond and Redding loads arrived they took the entire east side and our load took the west. The second load out of Winthrop joined us. They had extra chainsaws and fuel. At full strength we had forty-six jumpers and ten saws, about as big a jumper crew as I'd ever heard of.

Our strategy was basic: work the flanks building line behind the saws. If things went our way the wind would slow down, the night air would cool and, if we made enough progress through the night, we might earn a chance to cut across the head before the heat of the following day. In a blur of scenes lit by fire, sudden flare ups, and flashing headlamps, people felled snags, cut through logs, cut brush and small trees, threw debris out into the woods, dug and scraped line with shovels and pulaskis, yelled, pointed, cussed, guzzled water, ate dust and smoke and understood that, for the next few hours, that was the way it had to be. For me, it was running a chainsaw, filling it with saw-mix and chain oil, sawing again, on and on, the only real breaks coming when I had to stop and sharpen it. Rake and Johnny B. threw brush for me. They asked to trade off sawing but I was mad and needed to work off some bulldog and rag stuff. Besides, after landing in that big Doug fir, I was enjoying getting even with some of its relatives.

Dale and Willy, the two Winthrop jumpers in charge, kept us aware of snag hazards and the overall condition of the fire. Any differences felt during the morning welcoming committee were gone. We were just smokejumpers, working hard, needing few words to communicate. Most of the cutting was in downed logs left from the logging. Areas of young mixed fir and pine were from six to twenty-five feet tall, and thick as hair on a dog. The closer we got to the top the smokier it was. Sometimes the wind blew it toward us, other times to the far side. It was a typical ass-kicking, eyes-watering, snot-slinging, coughing, take-to-the-woods-for-fresh-air, pace-yourself deal.

Around 3:00 A.M. we reached the corner of the head, and the fire calmed considerable. It had run straight uphill, widening as it went but then narrowing near the top. We could hear the other crew's saws now. Our chance looked within reach. Headlamps flashed this way and that in the smoke. Soon we were aiming straight for each other. When we met, their lead sawyer and I cut right up to each other, then held our saws over our heads. Everyone cheered. The line was tied in.

Thirty yards back, right on the edge of the burn, there was a small clearing in the middle of a flat bench. The Winthrop jumpers volunteered to go back down and check the line. The rest of us gathered up on the little flat and made campfires and heated water in our Army tin cups, bleeped a few C-rats, and rested.

Johnny B. came over and sat down by my fire. Rake and Blue Leader came, too. Things got unexpectedly quiet. Light began to show in the east. We didn't say much, just ate and drank coffee and started getting sleepy.

I thought to myself, This smokejumping is, sure enough, strange. Two nights before I had been in Fairbanks, snuggled up with Sarah in her cabin by the pond. The night before we had slept on the floor of the Skyways Lounge in Seattle. Now, here we were way off in the corner of northeastern Washington, only a few miles south of Canada and just west of Idaho, dirty as pigs, pondering the brilliance of the morning star, feeling part of a small wonder. Other jumpers sat around their campfires, faces dangling like yellow masks, their bodies gray silhouettes against a crimson dawn. We had all come a long way. We had caught our fire. We had done it before.

Two days later at roll call, The Old Bull said he had heard from the Colville Forest and they were impressed that we caught their fire. PT came next. Not the do-it-on-your-own type we did in Alaska, but the line-up-and-love-it kind done by the welcoming committee. Starting with four-count jumping jacks, they didn't stop at the customary 50 but went right on. I was sure they would stop at 100, but they kept going as if the number meant nothing. Each exercise was the same, at least twice as long. Sweat poured from us thick-blooded Alaskans. Johnny B. started counting funny. Things like, one and two, how do you do, three and four, my ass is sore, five, six, where's the chicks, seven, eight, forn-i-cate. He said it loud enough that the PT squad leader heard him. An hour later half of us were out along the runway painting a line of yellow rocks yellow again.

"I reckon you just had to go and make fun of their PT," I said.

"Me?" Johnny B. said. "You were the one bitching about the mop-up standards."

"I don't care for shit like that," I said. "Standards are nothing but rules, and all they do is take away someone's chance to prove what they can do on their own."

"Maybe that's true," Johnny B. said. "But we're not proving much, out here in the hot sun, painting rocks. You need to shape up and try to get along with these guys."

I pulled off my ball cap, wiped my forehead, chuckled and said, "You can't just paint your ass white and run with a bunch of antelopes, then think you are one Johnny B."

After a while of rock painting, Rake said it was break time, so we made straight for the wash house and soaked our heads in cold water. While we were washing our hands, which by then were as yellow as the airport rocks, a pickup pulled in the parking lot between the barracks and the cookhouse. Out of a faded blue '51 Chevy pickup stepped two suntanned women, one dressed in Levis and a tank top, the other in overalls without no top at all, just that little Oshkosh B'gosh bib. In no time the truck was surrounded by Alaska jumpers digging for wallets. In the back of their pickup were crates of fresh picked apples, peaches, dark red cherries, big purple plums, and giant nectarines. In Alaska such fruit was consumed only in dreams, and so we purchased vast amounts. I bought three pounds of cherries, a half dozen nectarines and a bag of plums.

They came for the next two days, each time creating the same stampede. There were no fires, only rocks and paint, and chopping weeds in the hot sun. Thinking about the women and their big, round peaches gave us something to look forward to.

On the third day, whatever suspicions the North Cascades jumpers had about the Alaska crew were confirmed when Blue Leader came down with a case of crabs. By midday the barracks were emptied of all mattresses and sleeping bags, piled in a Forest Service stakebed, roped down, and sent to Wenatchee for industrial fumigation.

In the meantime Blue Leader kept to himself, sitting on a wooden bench on the backside of the big red Quonset with his pants down around his ankles, a magnifying glass in one hand, tweezers in the other, systematically tracking down crabs with homicidal intent.

To commemorate the day, Johnny B. ran up the Rumor Control chocolate cookie flag. I was impressed that had thought to bring it. That night the Alaskans slept on the lawn in newly issued sleeping bags. Blue Leader slept off by himself.

The next two days passed slowly. Few jumpers were out on fires. Only La Grande was busy. During our 4:00 o'clock break we were told that Regional Dispatch had decided to send us on to La Grande. That was good news. They had action in La Grande and, we hoped, no rocks to paint. We cleaned up our rooms, said goodbye to the cooks, shook hands with The Old Bull and all the NCSB jumpers, then loaded up for our flight. We took a Region Six Doug that had a plexiglas bubble on top of the fuselage right behind the cockpit. I climbed up there and rode along, able to see out over the wings, the motors and back to the tail. As we passed over Lake Chelan the Doug dropped its right wing and entered into a turn. Someone tugged at my pant leg.

"Aackk, change of plans," Quinlan said. "They want us back in Alaska."

# 17

At the Spokane airport we ran into another twenty-five Alaska jumpers, Big Al, and the BLM Lockhead Electra. Having come down right after we did, they had been sent to Redmond, Boise, and Missoula. Big Al was down to check on us. He was in Boise when Alaska got hit, and had flown to all those bases and picked up our jumpers. At the last minute it was decided to take us back, too.

Aboard the Electra there was renewed excitement. We were back together and headed home. Two poker games started, the players laughing and carrying on amid the background roar of the Electra's four huge turbines.

"I'll see that bet and raise you twenty," Mountain Puss said, his eyes bugged out.

"You're bluffing," The Legendary Rake said, "just like the last time we had a bet. Remember that? You ended up with hard-boiled eggs coming out your nose and your lips on my left butt cheek."

"Cut the history lesson, Rakowski. Bet or shut up."

Rake smiled and rested his hand face down on the firepack they had dragged into the aisle for a table.

"Hurry up Rake," Quinlan said. "I'd like to finish this game before we get to Fairbanks."

"All right then," Rake said. "I'll see your twenty... and raise it another fifty."

"Ha, ha," Mountain Puss laughed. "Who do you think you are, Butch Cassidy?"

"No, but I'm glad you asked," Rake said. "I'm the Legendary Fu..."

"We know, we know," Quinlan said. "But if you can't take the heat, get out of the kitchen... that's seventy to me, so I'll call. It's to you Al."

Big Al looked up from his cards, reached around and grabbed the whiskey bottle from the seat behind him, took a pull, smacked his lips, looked at his cards again, then tossed them.

Mountain Puss had a chug of whiskey, too, then dug out his wallet for the fifty.

"Ha, ha, I'm on to you, you frigging Polack. Let's see 'em."

Rake spread his cards out near the middle of the firepack. "Two pair, aces and jacks."

"Sorry Retardski," Mountain Puss said, laying out his three queens and reaching for the money. "Better luck next time."

"Hold it a minute, you lunkhead," Quinlan said, "I'm in too, you know. In that way I'm like you. But, unlike you, I'm going to win."

Quinlan lay his three kings on top of Mountain Puss' queens with great finality, then reached over with both hands and pulled the money in.

"Damn you, Quinlan." Mountain Puss grumbled. "You're cheating again. Nobody wins as much as you do without cheating. Every time we play you pull some bullshit hand out of your butt and..."

"Shut up and deal," Quinlan said. "This is a man's game. Not a whiners convention."

Besides the card games, others were gathered up telling stories. Most had come from Alaska just four days before. About half had made fire jumps. Together again, we were headed back to our favorite jump country, laughing and drinking and raising hell in high style.

I sat down in a seat beside Blue Leader.

"We may have no place to roost," Blue Leader said. "But at least we're in the air."

Out the window a strobe light blinked on the end of the wing. We were somewhere over Canada, airborne two hours. In four more and we'd be back on Fort Wainwright.

"This is what makes it great," Blue Leader went on. "Being part of something beyond control. Going with the flow, learning to surrender to humility, the value of trust, the freedom of letting go."

I thought about that a while, then said, "Did that medicine control your crotch crickets?"

"I think so," Blue Leader said. "The last one I saw was yesterday and it looked pretty dizzy."

Eyes closed, Blue Leader leaned back against his seat, smiling. I thought about what he'd said. To my mind, some things you might could let go of, but others you had to fight, like clueless managers, mop-up standards, and a case of the crabs. Letting go was downright difficult for me. Still, in spite of all that, I was beginning to see that going with the flow was not just a smokejumper survival skill. It was essential to the whole idea of enjoying anything. I believe that's what Blue Leader was talking about.

We landed at Fairbanks International at 3:00 in the morning and were back on base by 0430, back in the T-Hangar, unpacking gear, feeling like the whole trip south had been a dream. At 0800 the first fire call came in. I phoned Sarah and told her I was back home, that there were fires, that maybe I could see her in a few days. A second call came in and I was on the load. The fire was reported to be on Snow White Mountain, north of Christian, but after circling for a half-hour and not finding it, we headed back to Fairbanks with half the guys airsick from thunderstorm turbulence. Two hours later we headed east to a fire near Circle Hot Springs.

First in the door, Mitchell would be fire boss. By the time we got on the ground the fire was forty acres and rolling across a broad flat north of Beauty Mountain. All retardant was busy on other fires. Within the hour a smoke column stood 10,000 feet high. In the next hour all our line was lost and we hightailed it back to the jump spot to protect gear and improve a safety zone. The fire went big. Safety zone or not, our safety was in danger. At 3:00 a helicopter demobed us into Circle Hot Springs.

At the north end of the airstrip we set up a crude camp, ate C-rats, spread our sleeping bags in the warm sun and tried to sleep. Word was that Big Al was coming in a Doug from Fairbanks to pick us up. After an all-night flight of debauchery and booze, a dry run with airsickness, a fire jump ending in an emergency evacuation, and then being stranded on a lonely, dusty airstrip, our crew fell victim to a strange state of mind, some form of adrenaline hangover, I reckon. Though exhausted and needing rest, we were too wound up to relax. The afternoon wore on. Dark clouds passed over, bringing winds that blew dust and camp smoke in all directions. Still, no Big Al.

I lay in the dirt, tossing and turning and wishing I'd had a night in town with Sarah. By late afternoon the crew was grumpy and eager to get on with whatever there was to get on with. Mitchell decided to walk to the hot springs and call Fairbanks.

"You guys stay here," Mitchell said. "We'll probably jump another fire tonight, so we need to be ready. Everyone got that?"

Stuck in our gritty little camp, we tried to make the best of it. Some read, some did actually sleep, most others sat around the smoky campfires in a scene straight from a Civil War movie.

Around 8:00 PM a lone figure came walking the road back.

"Okay, listen up," Mitchell said. "Al dropped a load up by Steven's Village. He's in Fort Yukon with the Doug, but he can't find the guy with the gas key, so he's staying there tonight. He told me to take everyone into the springs and get rooms at the hotel.

Ah-uhhs, primate wah-barks and grunting filled the air.

"He also said to rent you bathing suits so you could swim in the pool."

Another round of male hysteria, then off we went, trooping down the road, happy about our latest good deal.

Circle Hot Springs was a rustic outpost 120 miles northeast of Fairbanks with a big, natural hot water swimming pool, a primary residence, and a handful of rustic support buildings. The old three-story hotel was attractive and well maintained. On the bottom floor, a large stone fireplace bid guests to relax in armchairs and couches. Moose and caribou mounts hung on the walls, along with wolf and bear skins. The registration desk, dining room, and bar occupied the remainder of the ground floor. Guest rooms were either on the second and third floors or in a half-dozen small cabins scattered up a nearby hillside.

Nice as the place was, none of its amenities could head off the crew's rush to the bar. Mitchell was left to register us, a process which required names, room assignments, bathing suit sizes, and handing out towels. Whatever fatigue, camp smoke, and a lost fire had done to crew spirit, the well-stocked tavern with its fine old pool table soon had it restored. Besides having a night off, a hot meal, and a good night's rest, there was swimming, maybe even women in bathing suits. Life had gone from dismal and dusty to hearty and freewheeling. To top off an already good deal, the bartender was a former Army Airborne, Korean War Veteran. First round drinks were free.

By midnight the bar was its own little Mardi Gras, with jumpers parading around in wet swim trunks, some barely hanging on, others too tight to button all the way. Locals joined in. Free drinks for the jumpers was the rallying cry. Johnny B., Rake, Bell, Quinlan, Kasson, Blue Leader, Mountain Puss, all of us, including Mitchell, swam, toweled off, shot pool, drank some more, laughed, yelled, pulled up our drawers, and staggered around half naked.

I put my clothes back on while I was still sober enough to do it by myself, and headed outside to take in some air on the front steps. At two in the morning the sun was just coming up good. Out over the flats, in the direction of Beauty Mountain, I could see a long streak of smoke from our fire. Thunderstorms tracked the chalk bluff on the Canadian side of the Yukon River, spitting lightning from great black-bottomed clouds whose tops were orange and purple.

I walked back to the airstrip at 6:00 AM, following the last stragglers as they ambled into the sun, trailing a cloud of golden dust behind them. Back in camp, most were still high from the dent they put in the Circle Hot

Springs booze supply. Stories and laughter filled the morning. Hot water boiled in honey cans over open flames. C-rats were ripped open.

"Looking after you guys is like herding fish," Mitchell grumbled.

"That bathing suit," Mountain Puss said, pointing at Quinlan. "Quinlan, you looked like a plucked chicken wearing a g-string."

Quinlan countered. "At least the bartender didn't have to call attention to my nut sack hanging out while I was shooting pool."

"Nobody, but no body," Mountain Puss crowed, "looked as funny as Bell. Bell you looked like Tarzan with a dead monkey tied around his waist."

"Boy," Mitchell said. "We left that place in a mess. I hope that guy doesn't get fired for all the beer he gave away.

We heard an aircraft approaching and everyone looked out over the flats where the Doug was turning final. It glided in over the end of the runway, touched down in a cloud of dust, rumbled forward, slowed to a near stop, then pivoted in front of us, its big wings reaching wide. Its engines shut down with a shudder as the propellers twirled to a stop.

The door opened. Big Al looked out and grinned, "Guess where you guy's are going?"

Normally it's not easy to get smokejumpers to pay attention. But when the subject of where they'll be going next comes up, their ears get as big as mules'.

"Boise, Idaho," Big Al said.

Back in the Ready Room we packed for our return trip south. The day before all hell had broken loose with lightning from Redding to Missoula. Most bases were jumped out.

"This is like déjà vu all over again," Mountain Puss said, "Yogi Bear said that."

"Not Yogi Bear," Quinlan sneered, "Yogi Berra."

"That's what I meant."

"Aackk," Quinlan quacked, "And was it not Quick Draw McGraw that said, 'Light travels faster than sound. That's why some people appear bright until you hear them speak.' "

"No," Mountain Puss said, "that was his sidekick, Baba Louie."

I tried to call Sarah but there was no answer. I didn't much matter. We had to be at the airport in two hours. Before we left, Big Al drew our attention to a letter tacked on the bulletin board.

To: Al Mattlon,
Base Manager, Alaska Smokejumpers

August 3, 1973

The afternoon of July 29, 1973, the men listed below jumped the Lake Minchumina Fire. The fire was initial attacked at thirty acres. Due to winds it blew out to 600 acres the next day moving toward Lake Minchumina. As Air Attack Boss I saw the outstanding effort made by the smokejumpers. At a time when the fire looked to be going big, they conducted a successful burnout along two creeks with minimum manpower. That level of fire knowledge and tactical action is to be commended. It reflects well on our organization. I will make sure a copy of this letter is put in their personnel folders.

Ron Dirkey
Air Attack Boss  Fire # 8558

I rolled over and looked at the big clock. It was 4:10 AM. Exactly one week before, I was in the same place, on the same floor, in the same flight service station at Seattle-Tacoma International Airport, waiting for the same Forest Service woman. And sure enough, she came with the news that, once again, there had been a change in plans. We were to go to La Grande instead of Boise. By 5:00 we were airborne, flying in the same Doug that was — only three days before — flying us to La Grande. We flew west, passing south of Mt. Rainier, and on across Central Washington. Brassy and orange, the sun hung above a smoky eastern horizon. Mt. Adams drifted passed, then the Yakima Valley. Crossing the Columbia River near Kennewick we flew over the Blue Mountains and began our descent into the Grande Ronde Valley.

The city of La Grande lay in a thin, gray haze between the escarpment of Mt. Emily and the Blue Mountains to the west and the Eagle Caps to the east. It was surrounded on all sides by a broad expanse of ranches and farms. The Doug landed and taxied right up to the front of the La Grande Air Center. As soon as we opened the door, the sweet smell of dew on alfalfa and grain fields filled the plane. No doubt about it. We were back in the Lower 48. The Air Center, a large gray-green building, had a set of big mirrored windows facing the ramp. We climbed down, stretched our legs, then started off-loading. We hadn't seen anyone yet. A voice boomed over their PA system.

"Arriving jumpers at La Grande are expected to off-load gear and bring it around to the north side of the building. Please keep between the yellow lines painted on the tarmac."

Our crew erupted in a fit of laughter.

"Check it out," Rake said, beaming. "These guys have a sense of humor."

Shouldering our packs, we headed over, taking various routes to different doors, knocking and demanding to be let in. Again, the PA blared.

"*Visiting jumpers.* Go to the north side of the building and enter there."

"You think they're serious?" Mitchell said. "Shit, we haven't even said hello."

I looked out along the runway and saw great, long lines of yellow rocks.

"See those yellow rocks," Johnny B. said, shaking a finger at me. "Don't start bitching!"

"Maybe you can refrain from bringing up Mohammad Ralph Louie, too," I said.

Davis Perkins and George Steele welcomed us at the north door, which actually was a big double door that led directly into the loft. With its four forty-foot rigging tables, walls of shelved parachutes and hanging tower, the place was neat as a pin and had that dry-nylon, wood smoke, sewing machine oil smell all smokejumper lofts have. Davis and George showed us where to cache our parachutes and gear. Both had rookied at Winthrop the year before, so we told them about our fire on the Colville.

"The Twin Otter comes on at 9:00," Steele said. "We should be rolling soon after that. The Eagle Caps got hit hard yesterday. Of the ten based here, there's just us and one squad leader left. The boosters got sent home two days ago. They'd no sooner left than we got hit again."

At 7:30 our crew met with squad leader, Jeff Lang, who explained the workings of La Grande standby and the general expectations of visiting jumpers.

"The public drops in once in a while for a tour," he said, grinning, "so we don't want anyone standing around looking lost. We have lots of project work and like to keep people busy. I know you guys don't do it that way, but you're here now."

"Are you the guy that talks on the PA system?" I asked, causing Mitchell and Quinlan to jump a little, then shift in their chairs.

Lang stared at me a moment. "No! I'm not. That would be Dean Dalton, he's the base manager. His office is up front. I'm the one that runs things out here. You'll be dealing with me. Dean works in his office most of the time. And since it's come up, no one is allowed in there but me, Dean, and the secretary. If you have a problem, then deal with me."

"I got one," Rake said, "I don't like assholes."

Quinlan and Mitchell really jumped then. A few Alaskans chuckled. Lang eyed Rake, then smiled.

"Funny boy, right?"

"More importantly, I'm The Legendary Fucking Rake. You've probably heard of me... or maybe you haven't been around that long."

"Look," Mitchell broke in before Lang could respond. "Rake's not trying to be funny. He's just tired. We're all tired. What's your plan for us?"

Lang smiled, rocked back on his heals, and said, "How about a little morning PT?"

After traveling all night, partying at Circle Hot Springs the night before, losing a fire that day, and flying the entire night before that, the Alaska bunch was beat and needed rest. But Mitchell didn't say anything, and soon we were all lined up out on the tarmac. Like the jumpers at NCSB, the three La Grande jumpers wore black Can't Bust 'Em jeans, white T-shirts and logger boots. Lang had his sleeves rolled up on his arm muscles.

"All right! Listen up," Lang said. "We start here with jumping jacks."

"Farm out," Rake said. "Can I do them between the yellow lines?"

In the back row, Johnny B. and I jumped side by side at first, but when we reached 100 I got dizzy and saw I was jumping in the weeds at the edge of the airstrip. Hopping back in line, I felt sick, and the world was spinning. Even Perkins and Steele were wearing down. When we finally stopped at 125 jumping jacks, I almost fell over. Then we did push ups, toe touches, helicopters, Hello Dolly's, and I don't remember what all. By the time we finished we were soaked in sweat, and I reckon Lang thought, satisfactorily humbled. We took off our shirts and cooled down with a hose on the south lawn. About the time we were good and wet, Lang came out and yelled, "Fire call. The Eagle Caps."

Our fire burned a quarter-mile southeast of the top of the ski lift on Mount Howard, about five acres, mostly under-burning in mature Doug fir, Alpine spruce, and pine. It was putting up a lot of heavy, white smoke but not crowning yet. The country was steep. A small, narrow clearing stretched along the top of a ridge 200 yards above the fire. That would be the jump spot. Perkins would be fire boss and jump with Steele. With the jump spot at 9,500 feet, our altitude out the door would be at 11,000, the highest most of us had ever jumped. The air would be thin.

The Winthrop Doug had been reassigned to La Grande, so it was made first ship, and everyone made the load. Perkins and Steele had clean exits, opened, and were in good position to make the spot. Although we weren't actually in the Eagle Cap Wilderness, from its north end we could look south across forty miles of rugged, snow capped mountains. Six-thousand feet below, Wallowa Lake glistened deep blue between two great glacial moraines. To the north lay the ranches and farms of the Wallowa Valley. High above it all, Perkins and Steele floated like gods in a land as beautiful as mortals could imagine.

I moved into the door, Johnny B. set up right behind me. The McGrath All-Star and I had jumped every fire together all season, and we'd stayed pretty much with the same bunch of jumpers. That was rare.

Lang grabbed the toe of my left boot and moved it out over the threshold farther than I liked. As soon as he let go, I pulled it back. When he grabbed for it again, I jerked it away. How much I put my boot out in the slipstream was my business, not his.

"Just do your job," I shouted. "And let me do mine."

On final he gave me a dirty look, and I had to wonder how smart it was to be fighting with the man who was about to put me out of an airplane at 11,000 feet with little but timber and rocks to land in.

"Get ready," Lang yelled.

I braced myself. The slap to my calf came fast and hard and nearly knocked my left leg out from under me, but in the next instant I was gone. After checking my canopy, I looked around to check my position. We were spotted well, nearly right over the clearing. At 400 feet an upslope breeze blew me backwards. The tops of great fir and spruce began to move in various directions, the gaps between them revealing the deep shadowy spaces below. Quickly I looked back over my shoulder for an alternate spot. In the next instant a tree top flew by in a blur. My canopy spilled air and sent me crashing forward in a nose dive. The next thing I knew I was sliding on my belly—head first—down a big buckskin log, through a bunch of small trees, until, after thirty feet of that, I crashed—still head first—into a giant root wad, flipped off to one side, and landed in a little open place filled with pink and white wildflowers.

Steele ran up. Perkins followed, stopping occasionally to talk to the plane on his radio.

"I saw you hit the trees and disappear," Steele said, out of breath. "I didn't think you'd be on the ground."

"Hell, I didn't neither. I had no idea where I'd end up. I slid a long ways down that log there. Chute's a might tore up, too."

"Don't worry about the chute," Steele said. "How torn up are you?"

"I reckon I'm fine. My fingers and toes all move, and there's a little hitch in my get-a-long, but I think I can walk all right."

"I was an Army Airborne Medic," Perkins said, walking up. "Let's have a look."

I unbuttoned my fire shirt and lifted my t-shirt.

"That's what I thought," Perkins said. "Your jump jacket's ripped pretty bad."

"I hit some limbs sliding down that log," I said. "More blood than anything."

Perkins wiped the blood away with his handkerchief. It was true. There were only a six or so half-inch punctures. The rest was just big scratches.

"George," Perkins said. "When we get to the jump spot, wash this with iodine, then bandage it. If he doesn't bleed to death, maybe we'll get some work out of him."

Perkins took off to scout his fire and we headed for the jump spot.

By the time Steele got me taped up, all the cargo had been rounded up and stacked in the middle of the clearing. Across the hill, out of the timber came Perkins talking on his radio and stopping here and there to survey his fire. He came straight to me and Steele. Rake and Quinlan gathered 'round. Satisfied with Steele's taping job, he said, "Look you guys. This is only my second season in fire, and my first time as fire boss. So, I'm wondering what you think would be best here?"

"Well," Quinlan, "I haven't seen it like you. What do you have in mind?"

Perkins didn't hesitate. "Leave two here with Len. Take the rest to the bottom and flank up both sides. Eight on the ski lift side, four up the other, one chainsaw with each. The three here on top can scratch some line and watch for spots. We've got a load of retardant ten minutes out. I'll direct that."

"Well," Quinlan said. "Based on what I saw from the air, that sounds like good start. Let Steele and Len take the top. Steele has a radio. That way we'll be in touch."

"Okay, good," Perkins said. "Let's go with that."

"Putting more on the ski lift side is good, too," Rake said. "That's your first priority. Same with the mud. If there's any left over put a couple gates across the top in the timber next to this clearing."

"Got it," Perkins said, tugging down the front of his hardhat.

I figured Perkins was a good man. It was rare in a world of big egos to find a firefighter who would admit that a fire might be over his head.

After all, the fire was in his jump country, he was from a proud Region Six crew and, over the years, the Alaskans' rebellious, oat-hogging ways had done little to enhance their reputation as good firefighters. That Perkins saw fit to ask for advice from our crew would take him a long way with us.

The fire fight on Mt. Howard was a study in the value of hard-hitting initial attack. After the air tanker had cooled down the left flank and painted the edge of the clearing in pink slurry, it disappeared back over the horizon. Chainsaws snarled in the timber below. Steele and I picked up a few spots, then cut a two-foot wide fireline along the outside edge of the retardant. That way, when the head burned out of the timber and bumped the ridge clearing, it would just smolder and hold. By mid-afternoon, line cutters and diggers came up out of the big woods to tie-in with our line just as an afternoon wind freshened. Flames crowned in patches of small trees, sparks sailed out into unburned woods. Line builders worked back down their lines, widening them, throwing dirt with shovels, eating smoke. Steele and I patrolled the woods picking up spots. By five the wind calmed, the fire began drawing in on itself, and fire boss Davis Perkins radioed in that the Mt. Howard fire had been contained.

Just before dark the last of us helicoptered down off the mountain to the airstrip at Joseph where our replacement crews were waiting to be moved up.

"Hell of a job," the local Fire Management Officer said to Davis, shaking his hand. "You guys got in here just in time. Thanks for all your hard work."

"Don't thank me," Davis beamed, "these Alaska guys did all the work."

# 18

After getting bused back to La Grande, even though it was midnight and we were bone tired, we went to work refurbishing our gear. Of the ten La Grande regulars, six had come in that day but then jumped another fire. With Perkins and Steele, and our twelve, that made fourteen. At least that's what we thought until we counted heads and only came up with eleven Alaskans. The missing crew member was none other than the Legendary 'You've probably heard of me,' Fucking Rake. Apparently he had told Blue Leader that he preferred to wait for our bus in the Joseph Tavern, and that we could pick him up there. Blue Leader forgot and then slept all the way to La Grande. It was embarrassing—the very thing that gave Alaska its reputation as a loose bunch of skunks. Jeff Lang, the squad leader, got pissed-off and started in on Perkins.

"Hell, it wasn't Davis' fault," I said. "You need to take it up with Rake."

"And you need to mind your own business."

I started to say something back, but Mitchell said my name kind of loud, and shook his head for me to shut up. Lang took Perkins into the main office. At 1:00 AM we took two vans to La Grande, and were checked into rooms in a dormitory at Eastern Oregon University.

By 2:00AM I had showered and was in bed. They gave us rooms alone so we could sleep better. But I couldn't sleep, no matter what. In my years fighting fire I had diagnosed three different levels of fatigue, each experienced during initial and extended attack—usually the first one to three days. Level one involved working a hard day and then late into the night. At some point the body wants sleep, especially around three in the morning. With a few hours sleep you're good to go again. That's normal fatigue.

But, as the second day wears on and the hard work continues, another set of demands come into play, especially on hot afternoons. The body gets sluggish, sometimes the mind. Slurred speech becomes noticeable— most often when talking on the radio. Knees begin to ache. I call that Level two. Still, important work can be done in Level two. Pacing becomes essential. Emergency adrenaline can still be counted on. Level Two is a slowed-down world, but one in which most tough fires are actually caught.

If, however, you have to work all the second day and into the second night, that can bring on Level three. Usually, not long after dark, the world slows another notch. There comes a mild nausea. Still, you can get a lot done if you keep busy and pay attention to what's going on. One time I hauled 60 pound packs of fire hose up a mountain all night in stage three. There were no good times, no bad times, just time. I moved up and down the hill about the same, just placing one foot in front of the other. Up the hill, down the hill. Steady and sure.

Recovering from the different levels is also different. Level one requires a good night's sleep. Level two requires a good night's sleep, a relatively easy second day, then another good night's sleep, plus plenty of food. Coming out of level three, though, can be rough. Once a person has the chance to sleep, they often can't. Then, when they do, they sleep what jumpers call the sleep of the dead. No dreaming, no memory, nothing. I'd done that lots of times, and every time I woke feeling like a zombie. After a tough season jumpers can take up to a month to recover normal eating and sleeping habits.

I wasn't in total level three, lying there in the bed at Eastern Oregon University, but we had been up most of four nights and fought two fires. I was feeling the sleep deprived part, though. My mind kept reviewing everything and wouldn't slow down, so I lay there thinking of one thing after another. I hadn't talked with Sarah for over a week. Maybe I'd have time to call her in the morning. I thought about Mort and Miles and could hardly believe they were real anymore. It was that way with Inspector Fentori, too. Everything in Alaska had stayed in Alaska and that was fine with me. Everything except for Sarah. I decided not to fight it and just lay there thinking about her long, black hair and how good she smelled. I finally fell asleep.

I dreamed another fear dream. I was beginning to have them more lately. As the season wears on and the more tired I get, the more they come on. In this one I wasn't at a jump base looking for lost gear while the other jumpers waited for me in the plane. They weren't all like that. In this one I was up in the sky somewhere, looking down into a deep, dark canyon at a Volpar slowly losing altitude, slowly descending to a point where I know it's going to crash. I am sick. I am helpless. Who are those on board? Just before the plane goes in I wake up. It's the same every time.

Mitchell came beating on doors at 0700 sharp. As Johnny B., Bell, Quinlan, and the rest of us made our way to the cafeteria, thunder cracked loud over town, then rumbled out over the valley. Lightning flashed above Mt. Emily. No one said a word. You could feel it in the air. It was rare to get lightning in the morning at all, much less first thing in the morning. This was a bust that was going big, and we were right in the middle of it. In the cafeteria we met the jumpers that had just flown in from the Siskiyou Smokejumper Base in Cave Junction, Oregon. Raucous and jovial, they were happy to be in on the action. The best part was, they dressed and acted like we did. As we finished eating, Rake strolled in, still wearing his dirty fire clothes. The Legend had hitchhiked to La Grande with a sheepherder and a truck load of sheep.

In the shade of the Doug's wing Davis Perkins, George Steele, Johnny B. and I lay sprawled out on our jump gear, trying to rest. We had just dropped the rest of our load on two fires in the Blue Mountains. We were told to fly to Walla Walla, Washington, and stand by. It was mid-afternoon and hot. The wind across the asphalt brought with it a weariness that, to me, was more than hot, it was sickening. Not just because of the temperature, but because of the nerves you get from waiting around to jump—especially in that country. Cave Junction Spotter, Mick Swift, came out of a hangar with a clipboard, twirling a forefinger for the pilots to turn the props.

The fire in the Wenaha-Tucannon Wilderness wasn't a bad fire; the jump spot, however, was a smokejumper's nightmare. Near the top of a jagged rim of black rocks, the fire was about a quarter-acre, burning at the base of a wolfy old Doug fir with a storm-broken silver top. The wind streamed smoke off the ridge, then rolled it out over a shear drop-off in ribbons that drifted above a canyon hidden beneath a blue haze. From the air the Wenaha-Tucannon looked like a dozen mini-Grand Canyons separated by narrow plateaus, all of them sparsely covered by ancient, old-growth pine and fir. In the low-angled light of late afternoon, its expansive ruggedness—completely free of roads or any sign of man—gave the impression of a land that time had forgotten.

Mick Swift knelt by the door surveying the scene.

"Hey there pardner," he yelled to George Steele, smiling his big, trademark Mick Swift smile. "There's a fair amount of wind and rocks down there, but we can do it, don't you think?"

Steele nodded. So did Perkins. I did not. What I was seeing was a good deal more than a fair amount of wind and rocks; it was the worst looking fire I'd ever seen. The only thing we had going for us was Mick. There are spotters, and then there are spotters. Mick was legendary at it. Even back East, when Cave Junction jumped fires in Tennessee and Kentucky, Mick could read what the Cave jumpers called the Gone-With-the-Wind winds, and get his crew down from the big spaces in the sky into the tiny ones in the trees. Still, the scene below was one of extreme jump country and wind, and after my last two jumps, I wasn't feeling all that confident. The spot was right next to the fire, near the top of a steep incline that crested at the black rocks. Beyond that, the country fell a thousand feet off the back side. Granite slabs lay here and there in what looked to be the best place to land. Right below the spot was a stand of tall, broken-topped fir; a sure sign that big winds were common in the Wenaha-Tucannon. On either side of the jump spot there was nothing but brush with big rocks under it. Drifting over the ridge was not an option. The first set of streamers did just that. The second also. The third set hung up in the wolfy old fir. Swift grinned.

"Okay gentleman. Hook up."

Steele took his place in the door. Perkins moved in behind him. The Doug pulled on final. Motionless and in perfect position, George and Davis stood in the door while Mick made his last minute decisions and the plane yawed left and right.

"Four-hundred yards of drift," Mick yelled. "I'm carrying you plenty long. Hold this side of the ridge and quarter down into the spot. Take a tree if you have to. There are rocks under the brush. Stay away from that snag patch. Any questions?"

They didn't have any. I figured it was because, at a time like that, there's only one question that's worth asking—How in creation did I go and get myself into a mess like this?

Mick gave them the slap and, questions or not, they were gone. Moving to the door I saw their two tiny parachutes drifting over the great space of the canyon. Mick was watching them and scratching his chin.

"They're holding just right. Go ahead and hook up."

I looked at Johnny B. After a quick high-five, we bumped butts and yelled a hearty Ah-uhh.

As the Doug turned onto base, I looked down at the place I would be aiming for, an alien point of earth onto which I had somehow to make my way—or else die. My heart was pounding. My breathing was rapid and shallow. The Doug pulled on final.

"Did you hear what I told those guys?" Mick yelled. I nodded. "Just hold this side of the ridge, angle down. Do a good job, there may be some women watching."

I nodded mindlessly, unable to process anything funny.

Mick Swift was in true form. Sensing my apprehension, he reached up, grabbed my arm and pulled me down, then drew his mouth up to the side of my helmet and shouted. "I know it looks bad down there. . . but you'll do fine. You can do this."

That was Mick all the way. Jumpers talked about Mick's fatherly sermons in the door. One time he reached up and kissed a scared rookie on the side of his helmet just before putting him out of the plane. Everybody loved Mick. He winked at me, still grinning, then thrust his head out into the slipstream to check the lineup.

"Get ready."

The slap came against my left calf and I felt myself lunging for the tip of the wing, eyes fixed on some mountains over in Idaho. This was no time for poor body position and twists. The turbulence behind the wing blew my feet up, then I pitched forward and could see straight down at a blur of bad jump country. A few seconds later I was drifting under my canopy, grabbing for steering toggles. I tacked into the wind initially making sure I had enough room between me and the cliff. Halfway to the ground, I turned and quartered down the ridge, braking to maintain my angle of approach. At 300 feet the wind picked up and I had to face more into it, more away from the cliff and canyon, but not so much as to run the risk of hitting the broken-top fir. At 150 feet my canopy got to rocking side to side. I pulled even brakes, held them steady and waited for the rocking to quit. Below the top of the big fir the canopy stabilized, then surged forward. I aimed for a point of open ground between two large slabs of granite. My feet would touch down just shy of the first one. By a grace unknown, I instantly surveyed the area of my landing zone, estimated my flight angle, struck a line in my head equal to the degree of slope, identified the touch down point, and made a critical decision. When my feet hit the ground, rather than follow through with a roll, I took some of the impact in my legs, then pushed as hard as I could to clear the first slab. Trouble was, the chute still held enough air to pull me forward into a headlong dive. In slow motion, I saw a picture in my mind of my body flying, belly down, parallel to the slope, Mighty Mouse style. My canopy began to collapse. I would hit with nothing but a partly-inflated parachute. I tucked my arms over my chest, resisting all temptation to flail. High-speed dirt came in a blur. The crash began with some helmet and shoulder plowing, then me flying end over end over end, and finally sliding feet first on my back.

I jumped up, threw off my helmet, and screamed like a West Texas panther. From the point where my feet first touched down until my shoulder hit, I had flown twenty feet, then slid another ten. Somehow I'd made it into the sandy area between the granite slabs. I began to unsuit, watching Johnny B. make his approach. He came in the same, but at the last minute oscillated sideways into the lower branches of the old fir where he hung up, then pulled loose to tumble eight feet to the ground soft enough to just flop over on his side.

"You guy's okay?" Steele yelled from down the hill.

He and Perkins had hung up in some smaller trees at the edge of the spot.

"We're okay," I yelled. "You seen those women yet? Swift said some might be watching."

"Women?" Perkins said. "Did you see some women?"

"Yeah," Johnny B. said. "There were four of them right next to this tree. But after they saw Len's landing they ran away. They're probably over the next ridge by now."

After the plane left the four of us examined my landing area. Johnny B. shook his head, then said, "Way to go, Len. You tore up enough ground here to plant an acre of corn. Good thing you did most of it with your head, otherwise you might have been hurt."

"Damn," Perkins said. "Too bad those women didn't stick around."

We started digging a line around the fire. It had mostly burned duff and forest debris and was only spreading near the top. It had not reached the base of the old fir yet, but was burning hot in a gnarly thirty-foot section of the tree's former top that had been broken off. We completed the line.

"This fire's going out on its own," Steele said. "We can finish it tomorrow. Let's go ahead and gather up our gear and make camp. We could all use a good night's sleep."

Just before dark we built a campfire and ate. The La Grande rations were better than C-rats with regular store-bought canned goods, crackers, peanut butter and Spam. It was a typical sit-on-your-ass-in-the-dirt smokejumper deal, but the best of all sauces is hunger, and who could deny the beauty of the scene as the last light of day played against the great thunderstorms that tracked east over Idaho.

It was good to be on a fire with George and Davis again. The year before they both had rookied at the North Cascades base in Winthrop with Dale and Willy, the two that ran the initial attack on the fire we caught on the Colville.

"Sorry you got in trouble over that deal with Rake," I said to Perkins.

"Oh, yeah," he said, chuckling. "It's all right, Lang will get over it."

"Well," I said, "he better. Seems like he's always looking for someone to jump on."

"Lang's not a bad guy," George said. "He likes playing the hard-ass, but he's a good solid jumper. If he has a problem with you, he'll deal with you face to face."

"He was an Army Lieutenant," Davis said. "George was a Marine. Did you know that?"

"So was Rake," Johnny B. said.

The more we talked the more we found we had in common. Five years before, Perkins had graduated as a newly minted paratrooper with the US Army. He was just nineteen and so full of fight he wanted to go straight to Vietnam.

"Graduation day, I remember standing with two-hundred young paratroopers while the first sergeant read our first duty orders. We all stood at parade rest, anxiously listening as our names were called. He called them alphabetically and 95 percent of the time RVN came right afterwards, meaning Republic of Vietnam."

Perkins shook his head and took a sip of coffee.

"When he got to the Ps, I was watching him like a hawk. He stopped and seemed uncertain. He read the order again to himself, then said, 'Perkins, Davis.' Here, First Sergeant! I said. He gave me a peculiar look then said, 'Arctic Paratroop Company, Fort Wainwright, Alaska.'"

Davis had a good laugh at that, and so did George.

"I was stunned. I had officially requested Vietnam. Then, before I knew what was happening, I found myself lifted high in the air by my comrades who had broken ranks and were cheering. It was like I was the one being saved. I was in a state of shock and damned disappointed. We'd trained together and I wanted to go with them. I guess it was lucky I didn't. Most were sent to the 173rd Airborne Brigade, which from mid '68 to mid '69 were always in the worst shit. Many didn't come back."

Davis quit talking a minute. We all just sat there, looking into the campfire. The broken top in the middle of the burn rolled a half turn and sent a shower of sparks up into a night filled with stars.

"I've often wondered where my life would have gone if I hadn't been sent to Alaska," he finally said. "That's where I first saw smokejumpers. I was looking out across the runways one day and saw a DC-3 taking off, and someone said, 'There goes those crazy smokejumpers. They parachute to forest fires.' I knew right then that's what I wanted. The way I see it now, getting sent to Alaska was a blessing."

It was late by then and I was ready to hit the hay. We'd been jumping fires for three weeks, including the trip back to Alaska, and it was beginning to take its toll. The warm little campfire, the beautiful night, and our quiet talk made me all the more sleepy.

"How about you, George," Johnny B. said. "How'd you get interested in jumping?"

"Oh," Steele said, coming out of some personal reverie, "After I got out of the Marine Corps in '69, I started my major in geology at the University of Oregon. The next summer I got a job with the Forest Service on the Rigdon District of the Willamette. It was right in the heart of the Cascades, and I couldn't believe I was getting paid to be in that country. It was a real busy fire year, 1970, and I got a lot of experience. My crew boss told some stories about the Redmond smokejumpers, and a former Cave Junction jumper also worked on the district. The more I heard about jumping the more I wanted to do it. I applied to Redmond in '71 but didn't get picked up. After another busy season on the district, I applied to NCSB and got picked up last year. That's where I met Davis."

"Are you still studying geology?" Johnny B. asked.

"Oh hell no," Steele said. "About the only chance I had of finding work as a geologist was to go to work for an oil company, so I answered to a higher calling and became a smokejumper."

George burst out laughing. We all did. Smokejumping. A higher calling, indeed.

Two days later we were back in La Grande. Roll call was at 8:00. Jumpers were busy refurbishing gear. The loft was full of parachutes that needed checked and rigged. At the time there was only one standing request. The pilots came on duty at 9:00, the planes at 10:00. The list showed our Alaska bunch as third load. All my gear was ready so I checked my mail. There were notes to call Sarah and Inspector Fentori.

On the back wall of a meeting room I got on a phone and dialed Sarah's number. A few other jumpers sat at tables filling out time slips, so I didn't feel too guilty for not helping with the chutes. While the phone was ringing Lang came in and give me a dirty look, but I ignored him. But then, following Lang was Dean Dalton, Bob Quinlan, and, of all people, Johnny B. Dalton was wearing an official Forest Service uniform shirt with a badge and patches on it and dark glasses, the kind with mirror lenses. They sat down and began to talk. Just as I had decided to hang up and get out of there, the phone picked up.

"Hello," a man's voice said.

"Hello," I said, barely above a whisper, "is this Sarah's place?"

"No, it's not."

"Is this 466-2261?"

"I don't know," the voice said. "There's no number on it."

"Well," I said, "I'm looking for Sarah Sheenjek, she used to live there."

"Still does... but it's not her place. Belongs to some old miner."

"Is this Melvin?"

"Yes, it is."

"Hell, Melvin, this is Len Swanson, and I'm calling from Oregon. How are you?"

"Oregon? I heard Don Bell went down there into Oregon."

"He did. We've been jump..."

"Where's Bell?"

"Melvin, *Bell's here*. But if Sarah's there I'd like to talk with her first, then you can talk with Don."

"Where's Bell."

"Melvin, I told you, Bell's here. But first I need to talk to Sarah."

"Who else's down there?"

I didn't say anything for a second. I needed to talk with Sarah, get off the phone and get out of there, but Melvin was wanting to take roll call over the phone.

"Melvin, listen. You can talk with Bell in a minute. Just get Sarah for me, okay?"

There was a scuffling sound and then, "Hello, who's this?"

"Sarah, it's Len."

"Len? Oh. Why haven't you called? Where are you?"

"I'm in La Grande, Oregon. We've been real busy. It's too crazy to explain. Look, Sarah, there's people listening so I have to talk quiet."

"I thought maybe you were. Anyway, it's good to hear you're alive."

"I been wondering how you are. You and the caribou."

"I'm the same. I'll bet you'd like to take another sauna. You had any lately?"

"Oh no. No saunas. I've hardly had a bath. We've been on the move. Since I've seen you I've been to Washington, back to Alaska, to Circle Hot Springs, and now back here to Oregon. We've had lots of fires, and I been so many places I don't know whether I'm coming or going."

I could hear Sarah chuckling. "You better come home so I can take you in the sauna and wash you up. Then you'd know."

"I wish I could. I might wash you up some myself."

"Why don't you come home?"

"I can't, I'm working. We're in the middle of a fire bust down here."

"Tell them you've got to go home and take a sauna."

"Sarah," I said, "smokejumpers just can't go home when they want. They can't go anywhere when there's fires."

"Melvin came home."

I didn't say anything to that. I knew she wouldn't understand. As educated and worldly as Sarah was, she was still Athabaskan in the ways she thought. To her mind, priorities could and should shift according to different needs in the present.

"When will you come home?"

"I don't know. It could be a week, it could be a month. But I'll call and keep in touch, then I'll come home. I wish I could now."

I didn't honestly mean that. I was in the middle of a smokejumper bust, and there was no way I'd go anywhere as long as I could to be part of it.

"No you don't," Sarah said. "You don't want to come home. Melvin wishes he was there, too. Jumping after fires."

I wanted to explain all that, to make it clear that fires weren't more important than her, but decided against it.

"How are things with you and the caribou?"

"Oh," Sarah said, after a long pause. "Things with me are good. With the caribou, not so good."

"What's the matter with them?"

"It's the fires. Melvin and my father and I have been flying up in the range and something strange is going on."

"Like what?"

"Too many fires. Right now there's three. The caribou are nervous about it, too. The calves run in circles sometimes when we fly over and the cows have to stand on their heads to calm them down. They're moving now, too. Early. South toward the passes. I'm worried they'll have to move away next year."

"The caribou are standing on their heads?"

Sarah laughed. "It's to calm down the calves. The calves see their mothers standing on their heads and then they stop and laugh and things are good again."

"Does BLM know about the fires?"

"That guy, Mort, he came up to talk to us about oil drilling plans. He says we need to think about moving the village. I couldn't believe he said that. I'm sure the pipeline company would be happy if we did. Anyway, when I told him about the fires, he said the fires were natural. I told him we saw three that had been rained out and they were all in a line, like someone had started them by dropping something from a plane. And, he said, lightning sometimes goes in a line like that. You should come home and I'll take you up and show you. My father wants to meet you."

Right then Quinlan looked at me and scowled. He wasn't happy about me on the phone, talking about taking saunas and caribou standing on their heads. I told Sarah to hold on while I asked Quinlan to go get Bell.

"Sarah," I said. "Listen. Tell your father that I'd like to meet him sometime, but I can't come now. I'm needed here. Try not to worry too much about the caribou. And as far as Mort talking about moving your village goes, that's plain ridiculous. I wish I could talk more but I've got to go. I'll call you when I can."

Bell walked up.

"Sarah, I have to go. Take care. I miss you... a lot. Don Bell's here to talk with Melvin. Goodbye."

I handed to phone over to Bell, and was walking away before I realized I hadn't given her a chance to say her own Goodbye. I felt like going back but I just went on into the loft to help check chutes. Our talk was all right I reckon, at least I'd called her. But I felt bad that I didn't tell her what I really wanted to.

Ten minutes later the phone was free, so I decided I'd better call Inspector Fentori. I went in the meeting room again, and Johnny B. and the overhead were gone, so at least I didn't have to put up with them. The number I had was the Washington D.C. number. He answered. He said he was happy to hear from me and that, after reviewing the case with his bosses, he intended to file a lawsuit against the Alnoka Pipeline company for damages and suppression costs on the Fort Greeley fire. He went on to explain that I would have to write up a detailed account of how I found the evidence, and then be ready to testify in court. He said I had no choice. I would testify voluntarily or by court order. I asked a few questions, told him about the fire bust and that I had to go, then hung up. I wasn't back in the loft two minutes when the siren went off and the first load of the day rolled. That left one load in front of ours. It was only 10:20 and my day was already ruined.

I didn't go back to the loft. I needed to be outside where I could be alone and think. On the south side of the building there was a big lawn. I grabbed my PG bag and went out there and sat down and acted like I was reorganizing it. Rake was painting a chainlink fence. It was gray and Lang wanted it silver. Not just the posts and stuff but each little wire square, too. Imagine. Right in the middle of a bust. I figured it was to punish Rake for missing the bus in Joseph, and then taking up with a sheep herder. Rake didn't give a shit, though. He was smoking a cigarette and painting away like he was Leonardo DaVinci.

About the time I figured I better get back inside and do some work, Lang came out, looked at me, shook his head and mumbled something, then went on towards Rake. Lang was handsome fellow with dark hair and a build that filled out his t-shirts in ways you could tell he was proud of. He walked up to Rake with a bit of swagger and started talking. I couldn't hear him but not long into his speech Rake turned, took a drag off his cigarette, blew the smoke at Lang, and said, "Speak up, speak up dammit. You don't have to be afraid of me."

I thought they might go to fighting right there, but Lang just frowned, did an about face, and stomped off.

An hour later a Twin Otter load launched to a fire over in the Imnaha River country. I checked the jump list and saw that the new first load was nearly all Alaskans. First on the list was this character named Eric Schoenfeld. Of medium height and build, he had dark hair, dark eyes, and a mustache that looked like it was trying to get away from his face. Eric chewed Copenhagen tobacco—day and night, and in massive quantities. He wore an old, tore-up looking black hat, and employed a style of attire that tested, not just the limits of the La Grande smokejumper dress code, but that of most civilized society. Although he wore the black Can't Bust 'Em pants and white t-shirt that they did, both looked like they'd been hung on a clothesline, then blasted with a shotgun. Besides that, he talked loud in a barking sea lion-type voice, in all situations, indoors, outdoors, and I suppose even in church, had he been the church-going type, which evidently, he wasn't. After Eric, all on board were Alaskans except Steele, Perkins, and Lang, who—beyond all belief—had taken the squad leader option of putting himself on the first load. In this case, in the place of Johnny B. Flabbergasted, I went looking for him.

"What in the hell's going on here, Johnny B.? Lang's my new jump partner."

"It was Dalton and Quinlan's idea," Johnny B. groaned. "One of their guys, Bruce McWelter, is taking Lang's place. I'm going to be some kind of liaison guy. You know, kind of like the organ grinder's monkey, running around with a tin can in one hand, picking my ass with the other, trying to keep these boosters in line."

# 19

The call came just before lunch. The fire at Unity Reservoir sat under a towering dark smoke column, rolling hot on ten acres of open, park-like pine woods and dry grass meadows. Eric Schoenfeld, or Eric the Black, as Mitchell had started calling him, stood in the door, wearing his road-kill hat, checking the scene below. Eric had begun his career at Cave Junction, and Mitchell had heard the Cave Junction jumpers call him that, and called him that every chance he got. To most of us, however, he was just Eric.

The fire lay in a flat valley surrounded by low hills with Unity Reservoir three miles southeast. Even with a light wind the fire had begun to suck in air along the ground, building fast. A four-acre meadow near the tail would be the jump spot. Eric's voice boomed inside the plane so that even those farthest from the door could hear everything he said.

"Wind's not a factor," he barked at the new spotter from Redmond. "One set of streamers should do it."

Though not yet a spotter, popular opinion was that it was only a matter of time until he would be. Unimpressed by popular opinion, Eric Schoenfeld acted as if that time had done come and gone.

"We could do four-man sticks, empty this bucket of bolts, hit this before it goes over the hill," Eric yelled above the engines. The spotter looked at him, hesitated and then nodded.

And so, after one streamer pass, we jumped in four-man sticks, emptied the plane in half the time, and were soon on the ground. Standing in the middle of the meadow next to his jump gear, Eric was busy suggesting the best approach for the cargo runs. Right then and right there, before God, Big Ernie, and everyone, as if by some planetary alignment or cosmic intervention, one of the great nickname events in smokejumper history took place; Eric Schoenfeld, officially and permanently, became Eric the Black. There were contributing factors, of course. First, the Cave Junction jumpers had started it. Second, his black hat was already notorious. Fedora style, it was all black, sweat, ash, and dust stained, creased on both sides to form a V towards the front. Both sides had shiny grease stains where he tugged at it. The hat was rarely seen unless on his head. Likewise, the top of his head was never open to public view except for those brief moments in the plane just before putting on his helmet, when he would pull off his hat and stuff it in a leg pocket of his jump pants. Microseconds after landing, almost before he had completed his roll, the hat was back on his head. Wind, propeller blast, running full speed, nothing could blow it off. Eric the Black's hat and Erik the Black's hair had evolved a velcro-type relationship. He slept with it on, ran with it on, packed parachutes with it on, fought fire with it on. As far as I could tell the only thing he did without it on—not that I knew that much about his personal life, mind you—was jump out of airplanes.

After breaking his leg skiing the winter after his rookie year, he had put in a summer as lead foreman of the newly-formed La Grande rappeller crew. He figured rappeling a summer from helicopters to fires would give his leg time to heal. When first seeing him at La Grande, we Alaskans knew that we had come upon one of our own wandering on foreign turf.

"Okay you brush monkeys," Eric the Black barked, beginning his fire briefing with the same volume he'd used in the plane with the spotter, "as you've probably noticed, this fire's no longer a smokejumper good deal. The Malheur wants it nailed chop-chop. Air tankers are rolling from about anywhere you can imagine. Dozers are en route. Engines, too. It's 1:30 now. This thing'll run 'til dark. Our big chance will be tonight. In this country it's a good idea to keep one foot in the black and keep hydrated. I'm not averse to taking advice so if you've got any, speak up. We'll split into two groups. Steele on the left flank, Perkins the right. First eight with George, the rest with Davis. I'll scout, direct retardant, tie-in with arriving units. Radios—Scene of Action Tac 2, Air to Ground Channel 2, Red."

The air war began with retardant drops across the tail to protect the meadow, then up both flanks. After each drop Eric the Black had but one thing to say to the air attack boss, "Keep rolling the mud."

We had been at it for four or five hours when the sun's afternoon light began radiating slantwise through the trees and the blue smoke and the brown dust of dry line digging. At times the smoke was thick and hot. We were tired. Faces, ears, and exposed hair gathered dust and turned them the color of creamed coffee. The fire was forty acres and still moving fast.

Mountain Puss ran the chainsaw up front, with me digging the initial line with a pulaski. Lang and Perkins came behind, improving it with the same tool. Bell, Quinlan, Rake, and Blue Leader brought up the rear, cleaning up with shovels. The work was simple—maintain the proper width, remove all pine needles, pine duff, rotten branches and pine cones, roots and rocks, clear down to mineral soil, toss burnables well outside the line. Extended fireline construction requires a certain mind-set. During critical hotline initial attack, breaks are only for a quick drink of water, a bite to eat, maybe some clear air. Then, back to work in a rhythm of grinding agony. Sometimes the brain needs to keep the pain and doubt signals from arcing too strong across into the misery of the moment, so you might get to humming a little song, or remembering lines from a poem.

Right after an air tanker drop back along our line, Quinlan did just such a thing. As the pink slurry cooled the air and knocked down part of the fire, he pulled out his handkerchief, wiped his brow and, after his trademark chicken-squaw introduction, began singing.

"A bold hippopotamus stood one day,

on the banks of the cool Shalimar.

He gazed at the bottom as it peacefully lay,

by the light of the evening star.

Away on a hilltop combing her hair,

sat his fair hippopotamus maid.

The bold hippopotamus was no ignoramamus,

so he sang this sweet serenade.

Mud! Mud! Glorious mud!

Nothing quite like it for cooling the blood.

So follow me, follow me, down to the hollow,

to wallow in glorious mud."

We all cheered. Quinlan beamed like a little kid.

"Mud," Bell laughed. "I can just see that old hippo right now, wading his big ass into the river, all the time making eyes at his fat hippo girlfriend combing her hair. Ha, ha. At last you sang a good song!"

"Speaking of mud, here comes another drop," I said.

After the air tanker completed its drops, I went to Perkins.

"The more mud they drop the faster we can push, "I explained. "The line doesn't have to be as good, just keep bumping someone back to check it. I'll scout up front so we'll know better where to put in the line. Maybe do some burnouts."

Perkins tipped back his hardhat, thought a moment, then said, "Take Lang with you. He's got the only other radio on this side."

Lang had worked behind me during almost all the line digging, and I figured he was upset with Eric the Black for picking regular jumpers to run things instead of him. But if he was, he had kept quiet about it, just working hard, just one of the crew.

I looked at Lang. He looked at me. Right then I was wishing he was Johnny B. Life sure was strange sometimes. My day could hardly have been more so with Sarah telling me about caribou standing on their heads, oil companies accused of starting fires, me dragged into a court case, and then, of all things, Johnny B. taking after management in La Grande, and finally Lang and I ending up jump partners, working side by side on a fire.

"I'll have Eric the Black bump a ground crew in behind us," Davis said. "If we're covered back to the tail, we can put all our effort into moving up."

Lang and I walked quickly ahead and came upon a spotfire the size of a swimming pool and immediately went to scratching line. While digging, we spotted another smaller one. I told Lang to take it, that I would stay and finish the first. Fifteen minutes later we met back again at the fire's edge.

"This is getting pretty shaky," Lang said, "us way up here, not tied in to secure line. There have to be spots we can't see."

"I don't doubt it," I said. "But we caught these two, and we'll have mud up here shortly. Maybe the rest will stay small until then."

"I don't know," Lang said. "We usually just work up the flanks and don't get into this leap frog shit."

"Look," I said, getting irritated, "this is no big science. To love this fire fighting you have to be good at it. To be good at it, you have to be aggressive. And to be successful at being aggressive, you have to know when to take chances and when not to. Strong initial attack is what makes good firefighters. Just look at what we've got here. We're working right on the edge of the fire, and the black's cool enough in places we could hold up in it if we had to. That's one thing. Another is that most of the spotfires left over from the blowup are inside the fire now. The fire's burned over most of them already or we'd be finding more. My thinking is that those left outside can be pretty easily be included inside an indirect line with some burnouts at these meadows. Frogs don't figure into it."

Lang laughed, and said, "Good fire fighting's fun all right, but I don't like the idea of getting burned up."

"Neither do I. So let's not let it happen."

After we lined a couple more little spots, I checked my watch. It was 6:15.

"Can I see your radio?" I said to Lang.

Lang drew it from its holster and handed it over.

"Eric the Black, this is Swanson on the right flank."

"Swanson, Eric the Black. Go."

"Have any Cats got here yet?"

"There's a D-8 unloading now. Why?"

"Lang and I scouted the head. Our guys are about 200 yards behind building line. A Cat up this way would be just the thing for turning the corner."

"Sounds good," Eric the Black said, Cat tracks screeching in the background. "We've got all kinds of toys coming our way. I'll head the Cat up as soon as he finishes securing the tail. How on that?"

"Perkins, this is Swanson. Did you copy my commo with Eric the Black about the Cat?"

"Roger, Perkins copied."

By the time Lang and I had backtracked to the jumpers, several things began to come together at once. A third retardant drop had reached the upper end of our hand line. A fourth was dropping straight across the burn from us, indicating that Steele's crew had moved up at equal speed. As I explained to Perkins what lay ahead, we took a breather for water, cold cans of beans, some jerky and candy bars. In the distance a Cat came clattering through the pinewoods, its tracks hammering against its idlers, its engine roaring inside its great iron body. I took a quick drink from my canteen, then got ready to meet 80,000 pounds of earthshaking, turbocharged steel bolted to a 16-foot dozer blade.

"This Cat's going to make a big difference," I said to Perkins. "If it's all right with you, I'll take it and head up. Have someone grid for spots outside the line. I'd like to take Lang with me to do some burning out."

"Fighting fire with fire," Perkins said. "Let's go for it."

Lang unbuckled his belt, pulled off his radio, holster and all, and handed it to me.

"Here," he said. "You seem to need this more than I do."

I nodded to him. "Thanks."

Dark came, the wind calmed. We moved up the flanks, spreading ever thinner, but able to do so with the wider catline, crews coming in behind us, and the cooler evening air. Perkins and his bunch burned out several meadows as we moved up, reducing the fire's chances of making quick runs at our line.

We were eating a lot of smoke and causing more for those bringing up the rear. Our burnouts moved slowly away from the Cat line at first, but when they got closer to the main fire, they caught its draft, sprang to life and ran through the grass and pine needles towards it. On average the fires met about 150 feet inside the line, slammed together, pitched high, then drew back down on each other. Now and then a clump of under-brush or small trees disappeared in white-yellow flames. An eighty-foot Doug fir, its resins vaporized by heat, exploded in a tongue of flame that danced 120 feet into the sky. In less than a minute, the tree stood out in the twilight, a torch of burning gases, its branches glowing red at the tips, its main stem a shimmering portrait of death by fire.

"Well, we got away with that one," I said to Lang, who just shook his head and grinned, like he thought me amusing.

"You don't like me much, do you?" he said.

"Well, I don't know if I'd put it that way. My Dad says you need to know a man for a while before you decide against him."

I stopped and thought a second about leaving it at that, but then said, "Mainly I don't like your rules about yellow lines, show-off PT, and bull-shit like that."

"Dalton likes a tight ship," Lang said. "Its a Region Six thing. A lot of pride comes out of Winthrop. That's where all this began. We've been doing good work a long time. We pack out of most all our fires here. We keep in top shape. Always have."

"That don't mean you have to make a bunch of rules. This is not the Army."

"Look, I know I'm pushy at times... but so are you. So is that Rakowski, the legend guy. It comes with the turf. But on fires I like to think we're all just smokejumpers, doing our best. That's all that matters, right?"

I thought about that a minute, then said, "You know Lang, we got a boss up north that taught us something this summer that you might ought to know about. He taught us that you don't have to push good people to do good things, that if you give people room to show you something on their own, they'll give you a lot more than you could ever get by pushing them around."

Lang grinned. "You must still be learning then, because I could say the same thing about you."

I couldn't believe it. Lang was turning out to be just as bullheaded as Johnny B.

"Besides, you have to have rules," Lang said, "or you don't have discipline."

"Shit, you can't discipline smokejumpers. You ought to know that. Too many rules don't accomplish nothing except get in the way of people learning their own strengths. And until they do that, they'll be scared to make decisions and take action on their own like every good fireman has to."

Lang didn't say anything to that, and I was ready to drop the subject, but said, "Which reminds me, why did you put yourself in with me? Johnny B. and I been jump partners all season."

Another tree flared up inside the burn and set a couple small fire whirlwinds dancing off into the middle of the burn. it. By then the Cat was a hundred yards ahead of us.

"I could have gone to the top of the list if I'd wanted to," Lang said. "But I thought it was only fair to take the spot of the guy I replaced. I've been stuck at the base for two weeks. I like to jump and fight fire too, you know."

"Well then," I said, "I'm glad you did. If you can put up with me, I guess I can put up with you. Now, what do you say we catch this thing."

Lang put out his hand. I shook it, then we shouldered our PG bags and moved up the line to fire out the next section. I liked what had happened. I'd seen it before. No matter the base, no matter how strict the management or how many silly rules they made up, once on the ground fighting fire, most all jumpers were the same goodhearted fellas.

At 10:00 I suggested that Lang check the line back to Perkins. Steele had a Cat plus two Forest Service brush engines halfway up his flank, wetting down the perimeter, refilling from a mother-tanker at the tail. Shortly after midnight I saw lights ahead through the smoke—Steele's D-8. The two Cats came together in a cloud of dust and smoke and mechanical chaos. Minutes later both sat idling while I talked with the skinners. The jumpers from both flanks came up and gathered around grinning, high-fiving, and swapping stories about the fire, the whole scene lit by firelight.

Perkins came tromping up with Eric the Black.

"My brothers!" Davis called out, happily. "How goes the war?"

"Fucking great!" Steele shouted, then let loose with a hair-raising rebel yell.

"We're tied in," Eric the Black croaked as he pulled out his Copenhagen can, tapped the bottom, pinched out some chew and tucked it under his lower lip. "But you don't trust the wind in this country. When you're finished feeding you're faces let's get everyone back down the line and spread out. Keep the D-8 here on the head. I'll take the D-7 back to the tail."

Eric the Black, Steele, Perkins and I went over how things had gone, what equipment was currently on the fire, what was coming, how many new bodies would be available come daylight.

After a quick bite to eat, we spread back out along our lines to patrol, look for spots, and fall snags. At 3:00 AM a big moon appeared in the eastern sky, yellow in the smoke, a few stars came out to the west. The main fire area calmed under an orange dome of light. After another look at the head, I went to find Quinlan, Lang, Rake and the others. They were hunkered around a campfire on the line, drinking coffee and keeping an eye on things.

We gathered at the tail of the fire mid-afternoon of the second day. Forest Service crews had arrived and were busy mopping-up. Two rigs pulled into the meadow, a Forest Service pickup and a stock truck with wooden racks that had been rented from a rancher. There was a fair amount of dried cow shit on the floor; we swept most of it out with our feet, but a lot was stuck in between the floor boards. Gear bags were stacked in the pickup. Two could ride back to La Grande in it, the rest would have to go in the stock truck. Everyone climbed in the truck, even Lang.

"Aackk," Quinlan said, looking out over the cab. "Behold the smokejumper way. Rudimentary yet not completely lacking in romance, either."

"Cow shit, Bob?" Mountain Puss chided. "Really? Cow shit's romantic? What are you, some kind of barnyard pervert?"

"Think of it as the romance of the old west," Quinlan crowed. "Rarely does one get to view the world from the perspective of the astonished yet resourceful cow."

The crew piled in. Down the road, at a little wide spot named Hereford, Eric the Black beat on the roof of the cab, yelling for the driver to stop. He and Steele went inside a little store.

"*Hereford,*" Mountain Puss said. "*Hereford, Oregon.* Can you believe it? We're demoding a fire in the back of a *cattle truck,* buying beer in a town named for a *cow.*"

Mountain Puss commenced to mooing and pawing the floor of the stock truck, which got us some strange looks from a couple old cowboys sitting on a bench under a tree, drinking beer. Minutes later Eric the Black and Steele came out with two cases of cold Lucky Lager. By the time we hit the main highway at Baker City the whole crew had a good buzz going and, once the stock truck got up to freeway speed, the dry cow shit began to blow every which way.

"Now you know what it means to be in a shit storm," Rake yelled.

We didn't care. We put our hands over our beers and stood up with the wind blowing our hair, laughing and carrying on like we had good sense. Eric the Black's black hat went to flapping in the wind but stayed right there on his head where it belonged.

# 20

Jeff Lang took up his old job right after the Unity Reservoir fire and Johnny B. stayed on as his assistant. For each of the next ten days the La Grande base was jumped out by supper time. Day after day those in off fires during the night were back at 0800, ready to go. Boosters from McCall, North Cascades, Redmond, and Cave Junction had stayed on. Our Alaska bunch had been in and out five times, averaging a fire every other day. The varied nature of the fires was typical, a two-manner on the Malheur National Forest, four dropped in the Seven Devils in Idaho, a planeload to the Strawberry Wilderness near John Day. Each jump mixed us up more and more, so that any given individual was likely to be on a fire with jumpers from Cave Junction, McCall, or wherever, the destiny of each written daily in the sky by air masses streaming thunder and lightning into the West from Northern California to Western Montana.

Fire busts are the heart and soul of smokejumping—the best and worst of it, as we like to say. Exhausted and running on willpower as much as anything, everyone had lost weight. After burning off our last bit of body fat, many were now burning muscle. I could tell because of the way my body craved food and the fact that I had lost 13 pounds. I was well into what jumpers call digging deep. Digging deep means finding that extra something to keep you going no matter how tired you are, how much you think you may be losing your nerve, or how much you'd just like to hang up your gear and go home in one piece. While some of that comes from the individuals themselves, I believe the biggest share comes from the collective spirit of the whole. Not just the jumpers you are currently with, but all those gone before, each one setting the standard and keeping the faith, all the way back to that first summer in 1940.

Whatever the deal, fire busts are always the same. Issues like yellow lines, petty bickering, and tight-ass management give way to no-nonsense hard work and a big amount of get-along and improvisation. While Johnny B. was liaison at La Grande, things loosened up considerably. With 70 jumpers coming and going, there was no place to rest, so Johnny

B. strung up tarps between the brace poles on the south side of the building. The names of each crew were written in fiberglass tape. Angled against the sun, they read: Redmond, McCall, Winthrop, Cave Jct, Alaska, La Grande. They were just the thing for a worn-out jumper that needed a chance to lie down in the shade and get a nap. Dalton was soon to catch on. Ice chests of cold juices, pop, and water appeared. Dalton, Lang, and Johnny B. acted like old friends. After a week of that, Johnny B. came back on the list. To my surprise he chose his old spot and we were jump partners again.

One morning Johnny B. and I were out on the lawn fiddling with our jump gear, and I couldn't stand it any longer. So I asked him what had gone on to change Dean Dalton from the uptight, keep-between-the-yellow-lines, hide-in-his-office base foreman to the way he was now. Turned out they had jumped a two-manner in Alaska one time and ended up jumping several fires together. The week before we came to La Grande, Dean lost his girlfriend, so he and Johnny B. had several heartache talks and drank half a pickup load of beer over it. Some days they would play guitars and sing songs in the meeting room just before quitting time. One thing did piss Johnny B. off, though. At La Grande they had these red five-gallon cans full of sand for people to put their cigarettes butts in. The word BUTTS was written on them in black letters. When Dalton heard that Secretary of Agriculture Earl Butz was coming to inspect spruce bud worm damage in the Blue Mountains, he had Johnny B. hide the cans in the fuel shed. He didn't want Mr. Butz to see BUTTS on butt cans, and that flabbergasted Johnny B. no end. The next day the Rumor Control flag—the white banner with a chocolate chip cookie and the words, *That's the Way it Crumbles*—appeared over La Grande Air Center, right up there below the Stars and Stripes.

By the last week in August most of the lightning had moved over into Idaho and Montana. Jumpers had regrouped at La Grande. Not all was laughter and good cheer, however. Word came from Big Al that Hairface, while jumping a fire in Southern Montana had hit a tree, collapsed his canopy, fallen fifty-feet, and broken his back. He was in a hospital in Jackson Hole, Wyoming. Every year it's the same. August comes. The busts begin. A week or two later announcements are made at roll call. So and so fell out of a tree up in the Bitterroots, broke his femur. Someone out of Grangeville mistook his harness for his risers, accidentally tied off to it, fell 40 feet, and was in a hospital in Boise. Joey Danner hit a big ponderosa down in California on the Klamath, broke an arm, and detached the retina in his right eye.

At best, Hairface just had a broken back. At worst, his life as a smoke-jumper was over.

With things slowed down and loosened up, I didn't feel so guilty about time on the phone, so I called Sarah every other day right after PT. She was back in Alatnuk and had been flying with her father to check on the caribou. The herd had begun moving into the foothills that led to the main passes south. I figured her father must be amazing. He flew a Cessna 180 as a fully licensed pilot. He drove a four-wheeler in summer, a snow machine in winter, but had never driven an automobile of any kind. Sarah still asked about when I was coming home. I was glad she did.

I was in the tower checking chutes when Quinlan came in and said, "Hey Len. Meeting in the ready room."

Right after I got there Lang walked in, clipboard in hand. Everyone quieted down.

"There's a request for sixteen to Missoula. They're jumped out. Dean's decided to send all the Alaskans plus four of our guys."

The four were Perkins, Steele, Eric the Black, and a fella they called Cowhide.

"Get your jump gear packed," Lang said. "We'll bag your extra chutes. Their Doug will be here at 2100 to pick you up."

At 2200 we roared off the end of the La Grande airstrip, climbed to 2000 feet, dropped a left wing and turned east. In no time most all the crew was asleep. I stood near the jump door. Jumpships in the Lower 48 fly with them open. We don't in Alaska because it's too cold and the flights are too long. A single strap was snapped across the open door about waist level. I stood there feeling the cool night air blowing through my hair, smelling the sweet smells of late summer, and looking out as we climbed above the Eagle Cap Wilderness. Moonlight lit the inside the plane. We began to fly in among craggy peaks and snow-fields bathed in faint blue light. Pinpoints of moonlight flashed across snow banks like diamonds. Lakes glimmered silver as the moon raced across them. Inside the plane the crew lay every which way on the floor, some flat out, some leaning against their gear bags. In the cockpit, tiny lights lit gauges and the instrument panel. The Doug's engines settled down to a steady drone and I could hear the air flowing beneath the wings. It was another one of those times when I couldn't help but know — beyond all doubt — that I was in exactly the right place, with exactly the right people, doing exactly the right thing. There we were, flying in a star-filled night, a small group of good men, swept away in an odyssey of movement and beauty.

The Missoula Smokejumper Base sat at the edge of the tarmac on the east side of the main airport. We landed at midnight. The place was empty except for a few support personnel and a half-dozen ex-Zulies who had been hired on emergency fire money to check and rig chutes. The Ready Room was littered with small sticks and leaves, discarded candy wrappers, and plastic bags of half-empty trail mix. Newspaper articles on the jumpers were pinned to the bulletin board. Two sets of crutches leaned in a corner. Dirty Lannville, his hair in disarray, sat red-eyed and coffee-logged at the Operations desk.

"Ah, fresh meat," he said as we walked in.

Missoula had been jumped out for two weeks. Besides their regular 120 jumpers, another 80 boosters had arrived. Some Alaskans were there too, including Big Al, who had come from Jackson Hole after handing Hairface over to his family. I looked at the list of fires and Alaska nametags: Bartell, Jimmie B. Pearce, Shearer, Striker, Fred Rohrbach, John Rohrbach, Bates, Wilbur, McGehee, Bruce Ward, Woody Salmon, Greg Lee, Bruce Marshall, and Dave Grendahl. All were on fires. Eight had been sent to the Grangeville base in Western Idaho.

Northern Idaho and Western Montana had been hit by dry lightning. The Bitterroot, Beaverhead, Clearwater, and Kootenai National Forests were hit hardest. The Bitterroot alone had 35 standing requests for jumpers.

"Dispatch isn't sure what to do with you, yet," Lannville said, scratching his head. "Get some sleep. We'll put you over in the barracks. Grab a sleeping bag in the warehouse. Take any room you want, they're all empty. Breakfast's at six in the cafeteria. Be back here at 7:00 sharp."

The barracks was even a bigger mess than the Ready Room. For two weeks it had been a one-night stopover for tired jumpers. Each night different ones bedded down in some Zulie's room, left everything as it was, just threw a sleeping bag down, slept, then moved on come morning.

The next day was the beginning of what became a nine day blur of flying over great mountains, jumping, digging fireline, climbing big trees for gear, three miserable, kick-ass packouts, and eating Missoula's plastic wrapped/soak-in-hot-water/pretty-good-meals that included dinners of mashed potatoes, roast beef and gravy, and breakfasts of French toast and ham.

Our first fire was a nasty two-acre holdover on ground as steep as a cow's face. Johnny B., Perkins, Steele and I worked it three days and then packed off down a steep, razorback ridge to the Selway River in the heart of Idaho's Selway-Bitteroot country. Halfway down Johnny B., ran into a small Doug fir with a yellowjacket nest hanging over his head. It broke loose and they got after us, making us drop our packs and run back up the ridge. We got stung anyway. Heat, sweat and yellowjacket stings are a fine fair-thee-well when packing 100 pound packs in rough terrain. The closer we got to the bottom, the steeper it got, until finally we had to get out our letdown ropes and lower our packs over several bluffs by hand.

Just before sundown we came to the bottom of the canyon, walked a hundred yards through six-foot diameter western red cedars, then out onto a wide, sandy beach, dropped our packs, tore off our clothes, and ran into the swift running, ice-cold Selway River. Shortly, a stock truck appeared on the road that ran along the other side of the river. We yelled for him to tell the ranger station that the jumpers were out on S.O.B. Creek. It used to be Son of a Bitch creek, but forest map makers, pressured by fussy city people, had changed it. That was true of lots of colorful names; places like Joley-Ass Joe, Squaw Tits, and Preacher's Prick, were changed to Joley Joe, Squaw Buttes, and Preacher's Point.

Two forest service men came with two pickups and a rowboat, then hauled us to Kooskia where we went wild eating hamburgers, milk shakes and cherry pie. We were back in Missoula a little after midnight.

The next afternoon the whole bunch from La Grande jumped a fire in Glacier National Park. We flew north from Missoula up along the east side of Flathead Lake. The regular national forest land was scarred with logging roads and cut blocks, but as we approached the boundary of the park all that was left behind and replaced by a vast tract of country, untouched and pristine, way up into Canada. Our fire was northwest of Lake McDonald about fifteen miles. Burning moderately in an area of heavy fuels — old downed trees and big snags — the fire was five acres on fairly flat ground. It had received some rain. Line cutting was slow with areas of jack-strawed logs. We worked until 3:00 AM, then went down for four hours sleep. By noon we had it lined. After two days of back-breaking mop-up, we were replaced by a twenty-man National Park fire crew.

Our next fire was on the Clearwater National Forest. At ten acres, the Avalanche fire stretched from a creek bottom all the way up to the top of a ridge where it had slopped over some. As steep as the SOB Creek fire was, it was nothing compared to the Avalanche. Our load came out of Missoula around noon. An hour later the second load arrived, then a third and fourth. In the meantime our load was busy digging line around the top so we could secure our gear and a camping place. The second load was from Grangeville, the third from Redmond and the fourth from McCall. I was patrolling for spotfires near the tiny quarter-acre meadow jump spot when the McCall load jumped. There was an elk wallow at the lower end about fifteen feet in diameter and filled with brownish-green elk shit and piss and what-all. A Boise jumper named Steve came in hot, oscillated a couple times, surged forward and bulls-eyed it right in the middle. His feet hit the ground at the edge of the wallow just before he was pulled headlong into a high-speed belly flop that sent up a big green bubble around his helmet. Don't bother asking what he thought of that, but it was clear from the raving and the cussing that he didn't care much for it. When his buddies ran over and pulled him out, he looked like the slimy swamp creature in a movie I saw as a kid.

Although the fire was tough, it turned out to be especially memorable. It was so steep we had to tie our letdown ropes together and use them like fixed ropes, so we could get up and down both flanks. We had to post lookouts to watch for rolling rocks, and all day long they came flying down through the burn with people yelling, *Rock!, Rock!, Rock!* But once we got it lined, the fuels were light over most of the fire and the smoke wasn't much. That first evening we made camp under the big timber along the narrow ridge. There were four large fire pits with a different bunch gathered around each one. That's when we noticed we had jumpers from every jump base in the country, except for Silver City, New Mexico, which was mainly a Missoula spike base. During the bust each plane load became so mixed that we had jumpers from Redding, Cave Junction, Redmond, La Grande, McCall, Winthrop, Boise, Missoula, West Yellowstone, and Grangeville. We were impressed. No one could remember that ever happening before.

Besides the beautiful country, a pair of shaggy mountain goats came around camp each evening just before dark to graze peacefully, shake their tails and occasionally look our way. Steve, the fella who landed in the elk wallow, had hung up his jump gear and dried it out. He washed his clothes in the creek, but still, when he was in camp, it was best if he kept downwind.

We worked the Avalanche fire for the next three days, then packed out to a road five miles down canyon, after which we were taken to the Kelly Creek District Ranger Station. Our bus ride home became known as the bus ride from hell. The seats were narrow with straight backs, and we drove in the dark for hours on washboard, gravel roads, heads bobbing, people leaning on each other trying to sleep. Not long after we hit the highway we stopped at a service station and nearly cleaned them out of soda pop, juice, peanuts, potato chips and candy bars. We arrived back in Missoula at 2:00 in the morning and, thoroughly exhausted, finally got to bed a little after 3:00.

While asleep I had another fear dream. In this one I was in my tent on a fire in Alaska. Something pushes against the end. Bear claws puncture through the fabric, a hole is torn, a black bear head appears, grabs the end of my sleeping bag, begins to pull. I am paralyzed, unable to move, to yell and warn the others. I wake up in a sweat.

The next morning we filed into Missoula's Ready Room for roll call, checked the jump list, and found that those in from the Avalanche fire were near the top. All except me. My name tag was down in the right-hand corner under the heading On Hold. I asked the Ops guy why, and the answer was that our boss, Al Mattlon, would be in at 8:00 to explain.

When Al arrived I could tell by the look on his face that something was wrong. We shook hands and he asked me to step outside on the ramp for a minute. Big Al took out a Marlboro, lit it, exhaled, looked across the runways, and said, "You're not going to like this. . . but I have to do it anyway. You're not on the list because I had them pull you off. Our District Manager called and wants you sent to Fairbanks as soon as we can cut a ticket."

Big Al glanced at me, then took another drag on his cigarette.

"Well," I said, stunned, barely able to speak, "I don't give a shit what he wants, I'm not going. I came here to jump fires. We're in a bust. It's my job, Al, and I intend to stay here and do it."

Mattlon didn't say anything to that. He just kept his eyes across the airfield.

"Tell him I'm needed here, Al, you know I am."

"I already did. We talked for ten minutes. He won't say exactly why, but I think it has something to do with the Fort Greeley fire."

"Well, I don't intend to go. You can fire me if you want, but I'm staying here where I belong."

Al paused again, like he always did when thinking on a serious problem.

"It won't do you any good. If you stay here, the only thing that will happen is that you will get fired and I won't be able to help you. I won't make you go back, Len. But... I'm asking you to."

I stood there feeling a sickness in the pit of my gut that no smoke-jumper should have to bear. Hell, we're expected to adjust to changes all the time. We are picked up and sent flying off in any direction, to all kinds of places, any time, day or night. Then we're asked to jump out of planes wherever they say, under whatever conditions they think safe. And we do it. That's the deal. But to be taken from the heart of the action for some high-handed, horseshit reason, was the sorriest thing that had ever happened to me.

"If you go back like he wants," Big Al went on, looking at me now, "I'll do all I can to smooth things over. We've had a great year. We've impressed some important people. You were part of that. I'll be up there by the end of the week. They're getting a few late season fires. We may all be up there before long. Like I said... I'm not telling you that you have to go, but my advice is that you should."

I heard the roll call inside and felt even sicker. My name would not be called. I was no longer part of it.

"Think it over," Big Al said. "Let me know by ten. Maybe we can get you home tonight. It's a rotten deal, I know... I don't like it any more than you do."

With that, Al Mattlon, the boss I had grown to respect so much, turned and walked away. A few jumpers wandered outside, laughing at some joke. Their laughter cut through me like a knife. I didn't even want to look at them. I had been singled out. I had been removed. I was an unnecessary and disposable part of all that had them feeling happy and full of life. All my hard effort had been reduced to that which could be hammered by some management jackass, and no one was going to step up and make it any different. I went to Johnny B. and told him.

"That son of a bitch, Mort," I said, unable to hold back. "This is all about him, and his bullheaded, twist and shout, ass-kissing with the oil companies. I can't take it anymore."

"I'm sorry, Len," Johnny B. said. "I really am. It's total bullshit."

"Yes, and I'm up to my neck in it. I've got to decide by ten."

"Hell, you may as well go. You're off the list. Why stay?"

At 3:00 that afternoon I was at the airline terminal, a half-mile down from the jumpshack, standing in line to get my ticket to Fairbanks when, of all people, Johnny B. walked in with his gear bag over his shoulder.

"What in the hell are you doing here?"

"I'm going back, too. I asked Al if he'd send me back. They've got a few fires. He knew what was going on but said yes anyway."

We got to drinking Jose Cuervo on the airplane between Seattle and Fairbanks and were drunk by the time we got back to Fort Wainwright. I called Sarah right off. I shouldn't have called her drunk, but I was feeling so low I had to. She laughed at me for getting sent home and calling her in the middle of the night.

"Now you can come here," she said.

"I don't reckon I can. We still have fires. I could be working every day."

She mumbled something about her father, then hung up. Johnny B. and I went right on drinking in my barracks room until two in the morning. I woke up with a God-awful headache and a sick stomach but showed up at roll call in the old T-Hangar just the same. Johnny B. was there, too, much to everyone's surprise. They had had a few fires and, with so few jumpers in Alaska, had kept pretty busy. Late season fires were the best, they said, with their fall colors, dark nights filled with stars, and sometimes northern lights. During roll call I was put on hold and told I needed to go see Mort.

When I walked into his office Mort was sitting at his desk, looking like a frog on a lily pad, waiting for bug.

"Ah," Mort said with a big smile," you're back. How was your trip?"

"It was cut short," I said, disgusted by everything about him. "I hear that was your doing."

"Exactly," Mort said, shuffling papers nervously. "A lot has happened while you've been away. Investigator Fentori thinks he has a case against Alnoka for the fire at Fort Greeley. But to pursue it would be a big mistake, don't you agree? I mean, we have clear direction from Washington to render assistance on the project, not hold it up."

"What's that have to do with me?"

"I'm considering firing you for insubordination, that's what. I knew all along you were the jumper he talked about. Much of Mr. Fentori's case is based on you and your hare-brained ideas about how that fire started. And that's the reason you're back here, and that's the reason for this meeting. I want you to write a statement that you've changed your mind. Say you were tired, made a mistake. That would do it. The case will probably be dropped anyway, but, with you having doubts, it's almost certain."

Be careful, I told myself. Be careful how you say what you say here. Could be Mort doesn't know that Fentori already went there, did his own investigation, or how he would react if he heard I had changed my mind.

"I was tired," I said. "It was late and smoky."

"That's right," Mort said. "Late and smoky. I imagine it was."

I almost laughed. There were a lot of things that Mort might imagine, but the Greeley fire wasn't one of them. I'd almost been burned up in a fire tornado, our whole crew, and the Cats we were with, had to abandon the line and run for it. Mountain Puss and Melvin had wound up hospitalized with serious burns. Imagine, my ass.

I went to the window and looked down on the parking lot. The same one Don Bell had roared around in the Red Lizard my second week on the job. A lot had happened since then. Mostly it had been great. But it wasn't going to end that way.

"When do you want the statement?"

"Let's see," Mort said, chuckling to himself. "This is Wednesday. Have it here by next Monday, first thing in the morning. Bring it personally. Until then you'll be on suspension and off the jump list. So, if I were you, I wouldn't get any ideas about running away again."

That afternoon, just before quitting time, Sarah's father, Albert Christian Sheenjek, flew his Cessna 180 from Alatnuk to Fairbanks, landed at Fort Wainwright and taxied up in front of the T-Hangar. Melvin was with him. Once inside, Melvin introduced his father to everyone in the building. Word of my suspension had not spread to the jumpers. Only Operations and Johnny B. knew. I had called Sarah right after my meeting with Mort, and she told me of her plan to rescue me. I filled out the paper work for three days' leave and we loaded up and flew northeast out of town, over the low hills towards the White Mountains. The sun slipped under a band of clouds and shafts of hazy, golden light angled down to pool on the earth as they might on the floor of a cathedral. In one summer I had come to love Alaska. Seeing it that way from the plane only made me more miserable. I was thinking my flight with Sarah's father would likely be one of my last in that wild and beautiful land.

# 21

Approaching Alatnuk I caught my first glimpse of the great mountains to the north. I could also see the narrow valley where the caribou would be coming through. At the far end lay a low band of drift smoke. Alatnuk was a typical native village with 50 to 60 log or framed homes and other buildings, all weathered and metal roofed. An old log church with a log steeple leaned over, one wall sinking into the tundra. Spruce trees, brush and tundra grew in among some of the buildings. Various dirt roads ran here and there. After a low pass over the village, Albert made a wide circle, landed on the gravel airstrip and taxied up to a half-dozen small hangars. A sign on one said, Welcome to Gwich'in Land. Sarah, her mother Anook, and several others were there, waiting with their four-wheelers. While they talked and unloaded the airplane, I tried to make friends with one of Sarah's cousins, a boy about six.

Are there any rabbits here?" I asked, smiling and waving my hand out over the country.

"No! No rabbits here," he said, shooting me a mistrustful look.

I thought he might have more to say, but he just kept looking me over.

"Well then," I said, still trying to make friends, "are there any lynx?"

The boy frowned like I was an idiot, and said, "I already told you, *there's no rabbits here.*"

That night, after a dinner of moose stew and homemade biscuits, Sarah and I went to her cabin, and got after a session of catch-up love-making. It had been nearly a month and, sauna or not, it didn't take me long to remember how crazy I was about her.

The next morning Melvin was up early, knocking on the door, saying that it was time to go flying. After a breakfast of pancakes, caribou steaks and coffee, we loaded up and flew north into the Arctic National Wildlife Range. Between the village and the mountains the country was mostly tundra. Along creeks, and up some canyons, stringers of black spruce, dwarf birch and willow grew as the farthest north of their species in that part of the world. We flew up the valley and could see the fire ahead. The smoke had thinned some during the night.

"This land's been recognized as important by white conservationists for over fifty years," Sarah said from the back seat. "Do you know about Bob Marshall?"

"Well," I said, "he was a conservation leader of some kind. I know they named the Bob Marshall Wilderness in Montana after him."

"He was a forester in the US Forest Service. In the early '30s he came here and spent time exploring this area. Afterwards, he went around speaking about it. In 1935 he and some other conservationists formed The Wilderness Society. In 1938, he presented a study to Congress recommending that all the land in Alaska north of the Yukon River, except for Nome, be permanently set aside and given special protection."

It was pretty loud in the plane, so we quit talking and just looked at the country. I'd flown over a good bit of Alaska, but this country, with its rugged peaks of mostly gray rock and open ground, separated by valleys tinted every shade of green, coursed by rushing streams, all of it running as far as you could see under scatterings of blue-gray clouds, splintered by shafts of sunlight, curtained in veils of distant rain, was on a scale of wide-open beauty the likes of which I'd never seen. Just looking at it made me want to get out in it, hike in it, sleep in it, wake up in it, and, maybe for just a moment, feel a part of it.

We came up on the smoke and beneath it I could see a smoldering fire-front and a few areas of open flames here and there. We flew on several miles and there was nothing but a black landscape and areas smoking along the creeks.

"It looks this way now," Albert said. "But we'll come back this afternoon and you'll see how it got this big."

Farther north, in different passes, we saw four other fires. All but one was rained out. On a couple, though, I saw something strange near what looked like the points of origin. I asked Albert to fly in low. In each there was an area of light colored ash, indicating it had burned especially hot where it first started. Still, without being on the ground and finding something obvious—like the Fort Greeley campfire—proving a wildfire is man-caused is nearly impossible.

"I don't think these were lightning," Albert said, "Lightning up here comes with lots of rain. Rain keeps the fires small. It was dry and windy when these started."

I shook my head and smiled. I didn't know what else to do. Lightning is funny. It does all kinds of things, and fires behave all kinds of ways.

Maybe they'd had a dry lightning storm or two. According to the jumpers, warmer weather and dry lightning had become more common the last few years. On top of that, even though I had no great love for oil companies, I couldn't believe they'd start fires to influence politics.

We found the main group of the Porcupine herd fifty miles north, in the hills that border the flat immensity of the North Slope. I was having a day of amazing sights, but best of all was the herd. Not the whole 130,000, but fifty to sixty thousand of them, flowing up and over the hills, a great dark, speckled mass of movement, more like the land itself was moving, thick as mosquitoes, covering the land, swimming streams, bunching up and fanning out again, an epic migration of thousands of years of instinctive stirring.

"Incredible," I said to no one in particular. Then, to Sarah, "I don't see any of them standing on their heads, though."

Sarah smiled, "They won't do that for you. It's the kind of thing they only let us see. They know you're up here. They're not sure they can trust you."

"You're too white," Melvin shouted from behind me. It was his favorite assessment of anyone not Indian. At least he hadn't call me a Meechameandu. He was sure that Rake was one. Quinlan, too.

"This is the sacred place where life begins," Albert Sheenjek said. "It's all connected. It's all necessary. If it's destroyed, our culture will end up like that, too."

We circled the herd for a while, keeping our distance, then turned back for home. In the village we had lunch and talked about caribou and the Range. Melvin's girlfriend, Jenny, was there. Back in his village Melvin had given up alcohol. Jenny was pretty with long, black hair, like Sarah's, and quiet and thoughtful, like Melvin. Even in the company of family, Melvin and Jenny rarely spoke.

"Like I was saying in the plane," Sarah said, "the Range has been recognized by non-native conservationists for fifty years. This man, Olaus Murie and his wife, they came here in the 1920's and studied the plants and animals. They traveled with dog sleds and boats. Also, Bob Marshall traveled and spoke of it. He died in 1939 and a great voice was lost. During World War Two, in 1943, the government made Public Land Order 82 saying that all the land north of the crest of the Brooks Range should be set aside for national defense... in other words, for the oil."

"Is that when they set up the national petroleum reserves?" I asked.

"No," Albert said, "that was later. And farther west."

"Then," Sarah went on, "in 1956, Murie and his wife, they came again and made studies on the Sheenjek River. The Supreme Court Justice, William O. Douglas, came too. He visited their camp and spent time exploring. After that they traveled and wrote and spoke of it to the American people. In the late 1950's a grassroots campaign began seriously. Alaska's Tanana Valley Sportsman's Association, the Fairbanks Chamber of Commerce, and the Fairbanks Daily News Miner endorsed what was called the Arctic Range Proposal. It was that same year that Alaska went from a territory to the 49th state. With statehood Alaska was granted the right to select 100 million acres for conservation purposes. About that same time legislation was introduced in Washington to establish the Arctic Range. It was passed by the House of Representatives but blocked by the Senate."

"Well then," I said after thinking a minute, "how did it get to be the Range?"

"That was the big change," Sarah said. "In December of 1960, President Eisenhower's Secretary of the Interior made 8.9 million acres a National Arctic Wildlife Range. It was by executive proclamation. It gives some protection to wildlife, wilderness and recreation values. That's the way it is now. But, it's too weak. We want it changed to the National Arctic Wildlife Refuge. As a refuge, someday, maybe, it can become a World Heritage Site. That would end the threat of drilling. After the discovery at Prudhoe Bay, it became clear they wanted to drill on the coastal plain, some of which is within the boundary. US Fish and Wildlife Service studies indicate it could reduce, or displace as they like to say, the herd by 40 percent."

Around 2:00 Sarah and I went to her cabin and made love again. Afterwards Sarah fell asleep. I wanted to but couldn't. I had too much on my mind. Just four nights before I had slept on a high ridge in north central Idaho under a sky filled with stars. The next day we hiked out and took the bus ride from hell back to Missoula. And that was the end of it for me. I wondered about the rest of the Alaska guys, Perkins, Steele, Eric the Black, where they were, and what kind of fire they were on. Hell, Johnny B. had come home on my account, just to make it easier, then I ran off and left him in Fairbanks. I was thinking of things like that when I finally fell asleep.

I dreamed that some caribou were standing around talking about the white man in the airplane, and laughing about how if they stood on their heads he wouldn't be able to see it anyway, so why waste time. But one stepped out in front and spoke to the others in a firm, calm voice. She asked them to be patient. She said that the man in the plane knew about fire and smoke. That he had a great-grandmother named Teneya. That she was Choctaw. That he may be too white, but he was not all white.

At 6:00 that afternoon we loaded up again and flew north, seeing more smoke right off. When we got to the fire, Albert flew higher up the slopes so we could look down on the head and keep out of the smoke.

"See?" Albert said. "The wind dies at night. In afternoons it comes out of the mountains and the fire goes with it. Melvin and some other guys came out here and tried to turn it off but they found out, even when it goes down, it comes back. It's the same every day."

I knew what I was seeing. We had dealt with it before on tundra fires.

"How far are we from the village?" I asked.

"About twenty miles," Albert said.

"What's the name of that creek we flew over on the way out here?"

"The big one's Victoria Creek."

I asked Albert to estimate how far the fire had advanced each day, and to measure the distance between the current head and Victoria Creek. The math was easy. The fire would reach Victoria Creek in three days, maybe sooner.

As we circled Victoria Creek, Melvin and I pointed out the window at the lay of the creek, agreeing that the fire would most likely jump it, especially if it hit it during the afternoon winds. In our favor was a small 30 foot bluff on the fire side of the creek. When we had seen enough, Albert turned for home. Dinner was waiting when we got there. Caribou and cabbage stew and hot cornbread served with lots of honey. I hadn't had cornbread since I'd left Texas, and I complimented Sarah's mother over and over on hers. Anook blushed and smiled a big smile just like Melvin's.

After dinner several men came and began talking about the fire.

"Well," Albert said to his neighbors, "the fire's still the same, coming every day."

Alatnuk, like most Alaska villages, had a fire crew, for both village fires and wildfires when called as EFF crews for the BLM. These men had a lot of fire experience. Some had been outside—which was what they called any place not in Alaska—to fight fires in the Lower 48.

"What do you think?" Albert said, looking at me, sipping his coffee.

I was surprised I'd been asked.

"Well," I said, taking a moment, "you folks know fire in this country better than I do. This is only my first summer up here."

"Melvin told me that in the smokejumpers you're the best... next to Don Bell."

"Well, I appreciate that, but Melvin knows as much about Alaska fire as I do."

I looked at Melvin. He was smiling, like he knew some secret joke.

"Melvin," I said, "you've been out there. You've seen how its burning. What do you think?"

Melvin kept smiling. Pretty soon he scratched his head and said, "Better turn it off at the creek. If we don't, it could burn up the whole village."

Melvin waited for someone to say something, but the room stayed quiet.

"We can fly some guys out there in Marty's Super Cub. There's a couple sand bars to land on. We can take some fusees I got from the paracargo."

For once I decided to keep my mouth shut. Everything Melvin said made sense. After some more silence and coffee drinking, he went on. "We can drop food from the Cessna. Maybe drop some more cornbread, for Len."

Everyone laughed. Especially Anook. Native Alaskans love to laugh and do it every chance they get.

"What else," Albert said, after the laughing stopped.

"I'll call my brother in Chalkyitsik," one of the men said. "Maybe he can bring his Super Cub, too. I'll call him tonight. We need to start tomorrow."

"What do you think, Sarah?" Albert said.

"It might work. But... if it doesn't, we'll need you here. If there's a big wind, the fire will come fast. There will be a lot of smoke and confusion. But with you here, it will be better."

The next morning the village had a fire meeting. Homes on the side where the fire would hit first would be most at risk. There was a grader at the airstrip. It could blade back and clear some areas around them. They would have the grader ready but not do it until after we failed at Victoria Creek. Shovels and rakes and buckets were brought to the Sheenjek home. That afternoon thick smoke rolled in for the first time.

I called the T-Hangar and asked to speak with Johnny B.

"Well, I'll be," Johnny B. said, "if it's not Len, my old jump partner. How's life in Alatnuk?"

"It's fine, I guess. I really like these people. But, we've got a problem."

I told Johnny B. about the fire situation. That took a while but he didn't interrupt, like usual. He just kept still until I was finished.

"Let me get this straight," he said, after a small silence. "You're on suspension but you're still fire fighting, just not getting paid. Have lost you're your feeble mind?"

"I reckon that's the deal, all right. But these folks need help. Talk to whoever you can. Maybe Big Al. The people here think that BLM has been told not to fight this fire. So they're not calling Fairbanks. I don't believe that's the case but hell, with Mort and his oil company ideas, I suppose it could be. Look what he did on the Peace River deal."

"I don't know, man," Johnny B. groaned. "Things are pretty weird here. All but two of the helicopters have gone off contract. Most of the dispatchers are down south. So with so few people and resources, some fires are being allowed to burn. It's a mess. Twist and Shout's got the jumpers ready to revolt."

"Forget him. Like I said, talk to Al. Maybe Rake."

"They're not here. Those guys are still in Missoula."

I thought to myself a minute. "Dammit, Johnny B., this is serious. I didn't call you up to argue. Talk to somebody. I don't care who, just talk to them, and tell them what I told you."

Johnny B., mumbled something about bulldogs, then hung up the phone.

The next afternoon we flew the fire again. It was advancing just as predicted. If the winds stayed the same it would run on Victoria Creek in two days.

My third day in Alatnuk was the last day I had for approved leave. In two days Mort expected to see my Late and Smoky report. Instead of going back to Fairbanks, and handing it in like I said I would, I'd be at Victoria Creek. At last I would truly be insubordinate, just like Mort always claimed I was. Whatever chance I had of avoiding a No Rehire in my personnel folder, it was gone now.

All day Marty and the man from Chalkyitsik flew firefighters in their two Super Cubs. The elders had decided that Melvin would be in charge. Albert would remain in Alatnuk and command operations there. Just before I left I met with Sarah at the airstrip.

"Sarah," I said as the pilot loaded the plane, "I want you to do something. Call Senator Jensen. Don't just leave a message. Insist that you talk with him directly. Tell him your Melvin's sister, and tell him what's going on up here."

Super Cubs are a light, high-powered, two-place aircraft. Most Super Cubs in Alaska's Interior are equipped with fat, low-pressure tundra tires that can land on areas of shallow tundra, not-too-rough open ridges, and not-too-rocky sandbars. Carrying only one passenger at a time, the flights to Victoria Creek took most of the day. Each trip included some gear. The last cardboard boxes of biscuits, cornbread, smoked fish and jerked caribou were stuffed in with me.

On the flight out I thought about how it felt to be flying to a fire in a plane and not jumping out of it. That added to the sorry nature of the whole mess. Things had moved fast since Montana, but it was time for me to face the fact that I'd been screwed and was looking at, not just the end of my jumping in Alaska, but the end of it anywhere. Mort would make sure of that.

Melvin was waiting on the sandbar with the rest of the men, sixteen total. The area of the pass where we would make our stand was a quarter-mile wide, so we would be spread thin. Depending on the wind when the fire hit, maybe too thin. We did have two pumps and some fire hose, though. The man from Chalkyitsik had brought one, and the village had one. Melvin set the pumps up and made sure they ran.

"Let's not put out hose until we see how it comes," he said.

With a couple of the fusees Melvin had swiped from paracargo, and, while the wind was still up but calming, we tried burning out the area closest to the creek on the approach side. That made for a lot of smoke but not much else. An hour before midnight we gave up and went back to camp.

The next morning we tried again but the humidity was too high, and all we did was make more smoke. We had done all we could. The near edge of the fire was about two miles out. I had seen it the afternoon before when we landed, a wall of fire with flames lengths of six to eight feet, much like we had during initial attack on the Mooseheart fire.

The wind began to pick up around 3:00 that afternoon. The smoke changed from a low band across the valley into a dark building column. When the fire hit the creek, the little bluff would hold the hottest smoke high enough that it wouldn't be directly in our faces. Also, the ground fire would have to burn down the bluff; that would slow it some. The bad part was that, with all the smoke, any idea about where to move the pumps would be pure guesswork. All we could do was hope for the best. I did a quick recon and saw that our own burnouts were rekindling, just like the main fire. In a way, that was good and would lessen its intensity when it reached the creek. Beyond our burns, there wasn't much to see. By then I figured the main head was about a mile out. Back with the crew, I briefed Melvin.

I think we both knew that our chances against that much fire were much less than we wanted to admit. About the time we had gone through all the things that were against us, I heard a familiar sound — one all smokejumpers immediately recognize — the distant drone of a DC-3. Out to the south we saw it, a jumpship, coming in low, landing lights flashing, heading our way. Everyone cheered.

There are beautiful sights in this world, but seeing that jumpship roar over with a spotter standing in the open door was as pretty as I any I'd ever seen. In no time orange and white parachutes came floating down. Then the cargo. The first man to the ground was Big Al himself, followed by Rake. Melvin and I ran to them. Once out of his gear, Mattlon lit a cigarette, and said, "Well, ah well, we brought three pumps and 2000 feet of hose."

I was flabbergasted by it all, but especially that Rake was there.

"We got back from Missoula last night," Rake said. "Most of us are here."

"Where's Bell?" Melvin asked.

"Bell's in the next load," Big Al said. "They should be here any minute. We made two low passes over the village. On the second one we dropped two radios at the end of the airstrip. We'll have contact with the village if we need it."

Ten minutes later a Volpar came winging in low, just like the Doug.

With the second load on the ground, the first thing Melvin did was to run off looking for Bell. In no time we were all at work laying out hose and positioning pumps. Thirty minutes later the big flame front hit, rolled over the bluff, and carried embers and other burning debris across the creek.

It was quite a deal. The fire on Victoria Creek was a junior version of the big stop we had made on the Minchumina fire, when it came off the big mountain and threw spots everywhere, except this time we didn't have helicopters and luckily, not quite as much fire. The best part, though, was that we had the same crew we had down south: Johnny B., Rake, Quinlan, Bell, and the rest. When they got back from Missoula the night before, the rest of the Alaska crew was out on fires. That very morning they went to the top of the list. Right after lunch Big Al conferred with Fairbanks Dispatch and made the decision — two loads to Victoria Creek.

By midnight all the spots had been picked up. Melvin was still fire boss. We stayed up until 3:00, patrolling perimeter, and making sure it didn't go around us between the creek and the mountain to the west.

Around campfires later that morning the jumpers and the village men laughed and told stories. By late that afternoon, after a day of dragging hose and pumping water, it was clear; aggressive action, though initiated later than was prudent, had stopped a fire that threatened an entire village.

Melvin had been talking with his father and Sarah on the radio. At midnight a helicopter came and ferried all but four village men back to the airstrip at Alatnuk. A huge group of villagers was there to meet us. The jumpers bedded down inside an old hangar. All except me.

The next morning, as the crew waited for their flight back to Fairbanks, there came the biggest surprise of all. A twin engine Cessna landed, and out came Senator Jensen and the Chief Editor of the Anchorage Daily News, the same one who had taken our photo after the Terror River fire. While I was surprised to see him, it was the long shot I had hoped for. Right after the village fire meeting, I made a radio phone call to Jennifer, the woman with the baby at the Terror River Ranch. I explained the situation and suggested that her uncle might want to send someone up to check it out.

There was a third man as well, Mort Twixtenblout, our beloved District Manager. Mort hovered around Senator Jensen, smiling, shaking hands, and acting decent for a change.

After a great fanfare of handshaking, the Senator wanted to make a speech.

"It's a real pleasure to be here again in Alatnuk," he began. "Here in this beautiful country you call home."

The Senator paused, everyone applauded, even Mort, but without much enthusiasm.

"But, best of all, it's good to be here with you celebrating this special moment when your people came together with our people and stopped a fire that could have been disastrous."

Everyone cheered, some clapped hands, Jenny hugged Melvin.

"I know of another instance when these smokejumpers came to the rescue this summer. I understand there was a third also, down on Kodiak Island. The editor here told me about that on the way from Fairbanks." The Senator held up again but people were tired of clapping and kept quiet.

"You must be extremely proud of Melvin," the Senator went on.

They cheered then, everybody and loudly. Jenny hugged Melvin again.

"I worked with him during the Lake Minchumina fire and, to me, Melvin is a hero. But, he's not the only hero here. This smokejumper crew... along with its foreman, Al Mattlon, are now also in my stable of heroes. I understand one jumper was here on his own time, and joined in the fire effort as well. When I get back to my office in Fairbanks, I will recommend each one for outstanding performance awards, even the one not on official duty. There can be no doubt... reports have come in from other areas as well. Our Alaska smokejumpers are an extraordinary group, and I intend to see that they remain a vital part of our wildland fire program. Thank you."

At that the Senator went to shaking hands again. When he got to me he said, "Aren't you the fellow I kicked that time?"

"Twice," I reminded him as we shook hands and laughed.

Mort had to get right in on the action, praising Al Mattlon and the jumpers, going on and on about it, just like the Senator had.

And so, for the second time that year, a fire crew photo was taken by the Editor of the Anchorage Daily News. He took another one of Sarah, her family, and the village fire crew.

When the planes came that afternoon to take the crew back to Fairbanks, I loaded on board the Doug and left with them.

# Epilogue

June 6, 2009
Smokejumper Reunion
Fort Wainwright, Alaska

I looked down at the old rails, half buried and rusted. From 1973 through 1978 the T-Hangar was home to the Alaska smokejumpers. The rails once formed the threshold of the main entrance on the east side of the building. These days they mean nothing to all but a few. Nine years after retiring from smokejumping I had come north from the family ranch in Texas to attend the 50-year celebration of the Alaska Smokejumpers.

Down on my knees, I dug at the old rails, scratching out crumbled concrete and dirt. I'm not sure why a grown man would do such a thing, but somehow it just didn't seem right that they were nearly covered over. Some strange melancholy came over me as I knelt there, my fingers getting sore. On the one hand I was grateful for having lived those years — all that parachuting and fighting fire, all those times we laughed and played and raised hell and got to be who we thought we were. Then, too, there was the undeniable fact that all that was far behind me now, becoming lost in the past. Adding to the whole thing was a big sense of loss for some truly exceptional people. There I was, a man of sixty-eight years, down on his knees, looking at a hand full of dirt, recalling the people and times of the T-Hangar Days.

Real life is not like the movies with clear endings, heroes, and villains. In real life, with its inevitable ambiguity, tragedy and loss, our stories are tied to the times we lived, the people we loved, and the adventures we shared. Some simply end where they end, leaving us no choice but to accept them. Whether swept away under a burning sky, killed in an airplane crash, taken by disease, or otherwise offered up onto some untimely altar of death, those people still live on in our hearts, and we owe it to them to tell their stories as best we can.

Back in Fairbanks after Victoria Creek, it soon became clear that our season was over. Mid-September came with light rain and snow. A big article came out in the Anchorage newspaper with another crew picture on the front page. It was picked up by the Associated Press and went national. Although we were really just doing our job, it was clear that, for most people, it was easier to see us as heroes.

Mort never spoke to me again. I reckon it was because of the Senator, but I don't really know. Mort only lasted one year as District Manager. By the beginning of the next summer he had been transferred to Alkali Flats, Nevada, to take charge of the Stinking Desert National Monument. The BLM and the Alnoka Pipeline Company made a deal and settled out of court with the company paying almost nothing for the fire at Fort Greeley. While we were down south jumping fires out of La Grande, Miles "Big M—little organ," Morgan, had taken a transfer to Pahrump, Nevada, I figured to help manage the National Jackrabbit Herd.

Everybody on the crew, including Big Al, got a Letter Of Outstanding Performance from Senator Jensen, just like he promised. Melvin also got one, plus a $1,000 dollar check from the Alaska Tribal Chiefs Association.

Whatever thoughts Mort had had of getting rid of smokejumpers ended with his departure. With the speed of the new Volpars, and the logistical troubles helicopters had with fuel supply, it soon became clear that smokejumpers would remain the primary initial attack force in Alaska. Now, thirty-six years later, the Alaska Smokejumpers are seen by many as the most experienced and professional wildland fire crew in the country. Their new standby shack, which they simply call "The Shack," is a multi-million dollar, state of the art facility with a spacious parachute loft, para-cargo wing, five offices, a weight room, locker area, Ready Room, and lounge. Bold and innovative, the Alaska smokejumpers pioneered the development of the new ramair square parachute, eventually fazing out the less maneuverable round chutes completely. Several modifications to jump suits, harnesses, and helmets followed. Jim Kasson played a big part in that, then quit, moved to Australia and started a business selling acrobatic kites.

Al Mattlon served as base manager for ten years, then moved up to the head of fire operations in Alaska. By the late '80s he was director of wildland fire for the state of Nevada. By the time he retired in 1996, he was at the National InterAgency Fire Center in Boise, Idaho, holding the position of Chief of Fire and Aviation for the entire Bureau of Land Management. A smokejumper leadership award has been created in his name. Many of us say he was the best boss we ever had.

Johnny B. and I have remained friends, although I don't see him much now. After jumping five more years, he enrolled in a wooden boat building school in Port Townsend, Washington. Two years later he moved to Fiji and started a school building traditional sailing catamarans out of modern materials, made it a big success, went native, and married a local woman and had three beautiful kids. Last time I talked to him the subject of Duke came up. Duke was still doing okay, but had lost one eye and most of his fur. Johnny B.'s still down there, navigating by the stars and learning the old ways of sailing the south seas.

Bob Quinlan had a long career as a smokejumper, then moved on, serving his final years as the Fire Management Officer for the Galena Zone in Western Alaska.

Don Bell and Betsy got an apartment in Fairbanks at Nanook Niches for the winter. Betsy got a bunch of dogs and took up dog sled racing. The next year they moved to a place out on Chena Pump Road they called — for reasons you might understand — Shit Acres. After three years Don told Betsy that she had to make a choice, It was either him or the dogs. She kept the dogs. Bell and I are still friends. He went on to have a series of relationships that I once heard him describe simply as "strange."

Of the ten-man 1973 La Grande crew, all but one transferred to Fairbanks and became Alaska jumpers the next year. Davis Perkins, George Steele, and Eric the Black were among them. Davis jumped fourteen years, then quit and became a career fireman with the South County Fire Department near San Francisco. He is now retired and a successful fine artist with his own studio, and paintings in the Smithsonian Air and Space Museum, the Pentagon, and the Alaska State Historical Museum.

George Steele jumped for 26 years, then retired to Colorado where he and his wife enjoy the outdoors and work each summer conducting statewide bird counts.

Eric the Black became Erik the Blak, which later evolved into simply Blak. He jumped 24 years, wore out three black hats, and eventually retired in the mid-nineties to a little town in Northeastern Oregon just twenty miles south of the now defunct La Grande base.

Melvin became a city fireman in Anchorage, then transferred to the Tucson Fire Department in Arizona, and finished out his career there. Last I heard he was retired and back in Anchorage, living alone in an old hotel. Don Bell and he are still in touch.

Gene Hobbs never jumped again, but had a long and successful career as a high school teacher and wrestling coach in Moscow, Idaho.

Rake went on to a career with BLM, then, to our great sorrow, passed away unexpectedly in 1998 due to complications with his heart. The Legend lives on.

And then there's Sarah.

After Victoria Creek, Sarah and I spent the winter living in her cabin by the pond. It was my first winter in Alaska and, although I never saw myself living in all that cold and dark, I eventually found the magic of the north country winter, with its cobalt blue skies, northern lights, and extraordinary people to be one of my best ever. Sarah continued her work with the Range and its caribou, making trips, giving talks and twisting politicians' arms. I spent time cross-country skiing with Quinlan and helping Bell and Betsy shovel dog shit. Sarah and I stayed together for two years, but then, with my smokejumping and her caribou, we had less and less time for each other. We finally broke up in the summer of 1975.

After Sarah, I didn't have anything to do with women for two years. In a way my life story, when it comes to relationships, turned out to be a lot like Bell's. I was lucky to know and love a handful of special women, but things just never worked out for me in that category. Looking back on it now, I think I failed to mature the way most people do. I suspect I never did get the difference between love and lust down right. Smokejumping for 27 summers didn't help, either.

While I didn't necessarily amount to much, Sarah went on to achieve great things with her people, her caribou, and what she called The Sacred Place Where Life Begins.

In 1980, after years of hard work, the Alaska National Interest Lands Act was passed. It doubled the size of the Arctic Range, changed range to refuge, and created the Arctic National Wildlife Refuge. Sarah had always wanted that. The coastal plain portion of the area, however, was excluded from full protection from oil drilling. In 1985 and 1986 the United States and Canada signed the US-Canada Porcupine Agreement, and established an eight member Porcupine Caribou Board—four from Canada, four from the US. In promoting this endeavor they urged that a new model for conservation be established—that of a Bio-Cultural Reserve, or Caribou Commons.

The battle continued with Sarah right in the middle. After the Exxon Valdez oil spill in 1989, public outrage killed a piece of legislation that would have allowed drilling in any part of the Arctic National Wildlife Refuge. Then in 1991, in the aftermath to the Gulf War, the George H.W. Bush administration proposed a National Energy Policy that called for full-scale leasing of the coastal plain. It was defeated after intense opposition from environmental groups and the Gwich'in Athabaskan Indians of both Alaska and Canada.

In the 1990s, Sarah traveled to Brazil, Ecuador, Nicaragua, and Guatemala, speaking about the plight of indigenous peoples, and, of course, her caribou. She appeared on CNN, the MacNeil-Lehrer News Hour, and CBS Evening News. She led several groups to Washington, D.C., crusading for the People of the Caribou and the preservation of ANWR.

Then, in 2002, as a member of the International Indian Treaty Council, Sarah Sheenjek, and two other lifetime members of the Gwich'in Steering Committee were awarded the Goldman Environmental Prize. The Goldman is an international award — the highest honor one can receive for environmental work.

The battle over oil drilling on the coastal plain still rages. Power politics and pro-development forces have continually pushed for drilling. Environmental groups and the Indians have continued to fight it. During his term as President, George W. Bush and his administration renewed efforts for drilling on the coastal plain, claiming it would keep America's economy growing, create jobs, and reduce our dependence on foreign oil.

According to estimates no one disputes, the likely yield of recoverable crude oil from the coastal plain would equal about one and a half years of total US demand.

I stepped up on the concrete slab and walked to an area that was about where the Ready Room had been. Standing there I thought back to all the roll calls, the meetings with Big Al, the I-Hear-You- Walkin'-Chair, the times coming back in after fires. Five o'clock taps played over on the parade grounds. So many people, so many stories. My time as a smoke-jumper during the T-Hangar days changed me forever. The playfulness, the joy, and the friendships that flourished in that old building were the direct outcome of each of us being allowed to be our own individual selves in an atmosphere of extraordinary acceptance and trust. Other great personalities aside, much of that credit must go to Al "Big Al" Mattlon.

I went out and took one more look at the old rails. Cloud shadows moved slowly across the airfield. A windsock rustled softly behind me. I picked up a handful of dust, looked at it through tears, then tossed it in the air and watched it drift away. I am growing old. My memories of the T-Hangar days and the people of my story get dimmer every year. Perhaps someday I won't even be able to remember their names. Their strong, laughing faces, I shall never forget.

# Glossary

**Air Attack:**
>   The airplanes and people that coordinate air operations over a fire.

**Air Tankers:**
>   Aircraft that drop fire-retardant chemicals.

**Backfire:**
>   Fire set to purposely influence the direction or rate of fire spread.

**Burnout:**
>   Fire set to eliminate fuels between fire and constructed line.

**Big Ernie:**
>   The smokejumper god. A deity with a twisted sense of humor. Determines good or bad deals for jumpers.

**Blowup:**
>   Catastrophic fire behavior, rapid rate of spread and mass ignition of large areas.

**Bush:** General term for Alaskan wilderness.

**Bust:** Intense period of jumping many fires.

**C-rats:** Army C-rations.

**Cat Line:**
>   Fire line constructed with crawler tractors (bulldozers).

**Contained:**

A fire is contained when its rate of spread has been halted by control lines or natural barriers.

**Controlled:**

A fire has been controlled when enough work has been done to insure that it will not escape.

**Crown Fire:**

A fire burning hot enough to continue to spread through the tops of trees.

**Demobe:**

Short for demobilization. The act of leaving a fire.

**Drift Streamers:**

Weighted strips of colored crepe paper used by spotters to determine wind speed and direction before a jump.

**EMT:** Emergency Medical Technician.

**Extended Attack:**

Work done after the initial effort has failed to stop a fire. For smokejumpers usually the second or third day.

**Firebrands:**

Large embers or chunks of airborne burning material.

**Fire Bust:**

See Bust.

**Fire Devil:**

Whirlwind of fire.

**Firestorm:**

A mass conflagration of fire.

**Fire-out:**

    See burnout.

**Flanks:**

    The left and right sides of a fire stretching from the tail toward the head.

**Fusee:** Railroad flares used to light burnouts and backfires.

**Head:** Hottest and most active part of a fire; determines the direction the fire is moving.

**Hootch:**

    Sleeping arrangement: mosquito net and rain fly, parachute.

**Initial Attack:**

    First effort to stop a fire.

**Jump List:**

    A rotating list that determines the order in which jumpers are assigned to fires. A jumper returning from a fire goes to the bottom of the list.

**Jumpship:**

    Smokejumper aircraft.

**Jump Spot:**

    Designated landing area.

**Loft:** Room where parachutes are rigged and maintained.

**Lower 48:**

    (aka down south) Alaska talk for the contiguous United States.

**Mop-up:**

    Final stage of fire fighting. Digging up all roots and burning material; putting out all embers and coals.

**Mud:**   Aerial fire retardant dropped by aircraft. Also called **retardant or slurry.**

**On Final:**
   For aircraft, the final flight path before jumpers jump. For jumpers, the final flight path as they descend into a jump spot.

**Ops:**   Operations desk. The nerve center of a smokejumper base. The jump list, aircraft list, and all other matters of business are managed by operations.

**Paracargo:**
   As a group, those who work to deliver supplies to fires by aircraft and parachute. As a product, supplies delivered in such a manner.

**PG Bag:**
   Personal gear bag.  During a jump, the PG bag hangs from rings below a jumper's front-mounted reserve parachute.

**PT:**   Physical training. Part of a smokejumpers daily routine.

**Pulaski:**
   Fire fighting tool. An ax with a grubbing hoe on the opposite end.

**Rats:**   Boxed Army rations, C-rations, C-rats.

**Ready Room:**
   Room in jumper facility where jumpers suit-up for departure to fires.

**Reburn:**
   A fire that is declared out, then later rekindles.

**Retardant:**
   See Mud.

**Rookie:**

> First-year smokejumper.

**Scratch Line:**

> Minimum hand line made quickly to temporarily hold a fire until the line can be finished.

**Slash:** Debris left after logging or chainsawing; limbs, cull logs, tree tops, and stumps. Can also be natural forest debris.

**Slopover:**

> The place where a fire crosses an established control line.

**Snag:** A dead tree, still standing.

**Speed Racks:**

> Racks on which jump gear is pre-positioned to facilitate fast suit-up.

**Spotfire:**

> Fire started outside the main fire area by flying sparks, embers, or rolling debris.

**Spotter:**

> Person who directs the jumping from the plane.

**Spruce Bough:**

> The top cut from a small (two to four inch diameter) black spruce. With all but its' short top branches removed, it is used like a broom to swat down flames on Alaska fires.

**Standby Shack:**

> The main smokejumper building. Includes operations, loft, ready room, paracargo, etc.

**Steering Lines:**

The right and left lines the jumper pulls on to steer a parachute.

**Streamer:**

Malfunctioned parachute.

**Tail:**   The back end or initial part of a fire. Usually spreads slower and with less intensity than flanks or head.

**Woodsman's Pal:**

Small machete-like tool carried by Alaska smokejumpers.

**Zulies:**

Missoula smokejumpers.

# Acknowledgements

For me, like most non-genius, plow horse writers, the task of initially writing, then spending thousands of hours rewriting, and finally finding a publisher is a daunting and sometimes discouraging endeavor. Thus, there are many people to thank here. First and foremost, my agent Dr. Syd Harriet of Agents Ink. Syd has patiently mentored my writing for the past eight years. First with The Rhythm of Leaves, and then the last five years with More or Less Crazy. As a University professor and champion of the written word, Dr. Harriet has helped many struggling writers move our ideas and thoughts out of our heads, onto the printed page, then on to the reading public.

Once again John Daniel brought his sharp mind, fresh eyes, and brutally honest pen to my editing process. If you've not read any John Daniel books, I strongly recommend you check them out. As an excellent human being and fine writer, it has been my great pleasure to work with him over the years on all three of my books.

Ex-smokejumper buddies, Davis Perkins, Rod Dow, and Jeff Fereday gave the manuscript a look and had several useful comments. Jeff Fereday was especially helpful with two complete line edits that added much to the quality of the writing.

Thanks also to Mike McMillan and his excellent fire photo website spotfireimages.com. As well as documenting the beauty and drama of wildland fire scene for ages to come, Mike was a great help in creating the cover.

A special thank you to all committed, and dedicated wildland firefighters. What you do—when you do it with great courage and pride—is both noble and ennobling.

And finally, thanks to the smokejumpers. Thanks to those who lived the story of what we called the T-Hangar days, to those jumpers gone before, those jumping now, and those yet to fill the ranks. Your outstanding work over the past 75 years has created a legacy of excellence unprecedented in the field of wildland fire. The effort to create this book came from my enduring admiration of who you are and what you do.

# The Smokejumpers

# About
# the Author

# Murry A. Taylor

For the past thirty-nine years (1975-2014) I've lived in the mountains of Northern California at the eastern edge of the Marble Mountain Wilderness. I built a log home there on forty acres of timber. My last year jumping was 2000. I was 59. Every year I passed the Super PT (physical training) test the first time I took it. I'm proud of that. Since 2004 I've spent January through March in a small village on the west coast of Costa Rica writing and wandering sunset beaches. I once envisioned myself doing this with only skinny dogs for friends. Turns out I'm part of a wonderful community as well.

My career eating smoke began the summer of 1959 on the Sierra National Forest on a slash disposal/fire crew. I started smokejumping in 1965 in Redding, California. For the next six years I took part in the Region 5 (California) refresher program. Each Spring we'd return to Redding for "Retread" training, a week of training units and practice jumps. Later, during periods of high fire activity, we'd be called in off our respective districts to jump fires. During my Retread years I worked as a forester for the U.S. Forest Service in both timber and recreation. By 1972 I was 31 years old, a GS-9, spending most all my time in the office going nuts and becoming increasingly disenchanted with the outfit. When they finally told me no more retread jumping, that fire was not for "professionals", and that I needed to get serious and focus on becoming a District Ranger, it occurred to me that I could simply quit, jump a couple more seasons, get it out of my system, then return to my Forest Service career and settle down.

In 1973, I became a Bureau of Land Management Alaska smoke-jumper. I loved it so much I never looked back. That season is the setting for the More or Less Crazy, and the beginning of what eventually became known as the T-Hangar Days. I jumped there until 1978. Those years were some of my greatest as far as people and jumping goes. I made as much money in a five-month season jumping as I did working year-round as a forester. And had more fun to boot. Unfortunately, it was during this time that my wife Kathy and I divorced. After that I spent my winters in Baja California and on the west coast of Mexico living on the beach. From 1979 to 1986 I dropped out of jumping so I could spend more time with my son, Eric. Eric lived with me during the last part of elementary school and most of high school.

In twenty-seven years as a smokejumper, I jumped fires in eight western states, all over Alaska, and the Yukon Territory of Canada. I made 375 total jumps, 205 to fires. The story of smokejumping is a story of extraordinary human endeavor; a story that strongly embraces the tenet that there is virtue in trying hard, keeping the faith, and never giving up. I will be forever grateful to those who, thanks to their character and courage, lived it then, and those still living it today.

# Murry A. Taylor's Other Books

## Jumping Fire:

Fighting fires since 1965, veteran smokejumper Murry Taylor finally retired from his legendary career after the summer of 2000, the worst fire season in more than fifty years. After three decades of parachuting out of planes and battling blazes in the vast, rugged wilderness of Alaska and the West, Taylor recounts in *Jumping Fire,* with passion and honesty, stories of man versus nature at its most furious and unforgiving. He shares what it's like to hear the deafening roar, to smell the acrid burn, to feel the intense heat, to breathe the thick fumes, and to finally run for your life with exploding flames two hundred feet high and a mile wide licking at your heels.

## The Rhythm of Leaves - A Novel:

*The Rhythm of Leaves* is a story of a small town in Southeastern Colorado that becomes split over the issue of whether it is appropriate to hold peace meetings Wednesday nights at a local church. Some believe the meetings are unpatriotic and do not support the troops in Iraq, while others say they are a matter of conscience in any war, especially one of questionable necessity. Clara Jennings, a 38 year-old, recently divorced, single mother, is the new pastor of the Church of the Holy Promise. She has come home from Alaska with, Joel, her fourteen year-old son and moved in with her parents to try to make a new life in the town where she grew up. After serious consideration, Clara decides to continue the meetings, while her father, Will, a Vietnam veteran still struggling with post traumatic stress disorder, is adamantly against them. Eventually the split that threatens the unity of the town also threatens the family.

As an in-depth look at what it means to be a good citizen, a Christian,and a responsible human being, *The Rhythm of Leaves* takes a close look at the costs of war. Not the cost of bombs and aircraft and munitions, but the costs of the deep wounding done to the individual human spirit, and thus that of an entire nation.

*The Rhythm of Leaves* is available on Amazon in both paperback and e-book form.

# More or Less
# CRAZY

is also available
in Kindle

If you liked
this book,
please review
it on
Amazon.com.

Thanks!

Made in the USA
San Bernardino, CA
28 December 2015